## PRAISE FOR SERHIY ZHADAN

"One of the most astounding novels to come out of modern Ukraine. *Mesopotamia* is seductive, twisted, brilliant, and fierce. It brings to mind our own fiction from a time when we still felt like we had something to fight for and a chance we could win."

**GARY SHTEYNGART,** author of *Little Failure* and *Absurdistan*

"To say that Serhiy Zhadan is a poet, a novelist, a rock star, a protester, a symbol of his country's desire for freedom and change, is to say the truth—but what is truth? Zhadan is a literary master of enormous force. At times he combines the energy of Jack Kerouac and atmospheric spell of Isaac Babel, at other times he is a balladeer of his country's struggle. 'Such strange things have been happening to us,' he writes, of the streets where 'winters are not like winters / winters live under assumed names.' In *Mesopotamia*'s nine stories and thirty poems we find ourselves in the newly independent Ukraine, stunned by its grit, its rough backbone—and its tenderness. What do we discover here? That 'Light is shaped by darkness, / and it's all up to us.' We also discover that Serhiy Zhadan is one of those rare things—almost impossible to find now in the West—a national bard, a chronicler. This is a book to live with."

**ILYA KAMINSKY**

"To know Dublin, read your Joyce, for Macondo, García Márquez, and for Mesopotamia, Serhiy Zhadan. Of course this Mesopotamia is not the Birthplace of Civilization (or is it?), it's Kharkiv, the Ukrainian Center of Nothing, located smack-dab on the Russian border, which, in Zhadan's brilliant vision, is smack-dab in the middle of life lived beyond the fullest because any second could be your last, creaming with joy, madness, war, orgasm, stupidity, and a blinding light that-smells like the essence of human spirit. We need to learn from Ukraine. Zhadan is a masterful teacher. The use of poetry as Notes—so far as I know, this has never been done before and is positively Nabokovian. This book is world-class literature."

**BOB HOLMAN,** author of *Sing This One Back to Me*

T0366486

"To say that Serhiy Zhadan is a great Ukrainian novelist of whom you might not have heard does not begin to cover it. Serhiy Zhadan is one of the most important creators of European culture at work today. His novels, poems, and songs touch millions. This loving translation is a chance to see Ukraine in terms other than the familiar, but more importantly a chance to allow prose to mend your mind."

**TIMOTHY SNYDER,** author of *On Tyranny*

"Unlike Joyce's Dublin, the cradle of Zhadan's civilization is a place of refuge for young people fleeing hardscrabble lives in the provinces, and a hardscrabble home for natives buoyed by desire yet adrift amid the flotsam of a spent empire. The men and women in these comic and heartfelt pages endure the dynamic paralysis that comes over those who are all dressed up with nowhere to go. They aspire, struggle, fight, fail, drink, fuck, and then they fight some more. Amid the city's detritus, they refuse to become part of it by continuing to love and dream. There is nothing marginal about them. They insist on being seen, heard, understood. They will charm and madden you. They will haunt your dreams, and you will never forget them."

**ASKOLD MELNYCZUK,** author of *House of Widows*

"Zhadan is the rock star of lyrical melancholy, and *Mesapotamia* is not just a book of short stories but a cosmos with Kharkiv-Babylon at its center. We meet its lovesick citizens at weddings and funerals; their visceral, fantastical lives unfold in the intensely prophetic atmosphere of the upcoming war."

**VALZHYNA MORT,** author of *Factory of Tears*

"With tales at once earthy and phantasmagorical, sentimental and anarchic, Zhadan is an exhilarating chronicler of a new kind of borderlands."

**SANA KRASIKOV**

"Serhiy Zhadan's dazzling novel—here fantastically well translated— evokes voices that get under our skin and take us into the rich inner life of people about whom we have long known nothing."

**MARCI SHORE,** author of *The Ukrainian Night: An Intimate History of Revolution*

"*Mesopotamia* offers a sublime experience of taking you right to the middle of a very specific world, where you eat and drink and love and fight and die with the characters, until you notice that that world has transcended the time and place and became part of the eternal human story."

**LARA VAPNYAR,** author of *Still Here: A Novel*

"*Mesopotamia* finds poetry in the most unlikely places — in the bars, tower blocks, and concrete boulevards of a Ukrainian city. By turns funny, shocking, and touching, weaving between the lyrical and the grotesque, Zhadan's stories provide a lesson in belonging."

**UILLEAM BLACKER,** University College London

"*Mesopotamia* is a portrait of post-Soviet Ukraine's lost generation, of people who came of age in the disorienting conditions of crumbling Soviet order and stagnating social transformation. Serhiy Zhadan gives voice to his generation from Ukraine's eastern regions bordering Russia. These are the people who have been missing from contemporary literature, whether in Ukrainian or in any other language. To understand the background to the crisis in this region, which has had such a major impact on the world recently, perhaps no other writer can provide insights as powerful as Zhadan."

**VITALY CHERNETSKY,** University of Kansas

"Serhiy Zhadan has written a love song to contemporary Eastern Ukraine — vices, passions, and ghosts included. His Kharkiv is filled with gritty stairwells, red nightgowns, raw love, and a bit of magic. Costigan-Humes and Wheeler have brought Zhadan's evocative prose to life for the English reader."

**AMELIA GLASER,** author of *Jews and Ukrainians in Russia's Literary Borderlands*

*Mesopotamia*

# *Mesopotamia*

**SERHIY ZHADAN**

**PROSE TRANSLATED FROM THE UKRAINIAN BY**

**REILLY COSTIGAN-HUMES AND**

**ISAAC STACKHOUSE WHEELER**

**POETRY TRANSLATED FROM THE UKRAINIAN**

**BY VIRLANA TKACZ AND WANDA PHIPPS**

YALE UNIVERSITY PRESS ■ NEW HAVEN & LONDON

A MARGELLOS
WORLD REPUBLIC OF LETTERS BOOK

The Margellos World Republic of Letters is dedicated to making literary works from around the globe available in English through translation. It brings to the English-speaking world the work of leading poets, novelists, essayists, philosophers, and playwrights from Europe, Latin America, Africa, Asia, and the Middle East to stimulate international discourse and creative exchange.

Yale University Press books may be purchased in quantity for educational, business, or promotional use. For information, please e-mail sales.press@yale.edu (U.S. office) or sales@yaleup.co.uk (U.K. office).

Set in Electra and Nobel types by Tseng Information Systems, Inc., Durham, North Carolina.
Printed and bound by CPI Group (UK) Ltd, Croydon, CR0 4YY

Library of Congress Control Number: 2017955589
ISBN 978-0-300-22335-4 (paper : alk. paper)

A catalogue record for this book is available from the British Library.

10 9 8 7 6 5 4 3 2 1

Nobody knows where they came from or why they settled on these rivers, but their affinity for fishing and knowledge of pilotage indicates that they arrived by water, sailing up the rivers, against the current. Their language seemed perfectly suited for songs and maledictions. Their women were tender and defiant, the kind that give birth to brave children and serious problems.

—*The True History of the Sumerians,* Volume 1

## CONTENTS

*Mesopotamia*

# Part I: Stories and Biographies

Translated from the Ukrainian by
Reilly Costigan-Humes and
Isaac Stackhouse Wheeler

## MARAT

Marat died forty days ago. Then spring came to the city. It had almost passed by the time we buried him, on Remembrance Day, at the beginning of April. Now overgrown grass had charred the hills green—summer was on its way. The traditional forty days of mourning were enough for us to calm down and forget about the whole thing. But then his parents called to remind us, and I thought to myself, "Yeah, I guess it's only been forty days." The dead don't have any outstanding grievances; it's the living who are always on your case.

A few friends and neighbors buried him. Most of his friends—and he had throngs of them, all over town—simply couldn't believe they were being invited to his funeral. They apologized for being so doubtful, and then they came to the cemetery and looked for Marat's headstone. That April was a rainy one; stray dogs trotted along after the van transporting the casket like an honor guard, occasionally thrusting their bodies at the black wheels of our Volkswagen hearse because they just couldn't stand to watch Marat depart for the kingdom of the dead. Solemn throngs of people walked through the cemetery, ascending hills where the low-hanging clouds pressed close to them, and then descending into the valley where the deluge pooled. They honored his memory as best they could, mixing alcohol with rainwater. We were the only people to show up at the cemetery with a dearly departed friend in the back of their vehicle, so we looked a bit out of place—it was as if we'd come to a music shop with our own grand piano. The fact that it was Easter made us feel all mixed up—our sorrow seemed inappropriate. Who dies on *Easter*? Typically, people rise from the grave.

■ ■ ■

Marat's death wound up being a lot like his life—illogical and shrouded in mystery. It was late Saturday night, or early Sunday morning. Marat hadn't gone to church, because he considered himself a Muslim, and a nonpracticing one, no less, but he had gone out for cigarettes in the middle of the night, wearing his slippers and clutching a 50-hryvnia bill in his fist. He'd gotten shot right by the kiosk. Nobody was there to see it happen; they were all in their respective churches. The clerk working the night shift said she hadn't heard any gunfire, but she could have sworn she *did* hear people singing and a motor revving up. She claimed she could identify those voices if she heard them again, although she wasn't sure if they'd been male or female. Also, she'd managed to write down the number of the supposed getaway car; however, it matched the plates on the ancient Zhiguli that had been parked outside the student infirmary for the past year or so. Nobody touched it but the street sweepers who stashed scraps of cardboard and empty bottles in it. "Well, looks like the mob has made a comeback," we remarked, thinking back to the tumultuous nineties. "Who's next?"

It didn't make much sense why anyone would have wanted to kill him. Marat didn't run his own business, he stayed out of city politics, and he didn't have any enemies; well, maybe he sometimes wouldn't recognize one of his friends and would walk right on by without saying hi, but come on, is that any reason to gun someone down? The city hadn't seen any street shootings for over ten years—well, that's if you don't count people shooting at cash-in-transit cars. But why would you? Do you know anybody who drives one? We could only guess what had happened that night.

Forty days passed; time pressed forward, the water in the rivers overflowed their banks and then receded again. The days had started getting warmer. I didn't want to go—I had even decided to call his parents and tell them I was sorry that I couldn't make it. But then I figured I'd be thinking about him all night anyway, so I might as well do it with my friends and relatives. It's always better to lose your mind in familiar surroundings. I left my apartment, passed my old school, stopped by the kiosk, and looked at their cigarette selection for a long while. I couldn't make up my mind, so I didn't buy any, and then I thought about heading back home after all, but I just kept going instead. I barreled down the steep hill by the Institute and skidded to a stop when I got to Marat's street. It was quiet. Lethargic canine bodies were warming up in the afternoon sun. Detecting movement near the house, the top dog lifted his head, his dark, attentive gaze lingering on me, then sank down again and closed his weary eyes. Nothing had happened. Nothing had changed.

Marat lived just a few blocks away from me, closer to the river. Just a three-minute walk. Everything you could ever need was right there: maternity clinic, daycare center, music school, army recruiting office, furniture stores, pharmacies, hospitals, and cemeteries. You could live your whole life without venturing outside our neighborhood, without even going to the next metro station—and we never did. We grew up in old apartment blocks that had been rebuilt and renovated countless times; in the morning, we'd run out of their damp stairwells. At night, we'd come back, to sleep under their leaky roofs, which were always getting patched up but were never really fixed. From our hill, hanging above the river, we could see the whole city. Standing outside our buildings, we could feel the rocks somewhere down beneath our feet, the rocks on which everything was built. In the summertime, those rocks would heat up and so would our bodies; in winter, they'd freeze and everyone would catch colds.

Their yard faced the TB clinic; their street stretched out all the way to the old warehouses. On one side, down below, beyond the city's rooftops, were the river and the bridge, black factory buildings, new apartment complexes, and Kharkiv's impassable maze of single-family homes. On the other side, atop the hill, were the city's main streets, churches, and commerce. I went through the gate, feeling the matter of my life beneath my feet—dust, clay, and heaps of sand so dense that not even the mighty grass could break through them. The walkway leading up to their house was paved with cracked brick and stones—Marat had been threatening to dump asphalt all over the whole damn place for years, but something had been holding him back, so everything stayed the same—two dilapidated, half-empty, two-story structures, built before the Bolshevik Revolution. There were flowerbeds in the middle of the yard, shrubs up against the house, apple trees toward the back, and then the blackened brick wall of a building that faced their neighbor's yard. Marat's family had hauled some tables and chairs outside; the neighbors had brought their own stools so they'd have a place to sit. Apple trees shone above the tables; white petals kept falling into the salads, adding zest and bitterness.

I said hello. The other guests nodded in reply; one of the women produced an extra stool from somewhere underneath her and handed it to me, so I squeezed in between two warm May bodies. Somebody immediately started heaping my plate with food and somebody else was pouring me a drink. I looked around, scanning the guests and recognizing familiar faces. Our whole crew had come—sitting across from me was Benia, who had cut his gray hair short. He gave me a genial nod and then returned to the main conversation. As far as I could gather, they were talking about the weather. Well, that's a pretty innocuous topic, so why not talk about it? At least nobody will get too riled up. Kostyk, who was sitting at the other end of the table, waved at me without turning his attention away from his meal. Apple petals were fluttering down onto his white dress shirt, dissolving against its fabric like snow falling into a river. Marat's frail neighbor who lived on the second floor was leaning up against Kostyk, though she kept getting edged off her chair by his sharp hipbones. Sem was standing off to the side, under the trees, next to Rustam, Marat's brother. Wearing rubber sandals and a new tracksuit, Rustam was pacing back and forth on the cracked bricks and talking to someone on the phone, occasionally asking Sem about something. Sem was wearing a tracksuit, too. They looked like two marathon runners who had taken a wrong turn and were now frantically calling the race organizers to get back on the course. It was the neighbor ladies who were doing most of the talking, but it felt like any second now somebody was going to put on some music and we'd all start boogieing. Occasionally, somebody would invite Rustam to join us at the table, but he'd wave his hand dismissively at us, as if to say, "Fuck off with all your Orthodox bull-shit," and then continue his passionate diatribe. Sem was nodding, seemingly on board with everything Rustam was saying.

I took a look at our crew. They hadn't changed much in the past forty days, but they hadn't changed much in the past ten years, for that matter, unless you count the wrinkles slicing up Benia's face, making him look even more like Mick Jagger. Decked out in a black sweater and fancy dress shoes, Benia was trying to look put together, using his last ounce of strength to do so. I was one of the only ones who knew that his company had been squeezed out of the market, so he was living off his savings. It was obvious they wouldn't last much longer, which probably accounted for why Benia's hair had started graying even faster. Honest businessmen had fallen upon hard times in Kharkiv . . . well, what can ya do? Kostyk had gotten even fatter, al-though that hardly affected his personality, since he had always been a pretty wretched human being. That doesn't change much over time . . . Kostyk worked on the railroad—i.e., he had some management position at the Southern Rail Station downtown. I wasn't quite sure what he managed; I suspect he wasn't either. As he put on weight, he started taking things too seriously. He stuck with us, his child-hood friends—he didn't hang out with anyone else. I guess Sem had changed the most. Well, he got a new tracksuit, that's about it. As a veteran cab driver, he could quick-draw his keys. He had a battle-ready stance, a suspicious attitude toward his passengers, and a deep-seated hatred of traffic cops. As for me, I could feel a warm clump of fatigue balling up somewhere between my heart and spleen, pushing upward. It was taking over more and more space in my body, compelling me to listen—something was going on underneath my clothes and skin, in my soul. Nothing—not my 9–5 office job, not even moving up the corporate ladder—could counteract that clump eating away at my internal organs like a piranha somebody had set loose inside me. Back in the day, I'd decided to stick to familiar territory, so I took a job at the local factory, just two blocks away from where I live. I worked my way up, and fifteen years later I even got my own office. The factory hadn't been operating for ten years, though; I was like a deckhand trying to get promoted on a sinking ship. In theory, it was possible to move up the ranks, but at the end of the day you're still gonna wind up on the bottom of the ocean. We turned the old labs into rentable office space and the old factory floors into rentable warehouses; I made good money and wore a suit that didn't quite fit. Just like my friends, I started having sleeping problems, and my first gray hair sprouted up a while back. I didn't see any point in griping about it, I just started cutting my hair short. The security guard ladies at the factory actually liked my crew cut—they started to respect me. Or pity me. All of us, Marat's friends I mean, had hit that age when life slows down and gives you more time alone with your fears and insecurities. Marat had only made it to thirty-five, but each of us could look forward to a long life and a natural death. Maybe from Alzheimer's.

Marat's mom and his dad, Alec, sat on opposite sides of the table, as if they were strangers. His dad kept quiet, while his mom was going on about the salads, making everybody wish she'd keep quiet, too. I sat there, only occasionally contributing to the conversation, trying to remember the good times. I put on a mournful face whenever I turned to talk to the mother of the departed, and I could feel moisture rising from the river, high enough to reach our old neighborhoods, thickly planted with trees and densely covered with gates, towers, and communal apartments. Sem and Marat's uncle Sasha had hung some heavy lamps on the apple branches, running long cords across the yard from the garage, and the yellow electricity mixed with the white blossoms and blanketed us in shadows. Once the sun had set, all the guests started saying their goodbyes, planning their next get-togethers, sighing, exchanging kisses and promises to be there for one another and lend a helping hand, then stepping through the gate, back to life.

The neighbors—the two women between whose wide hips I was nestled and the skinny one that Kostyk had been edging off her seat—were the first to leave, carrying their stools like Christmas presents. Blind-as-a-bat Zurab was next. Nobody had invited him in the first place, and he obviously wasn't in any hurry to get home; he lived in a metal shoe-repair shack on Revolution Street, packed with soles and boot leather. It was pitch black in there, not that he needed any light. He had some freakish talent for fixing shoes. Clearly, nobody was waiting up for him, but he decided to call it a night anyway. Maria, somebody's distant relative who had a deep voice and a once-elaborate hairdo that was now a frizzy mess, left after him. She sold vegetables at a stand on top of the hill, by the Revenue Service building. She was close to Marat's family; she had cried openly—hers had probably been the only genuine tears shed at his funeral. Her son Mark accompanied her in his white overalls with yellow paint stains. He left because he had to get back to the furniture-repair shop on Darwin Street to repaint a set of plywood shelves a couple of Armenians had brought in, to make them look brand-new . . . and Polish-made. Zhora, who was doing a trainee program at a pharmacy, was the next to go. He worked the night shift; when he got off, he'd raid the beer kiosks on Pushkin Street, pulling the clerks out of their murky morning slumber and demanding their attention and sympathy. The terror of our neighborhood's 24-hour convenience stores left, telling everyone to enjoy the rest of their night—he sure would. Tamara, our exhausted yet unstoppable homeroom teacher, left after him, taking a piece of pie with her, wrapped up in tabloid journalism. We were all tired of engaging her, so we just had to listen to her rambling, nodding in agreement and not bothering to interject with anything. Clearly bored by this one-sided conversation, she thanked Marat's parents curtly and disappeared, floating through the gate like a ghost. Then Pasha Chingachgook and his lady, Margarita, headed out. Marat had called them his brother and sister-in-law, but his wife didn't have any siblings, so it wasn't clear how they could be related. Pasha walked with a limp due to an old motocross injury; i.e., he stole someone's scooter and crashed it. Sometimes it seemed as though Margarita had a limp, too. Maybe it was because she was always walking arm-in-arm with Pasha, trying to adjust to his wobbly gait. They went on their way, like two merry sailors who had been discharged as unfit for service. Bob Koshkin and Sasha Tsoy, two guys who were part of our neighborhood gang despite being a bit younger than us, rose to their feet laboriously and slipped into the darkness. Koshkin had been weeping and pouring himself drink after drink because he was about to leave for Philadelphia. His dad's relatives, who had gotten stuck there back in the nineties, hadn't been responding to any of his family's letters, so Koshkin's dad, who went to synagogue regularly, decided he'd had enough of their nonsense. He figured he would send his only son to find out where the hell they got off ignoring him. Koshkin had even bought a cowboy hat with Hutsul embroidery patterns running around the band, which he figured would help him blend in with the locals. This was pretty much going to be his first time venturing out of his parents' home, if you don't count Pioneer camp—Koshkin's dad worked there, so when the summer session rolled around, Koshkin Jr. would feel like a repeat offender doing some more time in the can, where he would be greeted by the guards' friendly, familiar faces. Sasha had been itching to leave for quite a while; he was planning on going to a poetry group at some hip café, but he didn't want to admit he was into poetry, so he just sat there anxiously. Sasha was the son of a Korean student who washed up in Kharkiv in the early eighties. He didn't really get along with his father, so he kept his distance, living on his own and writing lofty philosophical poems. He rubbed some people the wrong way, so he was always getting into fights with poets he didn't know; he usually got his ass kicked, but that never seemed to get to him. Alla the Alligator took off after a while — we just didn't want to let her go; she wasn't dying to get out of there or anything, but she had to get up early, punch in at the TB clinic, check up on her patients — all that stuff. She was probably the one who was happiest to see all of us; she kept reminiscing — telling old stories and improvising when she got to the parts nobody could remember anymore. She shared her plans for the future with us, assuring everyone that her wild days were over now that Maria had gotten her a nursing job. Now she had a new and exciting life — the only problem was that patients kept dying on her. The electric light made the soft wrinkles under her eyes quiver; her dyed blond hair seemed bright with sparks in the twilight, and when she hovered over the table to whisper warm words of gratitude into someone's ear it would hang down into their wineglasses, turning it pink and damp. She was bouncing off the walls, blabbing away all evening, acting like this was her birthday party, and demanding everyone mark the occasion by drinking deeply and speaking kindly. She eventually had to get going, though. The closer she got to the gate and the deeper she stepped into the darkness pooling in the yard, the thicker the gloom hanging above her head became — it was as if, over there, out of reach of the yellow lamps, where the light dropped off, she had to breathe ash and clay and speak with the dead souls hiding out inside that clay. I watched her slide out the gate and suddenly remembered that she was the first woman Marat slept with — that's just how it played out. Well, she was Benia's first, too. And Kostyk's, obviously. And Sem's, for those keeping score. And if you really need to know, she was mine, too.

Then Rustam's lady friends headed out, holding hands — Kira, the older one, was annoyed at Olia, because she'd drunk too much, yet again. Olia was patting Kira on the back, giving her goose bumps, and making her shoulder blades ring in the cold. She was tearing up. We were all tearing up; frigid laughter was smashing up against our teeth, and we suddenly realized that everybody else had left. It was just Marat's family and us, like back in the good old days, when we'd all get together at Marat's place for birthdays or family gatherings. I thought about how we'd mostly come together on holidays, which might account for my oddly festive mood—I had this feeling that any moment now fireworks would soar over the neighbors' roofs, tinted gold and lilac by the evening sun that was still shining brightly atop the hill. But down in Marat's neighborhood, everything had burned out and the May air had cooled off. We started getting ready to leave, but Sasha asked us to stick around. He'd made the long haul out here just for Marat's wake, so he was planning on spending the night. He didn't feel like going to bed yet, and he felt even less like letting us leave.

"This won't do," he said in a serious tone. "This isn't how it's done. We can't just up and leave. We have to sit together and remember the departed. Otherwise his soul won't be at peace."

Sasha's words grounded us and we all started chattering at the same time.

"Well, obviously, come on. We'll stick around, Sasha . . ."

"We're not going anywhere . . ."

"It's not like we have anywhere to go."

"Nobody's waiting up for us . . ."

Marat's parents sighed heavily, but didn't object. They just said they'd be turning in for the night, because Alec's kidneys had been aching all day and his wife had to catch the evening news—it was as though she was expecting something big to happen. So they let us stay outside, asking Alina, Marat's wife, to bring us some food from the kitchen. Alina got right to it without saying a word. It was only now, after everyone else had gone home and the neighborhood had grown quiet and empty, that we became aware of her presence. Only now did we start paying any attention to her, even though she'd been floating around all evening—carrying things in and out of the house, putting up with the neighbors' weeping, writing down their baked carp recipes, calling Pasha and Margarita a taxi, and kissing everyone goodbye. Yet she seemed somehow solitary, displaced from the conversation, out there in the dark, on the other side of the perimeter of light the lamps threw on the ground. I had just noticed that she had a different haircut; it was short now. She kept trying to tuck her hair back, out of habit, because it always used to fall in front of her eyes. She was wearing a short black dress, black stockings, and sandals. All the people around here dressed casually, like they were heading out to the beach. The dress made the lines of her body slimmer, and the sandals made her footsteps inaudible. She hadn't taken off her wedding ring, and she never wore any other jewelry. Her hair was dark, as was her skin; it seemed that she would dissolve into the evening air any moment now. I felt bad about how we were acting. We were always nice to her, despite all the stuff Marat had told us; nobody treated her with disrespect, and I have to say that she returned the favor by being patient with us and putting up with our antics, even though we didn't always deserve it. Back in the day, when Marat introduced us to her, he was very firm with her, saying that we were his friends and she needed to be nice to us. She remembered that. She remembered every little thing Marat said. We'd forgotten all about her, though. Now our crew had finally started paying attention to Alina — probably a little too much attention, I realized. Benia darted after her into the kitchen, carrying some plates and dropping them along the way. Kostyk bolted to clear the table, mercilessly knocking the dirty dishes to the ground; Sem even pulled Rustam under the lamplight, though that didn't stop him from shouting threats about some fixed-rate mortgage plan or other into his phone. After everyone regrouped, Sasha tried to restore order.

He said something strange. He said that this was Marat's last night with us, so we absolutely had to say all kinds of nice things about him. Otherwise he would stick around. We went along with it — we even worked ourselves into a kind of frenzy when we started trying to remember some stories, but we couldn't produce anything coherent—we just kept on interrupting each other, yelling and arguing. Then Sasha told everyone to pipe down. Silence ensued, and I saw cold, sticky fog crawling through the gate into the yard. It was rising up from a black riverbed that the sun hadn't managed to scorch dry yet, as it does in summer. This weird feeling crept up on me—and everyone else too. It was beginning to dawn on us what Sasha had been warning us about as he sat hunched over the table, using his phone as a flashlight every time another round was called for—he was warning us that Marat was somewhere nearby, standing behind our backs, and that he wouldn't be leaving until we spoke the words he needed to hear. It wasn't a very pleasant feeling—straining to hear your dead friend's breath right behind you in the dark. Death had interrupted him in the middle of a sentence, and I knew so many un-flattering stories about him that it'd be much easier for him to choke me to death than trust me to keep his secrets to myself. Somebody touched my shoulder softly. I shuddered and whipped around—Alina was standing there, smiling sheepishly and handing me some napkins. I cracked a smile too and grabbed at those damn napkins, but they slipped between my nervous fingers. I cursed and bent over to grab them, banging my head on the table on the way back up, which brought everyone out of whatever trance they'd fallen into. Once again, everyone started jabbering at the same time; Benia was the loudest, so everybody started listening to him. Alina stopped dead in her tracks behind me, listening hard, which clearly threw Benia for a loop—he tensed up. He was struggling, trying not to say anything that might offend the widow. He was looking us all straight in the eye, as though he was asking for our support and sympathy. He seemed to be saying, "Well, you know what I mean, back me up here, guys. You were there, you know that's how it went down, you can vouch for me." We backed him up. We vouched for him. Alina stood there for a bit, leaned against the table, picked up some empty, lipstick-stained glasses; it seemed like she wanted to head to the house, but some-thing was holding her back. Something was compelling her to keep listening to Benia's story, which kept breaking off and starting from somewhere else. The fog was closing in on us, quietly and inexorably approaching her warm, dusky body.

"Lemme tell ya," Benia said, standing there under the lamp, holding a shot glass in his hand like he was proposing a toast. His speech was primarily directed at Sasha, whom the twilight was making ever more dark, sharp-nosed, and opaque. "The thing I liked the most about Marat was his manly ways."

His eyes shifted from person to person, waiting for our approval. But we didn't really see what he was getting at, so Benia turned to Sasha once again.

"I just wanted to say that Marat was always mature and responsible, just like a real man oughta be."

Everyone agreed with him, and Benia continued, "We all went to the same school, didn't we? We were all in the same class, weren't we? When Marat went out for the boxing team, I went along with him."

"Me too," Kostyk added.

"So did I," Sem and I chimed in together.

"Yeah, but we got cut. I know that down in the Caucasus, where you're from, every other guy is a boxer," he said, turning to Sasha. "Or a sambo wrestler."

"Or a mountaineer," Kostyk interjected, apropos of nothing.

"But Marat was a real fighter," Benia said, moving on and paying no mind to Kostyk. "No drugs or partying for him. He never missed a practice, even after he started dating Alina," he stated, now turning to her.

"Yep, that's right!" We all shouted to verify his claim.

Alina tensed up, the empty wineglasses in her hands clinking together. Everyone got quiet all of a sudden.

"Now I'm gonna tell you a story. You might not know this one," Benia said, pausing to catch his breath.

Then he started. According to Benia, Marat got his first pair of boxing gloves from his dad, before he could even stand up straight. In other words, Marat learned to honor his father and his mother, then to box, and only then did he get around to taking his first steps. He was an inspired and determined athlete, ready to box anytime, anywhere. The way Benia told it, Marat's fists knocked his rivals into oblivion, bringing his athletic club victory and glory. The coaches recognized his talent immediately, recruiting him without asking how old he was, where he went to school, or what his religious affiliation was. But they really should have, Benia stated gravely, because Marat's religion was a matter of great pride for him. He always had the holy relics which Benia had gotten for him in Sinai on his person, though nobody had ever actually seen them, since bringing relics into the ring during a match is strictly prohibited by the Olympic Committee. Moreover, Marat said *namaz* without fail, observed the Sabbath on Fridays, abstained from eating meat, and paid the tithe to the church. Benia didn't specify *which* church, deciding to stick to cold, hard, verifiable facts. Obviously, Marat's coaches realized they had a genuine prodigy moving up through their program, a boy who lit up their drab, pointless existence. They'd gotten really lucky with Marat, so they clung to him like he was all they had left, which made perfect sense. Who wouldn't want to mold a future Olympic champion? They all did, so they were going to make him a champion, whatever it took. Marat knew they wanted the best for him, so every time the clubs from his native Caucasus tried to lure him back there, he'd always say that he was trained here in Kharkiv and this was where he'd make a name for himself. Ambition gives you strength and stamina. Marat's painstaking efforts and grueling workouts, combined with setting clear goals, simply had to produce top results. Marat made the transformation from some unremarkable Chechen boy into Kharkiv's most promising sports star.

"Not a single opponent—in his weight class, I mean—could even last five rounds against him!" Benia proclaimed with inflated pathos. "Just remember how he'd prepare for fights! Abstinence and asceticism, prayers and meditation, submission and confidence . . ." Benia was off on a tangent again, and he wasn't coming back. "His skin became tougher over the years, and his bones became cold and hard. And when he was duking it out for the regional title, the city fathers stood in the stands, mesmerized by his fluid motions and triumphant shouts!"

"They sure did!" Sasha agreed, and a blue tear descended into his glass of cognac.

"Not a single defeat! Not one single defeat! He triumphed again and again, at every single training camp! His enemies' dried blood clung to his hair and their howls of pain marked his every stride toward glory! The most beautiful women threw themselves at his feet!" Benia said, getting flustered once he'd caught a glimpse of Alina. "I mean the women from the boxing federation. Unions, labor reserves, you know . . ."

Everyone started to feel a bit uncomfortable, everyone but Benia, who just kept going. I guess he didn't know what else to do.

"The story I'm gonna tell you happened at training camp, down in Yalta. I was there the whole time, that's why I can tell it in such detail. Nobody compared with Marat when it came to stamina or agility. Anybody who tried to keep up with him would just run himself into the ground or blow something out and have to go home. Nobody doubted that he had a great future ahead of him. Nobody besides Black Devil. I can't remember what his real name was. Nah . . . ," Benia paused, apparently racking his brains. "That *was* his real name, or at least his real name sounded like that. He didn't come from around here. His parents had moved here from out west, or maybe from really far east—I don't remember anymore. Now I bet nobody even remembers Black Devil. He wasn't much of a boxer anyway; Marat was the only one people ever talked about. Well, Black Devil just went off the rails one day at training camp. The coaches wouldn't even let their athletes go into town—the boxers had their morning calisthenics routine, athletic regimen, and all that stuff. Well, the whole entire coaching staff had to go to some sort of league meeting. That's when Black Devil went on the bender of a lifetime. He was just drinking by himself at first. Then he got the massage guys going. Then he got to work corrupting the younger dudes. Guess who was the only one who didn't drink with him? Marat! Black Devil egged him on for two days, tempted him for two whole days. He tried every trick in the book. He sent the massage guys over to Marat's room and even got the younger dudes in on it. But Marat didn't crack. So, let's drink," Benia said, trying to bring his speech around to some kind of conclusion, "to our friend Marat, to his manly nature." I saw that Alina hadn't bothered listening to the end of the story. She was heading toward the house, the fog coldly touching her calves as she walked across the yard. Benia kept going, he just couldn't help himself: "Let's drink to his commitment to the sport, his perseverance, and true manly friendship!"

Nobody was against having another drink; nobody had anything against true manly friendship either. Sasha, a skinny guy with a shaved head and a little, neatly combed mustache, looked like a chimney sweep who'd slipped off a roof but had his fall broken by a banquet table. He was quite happy with his lot because things could have gone much worse. As the sky got darker, the light shed by the lamps overhead became more disquieting. The darkness encircled us like water wrapping around motionless catfish it didn't dare disturb.

We all knew the real story. Nobody interrupted or corrected Benia while Alina was around, but as soon as she stepped inside, I started telling everyone what had actually happened down there in Crimea; everyone else started recalling parts of that trip too. Our crew was overwhelmed by a sudden sense of confusion. Even Rustam avoided making eye contact, took out his cellphone, and started texting angrily. The "Devil's" real name was Valera. He and Marat were kicked off the team on three separate occasions, but the coaches took them back every time. It wasn't because Marat was unbeatable or something—he never even won the regional crown. It's just that Valera's dad worked for the police department and he had a lot of pull; he'd go to bat for his boy and Marat whenever they got in trouble. They were at training camp together, right here in Kharkiv, but they decided to skip town and head to Crimea. Marat had been dating Alina for some time already, and they had been telling everyone they were going to get married soon. But all of a sudden, he went off the rails. It was March; black snow covered the city's squares and parks, the sky flared and burned, and Marat was itching to go somewhere, so he made up some story about another training camp down in Yalta. These two gymnast girls went along with them—I don't think they'd even turned fourteen yet. Marat and Black Devil, who were both eighteen, seemed so mature and responsible to them—two manly men who were man enough for anything. They stayed at Black Devil's friends' place—a cramped apartment in a big concrete prefab building. You couldn't even see the water from the balcony, but they couldn't have cared less about the stormy sea—all it was doing was inundating the beach with ice and seaweed. On day five of their trip, when they started running out of money, champagne, and bread, Black Devil and his gymnast were trying to drag Marat back to Kharkiv—but then it was like somebody had flipped a switch. That's how Marat would later describe what he had felt. He said that he didn't even know what had hit him or how it all started—his partner in crime, a shy, slim girl with nothing going for her but the prospect of a dazzling sports career, went crazy for Marat . . . and he'd gone crazy for her a while before. They locked themselves in one of the rooms, crawled into bed and didn't crawl out again for days, just wearing each other out. Marat told us that she didn't know a thing: he had to teach her the basics and show her how to make it last. The heat was on low in the apartment; they had to hide under thick blankets, so he hardly ever saw her naked—he studied her by touch alone. When he told the story, he would linger over how tender the palms of her hands were, how thin her veins, how dry her skin. It didn't take him long to teach her, and she soon forgot how awkward and painful it had been at first; she cried at night and laughed in the morning, grabbing him by the neck whenever he tried to free himself from the blankets wrapped tightly around them and run to the kitchen for another bottle of champagne. He'd come back to bed, slip under the covers, and they'd start going at it again. The alcohol made her reckless and tireless; she'd bite his skin and then lick his body's wounds, whispering tenderly in his ear. He'd be thinking about how to escape and take a piss. She'd conk out, mumbling something to her mom in her sleep, then he'd bring her back to consciousness. That went on for days.

Black Devil was the first one to panic. He knew the girls were under age. Sure, maybe that wasn't a big deal in and of itself, but he also knew that the girls had told their parents they were going to training camp too. They had to get home somehow, and fast, because if word got out, not even Black Devil's dad could get them off the hook. His girl started to panic, too; she broke down crying and asked him to get her a ticket back to Kharkiv. Black Devil tried reasoning with Marat. They were sitting in the kitchen and smoking their last few cigarettes. Blood was seeping out of Marat's fresh wounds, mingling with sweet saliva. Marat said that he wasn't going anywhere, he didn't want to hear it, he was afraid of going back home, she'd tell everyone everything, he didn't know what to say to Alina—she had no clue what was really going on and if she found out she'd die of a broken heart. So the best thing for him to do was to stick it out until the gymnast rode him to death or he ran out of cigarettes. Black Devil patiently presented some arguments, telling Marat that staying here wasn't an option because the authorities would start looking for them eventually and then it was only a matter of time—they'd be the ones dying, and not of broken hearts, either: the righteous would throw the book at them, and then start looking for something else to throw, and they'd wind up getting stoned to death.

"Nah, man," Marat protested, "you just don't get it. When things aren't going your way, when you're backed into a corner, it's best to just keep still. You just gotta stand there and take it till it passes." And then he went back to his room and started warming her cold, slim shoulders, then he warmed her palms and her stomach, trying not to think about anything in particular, trying not to think at all. For a few days, Black Devil tried to talk him into going home. He went to the post office a few times to call Alina and tell her that Marat said hello and that he was busy working out. Alina figured out what was up, but she didn't let on. She just said not to go too wild after practice. On one of the following days, Black Devil's girl gathered up her stuff, slipped out of the apartment unnoticed, hoofed it out to the highway, flagged down a car that took her as far as Simferopol, and made it all the way home by the next morning. It was only a matter of time until the cops showed up. Black Devil kicked in the door to Marat's room, pulled his girl out of bed, and helped her get dressed without saying a single word as she stumbled around, getting her stockings and socks all in a tangle. Then he dragged her to the train station. Marat stayed. Black Devil's friends came back in a few days, so Marat had no choice but to go home. Alina dumped him and then took him back. Marat's gymnast girl tried swallowing a whole bunch of pills, but it didn't work out for her. Well, she didn't die, I mean.

In the time we spent remembering that story, a thin, copper-tinged moon dangled itself over the yard. Partially concealed by the fog, the crescent was still showing through the damp air, moving quietly over the city's tin roofs and the black throats of its chimneys. Alina stepped outside and was drowned in the darkness that wrapped tightly around her black dress. Occasionally, her elbows and wrists would pop into view as if rising out of black milk. Everyone got really serious all of a sudden; Benia lunged out of his seat to help Alina once again, taking some bread and wine from her. Sasha started inviting her over to the table and she finally came, perhaps a bit reluctantly. The air was growing even cooler — it was as though a rain shower had just passed through and the smell of its even, frigid breath lingered.

Alina hardly said a word, occasionally asking the guests what dishes to pass them, and then she kicked back in her hard chair, gazing at the blue wine in the green bottles.

The next one to speak up was Kostyk, heavy and cumbersome, like he was all soggy from the fog and wine. He undid his tie and tossed it aside—it landed on some baked fish. He wasn't speaking all that clearly, yet his voice was loud with conviction. When someone talks like that, there's no disagreeing with him, even if he's talking nonsense. Kostyk realized that, so he tried to talk even louder. Sometimes it sounded like he was attacking someone, sometimes it sounded like he was defending them, and other times he broke into shouting, and then Sem would place his bony hand on Kostyk's shoulder, but then Sasha would nod gently at him, as if to say, "Let him be. Tomorrow morning he's not even gonna remember any of this crap he's spewing."

"Yeah, yeah," Kostyk said, clearly agitated. "I'd like to say something, too. Why aren't you letting me talk? Don't look at me like that." He got so riled up that he knocked over some wineglasses. The white tablecloth swelled with the dark weight of the alcohol, but Kostyk didn't pay that any mind, he just kept telling everyone to pipe down. "Having a warm heart . . . When a person has a warm heart, he has a completely different outlook on life. A man like that has eyes that light up from the inside, and people flock to him. Both men and women," Kostyk added.

"Here we go again," Benia interjected in a dissatisfied tone. "I told ya to cut him off a few drinks ago. Now that mouth of his is gonna get him in trouble."

Everyone knew what Benia was getting at. Everyone knew what to expect. First he'd start going on about the inner light, then he'd start holding forth about eternal salvation. He might break down crying or, more likely, pick a fight with someone. Kostyk got that way after his first stint in rehab. You generally think of drug users as mellowed out, but it's often exactly the opposite. Kostyk got hooked as an adult, when he already had something to lose, but he didn't quit until he'd lost all of it. He bounced around from one rehab clinic to another, not to mention all those spiritual counseling programs. He went back to his regular life after all that, but he had already started putting on weight. I figured it must have had something to do with his blood sugar. His drug use had led to some problems with his kidneys . . . and his head, for that matter. The drugs had nothing to do with his yelling and carrying on tonight, though. He was just as obnoxious at parties back when we were kids.

We didn't really like what he had to say, but the sloppily earnest way he said it won us over. All of our inner voices seemed to be saying, "That's it, keep it up. Open heart, men and women flocking to you." It looked like Alina was absolutely freezing; she picked up a shawl someone had left behind and wrapped it around her shoulders, shivering from time to time, as though she was reacting to a soft whisper only she could hear.

"Having a warm heart helps us get through our tougher moments and enjoy our happier hours when they come," Kostyk continued, inhaling a deep gulp of nighttime air, which made his white shirt puff up like a sail against black water. "It's all about having a warm heart, guys, having a warm heart!" With that, he started crying.

Then he wandered far afield, but it led us to a nice story that everyone could identify with; he spoke about hearts filled with goodness and hope, merciful and benevolent—those are the hearts through which mankind's conscience comes into this world, hearts with the strength to resist temptation and reject vanity. After a long and slightly garbled introduction, he reminded everyone how warm and splendid the weather had been that September, a few years back, when this incredible story took place.

"You know, you're talking about being a man and all that manly nature stuff," Kostyk blubbered. "Having compassion is the only true mark of a man, and being willing to administer first aid if it comes to that—that's the only true mark of a man too. Let's take Marat, for ex-

arm and pulling her against him. His movements were so sharp and unrestrained that she shrieked, and I wasn't sure what I was hearing in that shriek—outrage or surprise. It seemed more like surprise to me—and pleasant surprise, at that . . . although she did try to extricate herself, and she kept up her angry shouting, her teeth shining and her head bobbing, but then she thrust herself forward, crashing into Marat—with bewildered eyes, she studied his sharp, unshaven face, covered in scars and cuts, gray, fiery eyes, black hair, and hard skin. And the longer she looked at him, the more intent her gaze became. When the professor darted toward them to pull her away, Marat lost control, nailing his rival with a right hook like his coaches had taught him when he was a kid; he put his weight into it—and his heart too. The professor rolled across the floor, and the bartenders jumped on Marat from behind. All three of them crashed to the floor too. Marat's buddy and I tried to throw everyone outside, into the bluish-red void of the eerie park that had devoured the neon fire of the bar's sign. And there, amid Kharkiv's golden foliage, Marat pummeled the professor, the bartenders tried pulling him away from his victim, and we did our best to pull *them* back.

The police took everyone to the station—except the bartenders, of course. The professor was whimpering and calling out for someone to massage his heart before it was too late. His girlfriend was holding a handkerchief up against Marat's lacerated eyebrow. The professor and his girlfriend were sitting in one corner of the tiny cell, and we were sitting across from them. Nobody said anything; there was nothing but her nervous eyes, fixated on Marat, straining to parse every detail of his face, as though trying to memorize it. Then they were let go, but we had to stay. Marat asked me to use my one phone call on Alina to tell her that he had to report for a meeting with the president of the boxing federation.

"A meeting . . . at 2 a.m.?" I asked incredulously. "I'm gonna tell her we're down at the police station. Shit, man, we've gotta get outta here somehow!"

"Us at the police station?" Marat seemed hesitant. "She won't buy it—that's too believable."

"Why do we rehash things everyone already knows?" I thought. "Why do we curry favor with the dead by offering stories with so much blood and pain in them? It seems like everyone wants to re- member Marat just that way—in red boxer shorts with angel wings on his back and the Lord's benediction in his warm heart." I finally decided to leave. I turned toward Sasha. I was about to excuse my- self and dissolve into the fog when Alina leaned over toward me and touched my hand wearily.

"Hey, John, can you help me out over here?" she asked.

"Well, obviously, come on," I answered.

"I shouldn't even have come," I thought to myself.

Alina started gathering up the empty bottles scattered in the grass, passing them to me, then she took some dishes and forks off the table and headed inside. I followed, sensing everyone's eyes and voices behind me; I trod along the cracked bricks, amazed by how smoothly she moved, how deeply she plunged into the night, and how unexpectedly the light from the house's windows fell on her skin and dark hair. She opened the door and went inside. I went in after her. She took a slow look around her, quietly asked me to leave the bottles in the hallway, and then handed me the forks. They slipped out of my hand and crashed to the floor, sharp and cold like shards of ice. Somewhere deep inside the house, a door creaked. Alina put a finger to her lips, signaling for me to keep it down, since everyone was already asleep. She spoke in a whisper, which gave her voice a peculiarly trusting tone. She opened the door to the living room and took a few cautious steps. The light was off; I didn't see her so much as sense her—catching the sound of her breath, the slightly sharp walnut scent of her hair, and the slightly jarring creak of the old floor- boards under her feet.

"What's going to happen here in the dark when I accidentally bump into her, when I touch her in the void, when the forks and sharp knives in my hand wound her?" I thought. She passed through the living room and turned down a long hallway, finding her way by touch, her fingers groping from object to object. I knew this house — I played here as a kid. Its strange layout, which had changed a few times over the years, and its rooms cluttered with old furniture and tall cabinets reminded me of Marat, of slightly better circumstances, of the good old days. I've always liked the way it smells here — warm, comfortable clothing, wood, and tea. There were no books on the shelves, no pictures on the walls. Cramped rooms, narrow hallways, static shadows, invisible residents. We moved in the darkness, carefully weaving around chairs and bags, planters full of flowers, and shoes scattered across the floor. Suddenly, I realized that I didn't remember this hallway. It hadn't been here before, and I should know, I'd been here hundreds of times at different ages and in different states of mind. But I had no memory of this hallway that stretched on and on, gradually narrowing, overflowing with dust and darkness.

"They must have just done some more renovations. Yeah, that's it. Marat had been planning on knocking down this wall to merge his parents' bedroom with the little room in which nobody lived, but I don't remember him saying he was doing any remodeling the last time we talked."

We hadn't been doing much talking lately, though; I didn't have the time, desire, or patience to put up with the haze Marat lived in. Maybe he had built this hallway in his parents' dwelling so he could follow it out of this temporal world; he had broken open a channel of communication with the night, finding a place where the outer lining of the world was thin and permeable. He had finally taken advantage of this opportunity to set everything right. I stopped and listened hard. There was nothing to hear in that sheer darkness that enfolded and constricted everything; even Alina's breath was gone, as though she had drawn a gulp of air into her lungs and held it until she dissolved into the darkness like a lump of sugar in pitch-black tea. She was playing hide-and-seek with me. I remembered how Marat liked telling stories about his dad, about how his dad taught him to swim. He just picked Marat up by the scruff of the neck and dunked him; Marat would flail his arms, gasping for air and coughing up water. He spoke of those lessons with great pride—"The thing is, I didn't drown or go belly-up or anything. I kept my head above water. I lived to see another day, so now I know I'm gonna keep on holding it together— when death comes to take me, I won't just roll over."

But whenever he told those stories, his voice got so angry that it knocked the wind out of me. My mouth would suck in air greedily, trying to grab the oxygen out of it, as if I needed to make sure I wasn't drowning. This trap I had fallen into was awakening all my worst childhood stories. Fear overcame me.

"What's happening to me, how can I get out of here? Where does this damn hallway go?" I thought. I lunged forward, groping for the wall, and my hand connected with something hard—some kind of metal protrusions and dowels. I was beating one fist against black emptiness and still trying to hold on to the forks and knives with the other. I touched ripped wallpaper over cool, bulging bricks. I touched a wire hanger. I touched curtains and hats, kerchiefs and cellophane. Suddenly, my fingers stopped on something spongy and warm. I tried to identify it. Feathers—those were feathers—soft and weightless. Something like a recently stuffed bird, something packed with blood and memories. I touched it cautiously, probingly, trying to find out what this thing was. The darkness trembled at my touch and carried some faint reverberation, as if someone had sighed. I felt something moving. Horror seized me. Horror and desperation. I burst right into the darkness, fingers splayed out before me. I knocked the hanger to the floor, overturned some pots and pans. My hand struck a hard surface; the darkness burst open and harsh light hit me in the eyes. I stumbled into the old kitchen, where I had been a thousand times, where I knew every nook and cranny, where everything was familiar and elicited no fear or suspicion. Alina stood in the middle of the room, stirring something in a large pot. She gave me a surprised look. My expression was apparently a bit troubled.

"Where have you been?" she asked.

"I got turned around."

"You all right?" Her voice was skeptical.

"Yeah," I lied. She probably didn't believe me, but she didn't press the issue.

"Here, take this out to the table," she said after a short pause. She handed me a bowl of vegetables and I headed back.

By the time I got there they had just finished consoling Kostyk and were trying to remember where they'd left off and figure out where the conversation had broken down and why it had taken a turn for the worse. Kostyk was sobbing bitterly, his head in his hands and his hands on the baked fish. One might have thought he was lamenting over it—the fish, I mean. Sasha had moved over to him, laying a comforting hand on the back of his neck as if soothing a horse.

"It's gonna be okay, kid," he said. "There's no point beating yourself up over the dead."

Clearly offended, Kostyk sniffled, wiping away the tears and snot dripping down his face with his sleeves. With his sharp profile, Sasha hovered over him like a raven; Benia was smoking anxiously, tapping the ashes into a dish of marinated mushrooms. Rustam and Sem sat off to the side, still arguing about something or other. I sat down next to them, placing the vegetables on the table.

Then Sem told us a fascinating story. It was so incredible and so convoluted that even Rustam, Marat's younger brother, who was a witness to those events, threw up his hands in protest, opened his eyes wide, and shook his head disapprovingly, countering and correcting the storyteller—and boy, did he need to be corrected!

"None of us know," Sem said, sparking his lighter and making the scars on his broken and re-broken nose flare pink in its naphtha glow, "how close to us death is at any given moment. None of us can even imagine how deeply we have ventured into its domain." He may not have been as lucid as I'm making him sound—he took a few anxious drags and he stumbled over his words a bit, but his story was definitely about death, I know that for a fact.

"Death never meets us halfway; it can bide its time and pick the right moment. It stands in crisp, emerald grass—invisible and inevitable, observing how casually and imprudently we run into its shadow. Sometimes we're able to slip out of its shadow again. But most times, how we react isn't up to us. We are vulnerable in the face of death, paralyzed with fear and a sense of doom. Hardly anyone's capable of overcoming that sense of doom. Marat's situation was particularly strange. He wasn't afraid of death, and he loved women. One time they offered him a coaching position at some foreign club. You guys all heard about that. You know what he said to them? He said he'd die here, alongside his mom. Everybody knows how courteously and honorably he treated women. He might have gotten that from his mom, or maybe it went with his athletic discipline. Whatever the case may be, he basically worshipped women. One time, last spring . . . about a year ago, actually, Marat was drawn into a fight. He was just walking home after a match, descending the hill on Revolution Street, when he saw some prick hitting on this girl; he just wouldn't leave her alone. Marat got into a fight with him, obviously. You'd think it'd be easy for a professional boxer to knock out some joker on the street. But what that prick lacked in skill he made up for in stamina. His head was made of iron, you could bash him with a bicycle frame until it bent, and it wouldn't even faze him. They duked it out for two hours, grappling and then stopping to catch their breath and then going at it again. Even the girl lost interest; she tried to humor them, but after a while she couldn't take it anymore. She excused herself and went on her way. Neither of them tried to stop her. Eventually, Marat's boxing skills allowed him to emerge victorious—he knocked that meathead down. He was just lying there on the warm, evening asphalt, bleeding. Marat was just about to turn around and head home, but something stopped him, something compelled him to stay. He bent over, hefted that tough guy over his shoulder and started carrying him toward the bright lights shining by the metro station, thinking he'd just drop him off in front of a pharmacy. The guy was heavy and cumbersome—his legs were dragging along the ground, his jeans were sagging, he was breathing hoarsely and dripping blood down Marat's neck. But Marat forged on; he knew that an honest man doesn't leave corpses in his wake, he doesn't play dirty. He hauled that prick all the way over to the pharmacy and carefully set him down by the door. He was just about to try and get the night shift clerk's attention, but he decided to wipe the blood off the guy's face first. As soon as he leaned in, his rival opened his eyes, pulled a pair of long, shiny scissors out of his back pocket and drove them into Marat's side—then he just ran away. Marat tried to catch him, but the scissors were slowing him down a bit. Scissors still jutting out of him, he decided to head home, staggering from wall to wall and tree to tree through the night. It turns out the girl was a hairdresser."

And then they started chattering all at once, interrupting and deriding one another.

"He wasn't boxing anymore! He was already coaching kids then!" Rustam yelled.

"Whatcha talkin' about?" Sem said, shaking his head. "I went to all his fights. He didn't box like the old Marat, obviously, but that's just how it goes."

"What fights, what are you talking about?" Rustam asked hotly. "He would just loaf around on the couch for weeks at a time. He wouldn't even leave the neighborhood."

"That's right. He'd only leave to box," Sem declared.

"With who? Come on!" Rustam sprang to his feet, but Sem tugged at the sleeve of his athletic jacket to make him sit back down. "His heart was aching."

"Yep, that's true." Kostyk backed him up. "His heart ached with kindness!"

I said my goodbyes, shaking Rustam and Sem's hands, patting Kostyk on the back, writing down Sasha's phone number, and waving to Benia. Nobody stopped me. They were all exhausted, falling asleep at the table, but they held their ground—it was as if they were afraid of being left alone with all those stories. The fog rose toward the May sky, laying objects bare and hollowing out the darkness. Three windows on the second floor yellowly consumed the night. All three neighbors—the two heavyset women and the frail one—stared intently at my back, both presaging and foreseeing something to come.

I knew the hairdresser. Marat met her last March. He just happened to be walking by when he had some automatic reaction to the light sparkling on windows displaying pretty women's seemingly severed heads. He decided to stop in. It was the end of a cold workday, and she was the only one there. She was just about to set off into the night—what's the point of sitting around in a salon when real, juicy life is getting under way on the other side of the black windows? She had already shed her shiny apron with its numerous pockets stuffed with scissors, combs, and electric trimmers. And then Marat stepped inside. She immediately noticed the dark circles under his eyes, which alluded to all his sleepless nights and his tobacco-roasted lungs; she noticed his stubble, which, oddly enough, made him look younger and meaner than he really was. She noticed his bandaged right hand, which made her realize that this here was a guy that wouldn't back down if challenged, no matter what. Her eyes slid down his black hoodie, down his Nike gym bag, down his black jeans dotted with cigarette burns, all the way to his light sneakers. He looked like a movie hitman. The cops always find the distinctive footprints left by those sneakers, that's what gives them away. She put her apron back on and nodded at a chair, signaling Marat to take a seat. She walked over, examined him at length in the mirror, and ran her hand through his prickly, black hair. She readied the scissors carefully; there were sparks flying off Marat and she was afraid of getting burned.

Marat told us that her whole look was too pink and too bloody. Pink hair, bloody makeup, pink shirt, bloody nails, pink, fluffy slippers, and blood-colored underwear. When she touched him, he felt how impatient her hands were, how adept she was at touching men, feeling their heat and restraining the quivering tension of their bodies. Or not, Marat added. He spun the chair around and pulled her against him, but that pink apron of hers, weighed down by all kinds of hairdresser stuff, kept getting in the way. Marat tried pulling it off, but it clung to her body, determined to protect her from the caresses of strangers. Then she untied the strings and tossed it on the floor, and the ringing metal of scissors and combs flew under the chair. Now she stood before him and he looked at her bare stomach, which her tiny shirt did nothing to conceal, and then he jerked her down onto his lap, stripping off all her clothes, not daring to stop, not for an instant, propelled by some unaccountable urgency. She didn't even close the door of the salon; somebody peeked in while Marat was ripping off all her red straps and pink stockings, holding her against him to feel her skin grow warm from his touch and cold from the brisk March draft whipping in from the street. When she cried out and froze, he turned her face toward the light, trying to understand what had happened, why she wasn't moving, until he too froze and could do nothing but keep squeezing her and examining her hair and eyebrows up close, stunned at the brightness and color of this girl, imagining how many meticulous minutes of drawing before her mirror and draping herself in brilliant folds they entailed, and then marveling at how easily she had shed them all again. He was also surprised by how quickly and smoothly she quieted down. Her gaze was intent and detached, instantly disconcerting; he stood up, carried her across the room, tossed her onto the leather couch decisively, though not very tenderly, and walked out the door. He hadn't said a single word to her the whole time.

He came by the next evening. She was by herself, like before. Marat closed the door, standing there and waiting in silence. She knew where this was going; she turned off the lights. Outside the window, the street was infused with strands of light and shadow; they blended together and streaked apart, blurring and eroding the neighborhood's buildings away. She rushed to tell him odd and unexpected things, saying that she'd been waiting for him and that she knew he'd come, telling him about herself, reminiscing about her ex-boyfriends, quietly explaining what she liked and what she didn't, what she loved and what she feared until the wee hours of the morning, showing no signs of fatigue, not asking him a single question, doing everything he wanted, submitting to everything—they kept going until he let up and fell asleep.

For some reason, Marat liked her; he talked about feeling her heart speed up when they kissed and then turn slow and quiet again.

"Sometimes when we're together she acts like I'm not even there, even though she's lying next to me. Or on top of me. She looks right through me, at something only her eyes can see. Maybe she's just listening to my breathing or maybe she's just inhaling my smell. Couldn't tell ya," he said.

He seemed to like that too. At home, he wouldn't even bother hiding the fact that he was going to the salon. When he started going there more regularly he'd say that he needed to go to a salon to get a good shave, that a real man should always be clean-shaven. The trouble was, he'd sometimes shave before he left . . . He was crashing and burning, and all his relationships were falling apart—with Alina, his parents, and his brother too. He'd even started fighting with his hairdresser girl more often. One time he admitted that he was afraid to let her cut his hair.

"She's gonna chop my head off one of these days," he said ominously. That's pretty much how it all played out. Remember that story about the scissors? He made the whole thing up in my kitchen, with his hand pressed to the gaping wound. He was complaining that she had gone completely insane, that she wanted to kill him, that she was demanding the impossible from him, and that she was fucking him like there was no tomorrow. He tried talking to her, just to explain something to her.

"Do you realize that?" he yelled. "I just wanted to talk to her!"

But that caused even more drama; she just didn't want to hear it, crying and accusing him of God knows what. He got all riled up, screamed at her, demolished the chair, smashed the mirror, threw bottles of cologne on the floor, and bent some hair dryers in half. Well, that's when she drove the scissors into his side, right up to the handles.

"Just don't tell anyone, all right? Nobody can find out about this."

I didn't. Later on, he told everyone himself.

I asked him what was keeping him here. He had lots of relatives on his dad's side, and they were always offering him jobs back home, in the Caucasus.

"Well, how can I just up and leave? How can I quit on them?" He was referring to all his women, all his relatives, and all his friends and rivals. "There's just no way." But I knew that wasn't the real reason. I knew Alina was the one keeping him here—she flatly refused to leave with him. She said she'd die here—with his parents and in his house, an inconsolable widow—before she'd leave this city. Marat could act on any ridiculous fancy that popped into his head. He lived with whoever he wanted, he slept with whoever he wanted, he fought with whoever he wanted, he lost friends and made enemies, refused to make the *right* connections, and failed to uphold his obligations to anyone—by the end of his life he was at odds with everyone, even me. I hadn't spoken to him all winter. He owed Kostyk a lot of money. As far as I could gather, he wasn't planning on giving it back—plus Kostyk wouldn't have accepted it anyway. It seemed as though he was preparing for something important, some big decision, or some great event. He could cut himself loose of everything and still get by. Everything but Alina. I knew that for a fact. It made no difference how many women he had or how deep his pink hairdresser chewed into his skin, I knew that he would never leave without Alina. And I knew why.

Nobody besides me knew. A long time ago, Marat told me all about them, for some reason—how they met on the street somewhere or other, how he stopped her, how he didn't want to let her go because he already knew that this was the girl he wanted to live with. How she kept avoiding him, always hiding something. How he first went home with her and how all that turned out. How she finally agreed to move in with him—but before she did, she told him all about her mom, because she didn't want to keep anything from him. She said that her mom had to spend time in the hospital every once in a while— "Yeah, it's a drag. It's nothing too bad, but there's nothing too great about it, either. Sometimes she just doesn't recognize anyone. But that's nothing too serious, don't ya think? I don't always recognize everyone, either." So she always had to be somewhere nearby, somewhere not too far away, because of her mom and stuff. Marat had no problem with that, and he knew better than most guys do that his girl wouldn't be going anywhere . . . but that meant he wasn't going anywhere either. Because it's one thing to sleep in another apartment with another woman, but you just can't quit on someone who can't be left behind. That's just not an option. Not under any circumstances. At least that's how I understood their relationship.

"What's going to happen to her?" I thought to myself. "How's she going to get by? What's she going to do from here on out?" I passed the Institute, crested the hill, and stopped by our school. My old, four-story apartment building was directly across from it. It was so badly maintained that the front door wouldn't even close. Sometimes I'd wake to the sound of young voices coming from the stairwell—kids ducking in for a smoke break. I lived on the top floor; the only thing above me was the roof. Hundreds of pigeons lived up there—sometimes their cooing would seep into my dreams. One time, when we were already in high school, Marat dragged me up there to go "hunting." I don't know why he felt the need to do that. I don't remember why I agreed to go along with him.

"There are hundreds of pigeons up there," he said excitedly. "They're sleepy at night; you can just stuff 'em in a sack." We met outside my building in the evening. He had a gym bag with him. We went up the stairs. Marat stepped out first. I followed him. It was stuffy and quiet up in the attic. Only the eerie, invisible rustling of wings broke the silence. I took out my flashlight, but Marat stopped me just in time.

"Put that away, you'll scare 'em off," he said. He stepped forward. The pigeons were perched on the beams, sleepy and defenseless. He grabbed them and tossed them into his bag. They submitted with a chilling, doomed air, unable to process what was happening to them, unable to look death straight in the eye. Soon enough, the bag was full. It was rustling, as though two people were arguing inside. Marat walked over toward a window and stepped out, onto the ledge. He called me over and I followed him. We carefully positioned ourselves by the window, taking in the buildings down below. The city blocks where we were born and raised shone into view, dark and silvery—heavy conglomerations of structures and sprawling treetops. Apartment blocks with darkness pooling in the hollows between them, like water in the holds of sunken tankers, shone into view. Windows and balconies, antennas and ladders shone into view. Arches and doorways, telephone poles and kiosks shone into view. Bricks and tin, grass and stones, clay and nighttime earth shone into view. Spiderwebs, filling the air like thin veins, shone into view. Down toward where the river ran, the buildings dropped off and the roofs of warehouses and auto repair shops shone into view, and the cold mercury of its current shone into view, and on the opposite bank were the spectral pipe of the old windmill, the lights of houses, and the white smokestacks of furnaces and factories. Thick silver flooded the earth and the sky, and you could only guess who lived down there and what was happening. Marat looked straight ahead, entranced.

"You know what?" he said. "It'd be sweet to buy up all of this someday."

"What for?"

"What do you mean 'what for?' It'd boost my status. Can you imagine having your own house like that, all to yourself?" he said, pointing at the windows across the way. "When I grow up, I'm definitely gonna buy all of this. I'm gonna buy everything and everyone. Everything around here is gonna be mine." He thought for a second, then added, "Well, I guess it already is."

"Exactly," I agreed.

"Hey, you don't think I can do it, do you?" Marat was offended. "You'll see. I can do anything I want. How can you not believe me? You're my friend—and my student."

"Huh?"

"I taught ya how to box!"

"I don't know about that. You just knocked me around in the ring a couple times."

"It doesn't matter. I could even say you're my favorite student."

"Hey, why don't we let them out?" I asked, pointing at the bag. "Come on, man, this isn't cool."

Marat kept quiet—apparently vacillating—then he opened the bag and shook the birds out onto the slate roof. They rolled a bit, flapped their wings, and flew away into the nighttime air. Marat tossed the bag to the side. He sat there in silence. I didn't really know what to say then, either. Suddenly he turned around. The thin, reflected sickle of the moon glinted sharply in the cracked window behind us. There was so much light coming off it. It blinded and disquieted us. Marat extended his hand cautiously and broke off a piece of glass, as if he was snapping the moon in two. One half remained. It got darker.

## ROMEO

Two years ago, I could feel my heart waking me up every morning, "Come on, we don't have much time, we're gonna miss all the good stuff!" It would hop up and down impatiently, urging me to get moving. "Come on, how much can a guy sleep?" I'd get up and run outside, and then not a single one of the city's wonders could escape me. Two years ago, my lungs devoured the air ferociously, and I was sure that something extraordinary—white light, fireworks, and grand orchestras—was waiting for me just around the next corner, something like a holiday. Actually, there was nothing waiting for me except cold spring drafts, but that didn't get me down one bit. Twenty—that's the age when the devil pays you a visit to gripe about his troubles. All you have to do is sleep as little as possible. Well, that and use condoms. Then you're golden. Everything will fall right into place. Everything will happen just the way you want it to. Whether you want it to or not.

I got here at the end of May. I walked through town from the train station. I didn't have a lot of stuff with me—a leather backpack containing a few T-shirts, an old laptop, and a thermos of cognac I hadn't finished on the train. Jeans, Keds, and an aggressively green button-down shirt—I was here for the long haul, and I'd packed accordingly. My gait was smooth and buoyant from running daily that spring, my haircut made me look like Boney M.'s lead vocalist during their heyday, and the bountiful sun reflected off dark sunglasses covering half my face. I was a rock star—it was impossible *not* to notice me. At least that's how I saw it. I took a liking to the city—

quiet neighborhoods down by the station overrun with apricot trees and grass, outdoor garages, ramshackle additions, and condemned buildings (or at least they ought to be condemned) from which retirees, as slow as chameleons, would emerge from time to time—it was all all right by me. The smell of sugar and cocoa floating around the blocks down by the chocolate factory, the grim shop floors of the empty enterprises down by the market, iron gates, corner stores, and doctors' offices—it was all mine for the taking. I popped out by a river. "Huh, turns out this city has bridges. That's good," I thought to myself. "A city on the water is more calm and secure; life in that kind of city has its own order and sticks within its own boundaries." I later found out that there wasn't just one river here. The city lay between two of them, up in the hills; it might as well have been on an island, flashing its white and red buildings enclosed by hot May greenery. "All right, Kharkiv," I said, stepping onto one of its bridges, "are you ready to rock?"

The apartment building had four floors. It looked pretty dilapidated—i.e., like a place to call home. Overall, the area was quiet, although there were kids wailing despairingly in the schoolyard on the other side of the street. I pulled the front door open. I didn't even have to punch in a code—anyone could just waltz on in to any of the apartments and murder the tenants in their warm beds. I was feeling pretty chipper at the beginning of this endless, sunny day. The third floor was mine—a black metal door, a blue rubber mat, and what looked like a cute red coin serving as a doorbell. Sometimes the world forgets that we're in it and starts looking nice, for a change.

I rang and rang, pressing hard on the red button until I had squeezed out the last drop of its aggravating whine. Nobody answered—just my luck. I kicked the door, humming a cheerful tune to myself. I even thought about waiting at the neighbors' apartment for a while; I rang their identical red doorbell—they didn't answer either. What now? I didn't have anywhere else to go—nobody was expecting me in this town. I put my backpack on the floor, sat down on the mat, and opened up my thermos. "They'll have to come back eventually," I thought. "And they'll be sorry, you can bet on that."

In a little while I heard some light, untroubled footsteps and somebody humming. "It must be the downstairs neighbors," I thought. "But no . . ." My back was up against the door, and I could hear somebody walking on the other side. I sprang to my feet and reached for the doorbell. At first, the footsteps trailed off, but then they came closer, almost inaudibly. Somebody was eyeing me through the peephole. I stepped back so they could get a good look at my sunglasses. "You gotta nail that first impression," I thought. The door opened.

She had a perky haircut. Her hair wasn't simply dyed white—it was dyed all different shades of white—yeah, nice and perky. Her gaze was probing, yet languid. Dressed in red pajamas and a snow-white robe with a hotel logo on it, she looked like she'd just rolled out of bed. She'd thrown that robe of hers on carelessly, so it kept slipping off her shoulders, making her look like a boxer shedding his warmup gear and tossing it to his coach before stepping into the ring. She had green eyes, a heavy smoker's pale skin, a long, delicate neck, and bare feet; she shifted her weight from one to the other.

"Who are you?" she asked, peering over my shoulder.

"Romeo," I answered and looked behind me. "My mom called you."

"Your mom?" She looked confused. "Why'd she call me?"

"I'm going to stay at your place," I explained.

"With your mom?"

"Nope. By myself . . . My mom's at our apartment."

"At your apartment?" she asked, adjusting her robe as it slid down again. "What's she doing at your apartment?"

"Working on a case."

"Huh?"

"She's working on a case. She's a lawyer."

"Oh . . ." She finally figured out what was going on. "I remember now. You're Romeo, right?"

"Yep."

"Your mom's a lawyer."

"You got it."

"What's that thingy on your head?"


Her name was Dasha. My mom and her met a month ago at some seminar. During the day, they'd sit together, jotting down notes and guzzling coffee. At night, they'd go bowling with the other attendees, and usually get plastered. My mom knows how to butter people up; by the end of the first night she was hanging all over her new friend, telling her about how I'd transferred to a new school, so I'd be leaving her nest any day now.

"It's his last year coming up," she said, sniffling. "I get it—it's no fun sitting around at home with your mom. So he transferred. But what's gonna happen to him? Is he gonna wind up sleeping at the train station like a bum?" My mom wiped away her tears and ordered another round, which inevitably led to still more tears.

Eventually, Dasha interrupted: "What are you beating yourself up for? Why doesn't he just stay at my place? I've got my grammy-in-law's old apartment. She just croaked. Talk about great timing! I was planning on renting it out anyway. I'd rather have it be someone I know—at least he won't take off with the furniture—well, not that he could . . . there actually isn't any." My mom latched onto Dasha and her apartment; if she was going to let her little boy—meaning me—out into the big, wide world, she wanted to know where she'd have to start looking for the body. I was all for staying at her friend's place, but I would have found somewhere to live, even if Dasha hadn't come into the picture. I just really needed to escape from my room, which still reeked of children's clothing and schoolbooks. I had been planning on moving out for a while—living with your mom when you're twenty isn't exactly a boatload of fun. She drank more than a respectable lawyer ought to, and I spent too much time in the bathroom. Under the circumstances, we'd be better off living separately and writing each other heartfelt letters.

It didn't seem like I made much of an impression on Dasha, which bothered me, obviously. I thought I should tell her something about my mom, about what interested me, what I did, and what I was shooting for in life, but I didn't manage to get anything out.

"Follow me," she said. "Let me show you around."

She walked over to the other apartment, opened the door, and stepped inside. She didn't invite me in, so I stood in the doorway for a bit, but then I followed her anyway. There were two rooms. It looked like they'd been renovated not too long ago. And it looked like she had done it herself—the wallpaper was peeling off, warm water had pooled on the bathroom floor, and the ceiling looked as though it had been bleached, not painted. Dasha walked across the room, opened the window, and leaned out. She had nice legs. "I think I'm gonna like it here," I thought. She came right back.

"You don't have a sleeping bag?" she asked. "All right, I'll give you a mattress. And here's the kitchen," she said, steering me into the next room. There was a stove there . . . and nothing else. "Well, that's about it. You won't actually be needing any of this," she said, referring to the kitchen. "There's a pizzeria around the corner, just so you know. Here's the shower," she declared, carefully stepping over the puddles. "I'll give you a towel," she added. "Hmm . . . what else is there? Oh yeah, internet and utilities. You woke me up, so I'm kinda out of it."

We carried a large mattress with watercolors, playdough, and lipstick smeared all over it from her apartment into my room. Dasha had a slim body and a pleasing voice. "It'd be nice to sleep with her on this mattress. After all, why not?" I thought. "All you gotta do is make the right impression. It sure looks like she's single. She gets up at about noon and walks around the building in her PJs. She's definitely my type," I thought, looking at how lithely she was bending over the mattress to wipe it clean. "I just have to take matters into my own hands," I thought as I hurried off to the shower.

She ran over to my place again in the afternoon and said she had some stuff to do. She brought over some sheets, left me a set of keys, and told me that anything I could find in her fridge was up for grabs. Well, there was nothing in there but a head of cabbage—it was fresh, though. She was wearing a sand-colored suit that made her look a tiny bit heavier than she actually was, but those high heels of hers were so flattering they more than made up for it—Dasha was an older, self-assured lawyer with her bra showing through her snow-white shirt, a battle-ready haircut, sloppy makeup, and some serious coffee breath. She was talking so much and so loudly that I didn't even realize she'd left until she was outside.

I was kicking myself. "Just chill, it's not like she's never coming back. What could she be doing today? Maybe . . . going to a trial . . . or . . . I don't know . . . questioning some witnesses or identifying some bodies or something. She'll rip yet another unfortunate soul out of death's claws, sign all the necessary papers, and head home, to see me. Just don't let this one get away, seize this opportunity, and ride this wave of happiness rushing down the apartment hallway." In the evening, somebody changed the air like hotel sheets, turning the foliage dark and the window glass pink. Light grazed the floor and the bare walls; voices and children's laughter resonated beyond the trees. I felt the urge to follow those voices, walk among those trees, touch women's hands in the gloom, and catch the hefty green moons slipping off the branches under their own weight.

"How should I play this? Just how should I play this? I could go over to her kitchen, like I wanted a bite to eat. I'd keep my cool, announce I was hungry, and gruffly declare that I'd make us a meal. But I'd ask her to help out. Strong and silent, that's the key. I could show up with no shirt on—let her see my tan. I could show up barefoot. Nah, that's no good. She'll figure out what I'm up to and say, 'You might as well have shown up naked.' Okay, then . . . how about sandals? That way I won't have to mess around with any knotty shoelaces. Yeah," I nodded, giving myself a pat on the back, "that'll be perfect. I'll ask her to get me some spices from the top shelf—some cinnamon, cardamom, or pepper. And as soon as she reaches for them I'll come up behind her, calmly (keep your cool, man), and touch her legs. Like I'm giving her a boost. When she feels my warm hands on her skin, she'll know exactly what to do. And then I'll help her down off the chair, lay her down on the table, and start undressing her. Gotta get over there while she still has her suit on! She's been wearing it all day, she's gonna wanna get out of it—no, she'll help me pull off her jacket and anxiously hike up the skirt clinging to the warm curves of her hips. Only then will I step out of my sandals."

"Or," I was getting all excited, "I could show up and ask her for some little domestic thing. Like soap. Nah," I shot down my own idea, "then she'll figure out what I'm up to. No soap. A toothbrush is way better. I'll show up at her front door in sandals, with no shirt on, and maybe with my shades on too. I'll ask her for a toothbrush (keep it strong and silent, man), I'll be like, 'I forgot mine on the train—I was too busy helping all those women, carrying toddlers out onto the platform, and evacuating decrepit old people.' The toothbrush will probably be in her bathroom. And when she walks across the room in her suit I can slide on over and stand right behind her, and one whiff of my deodorant will do the trick. She'll freeze up, anticipating my next move, knowing exactly where this is going. Then I can touch her clothes, feeling her receptive body tremble, and I'll remove her jacket without saying a single word and help her slip out of her skirt, so she'll be standing there in her white shirt and colorful panties, like a naughty schoolgirl. I'll bend her over the sink—it will glisten like crystals of sugar—so she can look in the mirror and see all her wrinkles smoothing out and her pupils dilating with joy, fevered desire consuming her as she gasps for air. And I won't even need to take off my sandals for that."

"But that's not all. Not even close," I was really getting worked up now. "There's so many ways I could play this. I could show up with my computer and be like, 'I can't get on the internet. What's your Wi-Fi password?' Maybe she'll be sprawled out on the bed, too exhausted after a long day of questioning witnesses to take her suit off. She'll be lying on her stomach (you know she's the type that sleeps on her stomach) and watching television, preferably on mute. I could walk over, stand between her and the screen, and ask for the password. Just keep it strong and silent, man! 'You know, I don't remember anymore. Let me see your computer. I'll get ya all set up,' she'll say, patting the sheets next to her. 'Pop a squat, you'll be online in no time.' And then I'll calmly (calmly!) plop down next to her. Just make sure to kick off your sandals! And when she starts fiddling around with the laptop, I could help her, put my hand on top of hers gently, like it was purely accidental, and look into her wide-open eyes intensely, confidently. And then I'll wait for her to figure everything out and put my lagging computer off to the side—I wouldn't even have to do much—she'd hop right on top of me, taking off her jacket, yanking down the zipper on her skirt, biting my sun-tempered skin (if I didn't have my shirt on) or gnawing on its fabric (if I was still wearing it). Just gotta keep it strong and silent, be tough but fair, unstoppable and grateful."

With those thoughts racing through my mind, I fell asleep. Swallows flew over me in my dreams, describing menacing circles, but I wasn't scared.

I happened to wake up as she was coming back, sensing her footsteps more than actually hearing them. The front door squeaked open and then she stamped her way up the worn stairs, hitting the rails with her palms, resting between flights, peering down the stairwell, then finally pushing on. She was taking an eternity; I had time to chase all the swallows away, bolt over to the bathroom, wet my hair (everything had to be just right), and sprint to the stairs, coming face to face with her. She was staggering, holding a bottle of champagne in each hand.

Dangling precariously from her right pinky, her jacket was dragging along the steps behind her. Her shoes were stained with grass and encrusted with sand, and she was smiling drunkenly—Dasha was enchanting.

"Oh, hey," she said, surprised. "No slippers? Aren't you cold?"

"I'm fine," I said. Tough and reserved—keep it going. "I heard you come in."

"Were you waiting up for me?" She laughed.

"I wanted to give you your keys back."

"Wanna have a drink?" Dasha asked.

"Champagne?" I made myself sound as tough as humanly possible. "Sure, you oughta have some company."

She tossed her jacket on the floor, sat on it, and gestured for me to join her. It was painful to look at her skirt—everything was right out in the open. I sat down next to her, my bare feet feeling the nighttime chill coming off the floor. "I shouldn't have put my shirt on," I thought. "I could've given her a real good show." Dasha grabbed the bottle and began struggling to open it, shaking it and gnawing off the foil. Finally, it burst open; Dasha squealed but then composed herself quickly.

"Cheers," she said, taking a swig. The champagne soused her, running off her lips, under the collar of her snow-white shirt. Dasha handed me the bottle brusquely and started undoing the buttons, wiping the liquid off her skin. I was in a real state watching how delicately and fastidiously she touched her own body.

"Drink up."

"How was work?" I asked with an air of importance.

"All right. I have a stressful job. My clients always have one problem or another. But how can you work with people that have so many problems? They need a therapist, not a lawyer. What are you planning on doing here?" she asked.

"I'm just gonna settle in first," I answered, deciding to play my cards close to the chest for now. "Can I kiss you?"

"Kiss me? That's rich. Find yourself a girl your own age! All right, that's a wrap."

She got up, grabbed her jacket, stuck the unopened bottle in my hand, and went to bed.

What did I do wrong? Where was the error in my calculations? Was it the shirt? Or the sandals? Or maybe even my sunglasses? Everything should have played out differently. I should be lying in her bed right now and she should be lying next to me, gazing tenderly and languidly into my imperturbable eyes. Instead, I'm standing here in the kitchen holding a bottle of champagne in these hands that I don't know what to do with. What's she up to right now? Yeah, I knew it — she's walking around in the kitchen, too, feet pattering on the other side of the wall. I placed the champagne on the floor and pressed my ear against the wall. Now she's walking over to the window and opening it; all the twilight critters, all those moths and bugs, come rushing at her, so she shuts it quickly, walks over to the cabinet, takes out some dishes, tea, sugar, a mug, spoons, and saucers. All that metal jingles harmoniously; she puts it on the table right behind me — just an arm's length away, just one breath away — turns on the gas, places a kettle on the stove, sits down, gets up again, walks over to the window, opens it back up, and takes out her lighter. "Damn, she's smoking." She anxiously puts out her cigarette, exhales the smoke from her lungs, shuts the window, takes her phone out of her jacket pocket, checks for missed calls, and abruptly tucks it away again. The kettle starts whistling; she ignores it for a while, stands up, looks tensely at her side of the wall, in my direction, turns sharply, shuts off the gas angrily, sits down at the table and forcefully sweeps all the dishes and spoons into the corner. Now I can't hear her anymore. What's she doing? What's she doing over there? She's crying! Suddenly, it hits me — she's crying! She's sitting there and crying! Yeah, she's sitting there, all alone in her empty apartment, sobbing inconsolably, choking on her bitter tears after choking down a bedtime dose of bitter nicotine, and there's nobody there, nobody at all, who can listen to her weeping and ease her pain! Nobody besides me! Struck by this epiphany, I spring to my feet, knocking the bottle over—it tips to the side, slowly and mutely, like a freight train loaded with oil, and starts rolling along the scrubbed, cold floor, its squeaking violating the surrounding silence. She tenses up, there, on the other side—now she knows what's going on; she goes quiet and listens hard. The rolling bottle hits the wall and stops. I go quiet, too, standing still and listening to her silence; she holds it, knowing I'm here, that I can hear everything, that I've figured everything out.

It was a little before eight when she unlocked my apartment with her set of keys and shouted from the doorway.

"Wake up, sleepyhead!"

She sped down the hallway, poked her head into the bathroom, shot a probing glance at the kitchen, and barreled right into the room where I was sleeping, naked, as usual, so I finally gave her a good show.

"Ooo." She sat down next to me and touched my shoulder. "Whatcha got there?" she asked, examining my tat. "Is that a dog?"

"It's a dragon. It's not finished yet, that's all."

"Nah, that's no dragon. That's a dog. Look, here's its tail. It's a wiener dog." She touched my dragon again, sending waves of fire across my skin—but she hopped off the mattress before I could deliver a good comeback. "Come on, get dressed," she ordered. "I want to show you something."

I put my clothes on in a hurry. I'm generally a pretty confident dude, but after the wiener dog, I wasn't in the mood to argue with her. Dasha opened up the balcony door, stepped outside, stood there, and waved. "Come on," she said, "what's the holdup?" There she stood in her white hotel robe. Her hair was pulled back into a bun, and she had apparently slept that way, so it looked like an array of vegetables a chef had selected with exacting skill for the soup of the day. I walked over gloomily.

"All right," she said, looking around. "Let me show you the neighborhood and then you can go back to sleep. Look," she began, making room for me on the balcony. "You see that?"

I peered down. There was so much sunlight that it blinded me and blurred the objects near the ground. My eyesight came back to me almost instantly, though; things regained their shape and colors grew fuller. Greenery and heat were ushering out the month of May—fresh air was lying on the rooftops and pooling between the apartment blocks. Schoolkids were running down the street, a few other people were zooming around, and a street sweeper stood on the corner, his vest flashing orange. "Today is no ordinary day," I thought. "Today is something like a holiday."

"So, that's the school," Dasha said, pointing at the building across from us. "I didn't go there because I only moved here three years ago, but just so you know, some freaky stuff goes on over there. The principal often spends the night in her office, but not by herself—she has visitors . . . a car with diplomatic plates. They blast Italian pop music all night and stick their heads out of her office window to smoke. She has a red nightgown, just so you know. That's the beauty salon next door," she continued, pointing. "Those girls give each other nail extensions all day. They go outside for smoke breaks, take a seat on the bench—you see that bench up against the wall—whichever of them just got her nails done has to have her girlfriend pluck the pack out of her pocket. Then they sit there like owls digging their claws into the wooden bench. Check it out sometime. There's a real shady restaurant around the corner—every morning the owner walks around in a pink kimono, talking to somebody on his little girly cellphone. A little farther back, there's a sports bar where a bunch of Arabs watch the European soccer leagues. A while ago some Vietnamese guys opened up a seriously gross buffet—I've never seen one of them eat any of the food they make. Next to the Vietnamese joint, in the alley, there's a sauna that's just a front for a brothel—something to keep in mind . . . There's a vacant building next to that; bums hang out there in the summer months—kinda neat. Local artists have their studios next to the bums—make sure you keep 'em straight. And there's a TB clinic across the way. So, what else do we got?" She looked to the left. "There's a publishing house over there. I suspect they hide documents for companies that do under-the-table accounting—fresh packages of paper come in at dusk and corpses wrapped in Chinese rugs go out at dawn. The city fathers have a mansion a bit farther down—it seems like their mistresses are living out their days there. Sometimes I see them on the back porch—not the city fathers, obviously—their mistresses, drinking their tea mixed with rum. The youngest lady is about seventy or so."

"You serious?" I asked incredulously.

"I'm dead serious. By the way, she has a red nightgown, too. She's always just standing there, drinking her tea. Her rum tea. They just put up a new apartment block over there, but nobody wanted to move in at first. It was too pricey. So some construction workers lived there for a bit—they unrolled their sleeping bags, cooked meat on open fires, and rummaged around in the warehouses for something good to eat. I'm tellin' ya, they lived like a band of partisans. Down around the corner, there are a few convenience stores, but they're always closed for some reason. Nobody really knows what kind of business they're actually running. I've seen some young women go in there, but I've never seen them come out. There are some houses on small lots at the bottom of the hill—there's nobody living down there—but hey, there's nobody dying, either. There are tons of trees. Everything's in bloom this time of year. On the top floors, the lights are always on at night, and there's generally some kind of business—maybe a Xerox place, or a notary, or a place where they make headstones—on the lower floors. There's a gas station and some auto repair shops down the road—and the river, too. The army recruiting office is right below us," she said, leaning down. "I know a couple of secretaries who work there . . . it's a real tough job, it wears you down. Have you served yet?"

"No," I answered reluctantly.

"I see, well, last but not least, there's our building. All right, take a look." She leaned so far over the balcony rail she nearly fell, but I grabbed a flap of her robe just in the nick of time. "Two Armenian guys live on the first floor. Ya smell that cologne? They're goin' heavy on it. They've told everyone they're brothers, but I don't buy it. You see the windows and the antenna? Anfisa lives there, she's a journalist—well, she's the weather girl. If she invites you over just don't go. You won't be in there five minutes before her mom starts asking if you've set a date for the wedding. So don't go there unless you really need to know if it's gonna rain. There's an empty apartment on the second floor. The old owner—he was a big hunter—had a shootout with the cops. Vendetta!" Dasha shouted giddily. "I was just moving in when he was trying to fend them off. He used to be an artilleryman. He'd been mending clothes for a few years before that. He kept his gun loaded, though. Nobody moved in after him. It smells like death down there. Across the hall from the artillery guy's place there's Hutalin—he's a Communist and a real dickwad."

"A dickwad?"

"Yeah, a bigtime dickwad. He's a real louse, always flooding his downstairs neighbors' apartments. He acts like it's just our shitty plumbing, but I think he does it on purpose. Then there's our floor, you already know everything about that."

"No, I don't. How'd you wind up with two apartments?"

"It's none of your business," Dasha answered, "but I'll tell you anyway. My ex-husband left me the one I live in. His grandma used to live there. She didn't really like her grandson, so she left me her apartment."

"Where is that husband of yours?" I asked with some suspicion.

"In the Emirates, I think," Dasha answered. "Or Saudi Arabia. He moved all his assets overseas. It's too cold for him here."

"What about his grandma?"

"His grandma died. She was one tough cookie. She was a mail lady, and she stuck it out to the end . . . i.e., until she got canned. Oh yeah, upstairs," she whispered, "you hear those footsteps? That's Mr. Ivanovich. He's trying to sell some factory . . . has been for ten years already, but no dice. Hey, John!" she yelled into the sky.

Up above, a man—a bit under forty, a little too skinny, weary eyes, cigarette between his teeth, dark-colored suit, stale shirt— poked his head out. He nodded amiably at Dasha and gave me an attentive look—he had the air of a guy who just got back from a wake.

"Is that one yours?" he asked.

"Yep," she confirmed—it didn't seem like she'd understood his question.

"They grow up so fast . . ."

"Huh?"

"Forget it." He waved and went inside, shutting the balcony door.

"If you scream at night, he'll hear you. Well," Dasha said, adjusting her robe like the general of a defeated army tightening his greatcoat. "Soak it all up."

But how could I possibly *soak it up*? What kind of life would I have here? I couldn't keep my cool any longer. "I'm not gonna get any, am I?" I thought, standing by the window and observing the rising sun. "What's going on in that crazy head of hers?" I just stood there on the balcony till the afternoon and then lay around in bed till evening, when I went out to meet her on her way back from work, putting on the remnants of my stoic face and hiding my rage and despair behind my sunglasses. I prowled up and down the street—from the army recruiting office to the TB clinic, and from the beauty salon to the mistresses' mansion, going there and back—back and forth, over and over again. After yet another round trip, I saw her at the end of the street, walking slowly and looking at the fires behind the yellow windows of evening. I headed toward her, keeping it strong and silent. I said hello, asked her how she was doing, told her about my exciting day, and fed her some line about having a bunch of business meetings—"I was running around all day (yeah, in my sandals, why not?) and meeting with all my business partners (well yeah, with my shades on, obviously). It's a good thing we bumped into each other. Let me walk you back to the apartment. I'll carry some of those things for you." All she had was a glossy business magazine, which she refused to let me take.

She ascended the stairs without a word, clearly preoccupied; she even tried lighting the filter of her cigarette. "That's a good sign," I thought. "She's ready. She can feel it; she saw what she needed to see and now she's down for anything." I also noticed how different she looked in profile, like a sly fox, with a certain degree of suspicion showing in her eyes. "Huh, that's weird," I thought. "You can't see any of that when you look at her straight on. It's as though she's concealing her real face, pretending to be someone else. It's all in her lips—there's something odd about their color—no, it's the composition, but you can only see it if you look at her from the side. I guess that's just how it goes sometimes," I thought. "And it makes her look even better."

On our floor, the very moment I tried to block the doorway to stop her, get in her way so I could finally touch her, somewhere deep in the pockets of her suit her phone snarled, and she pushed me aside firmly, with one brief, iron-willed motion, just like a real lawyer ought to do. She took out her cell, tensed up, ignored the incoming call, and disappeared without so much as a "Sweet dreams."

But I had them anyway.

"My princess," went my song of praise the next morning as I lay there staring sullenly at the ceiling in my wrinkled jeans and stale shirt. "Why must you break my heart? Why must you toss it to the pigeons in the square? They play with it, perched up on the city's TV antennas, and I weep, my princess, while you paint your own portrait with only the most vibrant colors. Why do you keep me in these silver chains? Why do you put this black, suffocating collar around my neck and keep me from telling you all my thoughts about love and cruelty? My princess, where do you run off to every morning? In what burrows do you hide from me, you lovely fox? Why don't you return and let me go? Why do you hold me captive? Why don't you ever call me by name?"

I sang and sang as the street outside the window awakened, I sang as the building came to life, and I went on singing, not even trying to get out of bed. "I guess now I know what it means to be unhappy in love," I thought, despairing. "It can be painful, and it can put you in a rotten mood. Who would have thought? Who could have foreseen it?" Meanwhile, there was more and more sun, and the voices were getting more and more grating—the building was filling up with them, so I simply didn't have any more time for my suffering. I liked this building. It was like an electric organ. In the mornings, I'd wake to the workers stretching a cable along the cold, damp asphalt and connecting it to the blue waves of electrical current running through the apartment block. The doors were always open, and cold drafts pooled in the hallways, swaying like seaweed as soon as anyone ran inside. After midnight, when everyone was already asleep, if you listened closely enough, you could catch the chittering of mechanical alarm clocks, the dripping of water in the kitchens, the whispering of drowsy pigeons on the roof, and the women sighing quietly in their sleep, as though somebody was tuning all the cords and antennas, preparing for a concert staged to celebrate a holiday. In the early morning, the building would be set in motion and the first sounds would emerge—brisk air would whip through the windows and rooms like breath through woodwinds, the floors would creak, perky radio voices would echo, knives, frying pans, razors, and hair dryers would chime in as well as some toasters, irons, and loud ringtones, anchormen would deliver the latest news in their sweet, reassuring voices; you could hear dishes, you could hear water, kisses and whispers, people humming marches and reciting prayers, running giddily down the stairs, which finally woke all the balconies and hallways from their slumber—now it sounded like a piano was scraping across the floor,

and you were inside it, in the midst of the deepest sounds, in between
the most disquieting notes, listening to the wood and tin, iron and cement, glass and skin that held the floors and ceilings together. When
children ran into the building around lunchtime, their high-pitched
voices made invisible microphones screech, and booming sound rico-
cheted off the walls, and this music persisted—wistfully in the afternoon, adamantly at dusk, ecstatically at night—never slackening,
never pausing, just going on and on. The music made me want to die.
    I got right down to it.

    By the evening, alcohol was pooling in my blood, rising like thaw
water on the verge of flooding the empty streets of this defenseless
city. Everything I had drunk, everything I had dared to ingest, whatever I touched—bizarre mixes and curious combinations of champagne, sherry, and rum (disappointingly, acquiring them was as wild
as my imagination turned out to be)—all that fluid was inside my
heart, cooling it down, delaying the inevitable, like graphite in a
nuclear reactor, yet it gave me no reason to doubt that the inevitable
was waiting patiently for me, just up ahead. I loved myself too much
to have any experience with abusing alcohol, but I was too cocky
to call it quits. I went to a bunch of shady places, stopped by all the
basements and burrows she'd mentioned earlier, paid the Arabs a
visit, stuck my head into the Vietnamese joint, became best buddies with the guys that worked at the McDonald's, strolled into the
TB clinic and drank, arms intertwined, with the patients, ordered
champagne at Health, the local sauna, lost consciousness in a dark
basement across from the synagogue, regained it at a family restaurant (the waiters were busily setting up for some kid's birthday party
the next morning) by chasing milkshakes with herbal liqueur, asked
for directions at the pizzeria, died from cognac fumes in a bar run by
some Georgian dudes, and resurrected myself with some Madeira in
an empty supermarket. I was hanging in there, doggedly drinking her
health, insisting that everyone praise her phantom profile, drink to

her voice and her skin, and to the hairdresser who conjures up cosmic landscapes out of her unyielding hair. I stood there, wobbling like a cabin boy, and butted into conversations with learned proofs that no other woman in these parts had such green eyes, none of them could unleash a string of curses and then ask for forgiveness as eloquently as she could, and none of them had such high heels, such thin wrists, and such a thrilling biography. It's odd that the TB guys didn't beat me up. It's astounding that the Vietnamese people didn't mug me. It's nice that I got thrown out of the McDonald's. I only had a few hours left to live and I was determined to get something out of them, but I just couldn't.

She found me on the steps inside our building, leaning up against the door and blocking the entrance. She was angry and then scared. She hoisted me in her arms as best she could and carried me up the stairs. She was still lugging me along when I woke up; I tried to use my cellphone as a flashlight and get a better look at her, but just wound up dialing some random numbers, made what I thought was a good joke about her name—no, I'm positive it was a good one—asked her to marry me, and hung on to her, tenderly, at least I'd call it tenderly, hugging her with one arm and holding the railing with the other. She sat me down in the kitchen and told me to shut my trap, walking around and trying to decide what to do with me. At first, she thought about calling my mom. Then she decided to make me some strong tea. Then she got all anxious, suggesting we try to flush my stomach, hook me up to an IV—take a sleeping pill, take some vitamins, drink some cranberry juice, take some potassium permanganate, take some potassium permanganate with cranberry juice, take some potassium permanganate with a sleeping pill, hold the cranberry juice, or take all of them together and wash it down with some tea—no matter how you looked at it, she was taking care of me, which caused my heart to start pumping more blood; the liquid that flowed in was pink, what came out was dark, like blood ought to be.

While she was pacing up and down the room, rooting around in cabinets and drawers, Googling cures for alcohol poisoning, and calling her pharmacist and anesthesiologist friends, I started feeling sicker and lonelier. Her kitchen had been prudently filled with all sorts of herbs and spices, vegetables and seafood. I could easily distinguish the smells of cinnamon and cloves, the hot aroma of curry, the piercing scent of black pepper, the overpowering presence of garlic and lemons, the dark spirit of chopped meat, the bright juice of sliced vegetables, the briskness of ice, and the weightlessness of flour, the bitterness, resignation, and irrevocability of steak, the ghostliness of vinegar, the daydreams of soy, and the delirium of tomato sauce. The smells multiplied, swarmed above me like demons, nestling into my lungs and constricting my throat. They encircled me like an army besieging a fortress; they formed bizarre constructs above me, taking on curious shapes, baffling and suppressing me. My life smelled like frozen fish and my death will be tinged with the scent of Chinese mushrooms.

I was getting sicker and sicker. The sheer saturation of smells was killing me — and their overabundance was making my death an agonizing one. "Just not here," I commanded my body. "Not at her place. Go on home, don't bother her anymore, get the hell out of here," I whispered to myself. "Just not here." At that moment, she opened the fridge and I died.

Then she was standing over me for a while, holding my head under a cold stream of water. I turned my back to her, tried getting up and swatted her hand away, but she persisted in washing the pain and blackness of this world out of my body, holding me down and whispering life-giving words. Her clothes were completely soaked — I realized that she must be cold and that all this nonsense was the last thing she needed in her life right now and that I was being a real piece of shit. This realization opened the floodgates; tears came rolling down my face, mingling with the cold water on my skin. "What's wrong with me?" I thought, in a state of utter despair. "Why'd I have to go and screw everything up? What should I do now?" I said I was sorry and told her to let me go, pretending I was doing just fine, lying about how much I'd actually drunk that night, asking her to pour me another, coughing up some champagne and coke, coolly complimenting her haircut, and suavely inviting her to join me in my bed. She listened patiently to all my rambling, giving me a gentle smack upside the head whenever I started sharing my views on premarital sex, shivering ever so slightly in her wet shirt, and cracking a cool little smile in response to all my propositions.

As I trudged off, leaving copious wet tracks in the hallway, I felt the need to say something meaningful to her.

"You know, I'd be glad to give you a kiss. But I just puked all over your floor, so you can imagine how much my breath reeks."

"Run along now," she answered, neither agreeing nor disagreeing with me.

In the morning, I remembered every detail of the previous night—I hadn't forgotten a single word or a single touch. I remembered how she looked, how tentatively she held my hand, and how prudently she wiped the snot off my face. I hadn't forgotten anything, although it would have been better if I hadn't *remembered* anything. Flocks of startled swallows flew through my memory; it felt like bags of ice were pressing down on my heart, and I wanted to get rid of this body that wouldn't stop tormenting me. But I knew I couldn't waste any more time. It was now or never. I got up, somehow managed to get dressed, got my teeth all brushed after two unsuccessful attempts, burned my hand making myself some tea, spilled milk and sugar all over the place, and accidentally kicked over the trash can. "Now it's really gonna happen," I said to myself, and marched out of the apartment.

Once again, nobody was coming to the door. Once again, I had to stand there and listen hard for voices and sounds coming from inside her apartment. "What the hell?" I thought. "She doesn't wanna let me in, does she?" I started pounding on the black metal door, waking the pigeons perched on the roof. Then some keys started jingling, eventually sliding into the hole, and the door swung open heavily. I lunged forward and crashed right into a boy. He looked like he was seven or so, standing there in a T-shirt and soccer shorts—cut-up knees, scratched-up elbows, thick black hair, furrowed brow—he didn't inspire much trust in me. He was holding some pens and pencils and sizing me up. Dasha ran out of the kitchen to greet me, putting her hands on the boy's shoulders with affected carelessness; she was obviously flustered though.

"Oh, is that you, Romeo? This is Amin," she said, nodding at the boy.

"What's his name?" I asked, taken aback.

The boy looked at me, his eyes filled with hatred.

"Those are some nice pens you got there," I said in a conciliatory tone. "Is that a real Parker? I used to have one of those."

"You know how to write?" the boy asked scornfully, and headed toward the kitchen.

"School just let out," Dasha whispered quickly. "His grandmother dropped him off this morning. The thing is . . . what's he gonna do here all summer? He should be down south, swimming in the sea."

"Definitely," I thought, "he should be in the sea, somewhere out beyond the buoys."

I sat there in the kitchen—Dasha was bustling around, cooking something, showing how hospitable she was; the kid was watching with obvious skepticism. He didn't look like his mom, but he did look like he loved her very much. Clearly, I was just getting in his way. And he was getting in mine. Dasha became more anxious, some of the meal got burned, some of it got way too much salt, and some of it just wound up in the trash can. I was trying to break the ice with Amin, but he kept giving me lip. His mom scolded him, but he gave her some lip, too, which made her even more anxious. Eventually, she couldn't take it anymore; she grabbed her phone, ran over to the other room, and had a long conversation, while the kid indignantly drew monsters and serial killers in his school notebook. I got up and headed back to my place. The kid didn't even lift his head.

Things went on like that for two weeks. I'd wake up at the crack of dawn to the sound of her footsteps through the wall, listening to her running around the apartment, getting the kid up, making him breakfast, rushing to get ready, picking out her clothes, vainly trying to impose order on that hair of hers, frantically searching for her shoes, desperately calling someone who wasn't picking up, hopelessly pouring milk into cold coffee, resignedly running out the front door, tossing all her phones, pills, and sunglasses into her purse. She wouldn't be getting back until late, so I could bide my time. Her friends, neighbors, teachers, and babysitters would come by to keep the kid busy. One time she asked me to keep an eye on him, but the kid purposely (yep, it was on purpose, I know that for a fact) knocked over some pots and pans, called his mom (his phone was more expensive than mine!), and started griping and sobbing. She had to hail a taxi and race home. I told her my side of the story; she even seemed to believe me, but I wasn't asked to watch him again. I was pissed, cursing him to high heaven. "What's he even doing here?" I thought. "Why doesn't he go down south to the sea or some lake, or better yet a swamp, closer to nature and preferably some wild animals?" The kid kept ignoring me—he wouldn't speak to me or open the front door for me (he'd just stand on a chair and look at me scornfully through the peephole); he'd protest by making a big show of refusing to eat whenever I sat with them in the kitchen and blast his music whenever she talked to me on the phone. I even started to respect him for it. "He's taking a real stand on this one," I thought. "Actually, he's completely harmless," I assured myself. "Everything's gonna be just fine." But none of my attempts to reach out to him got anywhere. He really didn't look like a trusting, defenseless child; he had a grating personality and grown-up toys—pockets stuffed with indelible pencils and office supplies (I once saw him trying to staple my shoelaces to the floor—she didn't believe me, obviously), a used pepper-spray can he'd gotten from his dad (well, she thought it was all used up), an empty cigar case he'd gotten from his grandpa (I told her it didn't smell that empty to me, but she really didn't want to hear it), a stethoscope he found somewhere ("What does he need that for?" I asked anxiously), some borrowed shotgun shells, a Swiss Army knife he'd stolen from me (he stubbornly claimed it was his—she seemed to believe me again, but she didn't make him give it back). Worst of all, she'd practically stopped talking to me, although sometimes she'd stop by for a bit, keeping the apartment door ajar, as though she was always on the lookout—whenever I'd try to catch her on the stairs, strike up a conversation on the street, or lure her into some dark, cozy corner, she'd tense up immediately, turn falsely carefree, obtrusively friendly, or ostentatiously earnest. He was constantly lurking—waiting for her on the balcony, calling her as soon as my hand touched hers, waking up as soon as I tapped on her door in the middle of the night, cutting himself or burning his tongue, ripping his clothes on loose nails and getting in fights with the neighborhood kids, sticking spoiled food in his mouth and bringing stray dogs home—whatever he could think of to shift her attention away from me, get her back on his side, and elicit sympathy, tears, laughter, love, or at least frustration. She'd get mad at him constantly and fight with him more and more openly, perfectly aware of what was going on. "Well, what's the point of arguing with him. He's a smart kid; he's in the right—I'm the outsider here, and Dasha should be getting mad at me, not him." Nevertheless, it was him she got mad at. We gradually established an odd relationship based on leaving the kid with nothing. She'd try to call me after work so we could walk home together. At night, she'd send me texts, asking me about the weather and any breaking news stories. In the morning, she'd drop by for a second, just to say hello, and then vanish, leaving the sweet smell of freshly baked bread in her wake. The kid knew what was going on, he mounted a defense, setting clever little traps all over the place, taking her phone to bed with him, patrolling the neighborhood, plugging up the lock of my apartment door with playdough (good thing it was just playdough), and leaving me notes containing black spots and voodoo curses. All of this stuff wore me out, and I lost sleep and my peace of mind over it; at one point, I even thought about moving back home. I felt bad for the kid, as I was clearly bugging the hell out of him, her, as she was stuck in the middle of our feud, and myself, but I don't even want to get into that. That's how the summer started, and that's how all my hopes and dreams died.

On Friday, she stopped by in the early evening, running straight to my apartment and tossing her purse on the couch—business cards, notebooks, and her contact case spilled all over the floor. She paced around the room, consciously trying to avoid my eyes, talking about the heat wave that had hit the city, about the birds that kept her up at night, and about the water shortage. I tried to stop her, but she stuck her hand out rather forcefully, as if to say, "Stay right where you are," and then she got to it:

"Listen, Romeo," she said, examining the wallpaper, as if she was trying to find an error in its pattern. "My friend is getting married tomorrow. She invited me to the wedding, but I don't have anyone to go with. Why don't we go together?"

"To a wedding?" I tensed up.

"It's right around the corner," Dasha replied quickly. "I already got her a gift."

"What about the kid?"

"He'll stay home," she said harshly.

"Well, count me in."

"Just make sure you wear something decent," Dasha told me, grabbing her purse and vanishing into the hallway.

In the morning, she was standing outside my door—with the kid, obviously. Just my luck. She said that the nanny was sick, that an ambulance came for her neighbor last night, and that her friends were all being audited today, so there was nobody to look after him. Her face was a little swollen from crying, so she'd put on some big sunglasses. The kid looked at me triumphantly. A knock-off Rolex— a nice one, though—was sliding around on his wrist.

It would have been better if I hadn't gone, obviously. Who was dragging me there? Well, I knew exactly who. She was the one dragging me there. Wearing her black dress and carrying her little black purse, she was walking ahead of me, pulling the kid along and casting despairing glances in my direction. I was lugging the present (something made of glass—porcelain, at best), unable to take my eyes off her smooth gait, off her feet gliding across the warm, cracked asphalt; her body moved under that black dress as though the wedding had started already, as though the holiday had started already, and we should be celebrating right here, amid the acacia and linden trees, beneath the blue June sky, in this city that she'd told me so much about, in these streets where everyone greets her by name. I'd known her for less than a month, but I'd already gotten used to her hasty movements, her combative tone, the comforting warmth of her hands, and the bitter cold of her eyes. This summer will be long, the sun will be hot, my delights will be dubious, and my suffering hellish. This story will have a happy ending that nobody in it will live to see.

The wedding was held at one of the bathhouses in town, which didn't surprise me one bit—I've seen stranger things. One time, my friends got married in a high school gym, right under the basketball hoop, which was romantic, in a way. Here too was a hidden, mysterious place—car repair shop to the left, pharmacy to the right, and wedding tables in the middle. A metal gate with Olympic rings welded on it had been flung wide open; once inside, the guests found themselves in a large, open area with a decorative fountain in the center, which was flooding everything like a busted fire hydrant. This place didn't seem to have a name—I guess they couldn't think of one that would be appropriate for such a romantic establishment. The guests had parked all around—the newer, foreign-made cars were closer to the bathhouse and a few battle-hardened Zhigulis were parked out back. Under the morning sun, between the pharmacy and the black hubcaps outside the shop, the guests seemed particularly grand. They'd walk through the gate, look all around, and greet their friends. Meanwhile, servers were running, relatives were arguing, children were yelling, and there was a lot of sun. Dasha pushed her way through the crowd—everyone was glad to see her, stopping her, bending down to talk to the kid, and shooting appraising glances at me. I used the porcelain as a shield. I liked the look of the bride—about Dasha's age, petite, short, dyed red hair, weary eyes, cigarette constantly in her mouth, light-hearted smile—it was as if she was saying, "You can wait a little longer; it's not like you're gonna start without me." Sneakers poked out from under her dress. Dasha whispered back and forth with her for a while, dragged the kid over (to no avail, he bolted and crashed into the fountain without saying hello to anyone), and then brought me over too, introducing me as a relative of hers. The bride lunged forward to hug me and favor me with her tender nicotine breath; then the groom strolled on over—although he was older than me, his suit, which had clearly been tailored at the last minute, made him look like a high school senior going to prom. He had sharp features and gelled hair. His gaze was heavy, and he practically wasn't even talking to his bride-to-be, never calling her by her name, as though he was afraid he'd get it wrong. He was hiding behind his friends, who had formed a tight circle to protect him from any unwanted conversations. A lot of them had shown up in warmup outfits with the logo of some team or other on them; most of them were wearing sunglasses. I made a big show of taking mine off. Dasha dragged me away from the soccer guys almost immediately, telling me to go find Amin, which I did.

"Come on buddy, let's get back to the party," I said.

The kid didn't say anything, but he went with me. As soon as he saw his mom, he started whining—"I wanna go home, I don't wanna be here. I want some water. I don't wanna meet anyone new. I want love and I don't wanna share it with anyone!" I tried my best to keep him entertained, but Amin made a big show of turning his back on me and started bawling even more determinedly, putting his wounded mother down with one last shot to the head. Dasha pretended everything was fine for a while, but eventually she couldn't take it anymore—she walked away and dove into the crowd. The kid walked away, too, diving in the other direction, but what really got to me was that damn porcelain.

The guests were milling around outside, going into the bar, popping out of dark hallways, waiting for something and talking among themselves. I recognized John, the upstairs neighbor. He was standing next to some heavyset, diabetic-looking friend of his who was already a few drinks deep, making him look even more sickly. Older men wearing fastidiously ironed dress shirts and important-looking women with brightly colored makeup were mingling. Two guys who looked like taxi drivers—one of them was wearing a leather jacket and the other one had a bunch of prison tattoos—pushed their way through the crowd. "What an odd bunch," I thought. "It seems like they should be at the train station waiting for the morning express to come in, not at a wedding." Suddenly, I saw Dasha. She was leaning up against the wall, holding a glass of wine that couldn't have been her first, laughing and hanging all over some little runt of a guy. He had a bloated, olive-colored face, squinty eyes, fat lips, a stale white dress shirt, and expensive shoes that he didn't bother to keep clean. He kept trying to touch Dasha, leaning in to give her a friendly pat on the back, reaching for her hand, chuckling and excitedly shouting something or other. Dasha was pretending everything was just fine. Or maybe everything really was just fine. She wasn't looking in my direction, just yelling something back at Squinty Eyes and patting him on the back to rein him in, but she'd occasionally step to the side or back into the shade ever so slightly, as though that dude's breath stank. When he touched her leg right above the knee, either jokingly or accidentally, although he did it quite firmly, I couldn't take it anymore. I walked over to them.

"Oh, Romeo." She feigned pleasant surprise. "I'd like you to meet Kolia."

He extended his hand, not even looking at me.

"Hold this," I said, handing Dasha the porcelain. She was taken aback by my brusqueness, nearly dropping her gift, catching it rather awkwardly, and propping it up on her knee. Then Kolia finally acknowledged me. I took his big, damp hand, and he gave me a limp and reluctant shake.

"I'm Romeo," I said. "It's very nice to meet you. Dasha has told me so much about you."

"Like what?" He seemed puzzled.

"All sorts of stuff."

Kolia got all flustered and squirmy, patting me on the back damply and reluctantly, then disappearing down the hallway. She gave me a viciously disappointed look, threw the porcelain under one of the tables, and started berating me. She said that she was so sick of us, the kid and me, that we were a couple of nitwits, that we couldn't act our age, that she always had to break up our fights, and put up with us. But she wasn't made of steel, she could only take so much (she started crying, as if to demonstrate); she needed to be alone for a while, and she'd tell us when she wanted to see us again. In other words, "Get the fuck out of my sight."

"John," she yelled over my shoulder. "Got any smokes?" Shoving me aside, she grabbed our neighbor, who was charging ahead too, and led him away. The diabetic dude followed them. I lost it, but all I could do was head off in the opposite direction. It was a good thing the wedding party was all sprawled out.

"Where is your faith in yourself? Where is your joy, where is everything you've searched for in this world full of sun?" I asked myself. While the festivities continued outside, while dust rose and touched the soft blades of grass, green as salad, I was sitting in the bar, watching some damn sitcom. It wasn't worth going back out because I'd have to socialize, explain myself, and find some way out of this mess; I'd have to avoid locking eyes with her, make a point of not looking at her, and pretend I didn't see her. And right there, in the warm, early twilight, out of nowhere, a cowboy materialized — in addition to the hat, this character was sporting a light jacket, colorful shorts, and worn-out flip-flops. As soon as he noticed me, he detected all the sadness in my eyes and insisted I join him, saying, "Come on, man, whatcha doing bumming around here? The action is in the domain of the cold pools, in the sector of the water rides, in the black squares of the steam rooms, there among the hellish vapors!" He dragged me away because "you have to get into the spirit of things, you just can't waste this glorious day of celebration." He was a blisteringly fast talker, greedily devouring consonants and skipping between half-finished thoughts. His cowboy hat kept slipping over his eyes, sweat was pouring down his forehead, the anticipation was soaking his sideburns, but as soon as he led me through a few secret chambers to a massage room I immediately realized that it had been worth the struggle. All the action *was* right here — the instant we came into view, a group of fiery, naked bodies darted toward the cowboy, acclaiming him, rubbing up against him with gratitude, and they rubbed up against me too; when it was women I was happy, but when it was men I was seized by a disquieting feeling and the desire to clock one of them, which got worse by the minute. The cowboy took a fat, scented parcel — something precious, something wrapped up in a tabloid — out of his pocket, and everyone went wild; they hoisted him up and carried him out through the doors, right to the gates of hell. Then I lay down on the massage table in the room, looking at the cold pool electrified by bright lights reflecting off its green surface. Beautiful, naked women strolled by, smiling affectionately, and dignified-looking men wrapped in shaggy towels looked at me anxiously as they passed, seemingly trying to decide if I was one of them or just some interloper. Time meandered on, slipping by me and making my presence here even more random and devoid of purpose. When everyone had passed by me, left, and come back again, the cowboy reappeared, carrying a tray of cognac and lemon, forcing me to drink as much of it as I could—and then a lot more.

"When else are we gonna drink together, man?" he yelled. "I'm getting the fuck outta here man—Ukrainian airlines—before ya know it, I'll be halfway to fucking Timbuktu! No stopovers for me! Tomorrow, man! Out of invisible terminals! Down secret air corridors! Dodging all the customs agents, not declaring my jewels or my assets! Crusading through all the duty-free zones! Two days from now," he yelled with sloppy enthusiasm. "I'm gonna be sitting with a bunch of legit people somewhere out by Philadelphia (Philadelphia, man, the city!), with a bunch of bigtime stockbrokers (yeah man, brokers!), drinking some real kosher cognac, not this fucking swill!" He was screaming now, throwing back glass after glass. "Nah, no more of this shit for me." When the naked bodies spilled out of the hot room, headed over toward the cold pool, and hoisted him up once again, I decided I'd had enough.

I left the room and went back to the bar. The night had settled on the grass outside, the dishes were rattling, the women were arguing, and the singing was dying down. Somewhere behind me, a door creaked open. I looked around, catching a glimpse of the bride's dress. Someone shut the door. I stepped through the side exit. I was just about to head out when I suddenly saw Amin. He was standing there, up against the wall, sobbing. Kolia was looming over him, holding the Rolex. The kid was whimpering, reaching up for his watch.

"What's going on here?" I asked, walking over.

Kolia looked up with a start, but he calmed down as soon as he saw it was just me.

"Hey sonny boy, everything's all right," he said, narrowing his eyes even more. "I bought this Rolex off him fair and square, but he keeps bellyaching 'bout something."

"He didn't buy it." Amin started bellyaching again, still reaching up and trying to get his watch back.

"So what's the real story?" I asked.

"It's mine. I bought it," Kolia said coldly. "Run along now, sonny boy."

"Listen up, you fuckin' fag, give the kid his Rolex back," I demanded.

"Come again?"

"I said give him his Rolex back."

"Sonny boy, what's your deal?" Kolia finally opened his eyes all the way and looked at me as if he was seeing me for the first time.

I cut him off with a powerful punch to the solar plexus. Kolia doubled over, but stayed on his feet, trying to take a step back. I jumped on top of him. The door behind me burst open, and cheerful voices, invigorated by anger and excitement, spilled outside. I was slammed onto the asphalt before I even knew what was happening, taking a few hits to the kidneys and a few hits to the spine; it's a good thing I managed to cover my head in time. Then it all stopped as abruptly as it had begun. I tried to get up, but somebody's shoe was pinning me to the asphalt. Kolia was standing over me along with three or four guys. I didn't know them, but they seemed to know him quite well, that's for sure. Kolia couldn't decide whether to finish me off or leave me there. Then he finally let me go.

"Prick," he said in a conciliatory tone, spitting off to the side and heading back to the bar. The rest of the gang filed in behind him.

I got up. My leg was killing me, and my shirt was a total mess. The kid was standing next to me, badly shook up. The Rolex was just lying there on the asphalt. I picked it up, handed it to him, and then rested my back up against the wall. The door opened once again. Dasha ran outside, saw us, and walked over. Wobbling a bit at first, she regrouped quickly and regained her balance. She looked at the kid's teary eyes, saw my shirt, ripped to shreds, and then started yelling.

"What are you doing out here?" she shouted at the kid. "What the hell? I'm sick of your crap!"

The kid slouched against the wall, next to me—we looked like we were facing a firing squad together.

"I'm talking to you! Aren't you even listening?"

"Don't yell at him," I said.

"Butt out. What were you doing out here, huh? What the hell?"

"I said don't yell at him."

"Who do you think you are?" She turned toward me. "Since when do you tell *me* what to do?"

"Hey, go back inside, keep partying with those guys if that's what you're into. Go fuck their brains out, every last one of them, for all I care. Just don't yell at the kid, got it?"

"What did you say to me?"

She held a long pause, then splayed icy fingers whacked me right across the face. After that, she yanked the kid away and dragged him over to the bar. I darted after them, but the door was shut. I pulled it toward me, then rammed my shoulder into it, and finally pounded on it with my busted-up fists for a while. Of course, I could have just gone to the other entrance, but what the hell would've been the point of that? "What the hell?" Dasha's words echoed. I trudged home, went up to my apartment, threw my dirty clothes away, and packed my things, leaving my sunglasses on the table and walking back down the stairs. "I'll spend the night at the train station," I thought.

Everything I knew about this city, I'd learned from her. She was the one who told me all those farfetched stories, talking loudly and with conviction, listing names and places, recalling dates, drawing pictures in the sand with the sharp tips of her high heels to show me where the rivers flow and where they dry up. She told me about the city's fortifications and underground passageways, about the metal dragons that breathe fire in the dark caves of the trolley depots, and the impenetrable shells protecting the fierce animals that hide out in sandy burrows around the reservoir. She told me about the models of flying factories and engines of mass destruction manufactured by children at the Young Pioneer centers, mentioning something about fertile soccer fields and their strange plants that help you sleep and improve your memory, whispering jumbled rumors about the Polytechnic Institute's secret labs that loom unreachably on the horizon, the research institutions that have been trying to produce an elixir of youth for a good hundred years now, and the shortest trolley lines of all, the ones that run right through the city's apartment blocks. She mentioned something about the cold steel weapons cranked out by old factories, the trees plastering the sky in the summertime, and the fact that you couldn't see the moon or stars at night. That's why some people say there are witches living around here, and they're right, she declared. Things are just dandy for them, because Kharkiv is a pretty livable city—that's why people who have drowned or hanged themselves wind up here, floating down the rivers, penetrating the city through its train stations, multiplying, and improving the country's demographic situation. But in the winter, the moon hangs right outside your window—just reach out and grab it—it looks like cheese molded from clay and grass. She said it was easy to endure the long winters in the city because the factories always warm up the morning air. Come spring, thaw water erodes the foundations of old health resorts in the suburbs, the rivers run red and smell like medicine, so the smell of spring is ammonium chloride. She said they were shooting people in the streets, that there was still a war going on, and nobody was planning on surrendering. It will all keep going as long as we keep loving one another, she explained, as if offering a hint she expected me to pick up. There's enough love to go around. I didn't get what she meant by that.

## JOHN

The moment just before waking was long enough for Sonia to have a dream. It was short and unsettling. She saw a river and ships sailing up it—old and rusty, with yellow water-stained sides and black ash-stained funnels. They halted in the middle, their horns wailing despairingly. Sailors—tired and unshaven, which made them even more decisive and belligerent—were jumping over the side, swimming ashore, trudging onto the sand in their heavy clothes and worn-out shoes, walking along a quay, glancing angrily at the ships whose horns were blaring so loudly that she finally woke up. "Well, all-righty then," she thought. "We're gonna have a lot of guests today."

Everybody else in the house was still sleeping. She quietly slipped out from under the covers. The nights were warm, and they slept completely naked. She liked that, and she liked waking up and finding the room just the way it ought to be—everything felt light and exposed. He was a deep and still sleeper; his head faced east all night. "He sleeps like a Sunni," Sonia thought, putting on a T-shirt and stepping into the hallway. His relatives were sleeping in the living room. Yesterday she tried to learn all their names, but she couldn't keep them straight, it was utterly hopeless; they all stuck together, sleeping side by side like pilgrims and upholding a defined family code and set of hierarchical principles. Three guys were squished together on the couch, and somebody's nephew—a timid, chubby kid—was wedged hopelessly between his elders, like a bobsledder. The women were lying on camel-wool rugs spread across the floor. The men hadn't gotten undressed before bed; they were sleeping in their Sunday best—one of them hadn't even bothered to undo his tie, probably to avoid the hassle of tying it again in the morning. The women slept in warm robes, with the slippers they'd brought along with them from home by their heads. They turned in early, slept soundly, and didn't scream in their sleep. Sonia suddenly realized that she had nothing on but the T-shirt, so she shut the door softly. Her uncle Hrysha was sleeping like a real champ on the pull-out bed in one of the children's rooms. Sheets in disarray, he was frozen in some ludicrous position, his head buried under a pillow, left arm crushed by his skinny hips and right arm dangling somewhere under the bed. His blanket was lying on the floor, like a paratrooper's chute abandoned on the ground, the sheets were drooping like a flag torn off the enemy's headquarters, and his dentures were suspended in a glass of water on a chair by the bed. At night, she'd heard Uncle Hrysha tossing and turning like a sinner on the devil's roasting spit, moaning, whimpering, jerking to his feet occasionally to grab the glass with his dentures in it and gulping greedily, gargling, then spitting the water out again. He'd calmed down by the early morning, his blue lips whistling some obscure melody from the dreams of sleepwalkers. Sonia went into the bathroom and locked the door, took off her shirt, stepped into the tub, and turned on the hot water. "I have some time while they're all still sleeping," she thought.

The water touched her skin, making it warm and receptive. "I could use some tenderness," Sonia thought. "I could use sex and a nice cup of coffee, with milk." She bumped into Senia as she was stepping into the hallway. He must have felt that she was gone and gotten up to search for her. He'd been standing outside the door, waiting for her to finish, and now he shoved her back into the bathroom as soon as the door opened, pulling at her shirt. "Perfect timing," Sonia thought, giving him a hand with it. But as soon as he had gotten her propped up just right on the edge of the tub, holding her up with one hand and pulling his own shirt off with the other, somebody knocked tentatively on the door. They'd forgotten to lock it, so they stopped — Sonia listened hard, and he started grinding his teeth. Another knock.

"Damn," he hissed, releasing Sonia, tossing her the shirt, and opening the door. Looking even chubbier and more dazed after a good night's sleep, the nephew stood there in a women's nightshirt and blue sweatpants, shifting his weight from one foot to the other. Sonia had managed to cover up a bit by putting the T-shirt on her lap. But Senia just had one hand over his private parts; the nephew stared intently at him, clearly frightened and anxiously tapping his feet. Nobody said a word for a little while, but then he couldn't take it anymore.

"The toilet's next door, it's just the tub in here," he said forcefully, leaning out into the hallway, flipping on the light for the other room, fading back into the darkness, and shutting the door.

He tried grabbing her shirt again, but Sonia pushed his hand back firmly, pulled the shirt back on, and headed toward the kitchen. He stayed put. Sonia thought he'd been a little too rough with her when the kid started banging on the door, and he had thrown her the T-shirt too hard, as though he was trying to get rid of her. None of this felt like it was supposed to, but did it really matter? Nope, not one bit. Her wedding dress hung from a light fixture in the kitchen. Sonia got started on the coffee. "It's going to be a long day . . . and a fun one too," she added.

Their relatives seemed to all get up at the same time. Maybe his nephew had come back and spread the good news—the bride and groom were already up and about, so everyone should get moving and start this glorious day the Lord had given us. Or maybe Uncle Hrysha had struck a particularly high note and woken everybody up. Either way, no sooner had she slipped back into her room with her cup of coffee than stomps and voices started bouncing off the hallway walls. The men were shaving—all three at the same time, crammed into the bathroom, backing the boy up against the washing machine, not that he wanted to leave; male behavior is driven by the need for a sense of collectivity, so he just watched the grown-ups nick their skin with disposable razors, shedding their first drops of morning blood, wincing but not griping about it. The women were raising a great commotion in the kitchen, circling around the dress, throwing up their hands in despair.

"The dress is too short."

"We don't have enough time."

"It just can't be done. And what can be done just won't do."

They started frying and chopping; the smell of meat and sun filled the apartment. Uncle Hrysha, wearing a pair of long boxer shorts adorned with all sorts of white flowers, slouched out of his room, holding an ironing board under his arm, looking like a surfer heading out to the beach in the morning to conquer some big waves. Sonia was sitting in her room, looking out the window and drinking her coffee, which was cooling off all too quickly. She hadn't even gotten dressed by the time Senia came back.

"Ya nervous?"

"Sure am. It's like the first time all over again."

His face turned sour, even though she was just telling it like it was. At thirty-two, he was getting married for the first time, while she, at thirty-four, suspected this was her last try.

"Look, Senia," she said, turning toward him, "maybe we should just bag the whole thing. I'll make some omelets; we'll feed your relatives, and we'll send 'em on their way. Godspeed!"

"You've got to be kidding me! They'll disown me if we don't get married. You think today's about us? Come on, it's like they're the ones tying the knot."

"All right. Then let's go tie it already."

They all got ready very quickly, taking just the essentials, pulling his nephew, who had got it in his head that he needed a bath, out of the tub, and spilling out of the apartment. Senia was wearing a black suit, and his hair was gelled back; his relatives hadn't let him brush his teeth, so he stuck some gum in his mouth and started chewing angrily. She was in her wedding dress and white sneakers, carrying her light, high-heeled sandals in her hand.

"You're gonna go like that?" Senia asked, surprised.

"It's not like I'm gonna wear heels all damn day," Sonia answered.

After she'd seen everyone out, she turned off the lights and locked the door. The apartment where they lived was hers. She paid the electric bill, too. They went outside and started cramming themselves into a taxi. Those who didn't fit piled into a yellow Ford. Sonia put her heels in the trunk and sat down in the driver's seat. The Ford was hers, too.

She didn't want to get married—they'd already been living together just fine for a while, she figured if it ain't broke don't fix it. But all of Senia's many relations started getting on his case. They were Jehovah's Witnesses who would ride into town every weekend to go to church with all their kids and grandkids, wearing their freshly laundered dresses and suits. They looked like people who had managed to grab their best clothes before fleeing from their burning house. Their church services were held at an old building in town that was originally supposed to be a kind of combination cinema and concert hall, but there hadn't been any movies there for a while, let alone concerts. Senia would take his relations out to lunch afterward, just like the locals did. The men in town respected him and the women loved him. Everybody wanted the best for him. Everybody was constantly talking about Sonia, urging him to marry her. Senia lived in her apartment, she drove him to the metro every morning (just two blocks away, but it was uphill) and bought him cigarettes. Nevertheless, he started playing hardball with her, which really rubbed her the wrong way.

"You know, we've been living together for almost a year," Sonia said. "What else do you want from me? What's getting married gonna change?"

"Nothing at all, but my family's getting all worked up over this."

"Well, tell 'em not to."

But Senia kept insisting, and she gave in eventually, much to her own surprise . . . and his.

"All right, you're gonna get your wedding," she said. "But don't push it, my love has limits."

She rented out the Uzbek restaurant down by the river from the Tatars who owned it and tracked down one of her old classmates who now worked as a master of ceremonies at wedding parties. He didn't recognize her. "That's probably for the best," Sonia thought. She ordered a dress, gave her friends fair warning, and told them they were having an Italian-style wedding—meaning everyone should come dressed like they were in the Sicilian mafia. "Let's see them pull that off!" she thought, quite pleased with herself.

An odd bunch of people showed up for the wedding. They stuck around, too, which made things even worse. Sonia stood in the middle of the crowd, still in her white sneakers and matching dress, trying to figure out which of them she knew. Or which of them knew her, at least. Her whole office was there, including Dasha from the legal department, teary-eyed and exhausted, with her older and younger sons in tow. The little guy was probably the only one who was actually dressed for the occasion—he was wearing his school uniform and glaring at everything and everyone; yeah, he could pull off the role of a pint-sized gangster—though the boss apparently wasn't sending much money his way these days. He was wearing a heavy mechanical watch, which he'd probably stripped from the corpse of some debtor whose business the family had been "protecting." Their neighbor John was there to offer his best wishes, looking subdued as always and a little older than before. He glanced at Senia's hair scornfully, but refrained from making any comment. Some wacko in a cowboy costume had just crashed the party—from afar, he reminded her of Celentano—though that had more to do with his temperament than how he looked. Sonia didn't know him, but that didn't stop him from taking it upon himself to post up by the entrance and greet everyone as they arrived. Then a bunch of neighbors, school friends, and business partners started pouring in. Most of them knew what the bride liked and had a good idea of what to get her—after all, it wasn't her first time getting hitched, so everybody had kinda gotten used to it by now. A pack of Senia's grumpy relatives were walking around, not quite sure what to do with themselves. His nephew was the worst, he was really making a scene, knocking appetizer trays off the table and smoking with the Tatar guys. Then he crashed into the fountain, and who didn't see that coming? "And he's only ten," Sonia thought, thoroughly impressed. "He's barely gotten started and he's already a terror." The only relative she'd invited was her uncle Hrysha, who regarded himself as her godfather, for some reason, which helped give the festivities an Italian flair. "Whatever. Let him have it," Sonia thought. "He'd better head home after the wedding, though, I can't take him screaming in the middle of the night anymore." The rest of her relatives were either dead or off the radar. Her godfather more than made up for their absence, though—he was hitting on the women from the legal department, putting his skinny, yellow hands on their soft, supple thighs, pounding champagne, and occasionally taking out his dentures to clean them with wet wipes. Senia had invited his whole soccer team, too, at least the regular roster. They'd spent the last three years defending the honor of a local chain of hardware stores. The team had been on a real roll. They were always near the top of the leaderboard, so the players kept dropping hints— "Come on, Mr. Abramovich (he was the owner), if you spend some real money on us we'll win a corporate championship for you. It's all in our hands—well, not our hands . . . you know what I mean!" But Mr. Abramovich had his own plans; in winter, at the start of the second half of the season, he announced that the team had been disbanded. He'd gotten into some tussle with city hall and had a falling out with his guys in Kyiv, so he sold all his stores, bought a hotel in Egypt, and left for Africa to spend his days by the pool, counting camels as they went by. This was a huge blow for the team—they weren't interested in much of anything besides soccer, so they had no real skills. Nobody knew what to do next. Some of them got jobs, others went back to school, and a few of them, including Senia, were too down in the dumps to do anything. They all came to the wedding, though. Nobody adhered to the dress code, obviously ("Senia, don't be a fuckin' show off with that mafia shit"); however, they were all sporting sunglasses to go with their warm-ups. They said that was the look down in Sicily. Sania, their right wing, went to Sicily last Christmas; that's how all the Ukrainians there looked—Adidas gear, sandals, and black sunglasses. Just like the real mafia. They were apprehensive about all this wedding business, but they liked Sonia—her dark-red hair, warm lips, icy fingers, tan skin, slight, athletic build, lean legs, and expensive sneakers. They wouldn't have minded all banging her right there by the fountain, if they could. She wouldn't have batted an eye if they'd gone for it, either.

Danylo and Oleh were the last people to show up; it was already after noon. They stood there in the hot sun, smoking and thinking. Finally, Danylo suggested they head home.

"Let's go," he said, "this whole shindig is a joke."

Then Oleh took a drag so long he nearly fainted and wiped the amber sweat off his forehead with the sleeve of his leather jacket. He was thirty-six. Danylo was four years older, but most people would've pegged him for at least fifty. Oleh renovated old buildings, assembling crews of manual laborers and carting them around town to his various job sites. He'd always carry a small Panasonic camera with him, taking pictures of turrets and decorations on dilapidated buildings, zooming in to see details the naked eye couldn't. Oleh wore hiking boots, faded jeans, and a brown bomber jacket and had dark, unkempt hair. He hadn't shaved or slept in a while. Danylo wore athletic gear and had a bald, bruised head, but his wise gray eyes toned down his rough exterior. Nobody ever looked him in the eye, though; generally, all anyone ever noticed were his fists, blue with tattoos he'd given himself during his time in the service down in the Caucasus. All that ink made him look like an ex-con, but he really just drove a taxi, putting his Benz on the books at some state-owned company, giving rides to students and anyone else who was too drunk to drive. It was parked outside his apartment, across from the McDonald's; Danylo would wake up every morning, grab his thermos, and go sit in his car to get some more shut-eye.

"Hey, you positive we were invited?" he asked Oleh.

The surly Oleh thought for a bit, spat anxiously, and motioned, as if to say, "Get off my back." "Yeah, we were invited, obviously. We're their friends, aren't we? They just forgot to remind us."

"What's that supposed to mean?"

"They just forgot," Oleh said, nodding. "It's no big deal. I'll go remind them."

Danylo grumbled skeptically, but kept standing next to his brother.

They fired their cigarette butts through the warm air and drummed their palms against the outside of their pants pockets— "We got what we need, let's roll." They smacked around some wet-behind-the-ears punk, briefly but thoroughly, sized up some curly-haired guy in ripped clothes who was looking at everyone with utter disgust, shoved their way over to the bride, pulled some old-timer with red, drowsy eyes away from her, smacked the punk around a little bit more (he'd latched onto them after his first beating), and said hello to her. Danylo extended his hand, Oleh didn't.

Sonia was taken aback at first, but she quickly regained her composure, smiling at Danylo and reaching out to shake Oleh's hand. He blatantly ignored her, so she pulled him in and kissed him wetly on the cheek, scratching her face on four days' worth of prickly stubble. Flustered, Oleh apologized for showing up late, not dressed for the occasion, and with no present. He was getting even more flustered, but Danylo butted in, taking his keys out of his pocket and handing them to Sonia.

"Here kiddo, my Mercedes is all yours today. I'm gonna go grab a drink."

Sonia cracked a smile to ease the mounting tension and took the keys, something she wouldn't usually have done. "Join the party," she said. "I'll hold on to these for now. I don't want anybody playing bumper cars." Somebody was already pouring Danylo a drink; Oleh wanted to say something, but he just waved his hand dismissively and headed over toward the tables as well.

"Why ships?" she thought. "Where'd they even come from?" She'd been keeping a diary for the past few years. Some cheerful quack shrink would come to their office for sessions and hit on all the secretaries and accountants, but they all loved him, so he didn't get canned for it.

"You're in a good place, Sonia," he said. "You have a good job with prospects, and you've got your health. And it's a good thing you don't have a man in your life. Overall, everything's going well — you're in an excellent position to start worrying." So he suggested she keep a diary. "It'll be just for you, so there's no need to hold back. Write whatever you want — nobody else is ever going to read it."

Sonia went with it. It didn't usually take much coaxing for her to try something new. "But what am I gonna write about?" she thought. She immediately decided that none of the entries would cover her professional life. "What's the point of making the auditors' job any easier? And no love or romance either."

Love was the least of her concerns. Sonia was always the one who broke things off — none of her men ever had the guts to dump her. She'd been married twice, and her two ex-husbands had vanished from her life without a trace. Sonia would crack jokes about that, saying that she'd bitten their heads off . . . and some other things, too.

She had a lot of sex, plenty of interesting boyfriends, and a couple of girlfriends thrown in—women liked Sonia. She was always calm and had incredible stamina; they saw her the way they would have liked to see their men. Men liked her too, obviously; she was tender and open with them, and she always paid for her own drinks.

So she started logging her dreams, attentively and in detail. She described the rooms and buildings she saw and the faces that appeared, transcribed conversations, drew trees, flowers, and wild animals that didn't have names yet, sketching and carefully captioning meteors that had fallen on the city's old neighborhoods, diagramming systems of mines that had been buried under sand dunes, and mugshots of serial killers who'd been caught and sentenced to hang. The murderers in her pictures looked like the crew of a ship—exhausted, yet unbroken—they all had some faint resemblance to one another, as is generally the case with men who spend a long time together in a confined space. This had all been welling up for so long, eventually she couldn't restrain herself, so she showed it to her mom, who was still alive at the time. When she was done reading the diary, she told Sonia to burn it so she'd be able to sleep at night. She heeded her mother's advice and burned the diary, but then she started another one right away, filling it with more portraits of men standing in profile.

She and Oleh met three years ago. She had to do something about the facade of her office building, it was gonna fall off any minute; one of her friends (John? Yeah, it was John) recommended Oleh. He showed up empty-handed—these were the pre-Panasonic days—stepped out onto the balcony, climbed over the railing, and started making his way out along the ledge. But he came back before she could even start to panic, explaining that he'd needed to see everything up close. A few days later, his boisterous gang showed up, looking like a cross between a pirate crew and a penal battalion. They camped out in Sonia's office for a week, sleeping on the desks, eating ramen out of Ikea bowls, and using the sink to wash. They patched up the facade, drank a whole crate of Crimean cognac, and became good buddies with everyone. "At my age, people don't generally make new friends," Sonia thought. "There are some exceptions, though, and after all, it's exceptions that make life interesting."

They knew a lot of the guests but they still felt like outsiders. Family get-togethers can be pretty odd affairs—the more friends you have there, the less welcome you are. Danylo was sipping his drink carefully. He'd picked out some of the groom's friends—a bunch of Jesus freaks, fearless, committed missionaries wandering around a foreign city, saving souls like lifeguards at the beach—and struck up a conversation with them. The missionaries were a bit rough with Danylo, like a hairdresser is with a new customer. He liked that. He was always up for a thought-provoking debate. He told them a story about his friend who got mixed up with some missionaries; he had even given them the deed to his house in the residential neighborhood on the other side of the river. After that he got a year in the slammer for minor offenses, and when he got out three of God's servants were already living in his house—and they left him out in the cold, how do ya like that? "And then," Danylo added after a short, pensive pause, "he strangled them to death—all three of them—and put the house in some kids' name. They weren't his kids, obviously. You think a guy like that would have kids?" The story sent the missionaries scurrying off, and Danylo just let them go. His brother was sitting alongside him, sweating profusely, but he wouldn't take off his jacket—it was as though he was anticipating something or listening for some signal.

"What's your deal?" Danylo asked him. "Just chill out already."

"I'll chill out soon," Oleh answered cheerfully. "When the time comes."

"Yeah, sure," Danylo said with a laugh. "I don't know 'bout that."

Some older neighbor ladies kept coming up to them and asking how they were doing. The wedding was a free-for-all, and the kids were relishing the chaos, crawling around under the tables and pouring warm wine into people's shoes. Danylo actually liked it, but Oleh booted a few of the little munchkins in the ribs, and they crawled away into the dark and the dust in utter despair. Danylo had barely eaten anything. Oleh hadn't eaten at all. The bride came over a few times, holding some warm wine that not even her icy fingers could cool off, making conversation about the weather and launching into beguiling digressions. Women and men were standing behind her; the women held flowers and ice that they rubbed on their red hot faces and the men hid metal and stacks of cash in their pockets, keeping a cautious eye on the sun and not stepping back into the shade, determined not to miss anything. The kids were yelling, everything smelled like water and windblown grit; they were about to get to the really good part.

"Huh, this is so strange," Sonia told her mom. "I have a healthy lifestyle, I watch my diet, I don't do drugs anymore, I don't go to church—hell, I'm not even into yoga—but I keep having these dreams. I'm starting to think I'm doing something wrong. Like the one about the slaves. What could I possibly know about them? When did I even see them? It's not like I have any friends that are in captivity. But still, I have dreams about them—I hear their prison songs and their cries. I dream about them toiling away, cutting their fingers, following orders, resting after the day's work, and dying. Then they lie there in overcrowded graves covered with chalky earth, gritting their teeth, resentful and powerless."

"All of our dreams," said her mother, who had worked at a children's library all her adult life and had a deep-seated aversion to fiction, "come from the books we read as kids. The better those books were, the worse you sleep at night. Why don't you just get married?"

"I've already done that," Sonia reminded her. "Twice. It didn't really do it for me."

Oleh surprised her. One time, she saw how he made some fat-cat clients pay his construction crew for a job they'd done. Those clients commissioned a project and closely supervised the work for months, but then they kept ducking Oleh, and eventually told him to settle matters with their guys in Kyiv. Oleh arranged a meeting at a Georgian restaurant in town and invited Sonia. The clients showed up late, all sweaty and out of breath, didn't apologize for making Oleh wait, and complained that they could barely squeeze their way into the restaurant and up the stairs.

"It's crowded downstairs, like a damn town fair. Maybe they're giving out free stuff," they said.

"Those are my guys," Oleh answered. "They're waiting to see how this meeting goes. Getting out'll be even harder."

The clients slumped in their chairs, decided against ordering any food, asked for some still water, and signed all the necessary papers. "I wouldn't wanna be with him," Sonia thought to herself back then.

When a smoky haze started creeping out of the hallways and everything started to smell like honey, sugar, and cinnamon, and the sun set over the towers and antennas of the city's upper neighborhoods, while down here, at the foot of the south-facing hills, the evening air was cooling off the greenery, they decided it was time to take off. They saw that the bride and groom had gotten into a serious fight and that the whole soccer team had piled out and was now standing at the door and anxiously debating something or other, which also indicated that it was time to go. Danylo rose to his feet unhurriedly, went over to the bride's godfather, who had been sleeping upright in a chair by the bar, his head resting on a bunch of forks, and knocked him to the ground, slugged one of the soccer players who was trying to pick a fight with one of the servers, ran his heavy hand along the head lawyer's pale back, sending fire through her skin, and walked away without looking back, detecting the smell of charred sugar and wet tobacco that lingered behind him. Oleh headed out too, his hiking boot nailing Hrysha in the ribs, so he wouldn't ruin the reception, picked the fallen server up by the collar, clutched Dasha for a moment, feeling that everything in her was burning with bitterness, then kept walking, only looking at his brother's unwavering back, only following his bruised head, only trusting his brother, and only listening to him. They walked up to Sonia to get their car keys.

"You're leaving so soon?" she asked, clearly disappointed.

Danylo tried cracking a joke, while Oleh rooted anxiously through his pockets for his cigarettes, then Sonia grabbed Danylo's hand and placed the keys in his palm, but she didn't let him go, pulling him along, instead.

"I can't just let you leave like this," she chuckled. "You know I can't."

Danylo walked imperiously right behind her, while Oleh, quite guardedly, brought up the rear—he stopped in front of the kitchen door, grabbed the little terror who was now shadowing them (his relatives had only just fished him out of the pool, but he'd already managed to change clothes), turned him around, and kneed him in the rear end.

"Go enjoy the reception," he said gloomily, closing the door.

There was one thing she liked about Senia—he never even thought about saying "thank you" when she paid for him. He'd say that a man shouldn't have to grovel, and if he happened to be low on cash that didn't mean he had to apologize and thank his girlfriend up and down. That was his idea of a guiding principle.

"Principles force us to take action; they give us the strength we need," Sonia thought. "Or the weakness we need. Or both." When he moved all his stuff—T-shirts, cleats, shin guards, sweat-stained keyboard—over to her place, her life hardly changed at all. Not even her dreams changed; they continued as though nothing new had happened in her life—like she had been hooked up to some channel that only displayed outlandish educational dreams that she didn't always understand, so she often didn't finish watching them. Senia treated her with a certain restrained politeness, he didn't need a lot of attention, and he didn't say much—sometimes his continuous silence would make her anxious. He liked sleeping beside her and looking at her in the morning before she woke up, before she could start talking. After a night with her, his body looked as though he'd been fighting through briar bushes in the dark. With all those bite-marks, bruises, and scratches on his shoulders and back, he looked like a great martyr who had taken some serious abuse for his beliefs. Senia would stand in front of the mirror, looking at the blood ex-uded by his skin, and he'd get this inexpressibly sweet feeling. After practice, he'd stand there in the shower as the blood seeped out of his wounds and mingled with the cool water like wind hitting sheets of rain. His friends would make fun of him, and he'd get angry and dress quickly—but at home, before he collapsed into bed, he'd walk over to the mirror and examine his cuts, which never seemed to heal.

Where had everyone gone? Why had they left so early? Well, it was late in the evening—actually, you could say it was early in the morning, but who keeps track of those things at a moment like this, in a mood like this? There was nobody in the kitchen; light spread evenly across the shiny, sauce- and cream-stained stove, the metal surfaces of the tables and the tin insides of the sinks, and the heavy fridges and sharp knives stuck in the bloody cutting boards. Half-empty pots of leftover delicacies were everywhere, bright-green cabbage and ten-der salad greens littered the floor, the last slivers of precious beef lay in one of the sinks, and the table was covered with glasses, jars filled with honey and chocolate, and plates of something spicy and pep-pery, viscous and weightless.

"Come on in, ya lumberjacks," Sonia said, laughing. "There's nobody here. I haven't eaten anything all day. Man, that's at my own wedding, too! I'll grab something now. Take a seat."

Oleh hopped up on the table, snatched a stray cabbage leaf, aimed, and shot it into the sink. "Three-pointer," he thought, rather pleased with himself. Danylo was leaning up against the fridge, looking at his brother mockingly, and listening to the silence in the hall-way. Sonia started peering into the pots, sniffing around and fishing out something tasty—the last morsels of Mediterranean dishes, east-ern spices, and southern fish—rattling dishes, pouring gravy all over, lighting up all four burners on the stove, which flared like sea flowers, flinging lilac shadows all across the ceiling. She produced a block of cheese, found some lemons, took out an open bottle of cognac, and passed it to Oleh, who froze every time their fingers touched. She sat down next to him, taking out an apple from behind her back, and tossed it to Danylo, who caught it effortlessly. Sonia took a massive swig of cognac, passed the bottle back to Oleh, picked up some food and sliced it into equal portions with a big knife, sharing everything she had. Oleh started drinking hard, keeping a close eye on her. Sonia bit into a lemon, and its golden juice ran down her chin. Not a single muscle in her face twitched—only a few tears slid down onto her cheeks, but she wiped them away smoothly and then reached for the cheese and parsley. Her teeth ripped through black bread and she smoothly washed it down with cherry juice. Her fingers snapped bars of chocolate and she licked strawberry jam off her palms, laughing all the while. A white flame whipped across her mouth—her smile was wide and bountiful. That's the kind of smile only kids—not all of them, though—can have. The cherries left a bloody trail on her lips and the alcohol made her breath warm; eating gave her such a light and cheerful air that Oleh was instantly drunk, a sleepy kind of drunk. Something was tossing him up into the air. Now he noticed that it was cold in there; not even the gas stove could heat up the damp air hovering over the sinks and freezers. "She's gotta be cold," he thought, shedding his leather jacket and using it to cover her shoulders. Sonia wrapped herself up in it and breathed deeply, inhaling his smell, turn-ing to kiss him—she kissed him for a while, and her kisses smelled like lemons and honey. Oleh waited and waited some more, until he couldn't take it anymore, then he grabbed his jacket back and tossed it on the cold tabletop—Sonia went right along with him, dropping back onto the jacket, pulling his shirt toward her, still kissing him as he took it off. Lemons were tumbling to the floor, bouncing off the jam-stained tile, dates were crushed under his arms, making his skin sweet, alcohol was spilling across the table, hopelessly soaking the stray salad greens.

"I'm just wearing this dress. Like that's it," Sonia said suddenly.

"That right?" he asked, surprised. "Don't your sneakers count?"

But she just chuckled, taking his hand and showing him that she really wasn't wearing anything underneath. Who would have thought? As they were laughing together, Danylo walked quietly over to the door and switched off the light, taking out a pack of cigarettes. "It's a good thing I have some left, otherwise I'd have to bug my brother," he thought, lighting up, looking out the dark window, and cracking the faintest smile. He was trying not to bother them and trying not to look at them. Her skin was golden, her hair was copper, and her heels were yellow, like lemons.

Persistent fists pounded on the door. The iron was ringing dully, bombarded by men's heavy shoulders, but the locks were durable and the metal impenetrable, so over there, on the other side of the door, in the black hallways, there was nothing to be heard but sharp curses and frustrated cries. Danylo kept smoking, burning through one cigarette after another. Oleh jumped down onto the floor and started getting dressed in a hurry, trying to slide his hand into the armhole of his jacket, hopping on one foot, sticking the other one into his shoe, and looking around the room for something heavy.

"Take it easy," Sonia said.

She was sitting on the metal table, tying her sneakers unhurriedly. Hazelnuts and coins were sliding down the creases of her dress. Her hair looked like a red flame flapping in the wind. Her voice was calm, though, and her eyes tender. When they'd first started pounding on the door, Oleh had stopped and whirled around, looking at his brother apprehensively, but Danylo, hiding out there in the gloom, hadn't even flinched. Sonia had wrapped her arms around Oleh's neck, pulled him toward her again, whispering something in his ear—quickly, quietly, yet coherently—which brought Oleh to a sudden stop inside her, and then it stopped her too, but she kept whispering, overcome by gratitude, joy, and drowsiness.

"Sonia, are you in there?" His voice was odd-sounding—sharpness mingling with uncertainty, frustration with hesitation.

"What a guy!" Sonia said, laughing, and then she yelled. "Yeah, I'm here. Whaddya want?"

Senia was at a loss.

"Open up," he said dryly.

"All right," Sonia said to Danylo, "climb out the window, you two. Then I'll open the door. Are you listening?"

Danylo didn't say anything, and Oleh didn't respond, either. Everyone was listening on the other side of the door.

"Danylo, did you hear me?"

Oleh walked over to Danylo.

"What are we gonna do?" he asked quietly.

"Whatever you say," Danylo answered, just as quietly.

"I can't just leave her. He'll kill her."

He looked ahead, biding his time. Danylo hesitated for a second.

"Danylo," Sonia said, growing a bit anxious. "Are you listening to me? Come on, get outta here!"

"Don't think so!" Danylo said suddenly. "Like I'm gonna run away from those chumps."

"Yeah, for real, man."

Danylo patted him on the back, switched on the light, and opened the door like it was the gate of a besieged city.

They looked like a real soccer team, coming out of the stadium's dark tunnels and into the floodlights, geared up for battle and expecting another victory. As soon as the door was flung open, the whole squad burst forward, backing Oleh and Danylo up against the metal tables, forming a half-circle around them. Senia's nephew was poking his head between them, relishing the fact that he'd been the one to bring them all here, to the scene of the crime. Senia's relatives immediately rushed over toward Sonia, who had adjusted her dress inconspicuously, found Oleh's cigarettes somehow, lit one up, and was now coldly blowing smoke in the faces of some women as they yelled at her, doing nothing to hide their consternation and despair. The soccer players stood there, glaring at the two brothers, not knowing what to do; Senia's gaze kept moving from Oleh to Danylo and then back to Oleh, until he realized it was making his eyes look all shifty, so he turned toward Oleh.

"Hey, you," he said glumly, "let's have a little chat. And you," he said, nodding at Danylo, "stay put. We'll chat with you in a bit."

"Hey, you," Danylo mimicked his tone. "Go fuck yourself."

Senia wanted to respond, but the anger welling up inside choked him, and he charged at Danylo, who stepped out of the way, grabbed Senia's neck, and threw him against the table. Senia's chest slammed into its shiny metal surface, and he slumped to the ground, gasping for air. The soccer players charged at the brothers. Oleh clocked one of them, and Danylo took down another two. After that, the gang knocked them off their feet and went in for the kill. Danylo covered his head, trying to keep his breathing relaxed. Oleh was squirming, trying to fend them off, not saying anything and not thinking about anything, although he sure had a lot to think about.

Like his own misplaced self-confidence, how sure he was that everything would play out just the way he imagined it. He had taken a liking to her right away. He liked that she wasn't afraid of anything, especially being alone, and that she made a big show of carrying condoms in her wallet, right next to her business cards. He liked it that she sent the hearts of her potential business associates racing.

Back then, at the Georgian joint, after those two guys shat their pants and signed on the dotted line, he drove her home and then kept her in the car for a while, talking constantly so she wouldn't go anywhere; he could tell that she was tensing up and that she didn't like this whole situation, but he was so sure of himself that he continued holding her hand and cracking jokes, making her laugh and tense up even more. But when he casually leaned in, not even bothering to turn off the engine, she covered his lips with her cold palm and said, "Cool your jets, pal."

Then she got out, slammed the passenger door and headed over to her apartment building, swaying from side to side so angrily that he simply couldn't help but stare at her. "How on earth can someone walk like that without tipping over?" he thought. She opened the door to her apartment building and dove inside. He just sat there, unable to take his eyes off the black night enveloping him. A split second later, her silhouette popped back into the headlights, swaying back and forth, like before, approaching the car and opening the passenger side door again.

"Hey Rambo, are ya comin' or what?"

He caught up to her in the stairwell and tried to carefully lay her down on the landing, but she neatly slipped out of his clutches, mounting him and pressing him up against the cold stone floor. He felt a wandering draft, songs reverberating in other people's apartments, beasts and birds gathering around the building, reacting to the light and warm air, reacting to the loud cries she wasn't even trying to hold back.

"Keep it down," he said to her. "Your neighbors . . . you're the one who lives here."

"Uh-huh," she replied, not stopping. "I know."

She kept screaming after every jerky movement, stopping only once, when a door downstairs squeaked open — it sounded like somebody had come in from outside and quickly scurried up the steps; he tried getting up, but Sonia covered his mouth with her hand, which wasn't as cold anymore and now smelled like her warmth, and the pattering steps cut out a floor below them. A door opened, somebody said hello, everything quieted down, and then he couldn't hear a thing but her moaning. After that she ran up to her apartment, and he was left sitting on the steps until the early morning, lacking the resolve to get up and leave.

At first, the squad was dragging them down the hallway, throwing punches and ripping their clothes, and eventually shoving them toward the swimming pools. At that point, Danylo broke free and nailed one of the guys so hard he fell back into the water. Then the whole gang pounced on him and dragged him along, hungry for vengeance. When the whole crowd piled into the bar, John stopped them. A few locals were standing behind him. They had either heard about the fight or just knew that this was the only way this night could end.

"Whatcha got there?" John asked.

"Well, we caught these two troublemakers," they all shouted triumphantly.

"Just two? So it was all you guys against the two of them?"

"Well, uh, yeah," the soccer players answered, suddenly sounding less confident. "We caught 'em."

"And your fuckin' point is?" John said. "All right, you caught 'em, now let 'em go. Yeah, some troublemakers you got there."

"No fuckin' way!" one of the younger guys yelled.

"Come on over here." As soon as he did, John grabbed him by the collar, spun around abruptly, and slammed him against a half-open door. It swung the rest of the way, sending the guy flying, and the men standing behind John stepped forward. The squad started duking it out with John's guys, but they didn't realize what they were getting into, and it didn't go well; they all took a beating. John, punching randomly at bobbing buzzcuts, shouted to his buddies,

"Don't touch the groom. This is his big day."

Nobody touched the groom; he just stayed in the kitchen, crying, his face buried in Sonia's cold lap.

He could have thought about the fatigue that enveloped him every time he walked downstairs in the morning, sensing that the tenants in her apartment building were listening to his footsteps. Sonia never let him leave in the middle of the night.

"Don't go. I can't stand sleeping alone. If you go, I'll have someone else come over."

He was putty in her hands; he'd get mad and stay. Her screaming would lull him to sleep, but his body would keep moving, so she wouldn't even notice. He'd quickly snap out of it, unable to believe that he'd actually fallen asleep right next to her, and even though he couldn't see her face in the dark, he definitely knew when she was laughing, when she was worrying, when she was coming, and when everything was about to start all over again. You could tell by how she was breathing and what she was saying. She was always talking, always giving him warnings, explanations, and exhortations. He got used to her voice over time, but he could only stop and relax once she'd quieted down. Then he'd lie there, touching her skin.

The young soccer players were led outside and backed up against a wall. One of them tried breaking free, but he was knocked onto the asphalt immediately. Half the team stood there—the half that wasn't lying on the floor inside. Obviously, there was no point dragging them out. The locals stood there, making sure nobody could escape; John inspected them coldly; Danylo, holding his side, was standing next to him, and Oleh was next to him. Uncle Hrysha, who was stumbling but managing to stay on his feet, tried reasoning with John, nodding at the squad. The others could hear bits and pieces of the conversation.

"What the hell, man?"

"Why the fuck would ya . . ."

"Those goddamn morons."

"Uncle Hrysha," John replied, "go back to the bar and get yourself a drink."

So Uncle Hrysha slunk off dejectedly, not making eye contact with the team.

"All right then, ya little pukes," John started. "What'd I tell you? Was it that hard to just listen to me?"

The team didn't say anything. Danylo was readying his fists and Oleh was spitting out blood from a bitten lip. The rest of the guys were standing behind John and thinking, "Yeah, they deserve it. He *did* tell them. Was it really that hard to listen?"

"We gonna finish them off?" John asked, turning toward his guys. But before they could answer, a dry, deafening flash cut through the air, forcing everyone to duck their heads like turtles hiding inside their shells, and fireworks flooded half the sky, illuminating tree branches and roofs buried in the dark, reflecting in everyone's eyes, and fading into black ozone. People were hooting and hollering somewhere nearby, and our block chimed in, too. Beyond the trees and hills everyone was embracing the celebratory, celestial flame that scorched the insects in the air and blinded the passersby in the streets, making the night unbearably beautiful and our lives inexpressibly wonderful.

"All right, whatever," Danylo said, placing his hand on John's shoulder. "Who gives a fuck about these little punks? Let 'em go."

"Yeah, you're right," Oleh said, sliding his tongue along a chipped tooth. "Who gives a fuck?"

John thought for a bit and lifted his head, regarding the yellow and green flashes glowing in the sky above them, then he turned toward the team.

"All right," he said, "I don't give a fuck about you guys. You'll live to see another day."

Somebody suggested going around the corner to get a better view, so they did.

(One time, a hitchhiker tried to strangle Danylo. That was before he started working for the taxi company—it was pouring out and he saw some young guy on the side of the road, so he decided to stop and pick him up. It turned out they were heading the same way. The guy sat in the back, which was a bit weird, but Danylo thought nothing of it. While they were crossing the bridge, Danylo had to brake, and the guy leaned forward sharply, ramming his elbow into Danylo's neck, locking his hands together, and pulling with all his strength. The startled Danylo slammed on the brakes again, sending the guy flying, head first, into the windshield. Then Danylo heaved him over his shoulder and dragged him out into the rain. The guy looked at him, eyes all glassy, showing no hint of fear, no hint of any feelings at all. Sitting there in a puddle, he looked up at Danylo and muttered, his voice hissing with hate,

"Fag, fuckin' fag, you're such a fuckin' fag."

Danylo snapped—maybe he was just tired, maybe it just pissed him off that he went to the trouble of picking a guy up only to get called a fag. Danylo kicked the youngster right in the head, which he truly wasn't expecting from himself. He did it again and again, he just didn't have it in him to stop. The guy ducked his head, trying to cover it, and eventually tipped over. His head fell in the water, his eyes were bloody, and foam was coming out of his mouth. Danylo got scared; he even thought about just leaving him there, but something compelled him to lug the guy—all dirty and wet—back to his car and drive him to the emergency room. When he was talking to the doctor, he just said that he'd picked him up off the side of the road. The doctor took one look at him and figured it all out.

"Did he hit you or something?" he asked, seeing the bruises on Danylo's neck.

"He tried to strangle me," Danylo admitted.

"Did you do it to him, too?"

"Nah, but I kicked him a few times."

"Drugs. It seems like you knocked his eye out. He'll live, like that'll do anybody any good."

"What are we gonna do?"

"Nothing. We're not gonna do anything. You have to learn to control yourself. Sometimes our perception of the harm done to us pales in comparison to how much our conscience will torture us for the rest of our lives. But at the very least, you don't realize that until you're near the end of your life. Get going. You weren't here, I've never seen you before.")

He could also have thought about hurt feelings and jealousy, about the need for revenge, about the rage in his voice, about her scornful silence, about the disappointment she didn't even try to hide. He couldn't understand what she needed that soccer player for—he couldn't even tie his shoes—or where the hell he'd even come from. She shouted at him to quit sticking his nose in her business, that she didn't need him bossing her around, and that he should just beat it. He did, but then he called, and they argued until he ran out of money on his phone and she ran out of patience. Oleh was planning on tracking down that soccer player to tell him that Sonia was his, and he'd better make himself scarce; he was planning on it (he really was!), but he didn't follow through for some reason—maybe she talked him out of it ("Relax, it's just a little fling, you'll see for yourself"), maybe he realized that the soccer player had nothing to do with it, he wasn't the one breaking them up. She was the problem. You couldn't even talk to her; she was used to doing whatever she pleased, she was always the one calling the shots, and nobody had any sway over her—her dad was out of the picture, her mom had died a few years ago, and the therapist she saw every week, another object of jealousy for Oleh, didn't really seem to get her, so who had any sway over her? Who could reason with her? "Everything'll work out,"

Oleh said to himself. "She's a high-powered businesswoman, after all, she'll figure things out, sooner or later. She's not just gonna go and ruin her life. Everything's going to be like it was before—she'll keep ripping my heart out, writing me love letters in the afternoon, cursing me up and down in the evening, and telling me her dreams in the morning—they make no sense, they're too simple and too sublime."

They walked down the street and turned up the hill. They passed the Institute, dark buildings, and the empty schoolyard. They stopped by the kiosks. Danylo bought some sparkling water to wash his cuts—the bubbles hissed, as if his skin had come to a boil.

"Doin' all right?" he asked Oleh.

"Yeah."

"Ya sure?"

"Yep."

"Well all right, then." Danylo took out his cigarettes and handed one to his brother.

They had a smoke, patted each other on the back, and went their separate ways.

Then again, he could have thought about that morning two days ago or its low-hanging fog sticking warmly and waxily to the pines, making the forest invisible and treacherous. The dark skeleton of their building stood in a clearing, in the middle of a field, like a half-finished battleship. Oleh slept in the trailers, right alongside his construction crew, like a true captain, sharing canned food, bread, and alcohol with his cheerful and mischievous band of pirates. It was the alcohol they were most interested in sharing that night; it went on until the early morning, and then Oleh told everyone to get some shut-eye.

"No days off for us," he said. "This is a big client shelling out the big bucks, three hours of sleep, then reveille—we've got a construction timetable to think about."

But no sooner had he fallen asleep than he was awakened by his phone. It was Danylo.

"Did ya know," he started, "that your friend is getting married to that guy tomorrow?"

"What friend?" Still drowsy, Oleh wasn't following.

"Your friend, Sonia. Her wedding's tomorrow. I gave her relatives a ride into town from the train station. They had this fat jerkoffy kid with them, too. Did you know they were getting married?"

"Of course I did," Oleh assured him.

He got up and dressed quickly, putting on his work clothes and a jacket—a cold patch of air was coming out of the woods—woke up the foreman and told him he wouldn't be back for two days, and brushed his teeth with icy water, realizing that his breath still reeked of alcohol, so he'd have to take the train. "Well, it's no big deal. A five-hour trip and then I'll be home," he thought. He went over to the village and asked for a ride to the station. Someone agreed to take him, and they navigated the fog and murk. He'd missed the night train; the next one wouldn't be for another two hours. Oleh sat down on a bench and fell asleep. A cop woke him up, demanded to see some ID, spent a long time checking his picture, and called somebody to make some inquiries; it was only then that he got around to telling him that there wouldn't be any train today because it only ran every other day. Then they agreed that the officer would drop him off on the main highway. Nobody wanted to pick up some dude mired in the fog, dressed in heavy hiking boots and a shady-looking jacket. Pissed off and unshaven, he lay down in the grass, slept for a bit, and then called Danylo to ask for a ride. His brother had no problem with helping him out, but Oleh couldn't explain where he was standing, or, more precisely, where he was lying. A truck finally picked him up in the afternoon; the driver agreed to drop him off at the nearest bus station, refusing to take any money, because Oleh looked so worked up. When he got to the station, it turned out that the evening bus wasn't even going to run its route—there weren't any passengers. Oleh offered to pay the driver triple the regular fare but got turned down anyway. Oleh headed over toward the taxi drivers, who took one look at his stubble and the blood and cement caked on his boots and turned him away too, all but one of them, who said they'd be leaving at ten, because he had to wait for a regular customer of his who'd be arriving on the Rostov night express and bringing him a little treat. That's what he said—a little treat—like it was a chocolate cake or something. Oleh agreed to wait and then went over to the snack bar. The taxi drivers all followed him in, standing at the counter next to him and listening closely to his silence. They left at ten, driving slowly and stalling occasionally. The driver was anxious, and so was Oleh. They covered the first hundred kilometers. They were so close. Right at the city limits, as the car was struggling up yet another hill, it started smoking. The driver opened the hood so despairingly that Oleh paid him the full amount and started walking. "No biggie," he said to himself, "keep going at a good clip and you'll get to the metro in a few hours. You'll be there by morning."

He descended into the valley and then started climbing back out, feeling the city coming closer as he walked, and its breath becoming more and more palpable as its glow grew more and more intense up ahead of him. Trucks rolled out of the night, delivering fresh vegetables, frozen pig carcasses, grain, cotton, and contraband medicine to markets and warehouses. Some of the tankers had fresh milk sloshing around in their innards, some had stolen oil, some hid slaves being transported from market to market, singing their sorrowful songs, wondering who would buy them and where they'd ultimately end up. An endless stream of train cars loaded with fish and timber rolled down the tracks, and sleepy passengers peered out the windows, watching the sun flooding the grass of the outskirts with red flames. Barges filled with coal and ships with armed crews glided inaudibly up the rivers, trying to slip through the morning fog to the city's docks. The sun was poking through the fog, and the city swelled with light, voices, and sounds, rousing people from their slumber and releasing images from their dreams. The city lay up in the hills, flanked by rivers on two sides. Down in the valley stood the first of the houses where the workers lived and the schools where their children went, loomed the dark walls of the hospitals where the lepers were, glowed the white limestone walls of the prisons where they kept the thieves and lunatics. Beyond that were the great factory buildings where they made tanks and tractors, unrecognized churches, which it was forbidden to build in the upper neighborhoods, the black landing strips and the opium fields of the nunneries sprawled out before Oleh. Beyond the airport began the fences of bread factories and meat-packing plants that woke up in the dark to feed the residents of the city, followed by the gallows where they would hang local witches; the large hardware store was visible behind them, and in one of the hangars, hidden away from the security guards, pilgrims who had come from down south—the Donbas and Crimea—to venerate the icons of the city's ancient cathedrals slept on the concrete floor with pieces of cardboard underneath them. A bit farther along were red-brick houses with satellite dishes and secret wards that drove off swindlers and Gypsies. It was mostly people who worked at the markets and train stations that lived in those houses; in the morning, they'd set off for work, their boisterous children running after them, carrying backpacks full of hymnals and algebra homework. The women would stay home and take care of the housework, washing, sewing, making brews that cured the sick and kept men faithful, and pulling food out of their pantries and fridges—red peppers, green suns of cabbage, and yellow cheeses that looked like ripe moons. Smoke from factories and the fires where people warmed asphalt and boiled clean the clothing of the consumptive rose over the roofs of their buildings, and trolleys packed with factory workers, villagers, and couriers rolled past linden and poplar trees, goading along their fuzz that simply wouldn't settle on the ground, sending it fluttering up above the city's squares.

The old neighborhoods faced one of the two rivers, its smooth, level bank overgrown with cattails, where anglers hid, lying in wait for precious fish that were foolish enough to burrow into the silt of its shallows, where they shone like stolen silver dishes. The area around the bridges was mostly inhabited by alms-seekers who had set up camp in the old typography offices and pharmaceutical warehouses, prostitutes who rented cheap rooms at the dorms run by the railroad institute, jewelry dealers and Sophers who were hesitant to live in the residential area down by the river, so they raised large families in the Stalin-era apartment buildings along one of the main avenues. Sickly and childless women, homeless men, and unemployed teenagers peered at the city from the riverbank. Children tossed dead birds into the water, where they would float with the current, terrifying those living in the cottages that stretched along the left bank, behind the industrial area and the cemetery for prisoners of war.

A fortress wall, heavy and impenetrable, ran along the right bank, propping up the hills and keeping the city from expanding any farther. The customs office was behind the bridge—city guards in gilded armor and traffic cops wielding striped sticks stopped cars and trucks as they tried to pass through the city gates, checked their goods, and searched their trunks and the travelers' suitcases, looking for undeclared emporia and banned literature. The travelers were checked for syphilis and the plague, and the more suspicious of them were detained and quarantined at the gray barracks the Red Cross had set up by the bus station. The mornings were the busiest time for those officers; they had to catch merchants trying to worm their way into the Old City through underground passageways or stow away on metro cars, and sizable cohorts of sailors who avoided paying any tariffs or declaring any of their cold steel weapons who ascended the surrounding hills by dark footpaths that wound through the gardens and vacant lots behind the Polytechnic Institute. The travelers and men of trade who paid their taxes in full were admitted to the city and either climbed up the cracked cobblestone road, or the new asphalt one the government had recently laid, to the upper neighborhoods, where there was more sun but less greenery. Banks and stores, 24-

hour kiosks where you could always get a pack of cigarettes and 24-hour pharmacies where you could always get your particular drug cocktail lined narrow streets packed with advertisements and automobiles. Flashy dresses and jewelry burned pink and green in display cases, serving men carried heavy water jugs out of the stores, rushing to bring them to local kitchens, where cooks were lighting their ovens to prepare exquisite Italian and Arabian dishes for the heads of their households. Restaurants and coffee shops were welcoming their first patrons—those who'd arrived from other cities that morning or hadn't had the time to grab a bite to eat after a night on the town, or those who lived in hotels and nightclubs for weeks on end and just wanted to be around people, so they followed the alluring morning smell of cognac. Students gathered in cheap cafeterias, spilling beer all over their lecture notes, taking out hunting knives and vowing to gut deans and professors, catching up on the latest news, and reading protest poems aloud. Businessmen were sitting in expensive restaurants and closing deals, pricking their fingers and signing contracts in blood. The women standing on the streets smelled like sleep and love; the children were running to school, re-creating the magnificent stories they'd seen in their dreams the night before. Their screams soared up into the sky and disturbed the trembling currents of air—they froze and changed direction.

Up high with the rising morning air, among the solar fires and poplar clouds, there were enough churches, mosques, and synagogues to hold all the city's residents if danger were to strike, monuments to poets and university founders, sprawling parks where birds and beasts brought from Asia and South America roamed free, and theaters, palaces, the hall of burgesses, the municipal government building, and the main department store, all stacked on top of each other. In the mornings, street sweepers washed the steps leading up to monuments and concert halls, traffic cops despairingly stopped bicyclists who flew out into the main square, scattering flocks of pigeons and red, squawking parrots, and eminent professors and councilmen headed to their offices to attend to the city's needs, protect it against unnecessary fiscal risks and other threats to civilization. The city fathers walked out onto the high tops of their towers, surveying their neighborhoods, swollen with sundust, catching the nearly imperceptible smell of the river flowing from the south, gazing at the surface of the northern river glistening like an airplane's wing, listening to the birds circling over them, and lifting their heads to the heavens to ask the saints for mercy and intercession. The saints stood there in the blue, invisible space beyond the currents of wind and pockets of turbulence, feeding the birds of the air straight from their hands, listening to the voices down below; they were giving the city fathers an answer, and it went a little something like this:

"We are doing everything we can. We would like things to go well for you, but how they go is not entirely up to us, so you shouldn't rely on us alone. Most of our woes and crises of faith stem from our own unwillingness to separate our actions into two categories—good ones and bad ones. We have our love, but we don't always use it. We have our fear, and we rely on it more than we ought to. There are two paths in life—one leads to heaven and the other to hell. Those paths often cross, though."

## MARK

They set up their furniture-repair shop in the basement of the local utilities department. There was no sign, but the people who needed to find it could—turn after the metro, pick out the right building, duck into the brick archway, and you'll see the black metal door in the wall. Just knock or ring the bell. They'd stuck a sagging couch down there for the employees to nap on if they didn't have any work to do. Stationary equipment loomed in the middle of the room, and tables cluttered with jars, brushes, dry rags, pencils, worn-down sandpaper, and dull foldable knives with bent blades crowded up against the walls. A heavy, swaying lamp dangled from the ceiling and yellowed Soviet factory posters and a few wrestling plaques hung on the walls. The shop smelled of paint, varnish, old wood, and other people's homes, where all those chairs, wardrobes, bureaus, and bookcases had been before customers lugged them down here to get fixed or restored.

In the mornings, they'd open the windows, which faced an apartment complex overrun with grass and wild garlic. Fresh air and the muffled sounds of the streets would fill the room. There were some gnarled apple trees out there, and the furniture guys put a couple of benches in their shade—another place for naps. There were some wobbly little structures built against the sides of the apartment blocks a little farther away, beyond the trees, but it was no easy task fighting through the twisting ivy and tall grass to get to them. Even farther back towered a jagged section of brick wall—all that remained of the buildings that had once stood there, now ruined and forgotten. The wall ran up against a wide street that stretched uphill, past the

Polytechnic Institute, toward the center of town. In the summer, the block would be completely empty, and the grassy spaces enclosed by the apartment buildings would be as quiet as churches on Monday. There'd be even less work, leaving the employees with nothing better to do than listen to the radio on their cellphones.

Mark started working here back in the winter. In March, the shop was damp; he and his partner in crime would sit there, drinking their boxed wine, pairing it with scoops of the hard, dark snow that would linger on the ground under their windows until mid-April. His partner in crime, Yasha, had been at the shop since the beginning. He'd known the boss since the eighties—they were working at the bike factory, just going with the flow, then the nineties hit, they tried to start charting their own course, and the boss capsized. Loyal to a fault, Yasha waited for him faithfully, like a sailor's wife at the harbor. About ten years back, at the beginning of the 2000s, the boss got the green light to set up shop in the basement—he had to pull a lot of strings to make it happen, too. He'd find all his customers himself, buy all the used stuff himself, drop off salvaged material at night, stop by with some shady customers in the morning, casually raise the price on bureaus, make some calls, avoid some people in town, hardly socialize with anyone—hardly anyone liked him—but his heart wasn't really in it. Yasha, who had nimble fingers and a resilient liver, was the one who really kept the place running. But Yasha wasn't getting any younger, so he asked for an assistant. The boss wouldn't go for any outside help. After all, he barely trusted the guys he had. But then Kolia, one of Yasha's good buddies, recommended his nephew Mark.

"It's better to hire people you know. At least they won't unionize on ya."

So the boss went with Mark, and afterward he'd often say he'd done a good deed, but he later expressed remorse for his actions.

"Mark," the boss told his newly minted apprentice, "you have to honor your parents, even if you don't have any." Mark grew up without his father, who had gone up north with a lumber company and never come back, so his mother raised him. She did the best she could, which was pretty terrible. His uncle Kolia would step in at the most crucial moments—he bribed the draft board to get his nephew off the hook, got the college admissions committee to give him a slot in night school, and found odd jobs for him. But he kept his distance, never quite letting his guard down. Mark realized that, so now, at the ripe old age of thirty, he only trusted providence . . . though providence hadn't done much to earn his trust.

The job wasn't very interesting, but on the plus side it wasn't too demanding for the new apprentice—Mark hauled some furniture around, polished some things, and sanded some boards. Whenever the boss headed out to run errands, Yasha would go pick up some wine and Mark would sprawl out on the couch and flip through old newspapers, clearly dumbstruck by the kind of headlines he found there. The liquor store was across from the shop, built right into the factory's entry hall. Everybody knew Yasha there and nobody liked him. Yasha had the gentle touch of a true mentor, treating his student well; he even made all the alcohol runs himself. After a few drinks, the master would start talking about his life, and the apprentice would listen inattentively, not giving much credence to what he heard. According to Yasha, there were no women in the world he hadn't slept with, and no men he hadn't shared drinks with. Mark would show up to work in varnish-stained Keds, baggy white jeans with bright chemical speckles, and T-shirts his mom had scored at some Swiss charity event. He was calm, amiable, and a bit reserved; his heart wasn't really in it, and he would've quit months ago, if it hadn't been for Kolia. He was afraid of Kolia, whose imposing apathy had a debilitating effect on him. Otherwise, Mark was doing pretty well—he didn't have any friends and he lived with his mom, though they hardly talked because his mom didn't have any new stories and he didn't feel like hearing the old ones again. He enjoyed napping in the afternoon and he'd have some pretty exotic and menacing dreams during his siestas— snakes with women's heads and foxes with the voices of opera singers, buildings on fire, and rivers with dragons flying over them. He'd wake up in the late afternoon and climb out through the window to sit on a bench outside. Stray dogs would encircle him, ready to pounce, but they lacked the gusto to go for it—after all, what could you take from this odd character who smelled like varnish and wood? What could he have in his pockets besides nails, string, metal plumb bobs like machine-gun cartridges, and drawing compasses? Sometimes Mark would spend the night at work, switching on the table lamps, and bugs would be drawn into the room, only to be scorched by the bulbs and plummet to the floor. Mark roamed around the room, and the bugs crunched cheerfully under his feet like peanut shells.

He'd been up all night; he wanted to prolong that state that follows an extended stretch of sleeplessness, that feeling of being detached from the motion of the planets through the heavens. Thirty is the right age for learning to enjoy the passage of time and stop regretting that it passes so quickly. His habits had long since become fixed, his anxiety had dissipated, and he had comfortably settled into his addictions. The need to fight off drowsiness and preserve the eerie and fleeting quality of the world's darkness within himself hit Mark hardest in the summer months. At around 6 a.m., he'd completely lose the ability to orient himself in time; the sun was already over the trees, but the moon was still hanging up in the sky—it seemed as though the city had woken up a while ago and everyone was attending to important business, which gave Mark an unaccountable feeling of anxiety or anticipation, like the planets had perfectly aligned above him, hinting at the beginning of something important in his life, the kind of thing that ought to begin on one of these strange days at the end of June, when suns and moons multiply and hide in the air like foxes in warm grass. He shut the windows, walked outside, and took out his phone to check the time. At that very moment he got a call from Kolia.

Kolia owned two vegetable stands on Horse Lane and two more downtown. Mark's mom worked at one of them. He tried opening another one at the beginning of the summer, but it went bust, which caused his pancreas to start acting up. Kolia decided to steer clear of hospitals—alcohol was his go-to medicine. Yesterday morning he'd made a long haul out to some wedding—he had a classmate who had died a few years ago, leaving behind a solid legacy and an adult heiress. It was her daughter tying the knot. He came, congratulated the newlyweds, held forth about family obligations, hit on the women, and argued with the men. The pain flared up that night. He got taken to the hospital. He got pissed. He argued with the doctor too. He called his nephew as soon as she left the room.

"Markster," he said flatly, choosing his words carefully so he wouldn't sound too helpless. "I can't really talk, there's people sleeping here. Listen up, go over to my place, you have a set of keys. Grab my toothbrush, grab my razor, grab my hair dryer, grab my slippers, grab my towels, underwear, some magazines, my hot-water bottle, my cards (I'm talking about my playing cards, you know), a bowl, a spoon, my knife block, a few clean dress shirts and ties, handkerchiefs, my teapot, my thermos, my toaster—"

"Are you moving or something?" Mark interrupted.

"I'm in the hospital," Kolia answered brusquely.

Mark got scared. Kolia continued, "They brought me in right after the wedding, in the middle of the night. I didn't even have a change of clothes. Come on, Markster," he said coldly, putting some pressure on his nephew. "Move! Move! Move!"

His anxiety rubbed off on Mark. Kolia was always getting on his case—he was always riding everyone, he micromanaged everything, spinning a system of family relationships like a sticky spiderweb, taking deep offense whenever anyone would slip out of his tender yet firm embrace, and talking about his clan an awful lot—mostly good things—but he still treated them like debtors.

Kolia resided in a two-story building not far away; the whole first floor belonged to him. The building was buried deep in a nook between large apartment blocks, so you couldn't even see it from the street. The walls exuded moisture, the balconies were drooping, and the ceiling should have collapsed a long time ago, but it was still intact, supported by invisible braces and beams. Kolia arranged buckets and pots all over his rooms like he was setting cunning traps to catch precious raindrops. Back in the Soviet days, four families lived in the building. Kolia's family had two rooms on the first floor, next to the Pavlovs—Papa Pavlov, an engineer, Mama Pavlov, an engineer, too, and their busybody drama-queen daughter. Shalva Shotovych, a factory foreman up on Shevchenko Street, a lonesome unmarried jigit of Georgian descent with tons of connections around town, lived right above them. Some old Bolsheviks lived in the other corner of the second floor; Kolia could never tell them apart . . . or maybe they were just that good at disguising themselves. At the beginning of the nineties, the Pavlovs suddenly turned out to have been Jews all along, and promptly emigrated, selling their apartment to Kolia for peanuts. The Bolsheviks' ranks thinned over time. Eventually, there was only one old lady left, and she wasn't feeling too hot, either. She'd sometimes look in the mirror by accident and give herself a real scare. Kolia would sometimes stop by and give her some food. Shalva left, too, but without selling his apartment. Once every two years or so, he'd fly in from Hamburg or some other place where he was working down at the docks, air out the rooms, sit with Kolia in the evenings, tell him about his new life—he wasn't griping at all, but Kolia would still try to console him. Shalva refused to sell his apartment, for some odd reason. It was as though he was keeping one last corridor open in case he had to retreat, some illusion that all was not lost and everything could still work out in the end. So Kolia was all by himself—his parents had died, his sisters, Zina and Maria, got married, had some kids, and got divorced, but they were in no hurry to return to the nest. Between raising Mark and working for her brother, Maria had her hands full. Zina lived by the sea and hardly ever visited. Mark's mom got married, but it didn't work out. His aunt Zina got married, but that didn't work out either. He viewed this as some sort of family curse.

Kolia hid stacks of cash in his fridge, kept vegetables he'd bought from wholesalers in the hallway, and slept blissfully sprawled out on a sofa. He didn't have much luck with the ladies, and they didn't have much luck with him, either. Kolia had olive skin, squinty eyes, a heavy, mistrustful gaze, a dull smile, yellow teeth like an old stray dog, weak lungs, and a heart swimming in fat. He made himself breakfast every morning. No wonder his pancreas had started acting up.

Mark dug out his keys, opened the door, walked down the hallway, and entered Kolia's dusty domain, where herbs lay in a great heap on the floor. The air had the overwhelming smell of medicine and the muffled smell of burned food. There was a fancy new chandelier hanging over the table in the first room; only one of the bulbs worked, though. There were two washing machines in the corner; neither of them worked. There were wardrobes full of new, brand-name clothing and old children's books. The rugs were densely covered with potato chips. Then Mark stumbled over a loose TV cable and an unplugged extension cord with a toaster at one end. Kolia was clearly all about the latest technology, but he had some problems getting it hooked up. The curtains had been drawn, and the rooms were swaddled in murk. The air held so many smells and so much stagnant warmth within itself that Mark couldn't take it anymore and had to open the window for some relief. He took out his bag and started rooting around the apartment, gathering up Kolia's things: the thermos, towels, and underwear. Then he remembered about the toothbrush. The bathroom was on the other side of the building. He went through the room with a couch and two televisions (one had picture and the other had sound), past the closet where Kolia kept brooms and his hunting shotgun, into a spacious, messy kitchen; in the corner, partitioned off by a colorful Chinese screen, was a big, fancy tub resting on four bricks. He loved Kolia's kitchen—you could always find something interesting there, either in the fridge, which would shut off on its own sometimes, or in his grandma's old desk, where Kolia kept

sweets and sleeping pills. There were suitcases packed with magazines and cardboard boxes stuffed with Kolia's socks and supermarket
bags. A heavy piece of velvet was draped over the window like a flag,
which made the surrounding disorder mysterious, so Mark stepped
into the kitchen full of the foretaste of mysteries and riddles — with
good reason, as it turned out. A young stranger stood in the shower,
her back turned to Mark, fiddling with the hot-water knob. The screen
had been pulled slightly to the side; the stranger apparently hadn't
been expecting any visitors. Mark froze, took a half-step back through
the doorway, and then peeked in again. Light was streaming through
holes in the velvet, yanking colors and shades out of the twilight. The
radio on top of the fridge was singing with melodramatic sorrow; two
hoarse women's voices were telling some sob story about a downtrod-
den girl from a small port town who had learned too early about heart-
ache and disappointment. The stranger didn't even hear that somebody had walked into the room — she stood on her tiptoes, reaching
for the nickel-plated Italian showerhead that Kolia had attached with
blue adhesive tape, swaying slightly and listening to the sad women
as though the song was about her own life.

"There was," the first woman started, "nothing to do in my town
except pound beers all day and fuck your brains out all night in the
park by the jungle gym, the factories' white smoke, the workers' black
eyes, and duplicitous raspberry bushes behind the brackish nighttime delta."

"Yep, yep," the other woman chimed in, "nothing to do, no at-
tractions but dry southern wine and making love in the salt-parched
grass. The hammerers' black eyes and the fresh raspberries at the Sunday bazaars."

Mark stared hard, trying to get a better look at the stranger. She
was short and skinny with long, dark hair — weighed down now by the
water — standing on her tiptoes, muscles taut with strain, but she still
couldn't reach anything, and she kept on swaying so bitterly that the
song, already none too cheerful, became utterly hopeless.

"Everyone in town thought I was a tramp," the first woman cried, "everyone hated me for my dyed curls and the golden chain on my defenseless neck. Every good-for-nothing scumbag on the street tried looking under my skirt and pawing my hips in the dark movie theater."

"Yeah, that's right," the other woman continued, "black strands of hair glinted keenly in the dark pit of the movie theater, and forlorn men walked her home late at night, passing through the olive-colored evenings, mesmerized by the warm bronze gleam of her skin."

"They loved her," the other woman added, as though emphasizing an important point, "for her light heart and carefree nature."

Mark listened and looked. She had slim and weightless calves, soft hips, and dark skin, as though she had spent a lot of time working in vineyards, exposed to the sun, not hiding from the wind and rain.

Then the first woman continued, "Downtown was all decked out for the big holiday when I met him. He was a real gangster, plucking pigeons in streetcars, never parted from his Finnish knife, gunfights, hideouts, the whole shebang. But I'd given my heart to him—love's a funny thing. But he left me, withdrawing a step at a time till I was all alone in this cruel, cold world."

"Love, oh love," the other woman took over, "it made every day a holiday for her, when she'd rush downtown every morning, and the local men would pull their knives and fight over the right to buy her a bouquet of wildflowers. But only one of them could open her joyful heart like a bike lock; he removed its secret spring and deprived her of her voice and happiness. Where is he now? What streetcars carry him home? Why won't he come back for her?" She flung her hair onto her breasts, and Mark discerned some birthmarks on her back, so tiny they were hardly perceptible—he discerned her delicate vertebrae showing sharply under her skin like underwater rocks breaking the surface of a lake, rising to hold her up—she was so slim they could hardly feel her weight—he discerned her small, childish shoulder blades, unable to look away, bewitched as he observed them moving and then freezing again—he discerned her collarbone, her neck.

"Ever since then," the first woman, the sad one, intruded suddenly, "I've come to this mobbed-up bar to sell my love to postmen and longshoremen—to anyone willing to pay anything at all for it. After all, there's no such thing as a free lunch—nothing in life is free. When we buy our sweet love, what we get is just ripples on the water and blue makeup smeared on our faces."

"When we cry o'er sweet love," the other woman continued, "we pay all those postmen who don't bring us bad news with our sincerest appreciation. You have to pay for everything—every evening and every night—and our tears are just the blue hue of the air, blue ripples in the water, the gold of our joy, and the silver of our silence."

All at once, the song cut out, the fridge stirred and then froze. The stranger turned sharply and looked him straight in the eye.

First a wave of heat overcame him, then ice crippled him, and then he realized that his whole body had gone numb. The stranger was already smiling at him like an old friend. She found a warm, white towel, wrapped herself up in it carelessly, hiding almost nothing, stepped onto the soggy, squeaky hardwood floor, walked over to Mark, and extended her hand casually.

"Hi," she said, flipping her hair back. "Are you Mark?"

"Yeah, I'm Mark," he said, startled to remember his own name.

"I'm Nastia, Aunt Zina's daughter," she said.

Back at the hospital, Mark had to wait in the hallway—the doctor was trying to explain to a surly and uncooperative Kolia that he had to take his medicine. He offered the doctor a bribe to let him go, and she took offense and explained that nobody was keeping him there and that treatment at their hospital was entirely voluntary—unless you were a schizophrenic, of course. Then Kolia took offense, yelling that he could've sold half a truckload of bananas since they'd started haggling last night. The doctor burst into tears, Kolia apologized and tried stuffing some money in the pocket of her white coat, and she demanded that he lie down and stop chasing after her—he had an IV in his arm. Eventually, she left, glancing tearfully at Mark in the hallway. He walked into the ward and saw Kolia lying by the window, wearing wrinkled white pants and a stale dress shirt, his expensive, dirty shoes tossed under the bed. He looked exhausted, and after yesterday's festivities, his face, which was a bit puffy at the best of times, had swollen up and acquired a lemon tinge. Kolia had a bulging potbelly and stubby legs; Mark thought he looked like the bad guy in a Bollywood movie. Generally, those characters abuse their power . . . and the audience's patience. The way he looked now, with that needle in his vein, Kolia elicited dread rather than sympathy—what if he survives and seeks revenge? There were three other people in his ward: a bookish gentleman with glasses was lying across from Kolia, reading some newspapers and gnawing on a hard cookie; a guy who clearly worked at a factory, judging by his oil-stained hands and the bags under his eyes, with a coiled metal wand for boiling water, which was evidently central to his treatment; and a younger man in orange shorts, long, white socks like the kind golfers wear, a striped T-shirt, and headphones—he was lying there, refraining from talking to anyone or answering any provocative questions. It was as if he'd simply stopped by to rest for a bit and enjoy his favorite music. Mark immediately noticed that Kolia had already established his dominance—all three of them would occasionally glance at him warily, trying to anticipate his next outburst and figure out where the danger lurked. That's precisely why Mark found his uncle so intimidating: you could never tell what kind of mood he was in, whether or not he was joking, or when he was planning on busting your kneecap. Kolia's eyes scrutinized people through their narrow slits, and he talked as if he were ordering at a restaurant—you didn't feel like listening to him, but you couldn't interrupt him either. He spoke quietly, so you always had to listen closely to make sure you didn't miss anything. Once he saw Mark, he got up, yanked the needle out of his vein, and attached it to the IV stand with the Band-Aid that had been holding it in place.

"Ya got everything?" he asked calmly, as though he hadn't just tried to bully the doctor.

"Yep."

"What's new?" Kolia asked, apparently expecting to get some updates on the family.

"Zina's daughter's there," Mark answered, unsure what tone would please Kolia—happy, reproachful, or disgusted?

Kolia took one of the bags from Mark and dumped its contents out on the bed. Then he removed his shirt and pants unhurriedly, tossed them into the now-empty bag, handed it back to Mark, and started changing into clean clothes. Mark noted that Kolia's upper body was tan but he had pale, bluish legs, making it look as though somebody had mixed and matched body parts from different people to assemble a model Kolia, and now all you had to do was pump a little blood into him and send him on his way. Finally, he started talking again.

"Oh, Nastia," he said, "that's right. She was supposed to come by yesterday. How'd I forget?" He went silent, looked out the window, put his hands in his pockets, and then turned toward his nephew again. "I want you to keep an eye on her while I'm gone. Okay, Markster?"

"If you say so. But what for? She's not a kid, she doesn't need a babysitter."

Mark saw Kolia clenching his fists in his pockets.

"I realize that," he answered, clearly annoyed but trying not to let it show. "Just keep an eye on her, okay?"

"Okay," Mark said, trying to calm him down.

"I'm putting my trust in you," Kolia said, and Mark felt all the resentment packed into those words. "Pick her up something for dinner."

He took a wad of cash held together with a hair tie out from under his pillow, counted out a few bills, handed them to Mark, stuck the needle back in his vein, plopped down on the bed, and said sourly,

"We're all one big family. What keeps a family together? Trust. You got that?"

It was unclear how seriously Mark was supposed to take that, but he nodded just in case. On the way out, the headphones guy gave him a sympathetic look.

He stepped outside and mulled over that whole odd exchange for a while. He went to the 24-hour grocery store across the street and bought some frozen fish. He came back out and stopped dead on the sidewalk. He went back inside and bought some boxed wine. He left, then he went in yet again. He picked up another box, thought for a second, picturing Kolia's yellow face, then put it back. "I'll just make her some fish and get out of there," he thought. When he showed up at Kolia's place, his cousin was running around the apartment in a short light dress, trying to clean the place up. Mark noticed the striking resemblance between her and her mom—dark hair, bright clothes. Happy to see her cousin, she hugged him giddily for quite a while. She smelled like children's shampoo. Then she tossed the fish into the kitchen sink to defrost and told Mark it'd be ready soon.

"I'll whip something up in no time. I just gotta figure out what's edible around here and what we should steer clear of, you never can tell with Uncle Kolia."

She rooted around in the fridge for a while, fishing out chunky bags of milk, hard as set cement, pieces of meat the color of dirty shoes, and jars of dubious preserves that looked like witches' seasonings, tossing it all in the trash can, poking around in the kitchen drawers, standing on a chair to reach something on the top shelf, and calling Mark over so she could pass him some sugar, honey, and sea salt. He walked across the kitchen and gawked at her from below—in his eyes, the light filled up with sea salt, and what he saw brought tears to his eyes. Nastia loaded him up with sauces and preserves, rummaged around in the kitchen a bit more, plopped everything down on the table, and tried making some sense of what she'd pulled out of Uncle Kolia's hoard. Mark came out of his daze and started taking the kitchen knives away from her.

"Run along now. Go read some comic books or something while I get dinner ready. Then I've gotta get back to the shop."

"Do you even know how to cook?" Nastia asked.

"Yeah, but not very well," Mark answered, thinking back to when he mixed up some wallpaper paste for his buddy at the shop and nearly burned the whole building down.

"I'll teach ya," Nastia suggested, taking everything out of Mark's hands again. "It's pretty straightforward. It's all about the spices."

She took out the fish and vegetables, herbs, some dark-red powders and crushed roots, mixing and mashing, mincing and sifting, then tossing everything into a large pot that soon started boiling and taking on colors Mark had never seen before. He stood behind her, thinking about Kolia, remembering what his uncle had said about trust, and trying to figure out what he meant by it. He was unsure of how to act around his cousin, and he considered just leaving, but the thought of Kolia made him stay put. To keep his mind off his uncle, he asked Nastia where she'd learned to cook so well, which turned out to be a long, involved story. Nastia grew up in a seaside town, between the factory and the port, where she lived in the workers' dormitory with her mom. Nastia didn't have a dad, so the neighbors would take care of her whenever her mom rushed off to work.

"Our neighbors were real witches," Nastia said. They taught her how to use all kinds of dubious seasonings to make food that was nutritious . . . but not always edible. She remembered countless flavors and smells both fair and foul, fowl hanging dead in the kitchen, and the cold basement inhabited by slugs and packed with autumn vegetables. One time the neighbors accidentally locked her in that basement. She sat there until her mom came home in the evening.

"Ever since then, I haven't been afraid of the dark, not one bit."

"I'm not afraid of the dark, either," Mark said, thinking back to the time when he wound up spending the night in this apartment.

Kolia had set up a pull-out bed in the hallway and lain down on his sofa, struggling to fall asleep, tossing and turning, muttering and waking up when it squeaked like an accordion. Mark listened to the racket Kolia was making, timing the intervals between his screams; then he suddenly dozed off. He woke up, lifted his head, and immediately saw Kolia, who was standing in the kitchen by the window, stark naked, staring intensely into the black and lemon night. The moonlight made his skin green and his skull shiny. His breathing was heavy and predatory. He stood there, unmoving. Then he turned around and headed back to his room in the dark, not paying any attention to Mark. His heavy, wary steps squeaked on the hardwood floor like the first snow under the paws of a zombie hunting for prey.

Nastia poured her concoction into two bowls, went into the next room, took a seat on the rug, and set her food down. Mark followed her, carrying the box of wine. It blew up in his hands when he tried to open it—wine was everywhere, sousing the rug, seeping through its thick surface, touching its lines, and ruining the symmetry of its patterns. Mark came running back with some napkins and practically started licking the damn thing clean, but Nastia stopped him.

"Relax. I'll get the stain out later. I know an ancient Indian secret for cleaning synthetic Chinese rugs."

"Is that right?" Mark asked incredulously. "How'd you learn that?"

"A lot of foreigners would stay at our dorm—mostly sailors and amber merchants. They even taught me how to read. I learned Esperanto first, actually. Russian came later. Do you know Esperanto?" she asked, fixing her hair and straightening out her dress.

"Yeah, but not very well," Mark answered.

Then he thought back to when Kolia had to settle a dispute with some Poles the family was doing business with, which meant Mark had to conduct lengthy negotiations with them by telephone, in English. Kolia was touting him as their in-house interpreter, even though he didn't speak it all that well, and the Poles spoke it even worse. Mark could hardly understand them, and what he did get didn't please Kolia one bit. He stood next to his nephew, glaring at him, his expression cold and detached, constantly asking him questions, getting frustrated, which made Mark panic, so he understood even less. Finally, Kolia grabbed the receiver from Mark, gave him a real piece of his mind, and proceeded to negotiate with the Poles himself. He showed Mark the phone bill afterward, as though it were a list of the sins he had committed as a child. "It's all about trust," Mark thought. "Duh."

They seemed to have forgotten about their meal — Mark was just sitting there, remembering all the troubles he'd known in his life, thinking about the times he'd been too heedless, about when he'd trusted people, and about how hardly anyone trusted him, which made him feel even more troubled and unsettled. "She really does look like her mom . . . and my mom, too," he thought. "All the women in our family are alike — they talk so much that you can't get a word in edgewise. Then they think you're not listening to them." Nastia had curious eyes and a tender face, just like his mom. She dressed lightly, too, seemingly unafraid of drafts and unfazed by the cold, and she could find the right words just as quickly and enunciate them just as loudly and clearly, too. "I wonder what her dad was like," he thought.

Nastia got pensive and sad — her cousin was sitting on the bloody rug, immersed in his own thoughts and paying no attention to her. Or at least he was acting like it. She told him another story.

"I was really young when I fell in love for the first time. Everybody in my city falls in love really young, especially the women. He was about ten years older than me, just like you." She touched Mark, but he didn't pay any attention to that either, he just hunched his shoulders. "That's why it didn't pan out. I was very upset. I started thinking this was my punishment for falling in love so young. Long story short, I just up and got braces."

"How come?" Mark asked, confused. "Is she for real?" he thought to himself. "Trust."

"To repent," Nastia explained. "So I wouldn't be tempted to kiss anyone. I didn't kiss anyone for two years. Two whole years. Well, that was until I took those things off. But once I took them off . . . ," she said, fluttering her eyelashes.

"What?"

"Now I kiss everyone," Nastia answered.

"Everyone?"

"Yep, everyone."

At that point, Mark finally realized what she was getting at. "Trust," he thought, and kissed his cousin. He was really going for it, but he had no idea what was compelling him to do such odd things. He hadn't forgotten, not for one second, whose apartment this was and whose rug he'd just soused with wine. He hadn't forgotten, not for one minute, Kolia's heavy gaze and dry voice; he remembered where Kolia hid his knives and sharpeners, his threatening voice over the phone, his gray-brown face swelling up with anger, the veins bulging in his neck, his hoarse breath, the smoke and fire billowing out of his wide nostrils. He remembered, he was scared, but he couldn't help himself. Meanwhile, Nastia couldn't quite figure out what had gotten into him. She liked how clumsily he was kissing her, and how he smelled, but as soon as he touched her dress, as soon as he crossed the line, she slapped his hand warmly, tenderly pushing him away, emitting a short, admonishing shriek, and Mark tumbled back, but he immediately recalled all the blood and wine that had been spilled in this building, all the ashes and golden sand that had been flushed down its toilets, all the deaths and insults its walls remembered, and he touched her face once again, caught her hands, deprived her of her clothing. Nastia laughed and resisted; she was saying something, and he even answered her, without really processing her questions. At one point, she even started to regret that she'd gotten her braces taken off, because he was so persistent, this older cousin of hers, with all his fear and trust. She grabbed his short, fair hair, pulled his head back, and looked him straight in the eye. Then he pushed her hand away again and muttered something to distract her while he shifted closer.

She let him do just about everything, not stopping him, seemingly waiting for some signal. When that signal that only she could hear rang out, her elbows dug into the rug and her whole body arched as she slipped out of his arms and scurried away into the darkness. Mark caught his breath, calmed himself down, and then went for her again. That went on for a few hours, until she finally ran out of patience, and he hastily laid her down, unresisting, on the synthetic Chinese rug.

"What will I say to him? How will I be able to look him in the eye? He'll figure everything out as soon as he sees me. I won't even have to admit anything. He'll rip my throat out," Mark thought, "or break my legs—one at a time—or stomp my ribs in, or scalp me, or gouge my eyes out and leave me to beg for alms in the streets. I'll sit there on the warm asphalt with my McDonald's cup, asking for spare change, but he'll take it all from me at the end of the day and dump it into his capacious pockets. But first he'll tell his sisters—Zina and my mom—and they'll finish me off, doing what he wouldn't dare do—they'll deprive me of my manhood. Literally. They'll cut my private parts off with a pair of garden shears. What's my mom supposed to say to this? What does my mom usually say in these kinds of situations?" Mark thought for a bit but couldn't come up with anything. Well, he couldn't recall any situations quite like this one. Clearly, his mom would side with her niece, try to calm and console her. They'd sit there on Kolia's rug, trying to figure out what to do with Mark first—hang him in the hallway or quarter him in the kitchen. "Well, it's my own fault. I got myself into this mess; nobody made me drink with her on the rug, nobody made me listen to her stories, and nobody made me . . . well, come in her," Mark thought. He was holding Kolia's breakfast; he looked exhausted, his gaze was weary, and he had a few fresh scratches on his neck.

Kolia received him gloomily, nodded wordlessly as he snatched his breakfast, looked at the fish Nastia had prepared, clearly suspicious, and sniffed the herbs mistrustfully.

"Fish? She knows I can't have fish."

Something had clearly gone down. Kolia had apparently been showing the other patients who was boss—the gentleman promptly brought him and Mark two teabags, the factory worker passed him his heating wand, and the headphones guy turned toward the wall submissively. Kolia sat on his bed, looking at something behind Mark, so he could neither meet his eyes, nor look away.

"Markster," Kolia said, starting to put the pressure on, "children are not always born out of love. Sometimes their coming into this world is random and unplanned. Then their lives are full of hardship and adventure—but mostly just hardship."

"What's he talking about?" Mark thought in a panic. "Has he really figured everything out already? Why isn't he stomping my ribs in yet?"

"Hey sleepyhead, what's the deal?" Kolia asked, finally looking at him.

"I was up all night," Mark explained.

"Well, obviously you were up all night if you're sleepy," Kolia said. "How come you were up all night?"

"I had some work to do."

"Good, I'm glad you're keeping busy."

What was he talking about? Mark could feel himself starting to sweat profusely. What was he hinting at? As soon as Kolia reached for his food, Mark tried to wipe off those first beads of sweat dripping down his face in one swift motion before they could betray him, but Kolia lifted his head lightning-fast. He saw everything. Mark felt blood rushing up toward his throat, then even higher. He sat there in front of the dark and heavy Kolia, sweating bullets and blushing deeply. All he could do was keep sitting there, not knowing what to do with his hands or how to conceal the scratches on his neck. Kolia, gaze still fixed on him, rooted around in the bag, took out the fried fish, and started gnawing on it wordlessly, without even looking down. Sauce clung to the edges of his mouth and green flakes of garnish stuck to his chin; his eyes were all bleary and his face had swollen up. "He can't eat fish," Mark thought. "Maybe I can't either."

"How's your mom?" Kolia asked, chewing. He chewed slowly and methodically, the way conspirators chew up codebooks to confound their enemies.

"Fine," Mark answered reluctantly. He was absolutely convinced that he'd already been exposed and sentenced.

"Fine?" Kolia asked incredulously, continuing to masticate the fish with his yellow incisors. "Tell her to give me a call."

Mark nodded.

"The women in our family have always known how to make good fish," Kolia said, scrutinizing his nephew. He spoke quietly, but Mark had no doubt that everyone in the ward could hear him — even the headphones guy. "Fish takes time. The women in our family have always had time. Nobody has ever pressured them. I've never pressured them. I'd advise you never to pressure them either."

"I didn't." Mark's answer said more than he meant it to.

"You sure about that?"

"Yeah."

"All right, then." Kolia tossed the rest of the fish back into the bag, had Mark hold it, took a towel out from under his pillow, carefully wiped his face, took the bag from Mark, and stuck it under his blanket. "There's no need to pressure people," he continued. "There's no need to lie either."

"I'd better get going," Mark answered. "I've gotta get back to work."

Nastia was waiting for him, sitting barefoot on the steps. When he came over toward her, she got up, turned around, and disappeared behind the apartment door. Mark hurried after her.

She awoke in the middle of the night, moved his arm away gently, so as not to wake him, got up, opened the suitcase on the floor of Kolia's bedroom, found some pills, and took them with a sip of wine. Mark woke up and touched her skin. Nastia shuddered, but calmed down quickly; she turned toward him. Lying on his stomach, he rested his chin on her lap, considering her suitcase, reaching out to touch her things. "It's all up to us," he thought. "We can make it happen, if we want. I can't change anything now. This is how it's gonna be." He took out some books and started leafing through them. They were chemistry textbooks and detective novels. They typically use poisons in detective stories, so they're basically chemistry textbooks too. He picked up pieces of clothing she had worn, feeling how coarse the fabric was. Nastia didn't object. Then he picked up an icon. It depicted a female saint. With a dark face and bright clothes.

"Who is she?" Mark asked.

"Saint Sarah," Nastia said.

"What kind of name is that? Was she Jewish?"

"Uh-uh, she was Egyptian," Nastia answered, from out of the darkness. "She saved a boat with some important people on it."

"So what do you have her for?"

"I got her at camp. Ages ago. When I was a kid, I mean. My mom would send me to a Catholic camp."

"Why?"

"Well, she had to send me somewhere for the summer. She wouldn't keep me in town, she was afraid I'd run away. We didn't have the money for a regular camp, so Mom let the Catholics deal with me, and they gave me Sarah as a going-away present. You see that writing at the top?"

"What's it say?"

"Well, besides all the stuff about Jesus and the church hierarchy, it says that the greatest danger is hidden in rivers . . . but the most reliable protection is down there, too, because rivers separate friend from foe and partition light from darkness; they protect us from immediate threats and unexpected turns of events. All you have to do is hug the shore and be ready to administer first aid when you're out there on the water. Can you swim?"

"Yeah, but not very well." Mark didn't want to think about the time he and Kolia took their fishing nets out to the reservoir and he tumbled into the black rift of the water. Kolia had to fish him out and resuscitate him with alcohol, cursing him up and down all the while.

"I worked as a lifeguard for a bit," Nastia said, seemingly picking up on Mark's train of thought. "I administered first aid."

"To who?"

"The people I saved."

The next morning she patched up the knee of his jeans, fed him breakfast, and rubbed some kind of solution on his scratches, the old ones and the fresh ones she'd given him the previous night.

"Does that hurt?" she asked.

"I'm fine," Mark answered, feeling fire entering his skin.

"Yeah, whatever you say. There's no need to lie."

Peering out of his third-story window, Kolia caught a glimpse of Mark — it was like he was waiting for him. Mark gathered his thoughts and then entered the hospital. He ran into a patient in the hallway; there was something curious about him. He was standing by the doors tensely, thinking about something. It looked as if he'd run away from someone, but he could no longer remember who exactly. Some interns latched onto him, some elderly visitors bumped into him, and some mistrustful patients in their ragged gowns sidestepped him. He was holding a white suit jacket in one hand and a big paper bag in the other. He saw Mark and promptly stopped him.

"Got any smokes?" he asked. His voice was weary, yet unyielding.

"Nah," Mark answered. They stood there for a bit, looking at each other.

"Don't get your panties in a bunch. You got this," the patient said finally.

Mark thanked him.

Once again, he could tell that something had gone down in the ward — the headphones guy had disappeared, leaving only an unmade bed in his wake, and the gentleman was hastily tossing his things into some black bags, refusing to engage with anyone. Kolia eyed him with disgust, and the factory worker eyed Kolia with caution. Mark laid out some yogurt and milk in front of Kolia, but he didn't even look at them, immediately pursuing a harsh line of questioning—What's going on in the city? Do you have any news? How's your mom? How's work? He asked if the boss had been riding him, if he wanted to quit, and what he was planning on doing with his life if he did.

"Why don't you want to quit? You always have to be thinking about these kinds of things," Kolia said. "Life can really wear ya down. We've gotta have each other's backs, we're all one big family—aren't we? In our family, the men have always run the business together," he said through gritted teeth. "Nobody's ever even thought about bailing, you got that, Markster?" He didn't ask about Nastia, but Mark could sense that it was her he wanted to know about more than anyone else.

"Well, that's fine," Mark thought, deciding he had nothing to worry about. "He won't do anything to me—he doesn't have the guts." Kolia continued questioning his nephew, looking him straight in the eye, until Mark, brimming with hatred and anger, couldn't take it anymore—he met his eyes and studied him. Kolia looked right back at him, trying to extinguish the fire in his eyes, all of his dark weight bearing down on the kid, but Mark didn't buckle under the pressure, he stayed strong and kept resisting. At some point, Kolia started drifting, looking somewhere behind Mark's shoulders, barking something at the factory worker, and changing the subject to his antibiotics. Mark sat there facing him, pressing his palms against his knees; this was a Kolia he had never seen before, his skin yellowed like an old photograph, his gaze extinguished—he was old and crooked, hapless and broken, stale and uncertain, sick and hungry. Mark was even starting to pity him. "But why the fuck should I?" he thought.

"What kind of meds are they giving you?" he asked. Kolia thought for a bit, evaluated the situation, and spoke in a calm and conciliatory tone.

"They're giving me the right kind, Markster. It's just that treating me is like taking a guy down off the gallows and trying to patch him up—he's not gonna be in the best shape, there's a limit to how far therapy will get you. How've *you* been holding up?" he asked, squinting.

"I've been feeling all right," Mark said, without giving his answer much thought.

"What's with the marks on your neck?" Kolia asked casually.

"I cut myself . . . shaving."

"I see," Kolia said, nodding. "Do you shave every day now? Don't go slitting your throat. It's a good idea to have somebody around who can administer first aid. What if there was nobody there to help?"

Kolia's cold, wolflike eyes fixed on him once again. Mark got up, said a curt goodbye, and promised to give everybody Kolia's regards. Standing at the intersection, he could feel his eyes on him.

"What could he possibly know about business?" Mark griped that evening in Kolia's bathtub. "He can't even open a new vegetable stand."

Nastia sat on the edge of the tub in her gym shorts and a tight-fitting top, holding some dry towels, smiling and listening to her cousin.

"He can do anything he puts his mind to," she objected. "He just got taken for a ride."

"He just can't do anything at all! He can't even play cards."

"Everyone knows how to play cards. Even I do."

"Yeah, sure you do."

"Wanna play?" Nastia got up, tossed him a towel, and stepped out into the hallway.

Mark wrapped the towel around his body and left the bathroom, leaving wet tracks behind him. Nastia sat down on the rug, deck of cards in hand. "Well, now I know exactly what to do," Mark thought, remembering how ridiculous Kolia acted whenever he played.

"All right, let's go," Nastia said, smiling.

He lost three times. He was furious. Then he lost again, ripped the whole deck up, and went over to the kitchen. Nastia waited for a bit, then followed him out of the room.

"Hey, Mark, don't be so angry. You never had a chance anyway. I know all the tricks. I trained at the circus."

"For real?" he asked, turning toward her, thinking that might give him sufficient grounds to accept his defeat.

"Yep," Nastia assured him. "By the way, I know some other tricks, too. I can read navigational charts, just like Saint Sarah."

Lying next to her, distinguishing her every movement in the dark, Mark thought about how his mom slept the same way—pieces of clothing scattered around the bed, the alarm clock wound to a cold ring, the whole world forgotten. There she lay, not regretting a thing, not lamenting a thing, leaving all those tormenting nighttime thoughts to restless neurotics like Mark. He sifted through all the words he'd heard over those past three nights with Nastia, all her stories and promises. He made some calculations, tried to develop a plan, found some unexpected arguments in his defense, and searched for some level-headed answers. In the morning, the planets aligned—it's all up to us; our hearts dictate everything. No despair, no fear, and no excuses.

Through the sleepy reverberations and morning turbulence, he felt that there was suddenly more light, and someone's breath, muted and hostile, growing and growing until it filled and ruptured the morning void.

"Mark!" He hopped up, flipped over in the air like a cat, landed on his knees, sprang to his feet, slammed into the alarm clock that hadn't gone off, stepped on a plate of leftover pasta, knocked over some wine, spilling it all over the bedsheets, bumped into Nastia's suitcase, sending her maxi pads flying, and grabbed a pillow to cover at least some part of his body.

"Mark, you son of a bitch!" Kolia was an ominous figure in the doorway, wearing rumpled white pants and a yellow cycling shirt, his olive black skin pumped full of antibiotics and poisons.

His shout woke Nastia up, and she poked her head out from under the sheets. Recognizing her, Kolia froze, surging forward in rage, leaving his bags of hospital things by the door. Mark's reflexes were fast enough, but just barely—that bought him a split second, long enough to regroup, turn around, and tear through black hallways and dusty rooms toward the kitchen, with death at his heels. Kolia hopped over the suitcase, slipped on the pasta, banged into the wall, and then went flying in the other direction. Mark was stomping barefoot across the hardwood floor in the kitchen. Kolia got up and ran over to the closet—for his shotgun, what else? Mark ripped off the makeshift velvet curtain and tried opening the window, to no avail. Kolia had fallen behind, but not for long. He was going to catch up and start stomping Mark's ribs in. Mark retreated slightly, but there were heavy, frantic footsteps behind him. Mark looked back and saw Kolia feverishly stuffing shells into his Izhevsk over-under, intoxicated by the hunt. Mark hopped onto the sill and rammed his knee through the window. The glass shattered like ice in March. He jumped forward, leaving a trail of blood behind him. "He won't do anything to me," he assured himself as he ran down the street. "He doesn't have the guts."

Mark spent the day at the shop, nursing his knee, lying on the couch, and listening to the voices coming in from the street. He looked at the furniture scattered around, touched the old wood, and took in the smell of aging. "Most of the people who owned these things left a long time ago," he thought. "Something drove them out of this city, compelled them to leave their homes behind, pass through the fortress walls, get across the river, and dissolve into space. What was it that led them to that decision? Maybe it was all their misfortunes and failures. Maybe it was their need to be understood. Or their inability to endure the city's climate—clouds and rain blanket the sky half the year and its black flames scorch you for the other half. Some bolted after inner peace. Some wanted to rid themselves of it. The voice of faith beckoned some. Others fled, sensing danger. Why didn't they stay?" Mark thought. "What were they lacking? Inner peace? Confidence? Love?" Mark imagined how long it had taken them to reach that decision, how many setbacks they'd faced, and how much disillusionment their souls had imbibed. Some of them could only gather the strength slowly, and the process was especially painful for them, while others ventured out swiftly and effortlessly. Some people couldn't admit to themselves for the longest time that they were indeed ready—ready to give up everything they'd accumulated over the years and willing to move forward, beyond the river, into the darkness, among strangers. They had to make tons of arrangements, set all kinds of things up, find secondhand dealers and movers, say goodbye to their friends and relatives, take only the essentials, and shed everything superfluous. Furniture was superfluous. You don't set out in search of a better life with your own furniture. You leave it here to molder and die. Maybe I could flee and move forward. Maybe I could just bolt too, start anew, find my place in life, and claim my own territory. I might wind up in the big cities, live among the other refugees, look for my big break, test fate, and bounce around from place to place, forging on toward a blessed land where the sun will never set, where the raindrops will spare my house, and where the earth will be soft and the bread sweet. Of course I could," Mark thought. "But what about everything I'd have to forgo? What about Mom? What about Kolia? I don't like the idea of staying behind with them, but I like the idea of taking them along even less. What's more important?" Mark thought. "Finding a new place for yourself or leaving the old one behind? It's a good thing we always have a choice, that it's always up to us."

Nastia came by in the early evening. She was wearing a long, colorful, ankle-length dress and a see-through shirt. She was trying to act serious, though she couldn't quite pull it off. She saw Mark's swollen, bloody knee and got started on treating it. He took it like a man for a while, then he erupted with a scream. Then Nastia lay on top of him, as though taking cover from the evening heat, lying there and comforting Mark, lying there, piecing him back together, not letting him break down into hot chunks of clay. Mark was quieting down gradually and had even started to doze off when she spoke.

"Come with me. Leave everything and come with me."

"What am I supposed to do when we get there?"

"You could do just about anything. I can teach you to cook, if ya want. I can get you a job at the port, if ya want. I can have your kid."

"For real?"

"Yep, or I could not have a kid. I can interrupt my pregnancy. I can start it up again. I can put spells on spiders and scorpions. I can forge signatures."

"Well, I definitely won't be needing that."

"We'll live at my place. You'll help me take care of my grandpa."

"Since when do you have a grandpa?"

"It's a long story. He's really old. My mom wanted to put him in a home, but I felt sorry for him, so I started looking after him. He drools a lot when he talks. But he says some wise things that are worth listening to. So, whaddya say?"

"Nah," Mark said after thinking for a bit, "you'd better move in here. And bring your grandpa with you, too."

"Whatever you say," Nastia answered calmly. "It's your call."

She left in the morning, trying not to wake him up. She did, though. Kolia came by in the early afternoon. He brought oranges. He sat there in silence for a while, clearly wanting to ask something, but then deciding against it. Finally, he suggested Mark start working with him. Mark thought for a bit and then agreed.

## YURA

The deceased looked even worse in death than he had in life — gray hair, sunken eyes, pointy nose, sharp wrinkles on his sour face. His Adam's apple had protruded, his fingers had elongated, and his nails had turned blue. He had been silent for two days, apart from occasional coughing fits that would rip his chest apart from the inside. Then even the coughing was gone. He lay there, breathing slowly, like a fish that had been caught but not yet soused with cooking oil. His heart stopped shortly after noon. The young guy crossed the room, bent over the deceased, and examined him with great interest. One could have thought that he was studying the patterns on his hospital gown.

"Why don't ya take out a magnifying glass while you're at it?" Yura suggested.

"Why don't you?" The young guy got all offended. "What should we do?" he asked. "He's gonna start decomposing."

"He's just skin and bones. There's nothing there to decompose. Just leave him," Yura answered.

Yura figured that whoever told the doctor about the deceased would have to help carry him out, so he opened a *National Geographic* from last year that someone had brought him, and stumbled upon a piece on the fauna of Mesopotamia. "Mesopotamia . . . what's that? Something to do with water. Something made out of stones and sand," he thought. The fauna of Mesopotamia was hardly having a bad time of it, according to the article, at least. Most of the livestock belonged to the monasteries; the locals sacrificed animals to express their appreciation to the gods for the bounty they bestowed and pay off their debt to heaven. The word *debt* made Yura anxious, so he put the magazine off to the side. Dozing off, facing the wall, he heard the young guy shuffling around the room, circling the deceased. We gravitate toward death—especially someone else's.

He woke up in the early evening and peered out the window. Dark trees, early twilight, the beginning of July. The young guy was sitting on the next bed over, his eyes fixed on the corpse.

"Are we actually gonna sleep in the same room with it?" he asked, seeing that Yura had woken up.

"Sleep in the hallway then," he suggested.

But the young guy just shrugged his shoulders, clearly spooked. The young guy's name was Sania. He wasn't all that young, as a matter of fact—about twenty or so—he just looked inexperienced, especially compared to those who'd already died here. He was scrawny, yet fit, constantly biting his nails, making his fingers pink and raw. He had long black hair and a fractured shinbone—a soccer injury. When he got to the hospital, the doctors suggested a full examination, as per standard procedure, and an X-ray revealed that something was up with his lungs. Sania said it was all the stress that had worn him down. He'd been receiving treatment full time for about a month now, but he couldn't get used to the clinic. His mom would come to visit him. His friends on the soccer team would send their regards. This was apparently his first inpatient care experience. He was scared of dead people. Now here he sat in his soccer shorts and red T-shirt, veins standing out in his forehead from the tension, probably imagining what he'd dream about tonight. Yura couldn't take it anymore, so he threw a shirt on, stepped out into the hallway, and found the doctor. He had hit it off with the doctor right away, partially because the doctor didn't like any of the other patients here either. Who *would* like all those goners, constantly trying to spit out their pills and sneak alcohol into the wards? Yura nodded; the doctor rose to his feet laboriously and stepped out of his office. He was proper and rather friendly, yet much too lethargic for a man his age. He mostly kept company with the patients, and he could have easily passed for one of them, if not for his snow-white coat and the thin, gold-framed glasses resting on his pudgy face.

"Well, where am I supposed to put him?" the doctor said, stepping into the ward, sliding his chubby hands into his coat pockets, and nodding at the deceased. "It's only till tomorrow."

"Maybe we should carry him out into the hallway?" the young guy suggested timidly.

"Oh, great—then we'll have people stepping on him all night. All right, lights out."

"Whatever you say, Doc," Yura said, bumming a cigarette from one of the goners in the hallway and slipping out the back door. He took a seat on the edge of the fountain and found the lighter he'd stashed there. July nights are so short you can hardly finish your cigarette.

The fountain was in the middle of a large open area between buildings, across from the main entrance of the TB clinic. It was littered with last year's leaves and cigarette butts. There wasn't any water in it—never had been. The yellow building poked through the trees; the windows on the first floor were dark. Yellow blots of light ran down from the second floor, where the wards were, treacherously offering asylum to moths, only to snatch them out of the night's hands. The goners were getting ready for bed. Yura wanted to stay there, out in the night, but he stubbed out his cigarette and headed back inside. The young guy had waited up for him, and he tried to strike up a conversation, but Yura blew him off and plopped down, right on top of the *National Geographic*. Offended, the young guy hid under his blanket, casting despairing glances at the corpse, and Yura thought that the deceased's soul might be lying right beside it. There they lie, all cramped, like a married couple that didn't spring for a double bed.

Yura had been hiding out here for two days already. He immediately made the right connections, used the doctor's phone to call his friends, took plates and bowls from the nurses and never gave them back, and traded tobacco with the patients. He knew the ropes. It felt like the last week of your hitch in the army. Or your first stint in jail, the one repeat offenders always remember fondly.

It hadn't been the best of years for him. He'd poured everything he had into fixing up a recording studio, but somebody broke in and cleaned the place out right after it opened. Yura couldn't think of anything else to do but run himself into debt. He borrowed 20K from Black Devil, who told him not to worry, that he'd make it back. He got his business rolling again. A few months passed. It was time to pay his debt, but he had nothing to pay it with. Black Devil kept finding ways to make his presence felt, joking with Yura over the phone, showing up at the studio a few times, asking about his insurance policies, his fire safety precautions, and his family. Yura didn't have a family, though—he and his wife had gotten divorced, his daughter was all grown up and living in Canada, and he hadn't talked to his old man for ten years or so. He'd spent the ten years before that thinking about how to do him in. That's rock and roll for ya. Hatred and malediction come with the territory—and Yura had been in rock and roll forever. Long story short, when Black Devil started sending him blank texts, he went on a serious bender. When they carted him off to the hospital, he got his "chilling diagnosis," as they would have said on TV. "Well, is it really all that chilling?" he thought, standing at the entrance to the clinic, holding his fancy white suit jacket in one hand, and an X-ray, hot off the press, in the other. It could be worse. "Sometimes people are born without a voice or with a voice that folks would rather not hear. Sometimes people have extra body parts removed when they're babies, sometimes the extra parts start growing later. It's hard to say which is better. At least I can still control my bladder. All right," he said to himself, "don't get your panties in a bunch. Everything's gonna be just fuckin' fine." He bummed a cigarette off someone, turned himself in to the TB clinic (wearing his white suit jacket with no shirt underneath), went through a battery of tests, met the staff, and scored a spot in one of the three-bed wards. The young guy was already there. Some sports magazines were lying by his bed and somebody was decaying, slowly but surely, in the next bed over. "It's nice in here—it even looks pretty clean," Yura thought, and decided to stick around for a while. He immediately made friends with the doctor and started hitting on the nurse and smoking with the rest of the gang that hung around by the empty fountain. He turned off his cell, used the doctor's to call some of his buddies and tell them where he was, what to bring, and what not to say. Then his friends would show up and stand outside the window. They were too afraid to come inside.

"Oh yeah, ya call that stress?" Yura said on his first night in the ward, when the twilight made the young guy melancholy and he started griping. "Try being an electric guitar player in a hall where the electricity keeps cutting out—now that's stress, man. We're so used to complaining about everything. We've gotten real soft. We don't even know what our internal organs are made of anymore. And when you get down to them, you find so much evil that you don't even know if you *should* try to treat them. What's the use?"

That night, Alla, the nurse, came by his ward, called him out into the hallway, whispered at length in the moonlight, gave him her phone number, and ran on home. Yura went back to the ward and took out his cell, but then he remembered Black Devil and hid it in his pocket again. He just lay there, peering out the window in a dreamy haze. "Everything's gonna be all right," he thought. "I'll camp out here for a month and then take it from there." He liked hospitals—they were always clean. His apartment was never that clean. Over the past twenty years he'd spent his fair share of time in hospitals—two knife wounds, second-degree burns, kidney trouble, and all sorts of infections, not to mention going in and out of drug rehab. So he wasn't even close to panicking this time around—"just another brick in the wall," he thought, "just another corpse in the river." Time was chipping away at him; he was getting older, the last few morning IVs had made him woozy, and a wave of drowsiness was breaking over him now, mixing the smells of leaves and state-issued sheets. That goner was lying on the next bed over. His breathing had slowed like a river in the lowlands. He had two days left to live—a ton of time and a ton of sorrow.

That was the first night, and three days later, once the deceased had been carried out and his sheets changed, a new guy arrived in their ward. "Who's this chump? He looks like a damn gym teacher," Yura thought, looking at the new arrival—an elderly man in old yet neat and well-tailored clothing. He wore a freshly ironed blue cotton tracksuit with thin white stripes and polished pointed dress shoes that had a festive holiday glow to them. He made a good first impression, despite his odd getup. Maybe it was his kind, fat-lipped smile, maybe it was his big clown nose, or maybe it was those last strands of hair rakishly combed to one side of his yellowed skull. He came in with two bulging Hugo Boss bags, stuffed them under his bed, surveyed the room, instantly ascertained who was in charge around here, took a seat on the edge of Yura's bed, and nodded conspiratorially at Sania, as if to say, "Has this guy been bustin' your fuckin' balls, buddy?" Yura put his *National Geographic* aside diplomatically, expressing more or less the following sentiment: "Come on, if you've got something to say, then say it already." The new guy's name was Valera, and he looked Yura straight in the eye whenever he was talking to him, seemingly emphasizing his every utterance. His eyes matched his tracksuit—they were just as blue and ironed just as flat and they kept tearing up, as though he was griping about something.

"How is it here?" he asked. "Is it tolerable?"

"Yep," Yura answered, "for a while at least."

"I won't be here all too long. Only head cases hang around hospitals—they don't have to go back to work. I should know, I've been around them my whole life," Valera said confidentially. "I work at the circus."

"Are you a clown?" Yura asked immediately, for some reason.

"No," he said, not taking offense. "I'm a logistics manager."

He returned to his bed and started telling them his life story. It was packed with danger and adventure, obviously. Yura thought to himself that people with such wide and defenseless smiles generally fall into the deepest professional ruts. Their eagerness makes them so wide-eyed, they can't even see where they're going half the time. Valera told tales about the sweet and mysterious world of the circus, their strict regimens and harsh customs, their ancient rituals and professional hierarchies, throwing out dates, quoting poets, recalling the names of performers and tame tigers, and sharing special trapeze safety techniques. He was mainly addressing Yura, but the young guy was the one that was really paying attention—maybe he was a fan of the circus, or maybe he was just glad not to have a corpse in the next bed anymore. Yura humored Valera, nodding or shaking his head whenever the circus manager demanded that he bear witness to the truth of his utterances, but shortly thereafter he took cover behind his magazine, trying to focus on the birds and beasts of Mesopotamia. "How much longer is he gonna keep this up?" Yura thought nervously. "He's been talking for an hour already, and we're only up to his college entrance exams. How many more stories does he have?" Then Valera started reminiscing about the sunny days and purple nights of the sixties, their flashy shows and their sultry women who loved the circus more than the most devout Christians love their churches. It follows that they loved him too—after all, how could anyone snub *him?*

"And they never did!" Valera exclaimed, reaching into his bag and producing a meticulously filed collection of old color pictures in an envelope labeled *Unybrom*—Yura immediately remembered how photographic paper was sold in envelopes like that back when he was a kid, thinking about how old he was, how much useless nonsense he'd seen, how hopelessly he'd lost touch with the present, and how long it'd been since he'd gone to the circus. "Probably ten years ago or so. Or has it been even longer? Maybe it's only been ten years."

His little Mashka was already all grown up by then; she didn't want to go to the circus, but nobody had asked her, as usual. Yura had just come home from yet another bender and was trying to patch up his home life. The circus looked like the Reichstag after the Red Army took it—everyone was beaming with joy, but the building had seen better days. Cold hallways, women in fur coats, cognac at the refreshment stand, and the beasts of Mesopotamia in the gloomy ring. Mashka was crying. She felt bad for the lions. The women were laughing. They decided to walk home—they didn't feel like riding in the same trolley as those people. Now he was looking at the envelope in the old-timer's hands, glancing at his fingers—discolored by nicotine, warped by time and alcohol, battered and covered in scars, as though somebody had cut a notch into them for every year he lived. Seeing the effect his life story was having on his listeners, Valera perked up, pulled a picture—clearly his favorite—out of the envelope, and handed it to Sania, his gaze brushing over it tenderly yet brusquely.

"Here, kid, take a look," he said, barely able to contain his excitement. "That's me back in '71. See what I was like back then? Just take one look, how can you *not* love the circus?"

Apparently much enamored of the young Valera, Sania chuckled and passed the picture to Yura. He laid it flat on one of the pages of his open magazine, next to a wild desert mule. Valera had a fiercely independent manner, a proud stance, piercing eyes, and, most important, a thick head of hair, a cavalier mustache, and pirate sideburns. Yura involuntarily compared the two photographs—Valera and the mule. "There's definitely some overlap. No doubt about that." He gave the picture back to the young guy and kept listening to Valera's narrative for a bit, but once the circus people started delivering baby lions, he took cover behind his magazine, catching some familiar letters, arranging them into words, using those words to construct sentences, sifting through language to separate the circus guy's spoken words from the written ones on the pages before him, untangling the colorful, silk strands of stories, untying knots, and patiently rowing through

the sun's rays with a lifeline in his hand. He noted that in Mesopotamia nobody rode horses or used them as draft animals. They would
only hitch them to the chariots they took into battle or used to hunt
wild birds and predators that crept up to the city's outer walls. Meso-
potamians were tender and attentive with their horses—they valued
them and cared for them. The advice offered by their grooms was
touching and thought-provoking; they insisted that the owners of
these magnificent animals pay special attention to their diet and hy-
giene, spare them the strain of long, arduous journeys, let them into
their homes, if need be, let them lie down on the floor next to them,
so they could feel their breathing, cover them with warm fabric on
cold winter nights, pick up on subtle changes in their moods, and take
the time to listen to their tales of sorrow and hardship.

"Sleep makes us strong," the grooms said, "and vulnerable."
Zebras are another matter entirely. Generally, a zebra's route to the
circus skirted a few laws. They were transported across Asian repub-
lics under assumed names, their age, gender, and medical history
changing along the way. They were kept together in the circus's
own paddocks, quickly growing accustomed to large, rowdy crowds
and never straying from their herds. When one of them died, the
rest would encircle the body to keep the circus staff away. It was as
though they were offering up a sacrifice to the just gods presiding
over the heavens. Reemerging from this sticky stream of information,
Yura rose to his feet laboriously and plodded outside to have a cigarette. "What's the deal with those zebras?" he thought, disgruntled.
"Where'd they even come from?"

He waited for everyone to fall asleep, found the cute nurse, and
spent the night with her on the pull-out bed in the staff room. She
was so flustered she didn't know what to say, except that kissing was
off limits. Everything else was fair game, though. She tried to keep
quiet so they wouldn't wake up the goners in the clinic—the pull-out
bed squeaked like a ship's timbers. Her hair—blond and sunny—was
so long that different sections of it had different smells; hot wind

and dark river water mingled together. It seemed that her throat was delicate; she was always catching colds. She was weary and demure. "Sleep makes us strong," Yura thought as he was dozing off. "And vulnerable," he added, listening to her breathing.

The windows faced the shade cast by the trees whose branches touched the sills, catching and cleaving the sun's rays. Wasps would occasionally fly into the clinic, but as soon as they caught a whiff of the stagnant smell of chlorine and death in the hallways, they wasted no time flying back outside, where thick July spiderwebs would ensnare them. A police car pulled up at around ten. A pair of patrolmen had arrived, escorting Artem, a cheerful deserter who'd been caught about two months ago. Now they brought him to the clinic from his pretrial detention center every morning for treatment, and he relished setting off on these grand adventures with the fuzz as his lazy entourage. He said hello to Yura, yelled something spirited at the nurses, growled at the cops, and basically acted like going to a TB clinic was a lifelong dream of his, and he was over the moon to see it finally coming true.

Yura's friends came by in the morning and stood by the fountain, not talking to the locals. When he stepped outside, they gave him a full report. Zhora, who worked at a 24-hour pharmacy in town, had an authoritative air about him — he was a representative of the medical community, after all. His long fingers latching onto Yura's shirt, Zhora leaned up against him and whispered in his ear.

"Black Devil's looking for you. He's making the rounds of all your friends. He went to your old man's place."

"Well, what'd my old man do?"

"He threw him out."

"Good for him! All right, you better get going. Don't go blabbing around town."

Back in the ward, Valera kept bombarding him with questions about Alla, demanding details, expressing his support, and offering his assistance. Eventually the young guy couldn't take it anymore and disappeared into the hallway, slamming the door behind him.

"That's enough. Don't get all riled up," Yura said severely to the circus guy, thinking about all the distressing things going on with Sania. He seemed to like the nurse. Everyone here seemed to like her. But she rendered him speechless—Yura could see that perfectly well. The young guy would blush the instant she came into the ward. He'd look at her hair and manicured nails, clearly noticing the scar on her wrist and undoubtedly paying attention to her weary face, gold medallion, and absent wedding ring, her high heels and roaring laughter. She never stopped laughing; it was as though administering inpatient treatment was her idea of a good time. She had sharp teeth, the kind any man would love to get chewed up by. The young guy could only exhale after she had left again. Yura thought Sania must hate his guts. Maybe he did. Yura remembered hating his old man for bringing his girlfriends home and getting annoyed whenever he'd come home late and stumble over their stuff on the floor—stockings and sweaters, faded jeans and flashy dresses. Those warm pieces of fabric smelled like the bodies of grown-up women; Yura would pick them up and toss them into his dad's room, feeling their lightness— that pissed him off, but there wasn't much he could do. There comes a time in every boy's life when he puts a knife to his father's throat. The real question is where to go from there.

Meanwhile, Valera was at it again. As soon as the young guy had hopped in bed and rolled over to face the wall, he launched into another cock-and-bull story.

"The circus gave me everything I have," he said. "A job, an education, and love. The circus taught me to be attentive with children and treat my elders with respect."

"You talk like Mowgli," Yura interrupted, but that didn't rattle the old circus hand; he just smiled, making all his creases tighten up, and started talking about circus dynasties, glorious traditions, and techniques for applying clown makeup that were passed down

from fathers to eldest sons, painting pictures of the passions brewing in the dressing rooms, exposing bloody mysteries and divulging
secrets about mysterious conspiracies. He just kept going, on and on,
even when the staff started making the rounds; he told Alla about his
first wife, showed the doctor pictures of his daughters, suggested he
marry one of them—true, she'd already been married for years, but
he hinted that he could resolve that little hitch in no time. "Where
there's a will there's a way!"

"Huh, a dynasty," Yura thought, a few colored pills resting in the
palm of his hand. His dad had always wanted them to work together.
"Real men don't play music," he'd say to Yura. "Real men have enough
on their plates without music."

His dad was part of the country's migrant labor force, working
seasonal railroad jobs; one time he took Yura along. It was the middle
of the summer, around this time of year, during a heat wave, and his
dad was sitting there on the tracks, right on the ties, next to all the
other laborers, waiting for the foreman to come over and tell them to
unload some boxes of canned food from the train cars. Yura, wearing
his white shirt and dark work jeans, was sitting next to him; it may
have been the last time they sat so close to each other, out in the
open, in the sweltering heat, passing each other cigarettes. By sharing
his cigarettes, his dad seemed to be saying, "Now you're with us—
you're one of us now." They all shared their cigarettes and water—in
their simple clothes and beat-up shoes, they were real men with real
problems.

"Yeah," Valera drawled, as though he'd heard Yura's thoughts,
"beat-up shoes, sweat-laden warm-ups—we had to work day and
night, our whole life was packed in between those walls saturated
with men's odors and women's perfume. All those joyous nights and
bloody mornings! Insults and confessions were behind the making of
every performer—love was born and hope died behind every door;
the men fed the wild animals every morning, broke them, and soft-
ened their movements, while the women stood in cold hallways, nur-

turing treacherous plots in their hearts, scheming to escape from this troupe of roadside misfits. But you can't escape yourself, you can't escape your sorrow, so it lingered in their eyes and their movements in the ring were precise and unyielding."

Alla just couldn't fall asleep that night; she kept waking him up, pulling him out of his slumber. There was always a moment when he had no idea where he was; he immediately thought of Black Devil, but then he recognized her by touch, calmed down a bit, and asked for some water. He asked her to tell him about her parents. "I wonder what kind of dynasty she comes from. I wonder what they wanted from her," he thought.

"I don't remember my dad," Alla said. "He crashed before I went to kindergarten."

"Was he a pilot?" Yura asked diplomatically.

"Yep. A test pilot. He did two stints in compulsory rehab."

"Gotcha," Yura answered respectfully.

"I've always gotten along with my stepdad, though," she continued. "But something's up with him. He's a gardener somewhere outside of town . . . and he talks to the trees now."

"Maybe he just needs somebody to talk to," Yura conjectured.

"Well, obviously he does. The people he works for are Vietnamese, it's not like he can chat it up with them. So he talks to the pear trees, that's better than nothing."

After he'd returned to the ward in the morning, Yura tried to draw the young guy out a little. Sania answered curtly and brusquely, though; he wouldn't meet him halfway. He must have been pissed. Even Valera got quiet, sitting there and observing the action from his bed. Yura decided not to pressure him. "All right," he thought, "we'll figure this out eventually." He threw on a shirt and stepped out for a smoke. Valera caught up to him by the fountain.

"What's up with Sania?" he asked.

"He's all riled up."

"'Cause of the nurse?"

"Uh-huh."

"That's what I thought. What are you gonna do?"

"Well, I guess I gotta marry her."

"Are you for real?" he said, horrified. "Yura, you're kidding, right? Have you seen her?"

"Only in the dark," Yura joked.

"She definitely has another guy," Valera whispered despairingly. "A girl like that just can't be single. She's gonna wind up biting your head off, and Sania's too."

"Is she a shark all of a sudden? And why Sania too?" Yura asked, confused.

"Because misery loves company. I'm telling you, she definitely has another guy," Valera said, still all worked up. "She's keeping you on the down-low, you know that."

"Well, she's at work, man."

"Bullshit," Valera countered. "You wouldn't believe the kind of stuff I used to pull at work. Did anyone ever say anything to me? You'll see," he whispered, looking around, eyes apprehensive. "There's only one way to check," he said conspiratorially.

"Oh yeah?" Yura threw out his cigarette butt.

"Run away with her."

"Where would we go?"

"Wherever. The farther the better. My first wife and I did that once. Did I show you the pictures?"

"The pictures of you?"

"Nah, the pictures of her."

"Yeah, you did."

"Well, I pretty much kidnapped her right in the middle of a rehearsal. The firemen had to come and catch the tigers afterward."

"Oh yeah?"

"Then it was off to Crimea for a month."

"Who went to Crimea? The tigers?"

"Nah, we did."

"How come?"

"How come? I couldn't tell ya. We were scared—we panicked. Then we decided to make things the way they were before. And things went back to the way they were. That's to say, bad. But you won't come back. You can really do it."

"I don't want to go anywhere," Yura said anxiously. "I like it here."

"Here?" Valera nodded toward the clinic. "You like it *here?*"

"So, who do you live with, by the way?" Yura asked her a few days later, when her next shift came. They were sitting in the dark room— he was smoking, not even bothering to step outside. "I'll just burn this whole place down, with everybody inside," he thought.

"I have some animals at home," Alla said.

"Gotcha. What was your nickname as a kid?"

"Oh," she said, laughing. "I had an insane nickname. Everybody called me the Alligator."

"Because you had a lot of pets?"

"Nah, because of my smile. I had a special smile. And a ton of friends. I almost got married in high school. Everybody falls in love really early around here. Especially the women. He was a few years older than me. Just like you." She reached through the darkness and touched his hair. Yura shuddered. "That's why it didn't pan out. I was very upset, I thought I was being punished for my bad behavior. Plus he was a boxer, that probably didn't help. Then I flipped out—I just up and started sleeping with all his friends."

"All at once?" Yura asked, confused.

"Nah, one at a time."

"Are you a boxing fan?"

"What kind of question is that?" Alla was miffed.

Yura finished his cigarette and went back to the ward, saying that his roommates got anxious when he spent the night elsewhere.

She was gone for a couple of days. Yura approached the doctor, who explained that she'd asked for some time off because something was up with her father. Yura could picture it—the two of them standing there, chatting it up with the fruit trees.

"It would actually be nice to take her away from here," he thought. "Right now we're like a couple of college kids, crammed together on a pull-out bed. On the other hand, the last time a woman stuck around was five years ago. She wound up getting carted off to the looney bin." Yura wasn't sure he was ready for that kind of commitment.

The young guy had calmed down; he was keeping his suspicions and hard feelings to himself and avoiding Yura, opting to socialize with the circus guy instead, but the circus guy kept pulling away. Valera latched on to Yura, and whenever the latter would pick up his *National Geographic*, he'd simply roam the hallways and bother the staff.

Zhora showed up again toward the middle of July. He came over to the clinic right after his night shift at the pharmacy; the doctor hadn't even started making his rounds yet. He hid behind the trees and signaled Yura with a loud whistle. The morning shadows fell thick and cold. Yura put on his shirt and tiptoed outside so as not to wake his roommates. Zhora said hello and pulled Yura into the shade, telling him that Black Devil was getting more agitated and that he'd paid Yura's old man another visit and started threatening him. His old man didn't lose his cool, obviously, even though Black Devil had brought two other guys along. They promised to burn his house down next time.

"They'll do it, too," Zhora said adamantly. "They'll get away with it—they're firemen after all. Why don't you just give Black Devil a call? Maybe you can talk this out."

"What are you so worked up about? Did Black Devil send you?"

"Go fuck yourself," Zhora retorted. "Just think about your old man."

"All right, I will."

"Well, what's there to think about?" he asked himself. "I gotta get out of here. I gotta make a deal with the doctor so they let me outta here. I gotta calm the young guy down. I gotta figure things out with Alla the Alligator. I gotta call Black Devil. But what's he gonna do? Well, let him torch my old man's place for all I care. I'll bring him the lighter fluid. We're so used to complaining about everything. We've gotten soft. It's all because of our family issues. What's with our parents? We got one guy living on the street and another talking to trees."

It felt as though his roommates had been waiting for him to come back. As soon as he stepped into the ward, Valera poked his head out from under his covers, while the young guy ducked under his. Yura sat down on the circus guy's bed.

"So, what were you telling me about your first wife?" Yura asked, patting the old-timer on the knee.

Valera came to life, waking up all the way, clearing his throat, and shifting over to sit closer to him.

"My wife was a local celebrity, I'll have you know," he started. "Dining with her was considered a real honor."

"Did she take her tigers with her to dinner?"

"I'm being entirely serious with you," the circus guy said sternly, his feelings clearly a bit hurt by Yura's quip. "When I first joined the troupe, she wouldn't give me the time of day. She had so many guys to choose from! It was love at first sight for me, though. Then we ran away — I already told you that. But it didn't last long. I was young, I lost my way. I was a real pansy."

"Then what?"

"Then I lost her. It was my own fault. I just couldn't hold on to her."

"Like during a trapeze show?" Yura was confused, again.

"Like she left me, during one of our tours."

"What kind of tour?"

"Around socialist Romania. We spent a whole month there. I was young and self-assured, but I had no idea what I wanted and needed in life. I forgot all about her and started focusing on myself. She could feel that. She tried to fix everything at first, but I just wouldn't listen. I think everything changed after we got back from Crimea. She realized how much of a pansy I was, that I always back down right away, and that I wasn't willing to hold my ground for her. She didn't say anything, even though she knew it was over. Then during the tour she and one of our guys—one of the bosses—got together. I didn't even know what hit me. They came back here together. I wanted to quit, but I didn't have the resolve to do it."

"Yeah, Valera." Yura patted him on the back. "That's messed up."

Valera seemed to like that they were always talking about him. Even the young guy poked his head out from under the covers and started listening to the old-timer's love stories with a morose expression on his face.

"Don't I know it," Valera said. "I'm too ashamed to even think about it. Just imagine it—you're living with her, thinking this is gonna last and everything's just great. At some point, you stop noticing her and you forget that everything can change at the drop of a hat. Then that's exactly what happens. You don't even realize how . . . where was the error in my calculations? Well, you start blaming everyone else, even though it's your own fault and nobody else's. You start doing stupid stuff. You try and fix everything. You try to forget about it. But how can you fix something that doesn't exist anymore? And how can you forget about everything? You just can't. You can't escape from yourself. You can't escape from your grief."

The old-timer was a real mess at this point; Yura thought he shouldn't have made him dredge all that stuff up. They should have just talked about zebras. He wanted to get up, but Valera held him softly by the arm.

"Those tours . . . there's a different sense of time and a different way of doing things. They just forgot about us. Our month-long tour came to an end. Winter set in and we had to get back somehow. The bosses had just abandoned us. We didn't even have any gas left. Our guys sold it all to the locals."

"Why didn't you ride the zebras back, over the mountain passes?" Yura joked—but as soon as he saw the circus guy's distraught, fat-lipped face, he corrected himself. "The horses—I mean the horses, not the zebras."

"That just wasn't gonna happen," he answered bitterly. "They were circus horses, they couldn't carry heavy loads."

"Just like in Mesopotamia," Yura said.

The conversation died because there wasn't anything more to say and too much had already been said. Everyone just sat there, waiting for the doctor, not knowing what to do with themselves—and when he came into the ward, followed by Alla, pushing her cart, everything took a turn for the worse. The timing was so poor—something felt off. The most terrible thing was that Sania's mom had barged in too, right on the doctor's heels, bombarding him with questions and demands. An anxious blush was strolling across the doctor's face; he kept repeating, albeit a little too cordially, that she wasn't allowed in there, that it was not permitted, and that it wasn't safe, after all. But Sania's mom put on a mask and brazenly ignored all of the clinic's regulations, and the doctor, a gentle and proper individual, just couldn't bring himself to kick her out in front of her soccer star son. Actually getting inside the ward seemed to embolden Sania's mom—she started acting like she owned the place, immediately sitting on the young guy's bed, patting him on the back as if soothing a horse, taking out some candy and a cookie and asking him how he had been feeling. She acted just like a teacher—even when she asked you how you were feeling it seemed as though you would get marked down if she didn't like your answer—and she looked exactly like you would expect a teacher to look—appropriately enough, since she was a teacher. The young guy was anxious; he refrained from responding at first. Then he asked his mom in a whisper to leave the doctor alone, shooting mortified glances at Valera, hoping for some backup, observing Yura's reaction out of the corner of his eye, afraid to look at the nurse and getting horribly flustered when he tried to answer the doctor's questions. Sania's mom didn't even seem to notice the doctor. She was acting like she was proctoring an exam, simply waiting for the doctor and Alla to leave so she could spend some quality time with her son. So when Alla approached the young guy and saw his open palm (she saw its trembling and the beads of anxious sweat on his forehead, caught a glimpse of the bags under his eyes, so dark they looked like bruises, realized that he hadn't been sleeping well, that he didn't like it here one bit, and that he'd be more than happy to hightail it out of here, but where could he even go—his mom was at home, and it wasn't exactly clear which was better, staying here among the corpses or moving back home to be smothered by her love—she managed to see all of that in a split second, committing it to memory and feeling quite surprised), she dumped about a dozen pills into it, and his mom, paying no attention whatsoever to the nurse, was rooting around under the bed for her son's socks, chastising him for being so messy and disorganized. Alla tried to turn the whole thing into a joke, flashing her incredible smile . . . and the young guy just went berserk—there was some spring inside him, it had been there for a while, compressing, pushing against his heart until the organ finally popped out of his chest; he'd been holding back for too long, and everyone had been demanding too much from him. A month lying on this cot with these pricks—one of them had lost his marbles a long time ago, blowing smoke up his ass with his zebra and antelope bullshit, and the other guy was fucking treating him like some little bitch, like he was the fucking odd man out, like he should fucking take the goddamn fucking blame for fucking everything, like he was some little cocksucker who wasn't worth the fucking time of day! Fuck that shit! The young guy knocked those shitty-ass socks right the fuck out of his mom's hands, chucked the cookie at the wall (the doctor managed to dodge it and Yura got up, dumbfounded), and erupted, yelling at his dumb-ass mom to not fucking touch him, to leave him the fuck alone, that he'd do whatever the fuck he wanted with his goddamn socks, and that she could get her idiot ass out of here and never come back.

Everybody froze, at a complete loss for words. The doctor gently clasped Alla's elbow, while the young guy's mom stood in the middle of the room, bewildered—she was on the verge of tears, but she had lost the ability to cry after forty hard years in the classroom. The young guy was looking around at everyone, his eyes filled with hatred and despair, trying to formulate his next string of maledictions, when Yura suddenly interrupted him.

"Hey, quit yelling at your mother, ya clown."

"What do you care?" The young guy scowled at him, finally encountering a worthy opponent.

"Shut your trap!" Yura advised him.

"You shut yours." The youngster wasn't backing down.

Yura gave him a sudden, hard slap. Caught off guard, the young guy lost his balance, fell onto the bed, right onto the candy and pills, instantly popped back up, enraged and ready to charge at Yura, but his resolve faltered when he saw his rival's eyes. He just turned around and bolted out into the hallway, his mom in tow. The doctor waited a bit and then followed them. Alla gave Yura a harsh look and rolled her cart out of the ward. Valera saw a piece of the cookie that had landed on top of his sheets. He picked it up.

"Huh, I like this kind," he said, chewing.

She tried to keep him out. "Let's talk tomorrow. It's late," she said, clearly agitated, holding the door of the staff room shut. "You're gonna wake everyone up. Go back to bed."

"Bullshit," Yura countered, gently yet persistently pounding on the door. She eventually let him in.

"All right, all right," he said. "Quit acting tough. Why were you holding the door shut?"

"You don't even know when you're going to get out of here," she answered. "Or whether you'll ever get out. Isn't that true? Why start all of this now?"

"What do you mean I don't know when I'm gonna get out of here? That's up to me. I'm gonna get out. I'll get out tomorrow. That's the least of my worries. When the doctors were taking out my appendix and they forgot me on the operating table because it was Easter that day—now *that* was a time I wasn't sure I'd make it."

"Sure, they did. You're full of it. What'd you whack the kid for?"

"To teach him a lesson," Yura answered. "How's your stepdad hanging in there?"

"He's fine. They're going to start taking in the harvest soon. He's all worried."

"I can imagine. What else is there to worry about in the sticks?"

"When's the last time I talked to a woman like that, especially at night?" he thought to himself, sitting there, carefully shifting the sleeping Alla's legs into his lap. "I guess it must have been with taxi dispatchers. But sitting next to a woman, rubbing her feet, stroking her calves to warm her up—I couldn't tell you the last time I did that." He sat there, his head resting up against the wall. She'd conked out quickly, holding his hand for a bit and then letting it go; he'd risen to his feet and walked over to the window, glanced at the neighborhood—quiet and empty—faintly illuminated by the streetlights, and then come back to find her already sound asleep. He sat down carefully, leaning back against the wall. Her hand pushed through a dream and grabbed his, then released it again. For some reason, Yura thought of that one especially long and harsh winter, when all they had left in the kitchen was black tea and there was no use thinking about anything else, so they didn't. Life felt easy and endless; he was so young—his bones weren't so brittle and his heart wasn't so threadbare. Alyona took their financial woes in stride.

"It's no big deal," she said. "You'll be making money once you start filling arenas. We've got time."

They bounced around for weeks on end, sleeping on friends' floors and drinking on rooftops in the winter. "Those were our glory days," Yura thought. Everything came so easy when they were first getting started, and only their thoughtlessness and carelessness kept them from shaking the big, wide world down for everything that rightfully belonged to them. "We should have beaten and squeezed every last penny out of life, we really should have," Yura thought regretfully.

Who knew that everything would change so hopelessly and pass by so quickly? Alyona came down with pneumonia in early March; she was out of commission for a while. They ran out of money quickly and had no way to get more. They didn't have any medicine at home. They ran out of food, too. All the friends they'd been gallivanting around town with night and day had disappeared, evaporating into the icy, lilac twilight. Alyona started feeling even worse; she couldn't get out of bed for a few days, lying there, buried under all the blankets and jackets they had in the apartment. He sat next to her, holding her hand, like he was doing now in the staff room, holding on and feeling her body temperature rising, heat roaming around under her skin, flames scorching her from the inside. She wasn't griping about it, though; she merely asked him to keep holding her and not let her go. He kept holding her, never letting her go, up until the second she got better. Where did all of that go? How could all of that be forgotten? How could all of that be lost? He thought back to the last time he'd seen her—a few years ago, when he gave her a present to pass on to their little Mashka. Then he regretted the whole silly idea—her black, drained eyes, exhaustion and desperation, vulnerable, exposed neck, and icy fingers. No earrings or watch. Nothing to talk about, nothing to ask about. The weakness we harbor inside ourselves, the weakness that we cling to, kills us. It devours us from the inside like a virus—it keeps us from making the right decisions, from sticking by our loved ones—it makes us feel doomed, although we aren't really. Yura could feel himself dozing off. "It's a good thing I didn't have to kick the door in" went the thought that capped off his day.

They had to lock the doors overnight at the warehouses where they slept, to fend off the drafts and stray dogs. Packs of them were keeping watch outside, hiding in the frosty mist of the railroad yard, scurrying down the sidings, heads held high, howling into the cold Bucharest sky. Winter came early that year; hoarfrost lay on the wires and apple branches. Bonfires heated up the warehouses quickly. They burned cardboard from the train station or hay found in freight trains. Their animals stood, still and obedient, day in and day out, waiting for their food. The horses were spooked by the nighttime howling of the dogs, seemingly anticipating their death, which might come at any moment. Every morning, the local government would send them delegations from various churches or members of Parliament; acrobats and hypnotists would emerge from the warehouses and bargain with them at great length. But no command was ever given to send the circus troupe back home, so they kept guarding their props and grazing their tame beasts, occasionally launching brazen raids on food storehouses in the suburbs, stealing crops out of the fields, and returning to their warehouses with fresh provisions for themselves and their animals. They slept, curled up between lions and foxes, quenched their thirst with chicken blood, and made animal sacrifices, entreating the heavens to send them blessings and good weather. The locals resisted as best they could, desperately trying to protect their emporia and household treasures. Finally, given the sheer volume of written complaints—some anonymous and some signed collectively by the workers of local enterprises—the management of the train station put their necks on the line for the circus, allocating them a few economy-class sleeper cars. Shortly before

Christmas, they loaded up the animals and their requisitioned goods and the train headed east. The cars were laden with women's fur coats and Turkish carpets, crates of oranges and glossy synthetic coats from East Germany — a real find! The worst thing was that the animals kept multiplying, causing a serious discrepancy between their actual and documented population; the border guards grew anxious, railroad workers scattered back to their homes, and people shut the gates of their roadside towns, as if the plague were coming. Eventually, they were let through. They traveled for ages, traversing the Carpathian Mountains, getting delayed at small stations in Eastern Galicia for weeks at a time, exchanging their East German coats for sheep's milk cheese, and stubbornly pushing forward, homeward, to a place where nobody was waiting for them any longer.

Lying on a top bunk in the train, wrapped in a carpet, feeling birds' wings rustling and snakes' wise hissing, occasionally picking eggs out of nests and soothing the troubled sheep, playing cards with the trapeze artists and catching cheerful macaques as they raced between the cars, Valera could only think about one thing — he had to get back, return to the city that was waiting for him, nestled between the two rivers, up in the hills, open to the sky, buried under blue snow. You have to go back because there's no happiness on the road or common ground among outlanders. Everything falls into place at home: the timing is good, and everything feels right. You always have to return, otherwise what was the point of venturing away in the first place? Everything rests between the rivers and everything — everyone's stories and loves — starts here. The sojourner's alcohol fire trickled from lung to lung, leaving indelible marks, flashing and disappearing, vowing to return someday and serve as a constant reminder.

In the morning, Yura came back to the ward and packed his things, nodding at the young guy, as if to say, "Let's go have a chat." He was reluctant to step outside; they stood by the window.

"Hey," Yura started, "I'm getting out of here, and I don't want there to be any bad blood between us."

"What do you mean you're getting out of here? You haven't finished your treatment."

"I'll finish it somehow," Yura assured him. "Don't be goin' berserk in here, all right?"

"Whatever you say," the young guy assured him right back. "It was my own fault. I just snapped."

"When are they putting you back on the roster?"

"There's no roster to be on. The sponsor disbanded the team and sank all his dough into some hotel."

"Gotcha." Yura didn't know what else to say. "What now?"

"Don't know," the young guy said. "I'll finish up school . . . well, maybe."

"Sounds good. My old man's still riding me about not finishing school. I can't blame him, either. Why don't you write down my number? Call me up if you need a studio."

"Will do," the young guy reassured him yet again.

Yura quickly made a deal with the doctor, who obviously had misgivings, saying that was just not how things were done around here, that they were breaking the rules, that it would be unsafe and detrimental to his health. "All right, fine," he conceded. "But I won't be held responsible. Just make sure you come back for your pills."

He caught Alla in the hallway. They stepped outside, turned the corner, and found a sports bar. There were a few Arabs sitting there, watching replays of yesterday's soccer game. The bartender was talking with someone. A waitress came over—boyish haircut, attentive gaze. Yura asked her to turn it down a little. The Arabs protested, but the waitress coldly told them to give it a rest. Yura sent a thank you at her back; she turned around and nodded faintly, seemingly expressing her support.

"Why don't I give you my number?" Yura said.

"Okay," Alla consented quickly.

He took her cell and punched in his number, just in case.

"Will you call me?"

"I will."

"Are you sure you won't forget?"

"I won't."

"All right, looking forward to it."

While he was gone, the food in his kitchen had gone bad, even the canned stuff, and his flowers had dried out, neither of which was much of a loss. Yura milled around his apartment, turned on the electric kettle, took a shower, walked from room to room wrapped in a towel, leaving wet tracks on the linoleum, passing the mirror, and glancing at it—a veiny, battered, and scarred body, sparse hair, busted-up nose, resilient boxer's chin. He'd gotten pretty skinny, but not dangerously so. Missing finger on his left hand—the reason he quit playing guitar. Burns on his right leg. Dry, chapped skin. An angry, self-assured gaze. Same old, same old. Not much had changed over the past twenty years. He thought of Alla, took out his phone, turned it on, and started waiting. It rang five minutes later. Black Devil's number popped up on the screen. Yura hesitated for a split second, then jerked it up to his ear.

"Hello," he said.

## THOMAS

Everybody needs a good job, but nobody likes employers. Everybody hates paying taxes, but the first guy who actually suggests evading them gets put in jail. So what can liberate us? Well, maybe faith can liberate us, but that's about it. More often than not, religion is precisely what brings atheists together. Generally speaking, it's speculators and socialists who feed off of religion, so all the rest of us can do is pray. And make sure we balance our books. Thomas had those thoughts whenever he was struggling to set up meetings with potential clients, talking to them forever and waiting for them just as long. "What's the point of setting up a meeting in the first place?" he thought, disgruntled. "What's the point of checking and rechecking addresses, making sure my watch is accurate, and getting all anxious? Nobody shows up on time, nobody wants to pick up their feet, nobody keeps their word. Business is a crapshoot, you work for money then your money works for you, and we're all abandoned and lonely in this world—everybody needs love, everybody needs attention, and everybody needs a good job."

Thomas ran a small chain of mobile coffee stands (those brightly colored gas vans parked outside university campuses all over the country), managed poorly trained employees (students attending those same universities, who parked themselves at the controls of the gas chambers and sold brown poison in little cups), worked hard, and couldn't stand freeloaders. "There's so much work to be done in the world," he would say to his staff. "How can you just not have a job?" He had seriously high turnover. He didn't even have time to learn his subordinates' names. Nameless, they disappeared.

164

This time his clients suggested meeting at a restaurant. Over the phone they said it was nice and cozy, and that it'd be empty in the morning. Thomas knew the place they were talking about; it was two blocks from his apartment. He'd occasionally drive by that shady joint and see the owner walking down the street in his pink kimono and talking on his little girly cellphone. "Well, all right," he thought. "That place'll do." He arrived well in advance and parked, only to find that the restaurant was closed, and it wouldn't be open for two more hours. Thomas called his clients.

"Oof, is that right, it's not open yet?" they asked, surprised. "Well, wait for us somewhere around there. We're running a bit late, but we'll be there soon."

Thomas took stock of his surroundings. Empty street. Sunny July. There was a sports bar next door. "Oh, that's perfect," he thought. He'd been there a few times, he knew the owners and the bartender. One of the owners was doing some time for first-degree murder (he ran over his brother-in-law, but claimed it was an accident—first he hit him right outside his house, then he supposedly went back to administer first aid and wound up backing over him), so the convict's wife was struggling to keep the lights on at their business and cover all the legal fees. The bar was in a cold basement. Downtown Kharkiv, next to the metro, right on the way to some university buildings, always loads of students around. Painted walls, two plasma TVs. A pirate flag hanging under the sign outside. The patrons were a motley crew—college juniors and seniors who had afternoon classes, so they could bum around in the bar all morning, Arabs who weren't always allowed into classier establishments on account of how they looked, and a few neighborhood alcoholics who'd mosey on over in time for the second half of the evening's soccer match, since paying bar prices for two halves' worth of drinks would impose an unacceptably heavy financial burden. The bartender's name was Anton; he served drinks, waited tables, and called the police if things got out of hand. Thomas would say hello, and he'd always just nod in response.

A man of few words who never seemed to be in a hurry, he kept track of everything, meticulous when he added up tabs and genteel when he handled the alcoholics. He had a weird fashion sense, though, sporting orange shirts with green jeans, or white dress shirts with short shorts, or ripped sweaters with striped pants. Oh yeah, and he wore earrings in both ears, rarely shaved, and almost never smiled. The customers thought the bartender was a fag. The bartender held the same opinion of them.

Thomas came in and said hello to Anton, who just nodded in response, as usual. "Damn," Thomas thought. "He always greets me like he was hoping to see someone else." The bar was hopping, though it wasn't even noon yet. The Arabs were huddled around the plasma screen in the corner. They apparently didn't have enough money to fly home for their summer vacation, so they'd decided to spend their days down here in the basement. They were watching a replay of yesterday's match, sizing Thomas up: tall, slouched, dressed in an inexpensive yet neat suit and a sloppy tie—what he lacked in skill he made up for in determination—with a new cell and an old, spring-wound watch. They went back to their game. Thomas was glued to the screen, too, until he realized that he'd already seen this game, and he knew how it would go. He walked over to Anton and started chatting with him. A girl—long legs, dark jeans, white blouse, boyish haircut, nails painted black—popped out of the kitchen, greeted Thomas like they were old friends, took some glasses of juice out of Anton's hands, and brought them over to the couple sitting by the door. Thomas's gaze followed her and then settled on the couple. The man was anxious; it seemed like he was itching to smoke, but he couldn't light up inside. He took a cellphone out of the woman's hands and started entering something—slowly—he was missing a finger on one hand. The woman sitting across from him was anxious, too. Finger-wise, she was good to go, though. The girl brought them their juice and was about to turn around when the man sitting at the table clasped her arm gently and said a few words. She nodded, picked up the remote from the next table over, and turned down the volume on the TV. The Arabs squawked anxiously, but she responded briefly, silencing them instantly. "Man, she really showed them!" Thomas thought.

"What's her deal?" he asked.

"She's a waitress," Anton answered reluctantly. "'Her name's Olia. First week on the job. I just can't keep up by myself."

His clients called back again and asked where he was.

"In a bar, watching soccer."

"What's the score?" his clients asked.

"The final score or the score right now?"

"We're stuck right before the bridge. How do we get to the bar?"

Thomas started explaining, but then Olia came over.

"You can't be serious," she said to Thomas. "They're doin' road work over there. Tell 'em to turn left before the avenue, up there in the hills, and then right. Gimme the phone," she said, taking it out of Thomas's hands. She explained everything quickly, rattled off a few street names, listed a few landmarks — some stores they would be driving by, the school, the army recruiting office — gave the phone back, went over to the Arabs, and spoke to them at length about something or other. The Arabs looked concerned, but they didn't act up. Her calm demeanor surprised Thomas; when he thought of waitresses, he thought of drama. The Arabs seemed to really be berating her for something, but as soon as her hand grazed one of their shoulders, they turned mute immediately. She leaned toward another one of them to ask a question, and he started objecting and making excuses. Without even realizing it, the others started observing them closely, their attentive glances leaving hot trails in the air behind them, striking sparks against the ozone layer as they studied her face, catching her movements and listening intently to her insults.

The clients called back about fifteen minutes later.

"We're gonna have to take a raincheck," they said. "There was a pileup on the bridge and now they're waiting for the cops." They apologized and asked for an update on the score. Thomas said goodbye to Anton, then waited for Olia to come over, in the hope of saying something to her, but he got all flustered and tongue-tied, so all he could manage to do was extend his hand like this was the beginning of a business meeting. She started laughing and shook it, and he, unable to contain himself, hugged her in a slightly awkward yet exceedingly friendly manner, his hand softly gliding down her back but not exceeding the bounds of propriety. Thomas was beyond flustered when it turned out that she wasn't wearing a bra under her blouse. He scrambled outside, found his Fiat, sat down in the driver's seat, waited for a bit, and then dialed Anton's number.

"That waitress, Olia," he said, "who is she?"

"You still nearby?" Anton asked after a pause.

He stepped out of the bar a minute later and sat down in the passenger's seat, carefully shutting the door.

"Got any cigs?" he asked Thomas.

"I quit," Thomas answered apologetically. "I've been chewing gum. It doesn't help. Want some?"

Anton looked at the gum in disgust, but held out his hand for a piece.

"Well, um, Olia," he started, concentrating on chewing through the hard shell of his piece of Stimorol. It looked as though he was chewing through every single word. "You know, she used to be a prostitute, before."

"How do you know that?" Thomas started chewing in response.

"Well, she lives in the next building over. I've known her for years. I'm the one who got her this job . . . well, it's not as if there were a ton of people dying to work here."

"Uh, how come she's not a prostitute anymore?"

"How should I know?" Anton answered, clearly irritated. "Prostitutes are like boxers; their careers are spectacular, but short."

"Gotcha," Thomas replied.

He rolled down the window and spat, his Stimorol rocketing

through the air. Anton rolled down the window and spat his gum out, too. They shook hands wordlessly and went their separate ways.

"Is being a prostitute really that bad? Does it really mean your life's a complete wreck?" Thomas reflected. "What is it about these women that repels us? Society's scorn for them? Well, public prosecutors elicit much more scorn. If you think about it for a second, what kind of people decide to join the ranks of prostitution? People who've gotten a raw deal from fate and walked a troubled and uneven path through life. Jilted lovers, deceived brides, unloved children. Students deprived of their families' support. Workers tossed out of garment factories, single mothers, alcoholics, orphans, interlopers, and widows. Do widows become prostitutes? Probably. What else could they do? Who am I to judge? What grounds do I have for thinking poorly of them? Moreover, I suspect that most of them lead lives much more interesting than mine, packed with much more adventure and danger. It's self-evident — it's the women who want for love that go into prostitution, without a doubt. Who else? Women capable of sharing their tenderness, women capable of arousing jealousy and putting an end to depression. I'm sure that many highly educated and well-read individuals have dabbled in prostitution, settling upon this odd form to express their astonishment at the world and venturing toward a fuller and deeper kind of understanding. Obviously, most of them are well versed in human psychology and medicine and are capable of lifting fatigue and eliminating memory loss; most of them wear silk lingerie or have piercings in the most unexpected places. They are all fiercely passionate about music and their work; they are all trained to blend those two passions together. In the evenings, they run to their rooms to giddily apply their precious makeup, put on their masks and jewelry, and lay out their red sheets in anticipation of brave and generous men. They open up the windows to their abodes to let in round green moons that silver their skin and make their teeth as white as chipped porcelain. They burn herbs in their rooms that make men dream of foxes and black rivers with unknown cities on them; they stay awake at night and catch up on sleep during the day, like vampires. In the mornings, they gather on terraces wrapped in grapevines and talk of music and astronomy, pick out constellations on the black canvases of the predawn sky, observe the flight of birds, taking auguries for the upcoming days as they sip their sweet rum, and then retire to their homes, draw themselves cool baths, and lie there for hours. Their knees flash in the dark water like moons.

He came by the next morning, after struggling for an eternity to put on his best tie and nearly choking himself to death in the process. He parked under the pirate flag and called Anton, who ran outside, gloomy and preoccupied, shook Thomas's hand, and accepted a piece of Stimorol.

"In today?" Thomas asked.

"Yep, she is," Anton replied.

"I'm gonna stop in, all right?"

Concentrating, Anton started chewing.

"Listen, man," he said, then paused. "Do you really need the hassle?"

"What's the big deal?"

"I'm just saying, what do you need all this hassle for?"

"To balance things out," Thomas explained.

Anton got out of the car and slammed the door. Thomas sat there for a bit, waited, then followed him. The bar was empty. He nodded to Anton, who turned away, visibly irritated, and picked a seat across from the bar. The same soccer game as yesterday was on TV. Thomas realized he'd managed to memorize both teams' rosters by now. This was his third time watching the game in three days, but he was still on the edge of his seat. Olia ran out of the kitchen about ten minutes later, exchanged a few whispered words with the bartender, and then disappeared again without even looking into the seating area.

Thomas became anxious, watching the match and anticipating a 0–0 tie with disgust.

She came over a little later and asked what he would be drinking. Thomas was at a loss. "What should I say to her?" he thought. He asked a question or two, inquired about something else, and started automatically rooting around in his pockets.

"What's up?" she asked.

"My phone ran away on me," he answered, his voice surly.

"Lemme call it for ya."

Olia took out a battered Nokia held together with tape. Thomas told her his number, she dialed, they waited. Anton was scrubbing some dishes over at the bar. Thomas said something sheepishly as he was leaving, waved at Anton, and didn't even bother waiting for his signature nod. Well, there was no signature nod this time around. His cell was in his Fiat, lying on the floor under the driver's seat. Thomas picked it up, looked at the missed call, and dialed her number.

"What time do you get off today?"

"Why you wanna know?" she asked, not surprised one bit.

"I'm gonna come by and pick you up, all right?"

"Come on by," Olia consented readily.

He wanted to say something else, but what was left to say?

In July, these empty buildings appear especially desolate. The grass on the windowsills loses its freshness, dryly indicating the direction of the morning drafts. The trees that grow inside apartment buildings suffer from a lack of moisture. The bitterness of crushed stones, sunny, sticky spiderwebs, and stray dogs, as slow and sensitive as pregnant women—July stretches out shadows and burns out colors; long evenings fall suddenly and unexpectedly, old men sit outside in quiet neighborhoods, soaked with light, their skin becoming warm and their wrinkles deep; summer crests the city and descends on the other side, singeing the red-brick foundations of old factories and warehouses on the opposite bank. The sun drifts with the current like a burglar hurled from a bridge; flashes of light dot the horizon until nightfall. Old freeloaders die in their cluttered rooms at the end of July, starved of attention and love, since all the love to be had on those days goes to the young people. Girls, listless from the heat, descend into the water, hanging on to its freshness, wary of the plants along the shore. The streets are especially resonant, so every impertinent step and sudden outburst startles the pigeons on the rooftops and the weary, sun-drained urchins who inhabit abandoned, bombed-out dwellings in the summer. You want to speak quietly so nobody can hear you—or understand you if they do.

Olia was already walking up the steps before he could park. She saw his Fiat and sat down in the passenger seat. Thomas leaned over to kiss her; she touched his shaved cheek with dry ambivalence, like they were old friends or a husband and wife who'd just decided to get divorced. She was wearing a short dress, which made her legs look even longer. She kept fixing her hair, squinting into the evening sun.

"Mind if I smoke?"

"I just quit," Thomas answered.

"Good for you," Olia said, taking out a cigarette and lighting it. She noticed his look of despair, gave a skeptical snort and rolled down her window.

"Where are we gonna go?" Thomas finally overcame his anxiety and got down to business.

"Nowhere at all. Let's just sit here."

"Here?" Thomas was confused. "Sure, that's fine."

"Did you want something?" Olia asked without even looking in his direction.

"I just wanted to talk."

"Okay, talk away."

And then she turned toward the window.

Thomas realized he'd hurt her feelings. "Maybe Anton told her everything. Maybe she's figured out that I know. Maybe she thinks that I'm treating her like an ex-prostitute. Maybe that's what's weighing on her mind. Taking advantage of her past errors—what kind of swine would play that kind of game with her? She started a new life a long time ago, and here I am trying to pull her back into her old ways. Obviously her feelings are hurt. Telling her that you know simply isn't an option. Don't even hint at it, not even as a joke. You have to put her at ease and show her you're not planning on blackmailing her. Just make small talk."

"Tell me about yourself," Thomas said. "What were you interested in when you were a kid? Boys?"

*Damn*, he thought. *Now she's gonna tell me to screw off.*

"Chemistry," Olia answered.

"Chemistry?" Thomas was incredulous. "Okay, I get it. All those formulas, beakers, and acids. Did you have a lot of partners? Lab partners, I mean."

*Damn! Slipped up again.*

"Yep," Olia replied. "We had a big club."

"So were you actually doin' it at your meetings?" Thomas inquired. "You know, doing chemistry?"

*Damn! Damn!*

"We did experiments."

"You experimented together?"

*!!!!!!!!!!!!*

"All of us girls," Olia said suddenly, "were in love with our chem teacher. He was old and handsome. Do you like older men?"

"Nah, I don't like older men—I mean I don't like men . . ." Thomas was flailing, feverishly thinking about what to say next.

"He had beautiful fingers," Olia said, not letting him interject. "My skin would turn cold when he touched me, and then it'd start burning all over."

"He touched you?"

"Yeah. I was fifteen. I wanted to get to the bottom of all life's mysteries and enjoy all the delights of this world, so I chose him—an experienced, grown-up man with those beautiful fingers of his. He was my first."

"What do you mean?" Thomas asked, confused.

"My first, you know, sex-wise," Olia said, turning toward him. "We did it in the classroom after school. My uniform skirt was so short he didn't even have to undress me."

Olia took out another cigarette.

"And then what?" Thomas swallowed some saliva and loosened his tie.

"Then he died," Olia said, and explained without any prompting. "Not right away, of course — not right after we had sex, I mean. In about a year or so. Heart attack. Our whole class went to his funeral. He left behind a beautiful wife. She was a little pudgy, but still pretty good looking for someone her age. Can you give me a ride home?" she asked unexpectedly.

They drove in silence. It was only a few minutes away, though.

"Widows," Thomas thought, "widows — they've gotta be the ones who wind up being prostitutes. That profession welcomes them with open arms. Widows are the best lovers — they're the least calm and they have the most stamina." His first woman was a widow, which was pretty much the only thing she had going for her. She was his parents' friend. A full professor at the university. As a child, Thomas was convinced that the majority of people in town were full professors. Lecturers were in the minority. They had their share of lecturer friends, too, though. Thomas came from a respectable family, and he was raised with wholesome values. Given the sheer number of full professors in their social circle, it was hard to imagine his first time being with anyone else. His widow took the initiative, promising to help him get into college and offer guidance during the admissions process. They wrapped up one of their sessions at her home with some quick sex — excessively quick, as a matter of fact. Thomas just went along with it, thinking, "Sure, my first time can be with a full professor, why not?" Then she actually did help him get into college, although nothing else ever happened between them. "I hope it wasn't good for her," Thomas thought. Nevertheless, after that he was always cautious when dealing with widows. "You never know what you're getting into with widows," he thought, smoking on his balcony and taking in the golden light glowing inside the old buildings above the river. In fact, he was so cautious when it came to dealing with widows that he tried to only hire married women, preferably middle-aged ones. Preferably with gold teeth. That kept him in line.

That night, he decided to send Olia a text, something about how at such a late hour, when demons whiz by overhead through the sticky air and the smoke thickens in kitchens smelling of poppy seeds and cacao, he, like a grizzled old pirate, could spot the glow exuded by her apartment in the middle of the lilac night and sniff out the tender aroma of her skin with his acute, ratlike sense of smell, feel her fluttering down into a pool of dreams, as into fragile and weightless Christmas snow. Something about how he was keeping watch, protecting her tranquillity and warding off the demons with the smoke from his Cuban cigarettes while frosty crystals coalesced on her lips. He reread it and thought that the part about the poppy seeds was a bit much. He decided to destroy the message but pressed the wrong button, so it got sent to her after all. He stood there, waiting with trepidation for a reply. At around four in the morning, when the last few demons melted away in the morning twilight, his phone died.

She called after lunch.
"What were you texting me about cacao for?" she inquired.
Thomas got defensive, fabricating a mysterious, convoluted story about the events of last night, about shady characters and their family problems, about late-night calls and nighttime drama, about his futile attempts to comfort and reconcile everyone, about taxi rides and journeys across the city by night, about unveiled threats

and solemn oaths. Obviously, the smell of cacao had no place in this story; he got himself so mixed up all he could do was suggest they get together soon.

At the Georgian joint where they met up, she greeted the waiter, who responded cheerfully, seeming to recognize her, then nodded reverently at Thomas, immediately starting to recommend some specials and caution against ordering others. Thomas had made a point of dressing casually—a short-sleeved button-down shirt and khaki pants—so he was feeling pretty self-conscious without his signature tie, like a dog who'd been let off his chain for the night and was just dying to get back on it. "How does he know her?" he thought, looking at the waiter suspiciously. "Is he somehow part of her past? Just how many men are there in that past of hers? Is she going to be saying hello to all of them?" Thomas was anxious and he got hammered without even realizing it. Olia got a kick out of it all. "Good work, man," she said. "Keep drinking. You're more fun drunk." He drank but remained vigilant. "Just keep it under wraps. Don't let on that you know. Just don't drop any hints," he reminded himself. At first, he talked about work, said his clients just whored themselves out for money and then bit his tongue; he discussed politics, started telling a story about members of Parliament from the ruling party hiring young male escorts, then changed gears halfway in and recalled a gruesome crime scene from the paper—some priests had gotten busted in a closed sauna—but then she told him to cut it out. Eventually, he switched to sports, sizing up the waiter and saying that he clearly used to be a boxer.

"His nose is all flat and stuff."

"Yep, he did used to be a boxer," Olia said, confirming his suspicions. Thomas couldn't take it anymore.

"How do you know him?"

"Whatever happens happens," he thought, floating through a haze of alcohol. "I just have to know."

"What do you mean? He comes to our bar. He's a Manchester

United fan. He comes to my joint and I go to his. Isn't that funny? Sometimes it feels like most restaurant customers are just waiters from other places around town. Do you like waiters?"

"*Waitresses*," Thomas answered hastily. "I like *waitresses*."

"Oh, I like waitresses, too. I used to date one. Her name was Kira. She lived by the tractor factory, did yoga, and could go without taking a breath for a long time . . . a long, long time. You're looking at her and thinking, 'I gotta call the ambulance, get up, get dressed, and run down to the police station to report her death.' And then she exhales. I felt so sad and empty; I was eighteen and life seemed unbearable. That's when we met. Want me to introduce you to her?"

"I do," Thomas said, nodding his head sloppily. "I really do."

"All right, I will," Olia promised. "Want me to call her up right now?"

"I do," he said, sucking the last gulp of a Georgian red straight from the bottle.

He wanted to meet all her girlfriends, size up all her men, peer into all her acquaintances' eyes, hug all the boxers and duke it out with all the wrestlers in town, challenge all the bartenders to knife fights, and trounce all the valets at dice. He wanted to hear from her girlfriends what they said to her before she went to bed with them, what arguments they presented, and what they promised. He wanted to hear from her men about how she looked before she got that boy-ish haircut—what her natural hair color was, what she looked like in the morning—untouched by all that black makeup—what she said in her sleep after everything that had transpired the night before, how she spoke when she was drained by exertion and silence. He wanted to sit down with her teachers, he wanted them to tell him about her accomplishments, about her good behavior, about her passion for chemistry and sports, about the color and cut of her school uniform. He wanted to have a drink with her shop teacher and bond with her history teacher, gaze deeply into her assistant principal's eyes and smother her homeroom teacher with kisses, he wanted to be in her life, be next to her, close enough to feel the blood flowing under her skin. He wanted to be privy to all her secrets and all the riddles she had tucked away in the depths of her memory, know all of her countless stories word perfect, correct her mistakes, dispel her doubts, become part of the action, explore her life like a suitcase found in the attic of someone else's house, sit there and sift through precious evidence of other people's emotions, other people's laughter. He wanted to manage it all, he wanted to be involved in everything.

Once they were outside, she persuaded him, with considerable difficulty, that this wasn't the time for a scenic drive through the countryside. "All right, fine, but where are those waitresses of yours?" he asked. Their first stop was across the street, a place run by Turks, where he trudged through an endless love song, teaming up on the karaoke machine with some blubbery, mustached, glistening old woman, and then trying to tip one of the customers. All the patrons at this establishment were Turks, so figuring out who was an employee and who was a customer wasn't too easy. Then Olia dragged him from one shady establishment to another. They popped into all the burrows and basements she could possibly think of—paid the Arabs a visit, of course, stopped by the Vietnamese joint, naturally, became best buddies with the guys who worked at the McDonald's (they were used to this kind of thing by now), enjoyed a few rounds, arms intertwined, with the staff of the TB clinic, tried to order some champagne at Health, the local sauna, though their efforts were thwarted, reminisced about their respective childhoods in a dark basement across from the synagogue, and looked for escorts at a family restaurant where they were cleaning up the aftermath of a children's birthday party—he spilled a milkshake on his lap and kept trying to scrub the stains out with herbal liqueur. He asked for written directions at the pizzeria, and caught some cognac fumes back at the Georgian joint, because every other place was closed by then. They had live music, and he performed some Irish folk dances, getting in the waiters' way and driving her into a joyful frenzy.

Sometime after midnight, they wound up in front of his apartment building, and he said, firmly, or at least that's how it sounded to him, "You're not going anywhere. You have to stay with me. That's how it's gonna be." He made a convincing case, so she didn't even bother objecting.

"Okay. If that's how it's gonna be, then go ahead and show me the way, because I'm beat. I've been lugging you around all night."

He turned around and walked ahead, derailed by the July darkness and listening to the whispers in his own head. He kept talking and talking, so she wouldn't lose him in the night and drop back too far, so she'd gravitate toward his voice, moving along and sticking by him. He said that he wanted to see all her boyfriends' girlfriends, duke it out with the boxers, and trounce some valets. He said that he'd have a talk with her girlfriends and figure out who they slept with and what promises they made before doing so. He said that he knew everything there was to know about boyish haircuts, black dye, and drained teachers, implied that you couldn't hide anything from him about her attitude and behavior, stated that he absolutely had to kiss her shop teacher and drink with her homeroom teacher, dropped menacing hints about blood flowing too close by, questioned the veracity of her countless stories, and wrapped things up by holding forth about precious suitcases in other people's houses, demanding that they be brought to him without delay—he just couldn't give it a rest with those suitcases, discoursing on them with laughter and anxiety. He went on and on, thinking, "Just don't look back. Just don't stop talking. She'll gravitate toward my laughter as long as I keep walking and talking; she'll be forced to listen as long as I have something to say. She'll get to the end, she'll hear me out, and she'll stay with me tonight. After all, she has to know how this is gonna go; she has to wait for this night's culmination. Just keep talking and don't stop." He strode powerfully—more or less—over to his apartment building (gotta give him that!), flung the door open, stepped into the darkness with a sufficiently carefree air about him, ascended the steps laboriously, fiddled with his keys slowly, and didn't turn on the light (he was thinking ahead!); speaking and not looking back, passed down the hallway, kicked off his shoes, walked to his room, peeled off his shirt, and plopped down onto the bed.

She waited outside for a little bit. Once she'd heard the door of his apartment squeak shut, she exhaled and left.

He woke up early, in his own bed. He was surprised to discover a McDonald's flier in his pocket. Herbal liqueurs had seeped through his skin and there were blots of dried soy sauce on his shirt. Somebody called him from work and said their clients wanted to have a meeting. He thought for a bit and decided it'd be best to reschedule. Then he thought a little more and decided against rescheduling anything, but he took one look at his shirt and reconsidered yet again.

Olia started texting him in the afternoon, when he had begun to feel better.

"What was that stuff about suitcases?" she asked. "How are you hangin' in there? You didn't mug anyone, did you?"

"Don't think so," he answered. "But I couldn't tell you, honestly."

"You were scaring me with all that talk about suitcases," she texted. "I was sitting on a terrace wrapped in grapevines talking of music and astronomy with my girlfriends, observing the birds, and struggling to fall asleep. Not even rum could do the trick."

"Her life is so interesting and mysterious," he thought, as he slowly recovered from the previous night. "So many unexpected and mystifying things happen to her every night. What kind of life does she lead? Who are her friends? How many of them does she have? She probably gets along just great with them; they love her and they always have something to talk about. They reminisce about their travels and adventures, wild parties and nights of lovemaking, sea-coasts and the damp underground passageways of the city. They talk of love and betrayal, show off their new jewelry, and tell each other of their latest triumphs; their pockets are stuffed with cash and train tickets—they're always willing to skip town and dissolve into space, bursting toward the sun and escaping their fatigue and melancholy. I'd just die to have all of that," he thought bitterly. "I'd just die to have a chance to live like she does, easy, uninhibited, and inventive—I'd just die to not depend on anyone, indulge my every desire, experience real love, real passion, know that everything in my life is up to me. What have I seen in my life? Have I ever been in mortal danger? Have I? Have I ever been madly in love? Have I? I've never even slept with a waitress before. There was the restaurant owner's daughter, sure, but I've never slept with any waitresses, ever!"

The restaurant owner's daughter was his first wife. It just kinda worked out that way—they met at somebody's wedding, then went to somebody's wake together, celebrated somebody's birthday, and rang in the New Year in somebody's apartment. They slept together somewhere along the way and just kind of got used to each other. She suggested they get married, and he went along with it. Her dad gave him a Volkswagen as a wedding gift. Honestly, he'd rather have just taken the Volkswagen. It's a shame that he had to give it back after they got divorced.

The next day, he dragged Olia out to the countryside in the late afternoon. He talked to her about his job and told her some funny stories from his past, cracking himself up in the process. It was around eight when she asked him to take her home. Over the weekend, he invited her to his place. She turned him down, suggesting they just meet and chat somewhere in town. Once again, he told her some stories, trying to get her to loosen up. She'd make offhand comments, not always understanding what he was trying to say, but listening courteously. The next week was a busy one—he'd get off work a little after nine and call her up; she'd say that she couldn't meet that night because she was going out, staying with a girlfriend, or having some people over. They agreed to meet on Friday. They met. He kept blabbing about something or another, explaining what he thought were simple things in a convoluted manner, made some passionate reassurances, and kept stubbornly repeating himself.

"All right, fine," she conceded. "Let's go to your place. You can show me your suitcase collection."

She abstained from drinking, so he had no idea what to do. She asked him about his work; he started talking but quickly realized how sad he sounded.

"I shouldn't have dragged her here," he thought, growing more anxious. "I look like an idiot. And I'm acting like an idiot, too." Feverish thoughts raced past him—what tricks do I have up my sleeve? What should I suggest to get her out of here? Where should I take her to kill some time? Olia walked over to his bookshelf and picked up an adventure book.

"Do you have any kids?"

"Kids?" he repeated, surprised. "Nah, no kids for me."

"Why not?"

"Dunno," he said, getting even more flustered. "Nobody wanted to have kids with me, and I never gave it much thought myself. That's just kinda how it went. You're probably asking because of the books. They're mine, from when I was a kid. I've been meaning to throw them out, but my mom asked me to keep them. It wasn't too easy to get your hands on good books in the Soviet days."

"I know. Our elders read those books. That's for the best, don't you think? Boys should get used to bad literature when they're young, because that's precisely what teaches them how to be real men, be the top dog."

She took a book off the shelf and sat down on the floor, holding it. He sat down next to her.

"I was hung up on that as a kid," Olia said. "I thought, 'Huh, they all seem to be reading the same books. Maybe it's not just a coincidence, maybe there are a lot of important things I just won't get unless I read them too.' But I read all of them and I still didn't get it. But then later on, as I interacted with them, watched them mature, came into close contact with them, fell in love with them, I always saw things that seemed to come straight out of those books—something in their conversations, their behavior, and the dumb things they did. There aren't that many things that bring us together."

"Yeah, true. There really aren't," he said. "Even the books we all read don't always bring us together. You know, as a kid I never had any friends. I'd hang out with the kids my parents wanted me to hang out with. We had nothing to talk about when we were alone in my room. We'd sit there, staring at the fish in my aquarium. No books could bring us together."

"You know, I . . . ," she started talking about fish. And about other animals she and her friends would find out on the street and bring home. And about their parents who'd toss all those dogs, hedgehogs, and reed cats back out on the street, causing their children such distress that they would break down and cry. And about her older brothers and sisters who left home and started making their way in the world. And about how she wanted to be like them, how the rhythm and inner workings of their lives, their journey to independence, fascinated her. And about her girlfriends' personal problems, her guy friends' real, manly problems, complex relationships within families, and the convoluted structure of love triangles. By then, it was already past 3 a.m.; Thomas was hanging in there the best he could, but as soon as she started talking about those triangles, he took the book out of her hands without a word and started peeling her T-shirt off, still not saying anything. She was surprised and tried to get up, but he held her arms and pulled her toward him.

"What's all this? No, just don't," she said. But that merely riled him up even more. "Just don't stop," he thought once again, seizing her shirt. She tried objecting again, gently pushing him back, but when the fabric of her shirt ripped in his hand she erupted and kneed him right in the groin. Thomas emitted a shriek of despair and crashed to the floor. She crawled back, breathing heavily, fixing her boyish hair, and gradually regaining her composure. He eventually composed himself, too, lying on the ground and lacking the resolve to get up.

"How you doing over there?" she asked hoarsely.

"Fine," Thomas said, still not getting up.

"Sorry, I didn't mean to hit you that hard," she assured him.

"No biggie. It happens," he answered, nursing his injury.

"Well, I'm gonna get going, all right?"

"Let me give you a ride."

"I'll walk," she assured him. "Get well soon," she added, obviously referring to her own handiwork.

He waved energetically, as if to say, "I'm good to go, it could've been worse." As she was leaving he turned toward her and asked,

"You remember how you texted me about music and astronomy?"

"Astronomy? What about it?"

"I don't know. Just something about astronomy—and rum, and birds."

"You're making stuff up now," she said, laughing heartily. "All right, get better. I'll call you tomorrow."

He waited after he woke up in the morning. He waited after he got to the office. Then he couldn't take it anymore and dialed her number. She didn't answer. He called a half-hour later, then started texting her, then called once more. Now a bundle of nerves, he decided to stop by the bar to have a chat. Lacking the resolve to get out of his car, he called Anton first.

"I'll be right out," he said.

He came out five minutes later, walked over to the passenger-side door, took a seat without shutting it, and glanced at the pirate flag as though he was concerned that somebody would slip out of the front door unnoticed.

"She didn't show up today," Anton said, not even looking at Thomas. "I think she and her brother are butting heads again."

"What's that supposed to mean?"

"Here's the thing," Anton said, after a short pause. "She has a brother. He's a real prick. They have different moms but the same dad. He used to live somewhere up north, and then he came back about five years ago, when her folks died. You know, the older brother watching over her, blood relatives . . . all that jazz. He's always on her case. Everybody was telling him all sorts of stuff about her, so now he's not letting her out of the apartment. Was she at your place last night?"

"Uh . . . yeah." Thomas lacked the resolve to deny it.

"Uh . . . well, he might not let her out anymore."

"She's not a kid." Thomas was stunned at this turn of events.

"You should see this guy. He has cuts and scabs and scars all over, from head to toe. And he doesn't have a single hair on his body, not even on his head."

"Did you sleep with him or something?" Thomas snapped.

"I slept with her."

"Huh?"

"You really don't get it, do you? I slept with *her.* Just so you know, I like her. I don't give a flying fuck that she used to be a prostitute. Half of my old classmates are prostitutes now and the other half are jealous of them. I started chasing after her back in high school. I even started working out to get her attention."

"I know she likes boxers."

"What do boxers have to do with it?" Anton asked, agitated. "Her brother likes boxers. Whatever, what am I even telling you this for? I've always had a thing for her. Then just when things are finally getting going, her brother comes back."

"And?"

"And he broke my nose. Look here." Anton turned, his face now in profile. "Even the bridge is busted up."

Anton had clearly shaved that morning, but he might have been in a rush, or maybe he just wasn't used to doing it that carefully — there were cuts on his neck and stubble faded into his jaw line. The collar of his stale shirt wasn't starchy, and the earring Thomas could see had become darker over the course of time. Right now, what he wanted more than anything in the world was to hide out behind the bar and not let anyone in. "He can do that when I'm good and ready," Thomas thought resentfully.

"Do you have his number?" he asked.

"Why would I?"

"Do you know where he could be?"

"Maybe," Anton answered, reluctantly. "At his place, his garage, over on the other side of the river," he said, pointing down the hill. "You know those garages?"

"Yep."

"He has a repair shop there. The one with the dog skull nailed to the wall—that's his place. But do you really need the hassle?"

Thomas didn't answer. Anton waited a bit. Someone's head poked out of the bar—fearful eyes, unkempt hair, dark skin. Anton bolted, nodding goodbye and disappearing inside. Thomas left his car parked there, descended the hill, crossed a bridge, passed a factory fence, and stepped into a maze of garages, laid out in rows like storage units.

Clay, there was so much clay, it looked as though they were getting ready to burn something on a bonfire, as though nothing ever grew here and the dead came here at night to quench their thirst by imbibing dry, thick lumps of clay. Black tires, half-buried in the ground along the road, an unending white brick wall blanketed with Bible quotes—the clay gave way under his feet, and the scorching sun shone overhead, newspapers and dead cats lay in the grass, and the smell of hell and river water hung in the air. A rusty gate arm blocked the entrance, and the security guard's booth stood off to the side—broken glass, pocket calendars, random pamphlets, a taped-together length of hose, the door wide open, and black blood that had eaten into the cement floor. The security guard wasn't there. Thomas hesi-

tated, then peered inside the booth. The security guard smoked terrible cigarettes and didn't bother stepping outside to do it. He probably couldn't wash the smell of tobacco out of his clothes. A path
made of crushed asphalt ran up ahead; rows of white brick garages
stretched out to the left and right. Thomas thought for a second, then
hung a left, walking past metal doors and glancing at heavy padlocks
lining the sides of the path. Scrap metal was lying by the walls here
and there; some startled birds flew by overhead. There was nobody
around, and eerie silence prevailed. Thomas sped to the end of a long
straightaway, ran up against a brick barrier, turned right, reached the
next row of garages, noticed a side alley, and turned down it. He got
to the end and turned right again. The garages stretched out ahead
of him, without end and without hope. "Where is everybody?" he
thought. "There has to be somebody around here." He stopped and
listened hard. Little lizards were scurrying through the charred grass,
swallows were rustling under slate roofs, the wind was blaring, whipping through the frames of the metal doors, as if it were alerting the
drowsy city that unseen enemies were approaching. A flash of color
blazed by somewhere far up ahead. Thomas darted forward, realizing that it was somebody in a colorful shirt whipping around the
corner. Thomas ran to that corner, barreled out into the next row,
and caught a glimpse of the stranger's back as he walked quickly past
the garages, wearing a bright Hawaiian shirt and gray pants, his bare
feet in sandals. He appeared to be holding some heavy metal object.
Thomas was nearly at ease and was thinking about chasing down the
stranger; however, the man suddenly ducked into a side passageway,
so Thomas dashed forward, in a panicky frenzy once again. He ran,
turned, reached a narrow tunnel, sprinted down it, high walls on each
side of him, pounding the crushed bricks beneath him with his polished dress shoes and stomping on empty cigarette packs and used
condoms. The man wasn't getting any closer; somehow, he managed
to stay ahead, his shirt flickering in and out of view and his feet knock-

ing stones flying. No matter how much Thomas accelerated, the gap between them wasn't closing. Finally, Thomas decided to go for it, and yelled:

"Hey!"

His voice cracked and shattered in the overwhelming silence, but the stranger seemed to have heard it; he stopped and turned around. Thomas paused to think and then charged ahead. Then the stranger bolted, clearly trying to escape. Thomas bolted after him. Heavy footfalls filled the silence. The man ran up to the far wall, hesitated at the intersection up ahead, unsure where to go from there, then hopped off to the left and disappeared around the next corner. Thomas could hear his steps fading away, so he ran to the corner. The stranger was gone. Thomas ran forward, tearing past rows of garages, always hoping to catch a glimpse of the stranger's flashy clothes, but he had simply disappeared, as though he wasn't the one stricken by fear, as though he hadn't hesitated at the crossroads. Thomas was panting, yet he kept running forward, unrelenting, striving to reach the stranger, catch him, and finally figure out what was going on around here. At some point, he felt the path between the garages bend to the left ever so slightly—he must have been running around in circles for some time now. He'd already started thinking about stopping and turning back when his eye suddenly caught an open garage, with a small door visible inside it, also open. He stopped, caught his breath, walked over, and peered inside.

The smell of grease and burnt fur seeped through the darkness farther back as rays of sun poked through and sprawled out across the red, polished surface of an automobile—an old Kopeika. She had clearly given her owner many years of faithful service, but hadn't quite earned a peaceful retirement—there was something in her past, something for which she was atoning, even after her death. Thomas immediately realized that her death had been a terrible one—she was lying all over that garage, ground up like hamburger. Demons had intercepted that car, tossing it around like a rugby ball for a while and then hurling it into the hot sky over and over again. Chewed-up metal, junked internal components, black burnt rubber, finely shattered glass—the automobile looked like the body of a saint tortured by Roman legionaries. Thomas took a closer look. There was a felt blanket hanging behind it. Swaying in a light, invisible draft, it looked like a dark, heavy sail; evidently there was another unseen exit at the back of the garage. It was worth exploring. Thomas skirted past the dismembered Kopeika, cautiously pushing the felt partition to the side. Sure enough, there it was—another room, cluttered with paint cans and bottles of polish. He stepped forward carefully, saw another door up ahead, and opened it, entering the next room, which was much smaller. There was an office desk in the corner, covered in old, yellowed newspapers. He stepped in and surveyed the space. The next door was tucked away, a tiny hole in the wall, fading like an old scar. Thomas walked over and rammed his shoulder into the door, which wouldn't give at first, but eventually squeaked open. Hot, concentrated sunlight flooded his vision. Thomas ventured outside, raising a hand to shield his eyes from the painful rays and immediately sensing breathing nearby. He moved his hand away—still too blind to make anything out—crouched, backing out of the sun, and tentatively raised his hand again. He held that position for a bit, unmoving, still feeling a presence nearby and gradually regaining his vision; yellow balls and black planets were bouncing around in his eyes as they teared up and focused again. Thomas stood up. Right in front of him, no more than two steps away, breathing laboriously, dry tongues lolling, stood a pack of stray dogs, sniffing, moaning from the heat and their own exertion. The door slammed shut behind him with a clang of rusty metal. There was no way out. Their empty, hostile eyes aimed at him, the dogs came no closer, but they were clearly readying themselves to pounce on him any moment now and rip his throat out. The top dog, the most battered and muscular of the bunch, had gray fur, a scarred forehead, and a heavy tongue peppered with black dots. Two young hounds—both bow-legged, with tough, yellow coats—were waiting in the wings. Those two looked the most threatening, and they were clearly eager to pounce the instant their leader gave them the order. A bit farther back, behind them, a young bitch with cold fangs was arching her back fiercely, her head held high. A young pup, whose paws were incredibly powerful for a canine its age, was growling next to her, exposing some red spots on its stomach. An old stray with a mangled front right paw, eyes filled with hatred and despair, dried-up saliva around its mouth, and thorns sticking out of its gashed nose was limping off to the side. Yet another dog, young, shiny, and black, stood way in the back. A bit frightened, yet bold and fierce, not particularly worn down or battered and eager to demonstrate his ferocity, the strength of his muscles, the sharpness of his incisors, and the seriousness of his intentions for the only female around. She could feel that, too, but she didn't let on, turning her back to him and growling, reacting anxiously to each of Thomas's movements. His head inching forward, the top dog paused and started hoarsely exhaling all of his black aggression; Thomas realized that he was cooked, that everything was just about to go down, and that the leader had signaled to his pack that there was no point delaying any longer—they just had to rip this intruder to shreds. As the leader stretched out toward Thomas and softly dug his paws into the dead clay, Thomas thought, "I'm cooked. I'm really cooked, and nothing can be done about it. I just have to accept things the way they are, even if it's cruel, even if it's unfair." He looked the top dog in the eyes, so he would at least see the blow death landed on him. The top dog observed Thomas with a great deal of reverence, but no concessions would be made—everything must play out the way it's supposed to; everyone will get what he deserves, nobody will be saved—exceptions are degrading. Thomas gritted his teeth, clenched his fists, and took a half-step forward, preparing himself for a blast of salty dog breath on his throat—then an elderly woman appeared somewhere off to the side. She was tall and had dark skin on her face, a blue men's jacket on her torso, and heavy shoes on her feet. She was holding countless purses and shopping bags, which she was dragging along the hot clay. Those bags were stuffed with ancient clothing and empty bottles, food she'd fished out of dumpsters, and prehistoric kitchenware — bowls, knives, plates, and spoons. All that stuff rattled and rolled along, and it seemed as though her bones and joints were rattling along, too. Dust had settled around her. She smelled like an apartment where an older person had just died. Her empty gaze rubbed up against Thomas, as though he didn't even exist and she hadn't seen him at all. The dogs tensed up and stood still, continuing to growl and gnash their teeth, but their aggression was just riding its own momentum now. They didn't want to retreat from this victim who had just wandered onto their turf.

"Belshazzar!" the woman called to the top dog with the scarred forehead.

He was set to lurch toward Thomas; however, her voice had a strange effect on him, seemingly paralyzing his faith in himself and restraining his rage. Turning away from Thomas, Belshazzar stretched his muzzle toward the woman, who extended her dark, bony hand, rubbing his busted-up head and then stepping forward. The pack hurried after her, vanishing around the corner and leaving the smell of dry fur behind.

She called him in the early evening and apologized; they agreed to meet. He offered to come by and pick her up right then and there.

"You don't have to," Olia answered. "We'll see each other tomorrow, anyway." She thought about how men never stuck around for too long. Sometimes she'd notice them and pick them out of a crowd, touching their hands for the first time, peering into their eyes for the first time, remembering their wrinkles, uttering their names, permitting them to stay by her, noting their habits and behavior, listening to how they talked, patiently sitting through stories about their adventures, triumphs, and misfortunes, sharply and firmly thwarting their efforts to learn more about her than she wanted to disclose; she snickered at their bravery, let herself be perplexed and touched by their trusting nature, and harshly quelled their aggression. She adjusted to their breathing, urged them to take decisive action, lost her sense of time with them, left them exposed and alone with their troubles and distorted notions of love and loyalty. She missed them, thought of them, forgot them, refreshed her memory, and recalled everything they'd said to her, all their vows, and everything they did with her. She was resilient enough to never go running back to them and smart enough not to forget them forever, hiding some memento of each and every one of them under her skin—their brimming faith in themselves, their impetuosity, weakness, and unreliability, their caution, fickleness, and piety, their susceptibility to new love. "Those men," she thought, "were born to protect this city and lead campaigns of conquest in its name. They were brought up to value obedience and restraint. They were taught to endure extreme heat and cold, pain and hunger. They grew to defend the city's walls or build churches and warehouses, augmenting our city's riches and glorifying all the saints who watched over it. They're entrusted with keeping our city's gas lines and plumbing in working order, taking care of women and children, feeding stray animals, and keeping wild birds away from the fruit trees downtown. Spreading love is their vocation; the gods have opened the heart of each of them, making way for both love and hate, setting them up for endless joy and suffering, so all they can do is love and hope, believe and lose faith, wait and never retreat, express their gratitude and profess their views, lose everything they've accumulated and start anew, hoping that this time around love won't betray them, that death will retreat.

## MATTHEW

Ten years ago, time stopped for me, and it has been determinedly refusing to move forward ever since. My internal mechanisms paused and my heart took to beating like it was a service industry employee with a bad attitude — doing a passable job, but not making any guarantees. Everything irritated me, even the smell of my own clothes. Turning thirty was a trap. There was no fun to be had immersing myself in the unknown and no joy to be found continuing what I had already started. Just morning fire in my head, afternoon emptiness in my throat, harsh evening light, and my hatred, terrible and practiced religiously, for anyone trying to do something nice for me, and terrible vengeance to be exacted upon anyone who tried to help me. I'd already managed to get divorced twice by the time I was thirty. I would have gone for the triple crown, but I didn't have any takers. My habits scared women off. The fact that I hardly ever slept, and that I wouldn't wake up for a long time when I did, put them on edge. They sat by me in the cold twilight on old sheets, hovering over me, fearfully observing my breathing, taking my pulse, hastily calling their friends for advice, carefully touching my shoulder, turning me over so I wouldn't choke on my own bile. Back then, I'd dream of sand dunes. They flowed through my life, leaving no trace except the stifling heat of my room. I'd dream of snakes and ground-dwelling birds, I'd dream of signs written in dark clay, I'd dream of taciturn children who gathered poisonous berries among dry branches and offered them to me, seemingly exhorting me, "Come on, try one already. You don't know what you're missing. This is the strangest flavor you'll ever taste — only death tastes like this. It's better than any spice imaginable, it's sweeter than any drug cocktail imaginable. Just try it—wake up and try it." Naturally, that left me with no desire to wake up.

Sometimes the women couldn't take it anymore and they'd go run errands. Sometimes they'd just sit there, waiting courteously. But they'd all leave eventually. Sometimes they'd come back and continue to sit on sheets salty as sails. My sex life sure was incredible. In the afternoon, I'd compose myself and head to the radio station, switch on my battered, virus-laden computer, sift through some CDs, fecklessly try to clean up my desk, then get frustrated and wander out into the hallway . . . you know, for a cigarette break or a cup of tea. The flickering glow of the Polytechnic Institute, where my studio was located, towered over the trees, a few scattered lights shining in the classrooms. Darkness pooled between the buildings; the neighborhood smelled of early spring and damp alleyways. I never wanted to leave this city, and I never wanted to go back to the studio, not for anything.

Ten years ago, she graduated from college and tried looking at the world from an adult's perspective. The world was out of focus. For a while there, her parents thought she was still in school, so they would stubbornly wake her up for nonexistent morning classes. Her dad was a professional freeloader, and he seemed to be doing just dandy. Her mom worked at the post office, so she knew all the ins and outs of the postal system and could talk about it for hours—if anybody cared to listen, that is. In the winter, she started working at some charity foundation, but they turned out to not be very charitable when it came to paying their employees, so it'd be a bit of a stretch to call that a real job. Vadyk Salmonella, a big-time musician, brought her to the studio; they'd been dating for about a month, but Vadyk simply wouldn't acknowledge her in public, especially after concerts, despite everything they'd done together. He'd been through the wringer—nearly deaf, pumped full of shitty booze, his vocal cords absolutely shot, like a real rock star. He'd walk right by and blatantly ignore her. She'd break down crying. Apparently he liked this whole act, and apparently she did too. You can enjoy just about anything, even hanging out with complete assholes.

She came in after him, sat down by the door, took out her cell, her anger boiling over, and started texting confidently, snubbing everyone by not even saying hello. Vadyk tossed his leather backpack at her feet and made a big show of forgetting she was there. Fair hair, a white jacket that she'd tossed on the floor just like Vadyk's backpack, fingers burned pink by the wind, moles on her neck, a school uniform sweater exposing her sharp collarbone, a mistrustful gaze, tense movements, a childish expression on her face, filthy shoes, and pretty knees.

"That your daughter?" I said to Vadyk, nodding instead of giving him a proper greeting.

"Fucking what? Of course not," he replied in a surly tone; then our radio show got under way.

Vadyk talked about rock 'n' roll, the rebel's cause, the aesthetics of freedom, protest songs, and expanding your consciousness for exactly twenty minutes, not counting the breaks for music. She was sitting in the corner, just shaking her head discontentedly. She had a plastic bracelet on her right wrist—basically, she looked like she'd borrowed her mom's clothes for a night on the town. After the show, Vadyk and I stood out in the hallway, contemplating the glow beyond the windows. He produced some cognac; I passed—the idea of swigging from the same bottle as him was downright scary. You never know what you could pick up. "Poor girl," I thought.

"How old is she?" I asked Vadyk.

"How the hell should I know? Ya think I checked her driver's license?"

"Well, is she good?"

"Nah, man, she doesn't know a thing and she doesn't want to learn."

"Let me know when you split up. I'll teach 'er a thing or two."

"You betcha," Vadyk said with a chuckle.

I noticed how quickly he'd started aging. Burst capillaries, inflamed gums, and black teeth. "The fish rots from the head," I thought.

But what could I actually teach her? What did I know? How to shirk my responsibilities, play it safe, talk about things I had no interest in, and socialize with people who didn't really matter. What could *he* teach her? Nothing good. We'd make meaningless small talk, trying to keep up some front and acting like a bunch of cocky jerks, never really believing anyone and never really forgiving anyone. Vadyk tried killing himself a few months later, got all tangled up in the noose, and hung there for a while until some of his friends came by and brought him back down to earth.

Nine years ago, she showed up at a gallery opening with Hustav, patiently following him in and shoving her way through a thick mass of friends and casual acquaintances. A new camera dangled from Hustav's neck; he was snapping some pictures of old girlfriends— about two dozen of the notches on his bedpost were in attendance. We hugged for quite a while and asked for a detailed update on each other's lives, although we already knew everything there was to know—the world is small, life is short, and people tend to gossip. She'd changed her hairstyle recently, and the new one looked good on her. Her face had suddenly turned out to be much more interesting. Her features became more distinct whenever she looked away, as if a sheet of ice had cracked and water was flowing freely under her skin. She was wearing a leather jacket, bright orange stockings, and tattered ballet slippers to top off her outlandish getup. "Maybe she just walks a lot," I thought, glancing at her footwear. She intercepted my gaze and tensed up. She didn't recognize me, obviously, made no effort at small talk, of course, yet agreed to have a cigarette with me outside.

"Are you going to date every single one of my friends?" I asked.

No response. She was probably trying to figure out whether or not she should take offense; she decided against it.

"You have some pretty good friends. They could teach you a thing or two about manners."

"Huh, imagine that," I thought. "Someone who slept with Vadyk Salmonella is giving me pointers on etiquette."

"Don't get so defensive," I said.

"I'm not," she answered, and headed back in to warm up.

Hustav got some job on the mayor's PR team. Then he got fired a little while after that and sold his camera and his apartment, too. Life robs us of more than our illusions.

Eight years ago, she started going to night school. My professor friends griped that she didn't know the first thing about finance—not that they had a very firm grasp of the discipline they were supposed to be teaching either. "Nobody knows anything," they griped. "Nobody really knows what they're talking about. We're all faking it, pretending to know something, pretending to feel something; we live by illusions. But the problem is we have to pay good money to keep it going."

We wound up at the same concert a couple times, and we crossed paths on the metro once—she was with a pack of Hasidic Jews. As far as I could gather, she was giving them a tour of the city. They looked like a big family that had bought an apartment downtown and were disappointed to learn that it was still infested with cockroaches. She had long hair again, which made her look more experienced and grown up. Nevertheless, she was still resorting to the same mistrustful and confrontational tone, as though she were trying to prove something to the adults around her, as though she were attempting to convince all the Hasidic Jews in the whole wide world that the transaction she was facilitating was necessary and appropriate.

Seven years ago, I changed stations. This was a big step for me; it took me a while to pull the trigger. The new station could have easily tanked a few months after it went on the air, but this was a real job. It was time to make a move. I wouldn't even have considered something like that a few years back. But then one day, out of the blue, I started asking myself some tough questions—Do you really want to keep wasting away doing something you don't enjoy? Do you really want to keep breaking your back for some boss? How much longer can you be dependent on someone else and change yourself to accommodate them? "C'mon," I said to myself, "go for it. You're not some twenty-year-old punk. You're as old as Jesus was—it's time to work miracles and raise lepers from their graves."

I bumped into her downtown one May morning. She was sitting on the steps of a bank, still closed at such an early hour. There she sat, looking a bit lost, though she wasn't crying or anything, her head propped up on her fist, staring off into space. She had a tiny little watch dangling from her wrist, but I'm absolutely certain she wouldn't be able to tell you the time. She simply wouldn't process the question. She saw me and gave a weak, forced nod. Something compelled me to stop—it may have been that she nodded first. I didn't hesitate, sitting down beside her and asking her about her life, her studies, and our mutual friends. She nodded in reply and talked a little, quite reluctantly. Then she went silent.

"What's up? Did something happen?"

"Nah, not really. It's just that I was getting my brains fucked out all night."

"All night, really?" I asked incredulously.

"Yep, all night."

I didn't know what to say to that, so I waited for a bit. She wasn't saying anything either, though. I reached into my bag, pulled out a carton of milk, and handed it to her. She ripped it open and started sucking it down greedily. "Fucking all night must be pretty exhausting," I thought. I noticed that her fingers were trembling, as if she'd just done an intense workout at the gym. I noticed the veins bulging in her neck when she flung her head back to drink. I noticed dark circles under her eyes—the kind women only get when they're in labor . . . or when they haven't gotten enough sleep, I suppose. Well, at any rate, only women who are emotionally invested in what they do and afraid of slipping up can have those deep, translucent circles under their eyes. The weary and distant expression on her face indicated that last night had been nice, yet hard on her, that she was concerned about what happened, yet she didn't have the slightest regret. She smelled of warm shower water, morning cigarettes, and someone else's soap. It seemed as though the blood had deserted her fingers, flowing away to a safe distance. But those lips of hers—bitten and puffy—blazed darkly under the morning sun; she kept nibbling on them, as if she were thinking back to what had transpired that night, as if it had still not ended in her mind. It even seemed like she wanted that night to keep going, like something very important had withdrawn from her, something that she started to lament the instant that the dark of the night retreated—she'd been sitting there for God knows how long, for no apparent reason, lamenting the loss of something she'd just acquired. I must have been gawking at her lips—maybe that was why she choked on the milk. It ran down her chin. She quickly wiped it away, covered her lips with her hand, and started speaking, seemingly not even addressing me, talking in muffled and disjointed spurts, touching the wounds on her thin, vulnerable skin, stopping the blood that rushed to them after every outburst and question, growing anxious, and realizing that I could see it. She tried changing the subject; I kept the conversation going, trying not to look at her and feigning a casual and carefree attitude, yet constantly thinking to myself, "She was getting fucked all night! All night! She was willing to give love and understanding all night; she didn't sleep all night, she forced herself to stay awake all night, making utterances, listening to confessions, remembering promises, and screaming words of ecstasy. She was feelin' good all night—they kept her up all night—they kept her hot and bothered all night. She slipped into the dream world and was plucked out of it again, into the black air; she caught someone's breathing, felt someone's caressing fingers, tried to adjust to someone's movements, listened to someone else's heart beating, and got used to someone else's smell, someone else's voice, and someone else's love."

I took the milk out of her hands and started gulping it down too.

"You know anyone that's hiring?" she asked suddenly.

"I'll ask my boss," I promised.

I tried to pass the carton back to her, but she shook her head as if to say, "I've had enough for today." I got to my feet, said goodbye, and headed home, throwing the rest of the milk in a trash can along the way.

For some reason, my boss agreed to give her a job immediately. Now we were working in the same building. She sat in the next room over, copying out news stories from the internet so we could use them for our broadcasts. She hit it off with everyone, settled in quickly, and seemed to enjoy the company of her many new gal pals. She had a nice personality and a bad memory, almost never got angry, and almost never griped about anything. I'm not sure if she actually liked her job. I'm not sure if she even considered it a real job—endlessly surfing the internet, constant smoke breaks and phone conversations, soaking up the bright sun flooding through the wide-open windows, and hearing voices on the steps and car alarms erupting in the fresh morning air. She always seemed to be expressing a certain degree of appreciation for what I'd done for her, which I found pretty exasperating, because it rendered whatever prospects of getting with her I might have had nonexistent. We'd say hello in the morning, drink knock-off cognac at corporate birthday parties, and then she'd disappear again, and I'd pretend that was how things were supposed to go. I'd invite her out, suggest grabbing a drink together, and try talking about something besides work, and she'd agree in such an aloof and dejected tone that my desire to take her out would disappear.

"Don't sweat it. Whatever happened to not mixing business and pleasure? Just let her work. When you put in a good word for her with the boss did you really think that meant you'd be the one fucking her brains out all night?" I thought, really letting myself have it. "Yeah, admit it. You did. What else could you have been thinking about when you saw her that morning, drained and bloodless? Three years ago, you would have finished what you started, no doubt about it. You would have caught her at the office after hours and slipped your cold hands down her orange T-shirt, brushing up against the hard pebbles of her moles. So what if she resisted, so what if she complained to the boss, so what if she gave her two-weeks' notice? What would I care? Huh, that's exactly how it would have gone," I thought, agreeing with myself. "I don't even know what's holding me back now."

But something really was holding me back. So much so that late one night as I was passing her desk on my way out of the office, I discovered, much to my surprise, that she hadn't signed out of her email. I tried convincing myself to just walk away without reading her messages, but I just wasn't persuasive enough. I sat down at her desk and tried reasoning with myself once again. "What's wrong with you? You're gonna have to see her every day." Eventually, I got up, shut down her computer, and closed the door behind me.

And then, at the end of the summer, events took a surprising turn. It was an evening meeting that somehow devolved into everybody pounding booze. I'd been in a good mood all day. I was brimming with optimism, looking out the window where, cooling down in the twilight like radiators with no steam in them, heavy trees stood, drained by the white August sun. My spirits had gotten a lift that morning when I bumped into some old friends downtown, right in the middle of the street, taking an unexpected breather in the heat of a tough workday—drunken hugs and sweet memories of people I hadn't seen in ages, about those who'd disappeared and were now hopelessly lost, promises to keep in touch, demands to not be a stranger, exchanges of vows and unsolicited advice, tears, and the restrained singing of men. The point is I came to the meeting a few drinks deep, so I had a bit of a head start. Then once we'd settled all our official business and everyone was feeling more laid back, I refused to listen to any admonitions or appeals from my friends. She was sitting there the whole time, obviously, right next to me, at someone's desk cluttered with reports and newspaper clippings, and I could feel her warmth and her soft touch all evening, obviously, so I flew off the handle, obviously, because "When else am I gonna pull the trigger?" I thought. "It's now or never." I spoke only to her and listened only to her, told only her all my tales of heroism, and concerned myself only with her reaction. At one point, I was being ridiculously brazen about it, obviously, and she, being a person who was concerned about her reputation and did not wish to offend her good buddy, obviously, took the initiative and suggested we go for a little walk. She said that we could sit there in the office all night, listening to the trees breathing heavily outside. Nobody would judge us for doing so, obviously. The hour was getting late, though, which made absolutely no difference to her, since she lived nearby and did not depend on the city's public transportation system; however, she was clearly emotionally invested in my plans and my fate. Soon Kharkiv would close the luminous gates of the metro to its citizens, and she had no idea how I'd resolve my transportation woes then, obviously. What if it doesn't occur to me that I can call a taxi?

"Well, it's not gonna occur to *me*, it just won't," she said in a trusting tone. "But who says it's gonna occur to *me?*" I asked myself. "Yeah, it just won't," I told her and myself. So, she grabbed my hand and dragged me along the passageways of the editorial department and down old stairwells, walked with me through a black, neglected courtyard, under tree branches hanging low like winter clouds,

through an unexpected nighttime rain shower, ran across the street
with me, and popped into a park with me by her side. It was precisely
there that I tried to stop her and tell her everything that needed to
be said at that moment, and, well, do everything that needed to be
done. It was precisely then that two melancholy foot patrol shadows
emerged from beyond the trees. And that was precisely how things
came to an end. She flashed her press pass; I demonstrated my self-
defense techniques. She called the station and handed the patrol officers her phone; I tried taking their billy clubs away and handed them
a string of curses from the depths of hell. She tried paying them off;
I called them a bunch of whores. They took us back to the station,
obviously, the both of us; however, they complied with my request
to let her go immediately, suggesting I be their guest for the night.
She became hysterical, bawling her eyes out and pleading with them,
which gave me the strength to fight on. I snatched a can of pepper
spray when one of the patrol officers turned around to fill out some
paperwork and unloaded it at the ceiling with a cheerful whizz of
compressed liquid. Everyone had to step into the hallway for a bit,
and the officers punched me in the ribs a few times. She probably
would have liked to pitch in, too. Then suddenly she and one of the
officers started hitting it off—they were all looking at me judgmen-
tally, thoroughly irritated, all of them appalled by my behavior. I was
glad, though—I finally saw a glint of some sort of interest in me. So
what if that interest only amounted to wanting to slug me as hard as
she could? She was looking at me, she wasn't looking away, everyone
was looking at me, the whole station hated me; I was a real hero, and
that feeling made life worth living. They aired out the room, and then
we all went back inside. They demanded that I empty my pockets. I
complied reluctantly. She stood next to me and carefully followed
my movements, as though she was afraid of missing something, not
picking up on some sign. Her T-shirt and Keds had been soaked by
the rain shower, and she was quite cold, so she wrapped her arms
around her shoulders. Her eyes were frozen on me as I took out a

large ring of keys with a few machine-gun cartridges attached. You could say they were my good-luck charms. I had a lot of keys, since I had to look after two apartments downtown—the owner of one of them, my high school friend, was in the can, while the owner of the other, my former business partner, was hiding out somewhere, otherwise they would have thrown him in the can too. I had the keys to a few mailboxes, since I'd pick up my elderly neighbors' academic journals for them. They stubbornly kept their subscriptions up, although they hardly even left their apartment anymore. Their children never visited them—I may have been the only person who actually remembered their names. My address book flew through the air and landed on the table after the keys. One of the officers flipped through it, just for kicks, came across a few names he recognized, and placed it off to the side, rather uneasily. My address book contained the numbers of basically all the city council members. Well, enough of them to form a viable majority, at least. I could have called one of them and asked for help but I'd been stripped of the right to make my one call, and all three of my phones were now on the table in front of the officers. One of them had been stomped on during an International Workers' Day parade and then taped back together. The letters on the second one's keys had faded completely, so I could receive texts but I couldn't really send them. The third one was pink and covered in rhinestones—my sister had left it when she came to visit. I hadn't gotten around to throwing it out. The officers looked at all this stuff, their suspicion mounting with each new object I produced. I took out a bunch of business cards—some pediatricians I'd tried to help recently by inviting them to talk on one of our radio programs, some human rights advocate who'd make occasional appearances on the air and complain about stray animals being mistreated, a young lawyer lady who represented the employees at the trolley depot, and the owner of a Georgian restaurant in town who kept inviting me to his place for a barbecue dinner—but I stubbornly refused, knowing perfectly well what kind of dirty money he had behind him, what kind of business he was running, and how many scalps he'd taken. Next came a few flash drives, a dozen or so batteries, loose pieces of gum, cough drops, and, for some reason, a metal referee's whistle. The whistle caught their eye. They fiddled with it a bit and passed it back and forth. Finally, one of them, probably the junior of the two, who had a bullied look about him, simply couldn't take it anymore and he blew it. The other guy jabbed him. I was most concerned about the condoms in my back pocket. I was initially hoping the officers would let them slide, but instead they decided to wring every last cent out of me. She kept quiet, examining my wet, shaggy hair, black T-shirt with an anti-Parliament slogan on it, dark, coffee-stained sweater, jeans, and sneakers as if she was committing them to memory, as if she'd never noticed any of it before, never paid any attention to it, never seen that my sleeve was marked with traces of blood, never spotted the drops of hot asphalt on my shoes, never known what I did outside work, what interested me, who I hated, and who I was battling against. Just the condoms were left. Well, they were definitely the main problem. "On the one hand, it's a good thing she'll see I have protection on me," I assured myself. "That shows I'm a serious-minded and responsible individual, not some punk kid, that I've got everything under control and I'm ready to make a commitment. Commitment? What the hell are you talking about?" I couldn't help but object to my own faulty reasoning. "I'd say you're just preoccupied with sex—you're always carrying jimmy hats around, you even bring them to work. It's obvious what's on your mind and it's obvious what you want from her, ya dickwad. However," I continued, presenting new arguments to myself, "having prophylactics in your pocket attests to your constant readiness, tempered masculinity, and unmistakable grit. You're a real man, and it's just ridiculous to be ashamed of that. However," I reminded myself, "you've been carrying those prophylactics around for about two months now. They're so worn and shabby that desperation is what they suggest, not masculinity." So I made a big show of reaching for my belt, removing it, and handing it to the officer.

"Here, go hang yourself with it," I offered as a parting shot. She stopped listening to me and darted out into the hallway, slamming the door. I could take the condoms out now.

They let me go in the morning. They tried shaming me first, of course; maybe they were trying to provide a rationale for detaining me, though they must have known their excuses were pretty weak, so they were a little bit anxious, obviously. They returned my business cards, flash drives, and whistle. I showed up at work with the latter in my hand. She was at her desk. I asked her to step out for a little chat. She complied without saying a word, grabbed her coffee, walked out into the hallway, and sat on a wide windowsill. I positioned myself beside her.

"Sorry for losing it last night."

"It happens to the best of us," she answered, sipping her coffee, burning the roof of her mouth, coughing, and growing anxious. "I was just worried about you."

"Yeah, sure you were." I reached for her mug, burning my fingers, and placed it off to the side.

I tried kissing her. She made a big show of taking out some gum and started chewing, staring out into space. "Whatever," I thought. "You didn't want it enough. But actually you did. Of course you did."

She quit that fall. The boss's son filled her position. A special police unit raided us a month later, barging into his office and seizing all the station's documents. The boss encouraged the whole staff to stage a hunger strike. I agreed. I wound up being the only one. The boss weighed his options and went off to negotiate with the mayor. The good times were just getting started.

Six years ago, sometime in the winter, I bumped into her outside a jewelry store in town. I was racing to some meeting, looking at the ground, when I suddenly caught her in my peripheral vision. I recognized her immediately. She'd dyed her hair, and the new color didn't look good on her. A long fur coat that hung down to her heels (provided by some well-heeled individual, no doubt), high, black boots that wouldn't have looked out of place on a grenadier, and a tough guy in a leather jacket gazing at her with heavy eyes, yet holding her hand and not letting her go — none of it looked good on her. I nodded; she pretended not to notice, turned abruptly toward her tough guy and said something cheerful to him. I went on my way, watching his eyes narrow, like he was looking through military binoculars, his hand squeezing hers, his leather jacket creaking with frustration.

Five years ago, I saw her talking on some local TV channel. The caption below her name read "activist." She was advocating for some businessman to be released on bail. It turns out he'd done a whole lot for the city, and, it turns out, the authorities had apprehended him on trumped-up tax evasion charges, which, it turns out, she personally deemed to be an act of revenge by his competitors and an attempt to discredit his charity work, which benefited many residents of Kharkiv. She, it turns out, had already filed an appeal and approached the city fathers, with, it turns out, a petition. She's counting on them, those city fathers, although they've been acting like a bunch of pricks lately. She didn't explicitly say that, but it was the precise sentiment expressed by her eyes. She talked about the prisoner with such warmth in her voice that even the anchorman couldn't take it anymore and had to cut to commercial.

Four years ago, I moved away from the city without even thinking of her once. But then I came back and thought of her again.

Three years ago, somebody told me what she was up to. It turns out, after getting her night school degree and finding a respectable job, she took out a bunch of loans at an insanely high interest rate and bought an apartment in a new complex, intending to move in right away. But suddenly in the summer she sold everything, got all her savings together, borrowed some money from her aunt, and quickly settled up with her creditors. Then the financial crisis hit.

Two years ago, I bumped into her at the Georgian joint—sitting by herself, watching a movie on her laptop, and drinking dry red wine. She saw me, tensed up, yet waved, inviting me over to her table. I took a seat; she inquired about how I was doing health-wise, saying that she'd quit her job and started getting in touch with her spiritual side.

"Like karate class?" I asked. She started explaining. I was about to say something nice and high-tail it out of there when she suddenly clasped my elbow tightly and told me not to hold a grudge against her, that she'd always had warm feelings and a deep sense of appreciation for me, that I was a true friend, and she was an unappreciative swine who never valued my friendly attitude toward her. Now she was really down in the dumps, really hurting, because what she'd done just wasn't right and that's not how things should have been—friends are supposed to support one another and have a friendly attitude, because real friendship between friends is held together by friendliness and friendly feelings. It seemed like she was getting in touch with her spiritual side right there in front of me; I interrupted her, rather awkwardly, saying that I'd always had warm feelings and a deep sense of appreciation for her too and was happy our friendship had lasted so many years. I even gave her a half-hug at the end of our little reunion, nearly spilling her dry red wine. We produced our respective cellphones and exchanged numbers—hers was silver and polished, mine black and held together with tape.

A year later she called. Her number was no longer in my phone, so I didn't pick up for a while. I usually ignored calls from unknown numbers, but something hinted that I had to answer this one. My phone rang and rang; she waited patiently for me to come around. Her voice was tear-stained. She said hello and apologized, quite formally: "I apologize for disturbing you. I just didn't have anyone else to call. My parents are too old, I don't have a job—or any friends, as it turns out. My aunt's in a bad way right now—she fell and broke her leg. At her age that means death is just around the corner."

"Why are you calling me?" I was confused.

"You have some doctor friends," she explained. "I distinctly remember you were always talking to some doctors."

"They were pediatricians."

"What's the difference?" she snapped. "They said I could try and take her to a specialist. You hear that? I need somebody that specializes. I'm afraid they'll just butcher her in a regular hospital. Pull some strings, call in some favors, I don't care how, just make it happen!" Well, obviously at that point she burst into tears; I tried consoling her, but she'd already hung up. I pulled some strings. My friends actually did recommend a good doctor, asked me to wait a bit, got in touch with him, called me back, and told me they'd filled him in.

"Just make sure the old lady says she knows you."

I called her back: "Here's the deal, dial this number, tell them you know me, and you'll be good to go. And I'm gonna come over and help, okay?"

She stood outside the hospital, crying and dabbing her tears away with wet wipes. She rooted around in her purse with anxious, trembling fingers, pulled out her phone, pressed some buttons, flung some loose strands of hair—her hair was long again and scorched lighter by the summer sun—away from her face, darted toward me, and wrapped her arms around my neck, but it was such a cold and detached gesture that I wound up backing away from her.

"I don't know what to do—it looks like the operation went smoothly, but the doctors won't permit me to stay with her. What should I do? Do I just wait here?"

"Let me give you a ride home," I suggested.

She looked up at the hospital windows with a helpless expression. It was a late summer evening. Only two of them were emitting light. One of them went out unexpectedly. She finally gave in and decided to head home.

As far as I could gather, this was her aunt's place. My best guess was that she lived here too, on Theater Street, in a cluttered three-room apartment packed with books. Fourth floor. She hesitated for a moment in front of her building and then invited me in. Down below, between the trees, tangerine streetlights shone into view. The air smelled like rain, although there hadn't been any.

She drank tea all night and told some horror stories, primarily about the post office and then about her aunt—about how she had lost her husband at an early age. He was a jockey who was thrown from his horse during a race and died. This was a huge blow for her aunt; she just couldn't bounce back. She continued going to the track her whole life, taking her niece along. They'd ride over together, when trolleys still ran as far as the park, and sit there, never saying anything—her niece lacked the resolve to ask her any questions; they'd get off and walk over to the stands. She'd remain silent, looking at the distant, restless bodies of the jockeys, choosing who to root for as her niece read the programs with mounting anxiety, and then they walked home, upset and emotionally depleted. She never wound up getting remarried, although, as it turned out, she had many men in her life. Her niece, as it turned out, always suspected something was going on, while she, as it turned out, wasn't intent on hiding her relationships. The niece remembered the babyish faces of cadets, the shoes of trade schoolers, well worn, as if by the feet of active children, the adolescently slouching bodies of students and interns, and the chins of high schoolers and resentful deserters, nicked by cheap razors, like those of real adults. She didn't know a single thing about them; they'd occasionally surface in dark hallways, bump into her on their way out of the bathroom, shriek in the shower when she walked in on them, and smile at her as they stepped into the warm, smoky kitchen from the cold balcony. Her aunt never talked about them, and she never asked for any explanations. Whenever she would spend the night, her aunt would call somebody and make some arrangements or step into the hallway by the front door and speak at length with someone, in a firm and convincing tone, and then eventually return to her niece and read her an adventure book as a bedtime story.

Her stories and reminiscences, digressions and clarifications, lasted until the morning; every happy ending ushered in the next story, and every adroit plot twist warranted a continuation. All my attempts at cutting her off came up short, and all my efforts to say goodbye and make my escape were doomed to failure—she held me firmly and confidently, divulging numerous intimate details of her past, as if I were a close relative dying of cancer, like she was thinking, "He already knows everything about everyone anyway and he won't have time to tell anybody anything." But whenever I tried to touch her hand—gently, not trying to impose anything on her—she'd reach for her warm mug of tea, and as soon as I'd reach out to fix a strand of hair falling down into her eyes, she'd scoot back slightly and peer out the window, listening to the sirens wailing in the night, down by the river. She asked me to go with her in the morning. How could I say no?

I tried catching up on some sleep in the hospital waiting room. It smelled like iodine. It seemed like I was by the sea in April. She spent a few hours with her aunt and then left to run around from pharmacy to pharmacy looking for the right meds. I agreed to wait for her. In the early evening, the doctors told us that her aunt had lost consciousness.

"Who'd a thunk it?" one of them said, genuinely surprised. "It looked like everything was going smoothly. I hope everything will turn out all right, but be prepared for the worst." He took me aside and asked me to drive her home. I did.

She sat out on the balcony all night. I brought her tea. I brought her sleeping pills. I brought her wine. I brought her cigarettes. She thanked me, her fingers keeping a death grip on the balcony railing. I wanted to pry them apart and put her to bed, but let's see *you* try to

pry apart the fingers of a woman who's on the verge of losing everything. I brought her a blanket, wrapped it around her shoulders, sat
down next to her, and counted the meteors until morning. All two
of them.

The next morning at eight, the doctor called. He calmed her
down, said that her aunt's condition had stabilized, and asked us to
buy some more medicine. I suggested she stay home, promising to
handle everything. She rejected my offer, of course. The third straight
day on my feet was tough but the longer this went on, the less chance
I had of backing out. We spent half the day scouring every kiosk and
pharmaceutical warehouse in town; she spent the other half standing
outside her aunt's ward. We got home sometime around midnight.
Once again, she had deep, tender circles under her eyes from all the
crying and sleep deprivation. I had started hallucinating.

"Go get some sleep," I told her.

"Nah . . . but why don't you? I just can't sleep after everything
that's happened."

"Well, I'm gonna sit with you, then." The last thing I wanted to
do was leave her alone out here on the balcony. "How've you been?
How's night school going?"

"Good," she answered quietly.

"What kind of degree are you getting?"

"Tax assessment," she answered automatically.

"You'll be good at tax assessing," I assured her. "What exactly do
tax assessors do?"

"They assess taxes," she answered, reaching for my hand.

Then that feeling of lost time arises again, expanding inside you
like a reef, clogging your throat, tormenting and draining you. "I met
her ten years ago," I thought, as she let out her final cry, fell silent, and
looked at me, there in the dark, seemingly probing me for answers.
Would I tell anybody about her natural hair color, about her split
ends? Would I start bragging to my friends about seeing her fragile

and exposed? Would I constantly remind her about all her screaming and moaning, all her brusqueness and tenderness, all the soft curves and hard lines under her skin? Ten years ago, she was twenty years old; she didn't know a thing, but she learned quickly, reviewed all her homework assignments with painstaking care. Where had I been all this time? What was so important that I just had to do? Why didn't I find out about her habits and behavior back then—ten years ago? Why is it only now that I notice how she tucks her hair back and turns toward the window and how her nails dig into her palms when she wants to restrain herself from giving too much away? Why is it only now that I figure out she loves talking in the dark, speaking and reacting to voices and warm movements in the twilight? Why did it take me so long to muster up the strength to catch her, compel her to stay, compel her to do what she loves? Ten years—that's enough time to forget everything and fabricate another storyline, to break the sky down into its constituent parts and try to reassemble it, never doubting, not even for a split second, that your brash undertaking will succeed. What happened to all the time that had passed by? What had it been used for? What effect did it have on us? I closely examined the fine wrinkles under her eyes. People who smile a lot—who smile a lot and for a long time—are bound to develop wrinkles like that. Her face had acquired a certain sharpness and maturity; she had basically stopped using makeup, although she still always managed to look put-together. It may have been her expressive eyes, it may have been the dullness of her skin that wasn't getting any younger. Yet her collarbone was just as sharp, her nails, always engaged in active combat, were just as chipped; her knees were scratched, and her calves were bruised. She looked like a trapeze artist who'd been flying through the air for the last ten years, colliding with clumps and fragments of electrified emptiness as she reached out to grab them. When she had worn herself out, she asked for some water. Her voice was parched, her whispers hoarse and barely audible, as though she didn't want to wake anyone who was sleeping at such a late hour. She'd wet her lips, catch her breath, clearly delighted, and start searching for me in the damp, tangled sheets once again. At four a.m., all talked out and all calmed down, she started falling asleep. Her voice came through her dreams; she was recalling some names, gesturing toward some thin scars on her neck, taking out a cigarette, asking for a light, and falling asleep with it still hanging, unlit, in her hand. I carefully removed it from her fingers and placed it off to the side, on the chair, with her girlish bra dangling from the back and my unused condoms lying on the seat. I thought for a second, then put the lighter down, too. "She'll figure everything out in the morning," I thought. My third sleepless night in a row was making objects translucent, and the twilight came alive. My heart was hustling along like it was afraid of missing its train. It was bursting forward like a dog that had been chained to a pole for too long. Salty waves were gliding through my body, from my left lung to my right, colliding with the lining of my ribcage and rolling back, their efforts thwarted. Occasional sparks flashed in the dark and the occasional bug blazed by. I had to go catch up on some sleep. I gathered my things, struggled to dress in the hallway, found my shoes, and stepped out of her apartment. The stairwell was bright and ringing with sound, like a mine that had been stripped of all its coal and filled with glass and sundust. A dry August morning was breaking outside. I headed down the stairs, counting the steps, losing track and then resuming my tally. I heard movement down below, behind the trees. "Dogs," I thought. "Those are some stray dogs waiting to rip my throat out and avenge all those whom I have hurt in my life." I stopped, steeled myself, and kicked the door. It squeaked and swung wide open. A streak of light nailed me right between the eyes. It was like I'd finally escaped from the labyrinth I'd been wandering in for the last ten years.

There were a lot of them. I couldn't even see the ones standing in the back, but I could feel their warmth, which iced up my nostrils and throat. There were about fifty of them, maybe even a few more—my eyes still hadn't adjusted to the bright morning light—

their features were frozen black, as though they'd been etched out of old metal. They wore street clothes, all of them in their twenties or thereabouts—short hair, comfortable athletic footwear, light, hooded jackets, and dark, baggy tracksuit bottoms, standing motionless and clearly waiting for me to appear. "They've got me," I thought, leaning up against the brick wall.

They were all scrutinizing me, looking discerningly into my eyes and catching my panicky movements. Finally, one of them—clearly the top dog—spoke.

"You from here?" he asked, nodding at the apartment windows up above.

"Yep."

"Been livin' here awhile?"

"Not too long," I answered honestly.

"Do ya know Black Devil?"

I hesitated. "Who are they?" I thought. "What should I tell 'em?" I knew Black Devil, and he knew me, too. But I didn't know if that was good or bad. I decided to just be straight with them.

"Uh-huh."

"Do you know where he is?" the top dog asked, stepping extremely close to me and lowering his voice.

"Nope. How would I?"

"You sure 'bout that?" The top dog was right in my face now. He smelled like gasoline.

"I'm sure." I tried not to break eye contact.

"All right then," the top dog said quietly. "Let us know if you hear from him."

"Who are you guys?" I couldn't help but ask.

The top dog lurched back and took a look at me, genuinely surprised. Then he leaned in once again and started speaking quietly, almost whispering. I caught some words, while others flew past me hopelessly. I lacked the resolve to ask for any clarification; I listened, bewildered, and committed the bits and pieces I could hear to mem-

ory, because he spoke of important things. Things so important that
I didn't need to hear them—I already knew.

"We're tax collectors," the top dog said. "Tax collectors and sen-
tinels. We collect tribute from those who owe it; we collect it to main-
tain a state of perfect balance. There's enough to go around when we
take away the superfluous and return that which is lacking. We hunt
debtors and support the fearful. We receive duties from the thrifty and
generous, from the gullible and conniving; we collect them in the
upper neighborhoods and in the poor neighborhoods across the river.
We secure hefty monthly payments from bankers and entrepreneurs,
but we don't turn our noses up at the few coppers the factory workers,
cobblers, and secondhand dealers can scrape together. We collect—
coin by coin, bill by bill—documenting every wire transfer and pre-
serving every pay stub, since we know that everything must be paid
for. You can't leave anyone your debts, you can't leave this world a
debtor, you have to return everything that doesn't belong to you, and
you have to settle accounts for everything you have received throughout your life. But we don't just collect money and other valuables. We
collect unpaid anger every month, we collect rage and enmity, we
collect valor and brewing vengeance. Most important, we collect all
this city's unpaid love, every morsel of it, every last gasp of love. All of
us in this city are essentially love collectors. We collect it every morning, we seek it out every evening, then we find it every night, because
there simply can't be unpaid love, love bottled up inside, because all
that love belongs to the city, because the city is held up by that love,
filled with it, like its streets soaked with rain in the spring, warmed by
it, like its homes heated by coal in the winter. The city would die of
cold and thirst without it, without all that love; the city's last holdouts
would desert it, leaving it like a labyrinth, no longer able to wander
aimlessly up and down its streets and back alleys. So no matter what
transpires, no matter what happens to all of us, no matter how tough
fate is on us, and no matter what misfortunes fall upon our rooftops,
we are determined to continue collecting these large, unseen duties,

atom by atom, breath by breath, death by death. By finding common ground with those who don't conceal anything. By persuading those who don't trust us. By destroying those who get in our way. Just tell Black Devil that." The top dog slowly arched his head back, stepped to the side, turned toward his crew, said something to them, turned around, and made for the river. The rest of them followed him. Only puddles of gasoline remained, reflecting the faded sky of August.

She moved in a week later. She didn't bring any stuff with her, saying that she wasn't sure whether things would work out between the two of us. Things did work out, but she started an earth-shattering fight a few months later. It went how it always does—the first spark came out of nowhere, but the flame of animosity devoured everything, consuming all our memories like a massive fire at the docks, destroying every single ship. She yelled for hours, deeply hurt by something. I was deeply hurt too, but mostly by my own reaction. Heading out the door, she said she'd be changing her number so I couldn't call her. I asked her not to do that, promising her I wouldn't call. But I called in the early evening, just to check. She really had changed her number. "Well, this is a good thing," I thought, still angry at myself. "It's a good thing I'm dead to her. It's a good thing everything happened so quickly and we didn't drag out our failing relationship. It's a really good thing, really, really good. What's so good about it, though?"

She came back a month later and then left again in the winter, asking me for some time to think things over. She got married while she was thinking, but didn't sever ties with me, obviously. I started feeling jealous of her husband.

"What do you need him for?" I asked. "What are you keeping him around for? You're just putting him through a lot of pain." She agreed with me, but couldn't divorce him, obviously. Well, and he wouldn't just leave without a fight. I wanted to have a talk with him.

She forbade me to do so, throwing hysterical fits and saying she'd kill herself if he found out about me. She promised to sort everything out, obviously, promised me that everything would be all right. In the spring, they got divorced.

"What was the point of getting married in the first place?" I asked. She explained, saying something about debts that we have to repay to those who love us, about the love that drives all of us, about payments and settlements, about honesty and justice. I realized that they were still seeing each other, although she'd never said anything about it, obviously. That's how the summer started. In June, she said she was pregnant. It wasn't mine, obviously. It wasn't his either, obviously.

## BOB

"I'd say that America really is a country where everyone enjoys equal opportunity," Bob Koshkin wrote in one of his concise emails to his friends and family. "In my view, America's unshakable constitutional framework and sound democratic principles are foundational to that equality. I believe in the viability and flexibility of American liberalism, under the auspices of which big business and government regulatory agencies work together harmoniously for a better future. The only thing that's a bit unsettling . . . that's not the right way to put it—the thing that absolutely floors me—is that there are just so many black people everywhere."

He had landed at John F. Kennedy International Airport two months ago, at the beginning of the summer, boldly disembarked, and forged on, thinking, "This is how Columbus must have felt way back when." He wobbled through the terminal like a sailor walking on solid ground; just thinking about the vast ocean he'd crossed made his muscles spasm, but he'd reached American soil and it was high time to explore the continent and civilize the natives. Once Bob got into the city, he called his old high school classmate who had been hanging his hat in the East Village for the past decade or so. His classmate showed up in half an hour wearing a bathrobe, no less. Bob was decked out in a cowboy hat with Carpathian red deer running around the band, a light jacket, and flashy, colorful shorts. There's a chance his classmate wouldn't have recognized him without those shorts. They hugged, and even kissed each other, looking like two transvestites meeting again after a prolonged separation. The transvestite in shorts was happy to see his old partner, while the transvestite in the bathrobe would have preferred to put the reunion off as long as possible. Bob's classmate didn't invite him back to his place. They went to the Chinese restaurant around the corner and ordered some tea. Bob was counting on his classmate picking up the tab, so he sat on his hands until he did. Bob opened up his dad's leather suitcase, with the heads of lovely East German girls pasted all over it, and took out a souvenir plate that had Crimean landscapes on it, of all things.

"I got this for you," Bob said. His classmate thanked him, catching a glimpse of Mount Ai-Petri.

"Oh," he said, "that's the first place I got the clap, in Yalta. I was there for training camp."

"Should I take it back?" Bob asked, embarrassed.

"Nah, man. Oddly enough, I remember that trip quite fondly."

"The faculty of memory," Bob noted in one of his subsequent messages, "is capable of reconciling things that initially seem incompatible or mutually exclusive in terms of their logical content. Sometimes I think that our consciousness is built out of our most sorrowful and heart-wrenching stories and memories. The all-encompassing nature of memory and the irreversible experiences it contains are probably what drove humanity to invent sports, the arts, and anesthesia."

His classmate walked him to the subway and then went about his business, holding the plate under his arm like a fallen halo. Bob took a train to the hallowed city of Philadelphia later that evening. Tracking down his relatives proved surprisingly easy—there were only two Koshkins in the phone book, his aunt Amalia and his uncle Sasha. Actually, his uncle was listed as Alex here in America, but Bob wasn't about to let that stop him. He dialed their number and was greeted by a slightly shrill voice that turned out to belong to his cousin Lilith. Bob told her about the purpose of his visit and his place in the Koshkin family tree at great length, swallowing long strings of consonants and losing his train of thought. He sensed that his story lacked credibility, but he pressed on, appealing to their childhood memories and good old Koshkin hospitality.

"Yep," he yelled into the phone, "you got it. I braved a Ukrainian Airlines flight and crusaded through all the duty-free zones! I haven't eaten in two whole days! But I never doubted I'd find your family and hold you in my brotherly embrace once again!" Lilith gave him directions. She warned him that getting on the train without a ticket wouldn't fly here in the States, and that they weren't going to come bail him out if he got caught.

The Koshkins had settled in Philadelphia a long while ago and weren't planning on moving back to Ukraine anytime soon. They'd picked up the language quickly, but they hadn't forgotten their roots. Uncle Alex worked for a big food wholesaler. Aunt Amalia had been a teacher, though Bob wasn't quite sure whether or not she was gainfully employed in America. Their sixteen-year-old daughter, Lilith, the family's pride and joy, dreamed of being a dentist one day.

"Good for her, choosing a career based on a realistic assessment of her talents," Bob wrote in one of his emails. "That's why I've always dreamt of going to Brazil and becoming the queen of Carnival." The Koshkins, an ethnically mixed family, had an odd lifestyle. They took a selective approach to adopting American customs. Despite the many years they had spent in this faraway land, they still celebrated all the Soviet and Orthodox holidays—in addition to the Jewish ones, of course. Easter and International Workers' Day blended together smoothly. One year, Uncle Alex's friends from some weird Hasidic anarchist group persuaded him to march in their parade. The Koshkins celebrated the Fourth of July, too, because they regarded it as a Jewish holiday, for some reason. Uncle Alex's colleagues didn't question his rationale; he was getting into the holiday spirit and that was good enough for them.

Bob's unexpected visit caused much consternation in the Koshkin household. This alien from the East spooked his hosts; his thick sideburns and flashy shorts made them want to make doubly sure that he had a return ticket. Bob's family back in Ukraine had severed all ties with their relatives overseas. Uncle Alex didn't remember his older brother, Seva, Bob's dad, very fondly. In fact, he remembered him as a complete prick, for several reasons. First, Bob's dad was a Party member; second, he had a grating personality; and third, he hadn't given Uncle Alex any of the money he made from selling their parents' cottage. It seemed like Uncle Alex had buried that distant past a long time ago, only to have it turn up on his doorstep again. He just didn't know how to react. At any rate, Uncle Alex decided to prepare his special pasta dish, and then the whole family gathered around the long dinner table and started looking through the pictures Bob had brought with him, where the young Koshkins, Seva and his little brother, were looking life straight in its suspicious eyes, their teeth flashing whitely in defiance at their indeterminate future. Seva was fit and self-assured, while Alex was chubby and effeminate. The old photographs clearly disgusted the latter.

"We were all victims of that totalitarian regime," he said, pointing a yellowed fingernail at the black-and-white images. "Just look at that gut of mine." The womenfolk examined Uncle Alex's potbelly, saying he looked pretty well fed for a "victim."

"What are you talking about?" Uncle Alex protested. "I was in good shape. I boxed for years. I broke my nose in two places. Look, the bridge is busted up, too." The womenfolk took to Bob right away and excitedly kept the conversation going. The dry California wine did a number on Aunt Amalia, an ample, middle-aged woman. She was enthralled by the pictures dating back to the late seventies, all those scenes of picnics and beaches; she offered nasty commentary on the cast's silly hairdos and outdated swimsuits. Naturally, Uncle Alex got the worst of it. Like any couple that had missed their chance at an amicable divorce, the two of them nagged each other incessantly. Aunt Amalia was really letting the luckless Uncle Alex have it, berating him for his pretense to a lifestyle he couldn't afford. Uncle

Alex could only take so much. She was about to finish him off for good, so somewhere between the pasta and the coconut cookies he excused himself, wishing his nephew sweet dreams and declaring resolutely that America, the cradle of democracy, would make a real man out of him, the kind of man who could be a worthy member of an open society—i.e., he wouldn't repeat the mistakes of his nutjob father, Seva. Aunt Amalia suggested drinking to that. Lilith skooched over closer to Bob.

Bob found himself between two women—now he could relax. He had finally done what his father had asked him to do: he had restored balance to things, found the remnants of their family scattered across the world, gathered all the Koshkins together, and listened to the shared blood pumping through their veins. What is it that really ties a family together, after all? Remembering the deceased and procreating to secure your legacy.

"Speaking of procreating . . . ," Bob thought to himself, furtively eyeing Lilith. She took after her mother—she had the same wide hips, the same hairdo, and the same bright red lips. Her mom was looking about as good as could be expected, considering her lifestyle. You could plainly see what the future held for Lilith. The next twenty years or so were going to take a serious toll on her.

"A lack of transparency makes it unclear how one should pursue upward mobility," Bob speculated in one of his emails to his dad. "Faced with a lack of legitimate ways to climb the social ladder, we often resort to practices that are purely spiritual in nature, such as starting a family, joining a church, or even just daily meditation. Unfortunately, this journey usually ends in rehab." Lilith sat by him for a whole hour after that, inching closer and closer until he could feel the fiery curve of her hips. She criticized the locals and their proclivities, commended Bob for having such strong convictions, and chewed bubble gum; the aroma of her oils and lotions nearly overpowered him.

"Boy, I'd like to get her into the sack," Bob thought to himself, as he told them about his native city's struggle with xenophobia and the problems of post-totalitarian life. "But she's my cousin. What would others think about our relationship? Sleeping with your cousin may be frowned upon in the country of enduring democracy. That's something people only do in the East. There's something so hopelessly post-totalitarian about all this. Only we could think of doing something like that." So he turned toward his Aunt Amalia, still feeling the heat emanating from his cousin's nubile body and greedily inhaling the fragrant air through his nostrils. Meanwhile, Aunt Amalia was getting fired up, smoking her menthols and picking at the cold pasta like it was a dead patient lying on the operating table after a long and unsuccessful surgery. She told Bob about their family's trials and tribulations, about their long years in exile, about having to ride in boxcars and ships' holds, about transit zones, about having their clothes disinfected, about the scent of freedom, about equal opportunity, about squeezing the slave out of yourself, drop by drop, about enduring democracy as the foundation for inner peace, and about multiculturalism as the foundation for coexistence, even with black people.

"Obviously, we identify most with the ethnic Ukrainians and their moral code," she told Bob, her voice somewhat grating from the alcohol. "They're all nationalists. That's what draws us to them." Bob couldn't see any real logic in her claim, but he still enjoyed talking about nationalism in the abstract. When he was asked about the goings-on back in the old country, he gave them the following answer:

"Obviously, we have all witnessed numerous cataclysms that have left an indelible and irreversible mark on the city itself, and on its residents, for that matter. Clerics, ventriloquists, and street magicians fought doggedly for years, and eventually took control of city hall. Racing all the way up the social ladder before anyone could knock them down and getting to the top of the political hierarchy, they decided to tackle the most pressing issues. First of all, the city walls were reinforced, with special care being taken on the east side, where the threat of nomadic border tribes loomed. Also, two long avenues were built, one stretching from the eastern gate to the western gate and the other running from the bridges up north to the basin down south. A pyramid was erected where the two avenues intersect to symbolize the new government's commitment to tasteful architecture and fiscal transparency. Events commemorating the memory and legacy of our dearly departed ancestors have become a regular occurrence. Water from the city's two rivers is consecrated every Sunday for use by the utilities department. There are more flags around town now, too.

"The insignia they bear are mostly lions, jackals, and fighting cocks," Bob continued, "which are supposed to represent the government's firm commitment to further social upheaval. Although many reforms have been implemented smoothly and effectively, the problems of post-totalitarianism and xenophobia still haven't been eradicated. This new, post-totalitarian state has knocked all the social ladders out from under me, so I have no hope of moving up. I've been dealt a bad hand—I'm forced to waste away in the back alleys of the ghetto, fecklessly contemplating the ills of social inequality and religious intolerance.

"And those assholes," Bob exclaimed, crying and alternately tugging at Aunt Amalia's arm and leg, "are gonna keep me down, they're never gonna give me a chance."

Aunt Amalia was listening, biting her lip anxiously. Lilith was patting Bob on the back, which made him sob even more theatrically. It was only after midnight had rolled around, another bottle of California wine had been polished off, and Bob's tall tales had escalated to the realm of two-headed state employees responsible for education and burning witches in the central market, that Aunt Amalia had finally had enough. She suggested that everyone go to sleep, preferably in separate beds. Leaving the dining room, she assured Bob that he'd come to the right place, and that America, the cradle of multiculturalism, would make a real man out of him—if he acted like one, of course.

He couldn't even look at the pasta the next morning.

That's how his Philadelphia summer got under way. He didn't have much of anything to do because nobody had offered him a job yet—he had two months left until his flight back home, two months to explore the unknown and absorb his new reality. During the first few days, Bob took some pictures by the Rocky statue and stopped by the Ukrainian Cultural Center. Its young members, who had been born in exile, were discussing Ukrainian nationalism. They took Bob for an Irishman because of his thick accent and red sideburns, but they had no idea how this fuckin' Irish guy could know each and every member of the Ukrainian Parliament. They arm-wrestled a bit and sang some nationalist songs. Bob made a big show of not wanting to join in, but it didn't last—pure, Irish-bred love for Ukraine filled his passionate voice. Bob fell asleep toward the end of the meeting, slouched over in his chair. The other guys called him a cab, but they didn't know his address. They went through his pockets and found his cellphone. He had a picture of the Rocky statue as his wallpaper, so that's where they dropped him off.

Late at night, after his relatives had wandered off to their respective quarters, Bob would read emails from his family and friends back home.

"Dear Bob," his dad wrote, "never come back to this godforsaken city, no matter what! Do everything in your power to stay in the country of enduring democracy and stick by that brother of mine, life's really run him into the ground. This city doesn't deserve to be loved and remembered by you. It's already kicked me around enough. It's taken my faith, hope, and Party card away from me. Don't ever come back here again! But if you do decide to come back, please see if there are any Chinese guys down at the market that can get you some cheap blades for my lawnmower." His mom's emails didn't have the same degree of pathos, but they were just as troubling. There was talk of a default and another planned power outage.

"Supposedly, the ATMs only dispense large bills with some mysterious markings on them. Apparently, some mutated strain of *E. coli* was found in the city's reservoir. I don't know, Bobby—the government has been consecrating the water and all, but what's the use? What was the point of all that social upheaval of theirs? I've heard the city fathers have all gotten Chinese passports, so it's only a matter of time before they hand the keys to the city over to the Communist Party of China. Rumor has it that there will be a sugar and flour shortage soon. Life is chock-full of mirages and mysteries, and you have to have nerves of steel and a cool head just to get through the morning news—the things going on chill you to the heart. Anyway, your family and your ever-hospitable homeland wait eagerly to embrace you once more."

Zhora, his other cousin, who was employed at a 24-hour pharmacy, wrote the most interesting emails, giving him the full rundown. As a fully qualified practitioner of medicine, Zhora wrote in an eloquent and didactic tone, and he didn't turn up his nose at the opportunity for the occasional lyrical digression. He told Bob that their neighbor Thomas had started dating a girl who used to be a prostitute. Everyone in the whole apartment building was concerned. Well, and it looked like Mark, a distant relative of theirs through Aunt Maria, was doin' his cousin.

"You never know what unexpected turn fate will take next," Zhora wrote, referring to these odd relationships. "Just don't let it rattle you, and you'll be all right. Make sure to say hello to Lilith for me. She's such a sweetheart."

There was no need whatsoever to remind Bob about his cousin, though. Lilith had taken up residence in his heart and wreaked havoc. She'd be on his mind when he got up in the morning and she'd be on his mind when he turned in at night. In the morning, he'd lie there on his air mattress and listen to her getting out of bed and rushing to get ready for school, searching frantically for her clothes and phone and putting on her makeup. At night, as he lay there listening to her blabbing away on Skype and falling soundly asleep, his broken heart would nearly stop. He'd listen to her pajamas rustling and the movie stars and pro soccer players talking in her dreams. He saw her come out of her room, scantily clad, a few times. One time she asked him to do up her bra in the back, but he wasn't up to the task. Also, Aunt Amalia happened to be walking down the hallway right then, so they all felt a bit awkward. He'd occasionally see her panties hanging in the kitchen, which he took as proof that God and all the saints really did exist. Sometimes she wouldn't get back from hanging out with her friends until early morning. Aunt Amalia would start scolding her, and Bob would lie there on his mattress, mad with jealousy and boundless sympathy. They had a small Fourth of July celebration, just for the family. Lilith wasn't really into it—she hardly even spoke to Bob and outright ignored her parents. Bob was hitting the dry California wine hard, engaging Uncle Alex in a discussion of how the American democratic system affects the stability of the oil market. Aunt Amalia had been drinking since she got up, so she was definitely on Bob's side. That's how it was that summer. Aunt Amalia would back Bob, but Lilith wasn't coming around. Bob slipped into a serious funk. He stopped in at the Ukrainian Cultural Center a few days later. They took him for an Irishman once again, but this time they beat him up instead of singing with him. The sun hung high, seemingly detached from the city of Philadelphia. The air was saturated with utter hopelessness. He wanted to hang himself, preferably in her room, preferably not for long. He tried writing her love notes and camping out by her door at night. But all his efforts were in vain—summer was trickling by, dragging all his hopes and dreams away. Lilith was out sowing her wild oats, only coming home when she needed some fresh clothes.

Somewhere near the beginning of August, with a mere four days remaining before his flight back, Aunt Amalia suggested they throw Bob a going-away party. She and Bob were the only ones in attendance. Lilith blatantly snubbed them, while Uncle Alex got held up at work. He did call, though, telling them to start the festivities without him. Amalia drank and griped about the trials of family life—the callousness of men and the ingratitude of children. Bob backed her up as best he could, saying, "Yeah, yeah, callousness, ingratitude, and God knows what else." Amalia decided to call her daughter a little before midnight; she immediately threw a fit, yelling, crying, and making empty threats. Suddenly, she passed the phone to Bob.

"What's going on back there?" He heard Lilith's serene and slightly cold voice. Bob looked around the room. Amalia was crying in the corner, her fingers clinging to her menthol cigarette. An empty serving dish crowned the table.

"We're having a party," he told his cousin.

"Okay, here's what we're gonna do. You put her to bed. Then you go to bed, too. I'll be home shortly." Her voice didn't sound as metallic, and, moreover, Bob understood what she was getting at. "Of course," he thought. "This is it. She's planned everything out; she's thought everything through. She means, 'Go to bed, but don't fall asleep. I'll be home shortly. I just can't wait.' Did she actually say 'I just can't wait?' Obviously she did. I heard it with my own two ears." Bob helped Amalia ascend the steps to the second floor, and as soon as she collapsed on her bed, without even taking off her housecoat, he raced over to his room and started getting ready for Lilith. He put his dirty laundry away, took some dishes to the kitchen, lit a candle—setting some magazines on fire in the process—soused everything with water, hastily tried to air out the room, struggled to close the window (he just couldn't figure it out), and then finally lay down in his drafty room. Ten minutes passed, then twenty, then forty. Despair was gradually tightening its grip on him. His eyes grew tired of staring into the dark. Suddenly, something squeaked in the hallway. "The door! The front door!" he thought, immediately recognizing the sound. It was her. Timid steps pattered down the hallway; somebody bumped into the wall a few times, the door to his room squeaked open too, and a warm, female figure slid through the gloom and landed next to him. Before he could launch into his rehearsed speech about the insurmountable thirst for love and about temptation which, once yielded to, could not be renounced, he caught a glimpse of slightly faded curls, Aunt Amalia's curls—he was truly horrified when he noticed the menthol cigarette in her right hand, overcome with despair when he felt her left hand creeping down his stomach. But before Aunt Amalia managed to do anything nice or anything that would be of any use to him, his nerves snapped, breaking like guitar strings, and all the wistfulness and penitence that had been accumulating in him for the past few months came bursting out, severing all of Aunt Amalia's hopes for a long, sleepless night, severing all of Bob's aspirations to dig down to some golden intimacy. To her credit, Amalia didn't say a word. She merely settled in next to him, pulled yet another cigarette from the pocket of her housecoat, and started waiting. Bob talked the whole time, trying to adopt a flat and self-assured tone—not making any excuses, yet explaining everything to her, trying not to look silly, but still aiming to have them laugh it off.

"Extended abstinence," he explained. "Meditation and vows of self-denial. We warrior monks handle cold steel weapons more often than women, so it should come as no surprise that such an unfortunate mishap occurred. But do not, on any account, reproach yourself," he told Amalia, "don't assume any of the blame—you did everything right, you did everything you could, you did everything as you've grown accustomed to do, you poor, hapless woman." It's just that he'd grown accustomed to slightly different types of relationships and a different degree of passion, which he'd demonstrate presently—Bob spoke with a great deal of confidence, since somewhere deep down in his heart, which had been broken and haphazardly pieced back together, he felt a certain eagerness to continue this struggle to which he was already committed. So he intercepted her left hand and placed it on his stomach. Amalia was about to get frisky—she even put her cigarette aside—but as soon as she touched what Bob had been pontificating about for the past forty-five minutes, everything played out much as it had the first time around. Dejected, Amalia merely wiped her hand on her damp housecoat, while Bob despairingly scrunched himself up under a heap of pillows to hide his shame and hopelessness. Suddenly, the front door squeaked open. This time it actually was Lilith. Bob heard a cold, crystalline jingling somewhere beneath his throat. That was the last remnants of his heart breaking. Amalia got up and stepped out into the hallway, making no effort to be discreet. She asked her daughter something and told her something. Lilith laughed buoyantly and then headed to her room. The inside lock of her bedroom door slammed down with a thud in the silence of the house.

In the morning, Bob informed everyone that he had to leave right away, since he'd arranged a bunch of important business meetings in NYC before his flight back home. He simply couldn't waste another minute of his precious time. He thanked everyone for their hospitality, offered to pay for the broken shower head, and promised to write. "No big deal," he thought feverishly. "I'll camp out at my classmate's place for the next three days. Just get as far away from this shameful debacle as possible." Oddly enough, his relations were saddened and moved by having to say goodbye, encouraging him to come back anytime, even tomorrow, if he wanted, trying to talk him out of leaving at all, tempting him, and providing him with unsolicited advice. For some reason, Uncle Alex was the one who was beating himself up the most over Bob leaving them. Lilith was the least affected. Amalia walked him to the front door and gave him a tender kiss on the lips.

"Women, it's all because of them," he thought, as the train ripped past the grim outskirts of Philadelphia toward the expansive horizon. "It's our interactions with them and our interest in them that change everything in our hearts. Life never makes any guarantees — in most cases it asks you to take it at its word. When you do trust it, when you open up and leave yourself defenseless, life sweeps away all your hopes and dreams like a raging river sweeping away a fishing village. My path of conquest across America, that wild land to which submission is utterly foreign, was severed by a woman's tender yet firm movements, by the exceedingly deep and smoke-filled breaths of one woman and the slightly immature — scratch that — the incredibly childish, reckless abandon of another. Who will rescue me from this sad predicament? Who can I depend on? My family won't be able to help me at all — it's not their job to fix my premature ejaculation. My friends won't solve my problems; they'll merely commiserate with me for a while, then dump their own troubles on me. What stories could they tell? What advice could they give? One of them is sleeping with his first cousin, and one of them is dating a former prostitute. What do prostitutes have to do with me?" Bob pondered, getting even more riled up. "What is prostitution, when you get right down to it? Undoubtedly, it means your life's a complete wreck, that you've fallen and given in to meekness. Then what is it about those women that attracts us? What compels us to lend a helping hand? What drives us to find common ground with them? Society's scorn for them? Undoubtedly, it's society's scorn for them. Courageous and valiant men are the last to pay any heed to society's sanctimonious double standards. It's just the opposite, they defy religious and moral dogma. They find women who are no less courageous and valiant, then they stick with them, since it is alongside these women that they experience the fullness of life and the depth of feeling. What kind of people decide to become prostitutes? Those blessed by fate. Strong, complete individuals. Tameless lovers, happy brides, children showered with love. Heroes of Socialist Labor, straight-A students. Mothers with many children and inexhaustible reserves of tenderness, widows who adopt orphans and love the dry breath of champagne. So who else should I be thinking about?" Bob wondered, bouncing around in between train cars on his way to NYC. "Who else should I exalt in my daily quest to get in touch with my spiritual side? After all, most of them lead much more meaningful lives than I do, lives charged with social significance and public-spirited activism. I'm sure that their ranks are mostly filled by environmental activists and politicians, managers of institutions of high culture, and church choir singers. Undoubtedly, most of them are well-versed in the fields of political economy and public relations; undoubtedly, most of them tend to identify most closely with the neoliberal model of economic development and the Bologna Process. They are all fascinated by choral music and team sports; they all successfully juggle their interests in surfing, tennis, and healthy morning runs. In the morning, they gather at their local swimming pools and gyms to praise providence for the opportunity to be part of time and space, for the joy they derive from being immersed in the dark river of this epoch, for the sweet honey on their lips and the roses at their feet, and the joy of socializing with the most renowned visionaries and inventors of this heroic age." Suddenly, Bob understood that he was raving, possibly even out loud. It's a good thing there were only black people around—they could never understand him anyway. White people couldn't understand him either, as a matter of fact. Nevertheless, he was coming down with something, which was to be expected, much like the rain in November. He had to nurse this cold. He had to get back home.

At the train station, a few meek yet cheerful Chinese women sitting at a fast-food joint located on the floor above their noodle place caught his eye immediately. Their porcelain necks bent over their food, as if enacting a movement they had been trained for, seemingly serving as a testament to female placidity and submission. In the subway, he came across a group of Italians examining a city map so excitedly and arguing so heatedly that one would have thought they were reading one of the early Futurist manifestos aloud. They emitted heat and the smell of tender, nearly imperceptible sweat, which reminded Bob of swimming in the rivers and manmade lakes of his hometown, the little booths to change in, and the August beaches with all their sun and unsanitary conditions.

His classmate wasn't picking up the phone or responding to texts. Bob found his address online and went by his place, but he was out, just as Bob had expected. "No biggie," he thought, trying to keep his cool. "I'll camp out here until tomorrow. He's gotta come back eventually." His passport, return ticket, and last hundred bucks were in his shorts pocket. He didn't feel like springing for a hostel. Bob dragged himself down the city's hot streets, believing he'd soon receive a sign from above, his faith in mankind's higher vocation never wavering. A wild Puerto Rican girl's black flowing hair slapped him as she crossed an intersection. On his way out of a small Greek restaurant where he'd bought a bottle of water, a scantily clad German girl with fair hair, soft peach fuzz on her lean body, a rock-hard stomach, and a piercing dangling from her nose like a band attached to a tame dove's leg pressed up against him. He was lugging his suitcase around—it was getting heavier as the day progressed—dreaming about taking a short respite, hot tea, and a woman's cold skin. He stumbled across the local Ukrainian Cultural Center in the early evening. Some Poles got him sloshed. A few drinks in, he tried paying for himself and his new friends, but the Poles refused to accept his offering, assuring him that it was an honor to carouse with such a hellishly jolly Irishman and that Ireland was Poland's sister country.

"Dude, the women in your country!" they yelled, looking at Bob's thick sideburns enviously. "Dude, the women in your country! They have fiery red hair, like squirrels. As pale as jellyfish! As tall as mast pines! Spangled with freckles like the constellations captains use to guide their ships!"

They didn't take Bob back to their place for the night, however — they limited their appreciation to words and expressions of their deep admiration for Irish women. "What are they telling me all this for?" Bob thought, weeping and lying on a bench warmed by the hot sun outside a Protestant church. "Why are they wringing my heart out? What do Irish women have to do with me? I've never been with an Irish girl. I've never even been with a Northern Irish girl! I've never been with a Puerto Rican girl, a Brazilian girl, or a Peruvian girl, either. I don't know what their love tastes like, what it feels like, what it sounds like coming from their lips. I just want to go home — to that city of sun that I left so heedlessly. I've drifted dangerously far from it, completely lost the sensation of it. I lost all sensation a while ago." This thought raced through Bob's mind because it was actually true — he couldn't feel his throat, his tongue, his pain, or his life. That's how he fell asleep . . . He dreamed of the queen of England.

The morning brought hope and relief. His temperature had gone back down; his blood, stagnant during the night, was now bubbling throughout his body, and pigeons were sitting on his suitcase, pecking out the eyes of the East German girls. A young dark-skinned girl was doing some unbelievable exercises in the park across the street. Her legs were tangled up in such unfamiliar knots that Bob's cheerful morning mood was wrecked instantly; yesterday's wistfulness and uncertainty had returned. He headed for his classmate's apartment, taking great pains to dodge the sunny waitresses carrying chairs outside and unfurling snow-white tablecloths and the elderly postwomen looking at passersby with tremulous attention, as though they were potential addressees. He dodged the ancient nuns flashing their ceramic dentures and the portly policewomen — their powerful arms made him want to give himself up to their embraces and their handcuffs made him want to be fettered for the rest of his life. His class-

mate still wasn't home. Making inquiries with his neighbors didn't do
any good—if anything, it made matters worse. A Japanese girl sprang
out of the next apartment down, poorly concealing her private parts
with a blanket. Actually, she was just waving it around like a flag. Bob's
eyes unconsciously, yet unwaveringly, slid up her dark, shaved calves,
her hips, tinted gold by the light, and everything else she had to show,
although that wasn't a whole lot, considering her age. Nevertheless,
it was enough to send him into a deep melancholic state; he thanked
her vaguely and said goodbye, slinking off to a nearby park, where he
bummed around all day. In the evening, he found a soup kitchen,
had a meal, and told the women dishing out the food all about his
trials and tribulations. They listened attentively but didn't offer him
seconds. "Those whores! Is this what their faith teaches them? Is this
the kind of behavior their pastors recommend? Why couldn't they let
me stay in that damn soup kitchen until morning? Bunch of whores,"
he repeated to himself. "Yeah . . . whores! Prostitutes are the only ones
in this city who could possibly understand me! They're the only ones
I can count on. They're the only ones who could actually help me.
I've got this damn hundred-dollar bill in my pocket—am I just gonna
take it home with me? No way!" He tried thinking it through logically.
"Souvenirs? I can get the same souvenirs cheaper back in Ukraine. A
hostel? They're for wimps. I just have to find a woman here. I have to
fix everything, start anew, like I'm filling an old riverbed with fresh
water. I just have to nab some Surinamese girl. Or an Ethiopian girl.
An Ethiopian girl would give me a breath of joy and serenity. She
really would. Or a Japanese girl," he kept pondering, still lying on
the same bench, head now resting on his suitcase. "Japanese women
can resurrect the dead with their tongues. They'd raise me up like
Lazarus, dust the clay and dark seaweed off me, and set my internal
organs, stalled like frozen steam engines, into motion. Or a Brazilian
girl," he thought, already sound asleep. "The queen of Carnival, with
feet like red-hot coals and palms as damp as rocks on the shore in the
morning. She'd have incredible stamina and flexibility; she'd take me

to where the gates of the airport stand open to travelers, make sure I got on the correct flight, and then send me short, funny letters about nothing." That night it started raining. Bob woke up with a stuffy nose, and his temperature had come back. There were twenty-four hours left until his departure.

But even his stuffy nose could detect all the smells and smoke of this city, its August skin, scorched by the sun and bleached by the ocean. He looked at the pigeons, surprisingly calm in the constant commotion, the yogis and monks, observed the dragons on the rooftops and the hyenas rooting around in the dumpsters, shielded his eyes against the bloody rays of the morning sun, and wrapped his sodden jacket around his shoulders, but he wasn't getting any cozier. Just as the thought of heading to the airport and waiting out the last twenty-four hours before his flight popped into his head, a bunch of jovial drunkards, who had noticed him earlier yet decided against tearing him away from his brooding and melancholic morning reflection, understanding the true delicacy of the matter, as jovial drunkards so often do, shouted to get his attention. Once they saw that Bob was really hurting and the demons of morning blues were absolutely devouring him from the inside, they hollered at him to join their merry festivities and hospitably handed him some strange beverage. The natives themselves didn't know what it was called; all they could tell him was that some Poles sold this poison at their nearby store, though not even they could pronounce its name.

"Polish has so many hushing consonants," they shouted excitedly, pouring Bob drink after drink. "One shudders to imagine how their church services sound! Hymns cluttered with all those consonants have gotta wake God up in the morning!" They were talking to Bob, and he even answered them, but nobody was listening to him; they kept talking and talking as the hyenas scurried into the shade and yellow snakes wove nests in the metal trash cans. The sun was blazing over church bell towers and billboards, bouncing off the windows up where the city's warm air hovered, where rooms were filled with life and August drafts were skipping down fire escapes. The women walking down the street smiled at him, waved their hats and kerchiefs amiably, shouting cheerful and tender words, exclamations so tightly interwoven with hushing consonants and palatized vowels that Bob didn't dare touch these nodes of language, golden, like cells in a bee-hive, packed with joy and delight. Joy and delight were just what he had the direst need of when he woke up that morning and found his dad's old suitcase unscathed; it was for the sake of joy and delight that he charged into the late evening twilight, searching for public trans-portation and brotherly love.

He made for the Bronx, crossed the river, and found them. They were standing outside some banks and clothing stores, closed at such a late hour. One might even have concluded that they bought their outfits at those very stores. Bob stood still, warily sniffing around like a seasoned stray dog, thinking about turning back . . . but then he real-ized it was now or never: "I'll keep reproaching myself for being so weak-willed and I'll continue to search for some sort of justification for my fears and insecurities if I don't go for it. C'mon, Columbus, move your flippers," he said, pushing himself toward all the Puerto Rican and Surinamese girls of the Bronx. There's plenty of fish in the sea, and he soon came upon one, a short, rail-thin woman with dyed black hair, a sharp nose, and an improbably large bust—which made her all the more tempting. Her velvety voice halted him, causing his heart to spring back out of the realm of oblivion.

"Wanna chill out for a bit?" Her tone inspired trust.

"Chill out how?" Bob answered with a question, his heart aflut-ter, listening to the falling tone of her voice.

"I'll show you a good time for fifty," she promised, moving her hand back and forth as though she were brushing her teeth. "Two hundred for everything else. Don't worry, I'm on the level and it's all legal. What's your name?" Bob answered; she didn't even bother try-ing to remember, immediately introducing herself as Mel.

"Mem?" he asked.

"Forget it," she said. "It doesn't matter."

They settled on fifty bucks. Mel-Mem took him by the arm with an air of confidence and led him down the street. Her girlfriends avoided making eye contact with her.

"We almost there?" Bob asked.

"Another quarter-mile," she assured him. "It's slow going in these heels, though."

Bob finally noticed them. It probably wasn't too easy for her to walk . . . but they had to keep going. "Let me get us a cab," she suggested. Bob tensed up, but didn't object. She waved at a taxi that seemed to be waiting for them. They hopped in, drove half a block, and stopped.

"Pay him," she said quietly. Bob handed the cab driver a ten-dollar bill; he thanked them cheerfully. For some reason, the cab driver put him at ease. "He could have taken us outside the city," Bob thought, "and dismembered us. Well, that's what I would have done at least." They passed a Chinese restaurant, then ducked through an arch, crossed a courtyard, skirted some shiny metal dumpsters, ascended some stairs, and opened a dark, inconspicuous door. Two security guards were sitting on chairs by the entrance to the building. Their unfriendly, inattentive eyes slid down Bob and Mel-Mem, and then they resumed their conversation. She snatched a key from one of them and dragged Bob up another steep flight of stairs. There were red lamps hanging on the walls and the floor was covered with shaggy white carpeting. The place felt like a darkroom. It smelled like one, too.

They walked to the end of a hallway; she opened a door and stepped through. He peered inside—the room was gloomy and dank. There was a small, empty desk off to the left, while a large bed with some strange curly wooden banisters, silk sheets, and other crap loomed off to the right. "Uncle Alex's bed looked just like this one," Bob recalled suddenly, which made him even more dejected. Off to the side, an open door led toward a small shower. The lights were on, and there were clean towels hanging up. She immediately took charge, like a chipper hostess.

"All righty then, do you want to take a shower?"

"I've been wanting to for three days now," Bob answered.

"Okay. Give me some money and I'll get us something to drink. You have to buy drinks here," she explained. "What do you want?"

"Is there any Polish booze?" Bob inquired.

"I'll find out," she said, taking his money. "What's the matter with your nose?" She was referring to Bob's sniffling. "Drugs?"

"Boxing," Bob explained. "The bridge of my nose is all busted up." Then she turned around and left without saying a word.

"She's not coming back, obviously," he thought, lying on the bed and contemplating the shadows on the ceiling. "She's clearly left this building and evaporated. She's long gone. I probably won't ever see her again. Obviously, I won't even recognize her if we do cross paths again. Mem, oh Mem, where have you gone? Why'd you drag me over here onto these fiery sheets? Why'd you ditch me in the middle of the stuffy summer night—without any love, without any compassion, and without any alcohol to boot?"

The door opened quietly, and she slid inside.

"How ya doing?" she asked. "How's the shower?"

"It works," Bob answered succinctly. Not sure what he was getting at, she simply handed him a glass filled with golden poison. "If I don't die, I'll inherit eternal life," Bob thought, and drank it in one gulp. Then she got down to business. She had a certain fierce intensity about her. But there was something mechanical, disheartening, and utterly unpromising about that intensity; too many frills, too much facade. At first, she made Bob lie down and keep still, as if she didn't know what to expect from him, and the mere fact that he could move of his own volition was unnerving. She followed his changing facial expressions warily, listened closely to the gurgling sounds coming from the back of his throat, and groped at his crazy-ass shorts, either to please him or just because — or to check if he was packing some psychotropic substances or, at the very least, some kind of knife or switchblade. She started moaning immediately — without interrupting her task. She was moaning with stubborn passion. At one point, Bob started feeling like an infant being rocked to sleep. He even lifted his head to make sure she was doing all right. Unlike him, she was doing just fine — she was toiling away, two-handed, as though she were trying to light a fire with soggy kindling. Eventually, she lifted her head, too, intercepting his gaze. She stopped brusquely and tossed back a strand of hair that had fallen into her face.

"What's the deal? Too much alcohol?" she asked.

"Yep, that's part of it," Bob answered dejectedly.

"Well, how 'bout this . . ." She took her job seriously, and something about this cowboy with Irish deer running around his hatband had gotten to her, so she wanted him to get his money's worth. "Throw in another fifty bucks and I'll let you touch my breasts."

"What will you let me do?" Bob didn't understand what she'd said. But she was already releasing her incredible, cosmic, synthetic bust, dangling it in the bluish pink twilight of this darkroom. What else could he do but go with it? "I'll bum a ride to the airport," Bob thought.

"Mem," he said quietly, yet firmly. "This is all I've got left. I don't have fifty bucks . . . but I don't want anything else. Come on . . ." She agreed, snatching his last few crumpled bills and getting back to work, just like last time — firmly intent on not giving up until she got to the finish line. When that didn't help she took a short breather, and then informed him in her dry yet still deep and velvety voice, like an employee at the DMV, that if he didn't come within the next hour he'd have to pay extra, and since he was out of cash (she knew that for a fact!) there was no telling where that would lead. Well, you know how these kinds of things generally play out — you'd think some secret, some hidden and unspoken visions and stirring experiences would surface, and he'd see the faces of the most beautiful women imaginable in the translucent, placid darkness and recover his great-est hopes and dreams from the back alleys of his past. But none of that actually happened. The mechanics of a woman's tender touch and lengthy intimate labor can generally be relied upon to work their sweet magic, so after a few short minutes all those involved reached a happy ending, without any financial complications, any unpaid debts or unperformed duties. She wiped him off with some paper napkins, he looked at her dark silhouette and thought of how his fingers had come upon the thin, tender, and nearly imperceptible scars under her breasts, left behind when she pumped them with all that gel, making them soft and bouncy. The scars didn't go away, though. And they never will.

Then she sat there with him in the dingy room for a bit, mightily pretending that she was in no hurry, that customers were treated with respect around here, that she wasn't just interested in making *that* happen (who could be, really?), but also in what was on his mind. She tried making conversation, told him about herself, saying that she was one-hundred-percent American, born and bred ("Well good for you," he thought), was raised with wholesome values ("I can see that"), graduated from a respectable community college ("about thirty years ago"), then got married ("to some fag"), but then she wound up here ("It could have been much worse"), and now she has to do this de-grading work ("Well stop fucking whining and do it, then"), but she still believed that everything would work out ("I highly doubt that") and she'd eventually go back to school and get a four-year degree ("Yeah, maybe if you buy one in Ukraine, Mem").

"What are the women like where you come from?" she asked Bob.

"Our women have one odd trait; they can get pregnant without having sex."

"Huh? How does that work?"

"They can . . . they are impregnated by the wind and rays of sun-light, just like flowers. They use bees and butterflies to conceive; in the spring, they expose themselves to the sun and moonlight and they bear their fruit gladly and easily, like knowledge imparted by an institution of higher learning."

"Yeah, but what about sex?"

"They perceive sex as the highest demonstration of their love, as the finest line showing their deepest affection—a line so fearful to cross, but so hard to spurn. They grow up to love; they're raised to prepare themselves for their glorious time of love and devotion, for that heart-wrenching dependence on waiting for and parting with loved ones. Our men know this, so they prepare themselves to take on women whose tenderness is inexhaustible and whose passion is unmanageable. There's so much love where I live. The men see no point in leaving their women, because they'll fall in love with them again sooner or later anyway, so why bother?"

"Are you sure you're not on drugs?"

Somebody was already waiting for him outside, at the arch leading back to the brightly lit street. He was a large Surinamese or Ethiopian man—it was hard to tell because it was so dark and foreboding in the courtyard. Bob stepped out of the building, and the guy simply blocked his way.

"Well hello there, punk," he said as Bob tried dodging him. "You knew I was coming for you. You're not gonna get off that easy." Bob stopped. The dark-skinned man was barely visible, so it seemed as though emptiness was meshing with emptiness and emptiness was speaking out of emptiness.

"All right, now empty your pockets," he said to Bob. "I know you're a boxer and all. You think I'm dumb or something, don't you?" Bob didn't think he was dumb at all. Bob couldn't even see him—he could only hear him. But the man's self-assured tone made him realize that he simply couldn't back down. Also, he couldn't count on anyone else in this part of the world, amid this darkness and emptiness. He realized that fate, that conniving witch, had thrown him so far away from home that there was nothing left beyond him—the universe was breaking off, coming to an end; a little distance away it was simply absent. The only way to go from here was back the way he came. But first he had to settle things with this Surinamese guy—Ethiopian guy, rather.

"I don't have anything, you know that," he said wearily.

"I don't know what you're talking 'bout. Empty your pockets, otherwise you'll be stuck here."

"All right, screw you. I've got something for you." Bob produced a slightly tattered, yet rather fragrant parcel from some secret pocket in his shorts—clearly something precious, something carefully and skillfully wrapped in tabloid journalism, printed in some other-worldly language, a language from the other side of the planet that nobody here could use to communicate or profess their love.

"Death," Bob wrote as he waited to board his flight, "often throws us for a loop. Sometimes we take its presence as a sign that it has come for us, but sometimes its appearance doesn't have anything to do with us. Death is just as present in our lives as love, trust, or nostalgia. It comes up out of nowhere; it moves along its own route, so you shouldn't even dream about being able to alter that route. All you can do is believe and hope. All you can do is love and accept life the way it is—as something unbearably incredible . . . or rather as something incredibly unbearable."

## LUKE

At the end of August, she called again.

"Did you hear about Luke? Throat cancer. But he doesn't want to get any treatment."

"Yeah, I sure did," I answered. "Is that what you're calling about?"

"Yep. His birthday is the day after tomorrow. He wants everybody to come to his place. I think he wants to say goodbye. Are you going?"

"Well, since he asked, I'm definitely going. What about you?"

"That's why I'm calling. Let's go together."

"All right," I agreed immediately. "You driving?"

"Wasn't planning on it. I was gonna take the train. That's why I'm asking you to come along."

"Good thinking. Who drives to a birthday party? Ya can't drink."

"Come on, Matthew, you think I'm gonna be drinkin'? I'm three months pregnant," she said indignantly.

She was waiting for me by the ticket office. Long hair pulled into a tight bun — reliable, safe, comfortable. Sneakers, denim overalls, warm sweater. Showing, but just barely. Serious face. It was sunny, but she'd dressed as though we were heading out on a long, nighttime hike through the mountains. Standing next to her in my threadbare T-shirt, I felt like a beachgoer hanging around in a hotel lobby. At first, she just extended her hand formally, but then she quickly dropped her air of restraint and wrapped her arms around my neck — not going far enough to give me the wrong idea, but expressing enough genuine emotion that I wouldn't forget where we were going.

"Do we need to get him a gift or anything?" I asked, without letting go of her.

"A gift? Like what?" she answered, clearly surprised.

"Flowers or something like that."

"You might as well buy him a wreath. We'll pick up some wine at the store by the station," she added in a conciliatory tone, pushing me back like she was propelling herself off the side of a pool.

She chose her seat in the half-empty train car, on the sunny side, facing the direction it was moving. She sat down and watched as we rolled out of the station, leaving the last of the city's seemingly endless chemical tanks behind; the greenery of its streets and parks blotted out its brick buildings, the leafy horizon suddenly burst out from behind factory fences, the suburbs cropped up, more stations popped into view, and passengers—fishermen, secondhand dealers, and people heading to their cottages—were milling around out there, exposed to the afternoon sun. The train pushed forward, past pine trees, quietly, as though it was afraid of attracting someone's attention, freezing momentarily at railroad crossings and making longer stops at sand embankments. She wasn't saying anything. I couldn't quite remember where we'd left off or decide how to go about resuming our ongoing conversation. We passed some lakes and wove in between some clusters of cottages. A forest came into view through the window; the sky was generously heaped with low-hanging clouds. Then suddenly there was so much sky—it was everywhere. "Man, August is almost over, time flies," I thought.

The train stopped; we stepped out onto the platform. It was quiet; wide, slanted rays of sunlight tinted the air gold, making it difficult to see things as they really were. It was three o'clock in the afternoon. There wasn't a living soul in sight. Just the right time to pay a ceremonious visit to the dead. We picked up some boxed wine at the store by the station and headed down a sandy path along the tracks. She was walking up ahead, although she didn't know the way. Her gait had changed—she mostly looked down at her feet, as though she was afraid of going off course. This went on for quite a while. She stopped to rest a few times. A pebble got in her sneaker once; she leaned on my shoulder, hopping on one leg, laughing and shaking it out. We reached the village; I asked for directions, and we started looking for Luke's place. The road deposited us right beside a riverbank, a little below a confluence, and the current looked like marble—light veins crisscrossed with dusky ones and murky water with clear. We were completely lost at this point; it was time to ask for directions again; she took out her cell and called someone.

"Well," she said, pointing at the house across from us. "This is it."

It was behind some old trees; you couldn't even see it from the road. There was a fence, there were a lot of flowers, there was silence. We opened the gate and walked across the yard. It seemed like Luke hadn't been neglecting it; his lawnmower was clearly still seeing plenty of use. The yard looked like a soccer field—admittedly, one nobody was permitted to play on. The house wasn't too big; it looked like it had been assembled from disparate parts—decent-looking window frames and doors lugged there from somewhere else. Red-brick foundation, speckled with white. Wooden beams and metal fasteners. It was as though somebody had knocked down a few buildings and assembled them into a single new one, and not a great one, either. She walked over to the door and pulled, but it wouldn't open. She knocked. I peered in through the window. There was a bed by the wall and an empty table covered with tissue paper by the window. An apple fell off a tree, its descent heavy and steady. We looked around. There he stood, looking back at us, not saying anything. His face was more wrinkly now, and he'd apparently trimmed his own beard. A dark green shirt with the sleeves rolled up to his elbows, battle-scarred jeans, worn at the knees, sneakers fissured by constant walking. Puffy eyes, bitten lips. Black hands, long fingers, yellowed nails. Skin the color of dry clay. Sixty years behind him. Death and dissolution up ahead. It was four o'clock now. There wasn't much sun left for us today.

Twenty years ago, he didn't have that beard, and he had dramatically fewer wrinkles. His hands were the same, though—darkened by hours of labor, paint under the nails, palms all cut up, and veins bulging with tension. It looked like he'd been finger painting. Not much else about him had changed—always in jeans, even at gallery openings and formal events, always in sneakers, always standing behind you, as if to say, "I've got your back if you fall." He was young and belligerent twenty years ago, not afraid of anyone and never asking anyone for any favors. He didn't seem to be afraid of anyone now, either . . . but nobody was afraid of him now, either. Back then, twenty years ago, he was a force to be reckoned with; there was just no ignoring him. In the eighties, he worked at a children's center in some basement downtown. He taught kids how to draw. The nineties were tough economically, but kids still wanted to draw, so he kept teaching them. The center was shut down toward the end of the decade; he'd been out of work since then, and he seemed to be doing just dandy. Everybody in town knew him. He had a ton of friends. Even the cops got along with him. He had a lot of lovers, too. I personally knew a few of them. They brought him food and fresh clothes when he was working in his studio. They'd clean his shoes and console each other whenever he left town without a word to anybody. His son from his first marriage had his own business, always looked nice, and really loved his dad. Luke didn't put his art in any shows, but everyone had a couple of his pieces hanging up at home. He'd spent the last couple of years building that house. He bought somebody's orchard and nested between its trees. His son helped and offered to build him a regular house; he even offered to pay for everything, but Luke turned him down, saying he wanted to do it all himself. Some friends helped him out anyway; sometimes his son would come and move bricks for him—he'd turn his phone off for the weekend so nobody would bother him. Luke was in no hurry; he seemed to like the process of building something. Last year, his son brought in a construction crew and they finished the job in a month. In the spring, Luke decided he was going to live there, or, more precisely, die there.

"Luke!" she shouted, and rushed toward him.

He chuckled in response as she wrapped her arms around his neck, hanging on him. I followed her inside. He lowered her onto the floor and hugged me too.

"You're the first ones here," he said, still laughing. "Hope you're not the last ones, though."

We weren't the last ones, that's for sure. His son pulled up in his Jeep, packed to the brim with food. He brought Luke a tiny children's tape player and loaded it up with batteries so his old man could listen to his favorite music no matter where he wound up—like a hospital bed, just for instance. He brought two of Luke's old friends along with him—Zurab, the blind-as-a-bat old-timer who'd lived with Luke in a communal apartment on Revolution Street, and Sasha, a tall, skinny guy who'd commissioned Luke to decorate some public cafeterias way back in the eighties. It seemed like Zurab didn't really know where he was, but he greeted Luke courteously, giving him a long, firm handshake, patting him on the back, and even shedding one rugged tear from one half-blind eye. Sasha was a lean guy sporting a military haircut, his signature thin graying mustache, and a jacket, black like that of a chimney sweep. He knew exactly what was going on, so he tried to keep his feelings and need to show compassion in check, hugging Luke and Zurab and jabbering away about something or other.

Eventually, Luke's son couldn't take it anymore, so he said, "All right, you guys catch up while I go get the spread ready." He started carrying some grocery bags over to a large empty table under the apple trees covered with the same tissue paper.

"Let me give you a hand," she said, getting down to business.

"Don't worry," Luke said. "Let them get everything ready. Come take a look at my apple trees."

Zurab and Sasha stepped forward; I was about to follow them, but then Luke reached out and held my elbow gently.

"How are things between you two?" he asked, voice low, nodding toward her setting the table.

"I don't know yet."

"She pregnant?"

"How can you tell?"

"You just can. Pregnant women are calm and reflective. She never used to be like that. What do you think about all this?"

"Don't know what to think."

"It isn't your kid?"

"Probably not."

"Whose is it then?"

"Don't know."

"Does she know?"

"Not sure."

"Stick with her. If you quit on her, you'll regret it. Try to hold on to her. She's worth it. All right, c'mon, let me show you my apple trees."

Warm apples lay in the grass. Luke picked up a few, holding them in his hands for a moment, and then putting them back on the ground.

Everybody started trickling in. Maria, who was everyone's acquaintance, showed up, tired after work, with a big bouquet of flowers. Zhora had made the long haul out here. I hadn't seen him since spring, when he was constantly griping about his trainee program at the 24-hour pharmacy by the metro. He wasn't sure if they'd be taking him on full time, but they did. Everything went smoothly; Zhora looked confident and happy and kept giving everyone unsolicited medical advice, which was a bit inappropriate under the circumstances. Nobody really acknowledged the circumstances that had brought them together that day, though; everyone was taking in the fresh August air, the river flowing by a few dozen yards away, the ripe apples, and the evening sky. Zhora's cousin Bob had tagged along with him. His hair neatly combed, dressed in a fancy suit, he looked like a young Protestant missionary. Bob had recently returned from a trip to America, but from the way he was acting, you'd have thought he'd just returned from the depths of hell, or someplace much worse. He was bubbling over with stories to tell. He gave Luke a bottle of dry California wine. Sasha Tsoi, a young rebel, the son of Korean exiles, an active member of the poetry club at the Jewish Center back in town, and Bob's best friend, showed up soon after and bestowed one of his manuscripts upon Luke. Luke promised to read it when he had the time. Pasha Chingachgook limped over with his wife, Margarita, who was carrying a big basket of fish; she immediately scurried to the kitchen to start cooking, leaving Pasha to hobble around by himself among the trees. Alla the Alligator, the apple of everyone's eye, and the muse of the poor and the humiliated, made an appearance, sending them all into a frenzy. She brought a chocolate cake and hugged Luke, holding on for a long while. He looked at her, his gaze full of tender sadness. I remembered that a billion years ago, at some drunken party, Luke had confided in me that he was the Alligator's first man, that he'd taught her everything she went on to share so generously with all her friends and acquaintants.

"She came over wearing her mom's dress. Can you believe that? She didn't have any grown-up clothes," Luke said.

"How'd you know it was her mom's dress?"

"Well . . . I was with her mom for a while."

Alla was with Yura, my old friend, a former guitar player, with a finger missing on his left hand. He had a resentful yet open expression on his face. He wouldn't drink with us, saying that he was taking medication. He didn't specify what it was for, but everyone already knew—TB. Luke's friend Kira came, too. She looked sad and lonely, a silver ring dangling from a chain around her neck. She'd also brought

Luke flowers. He asked why she'd come by herself. Kira explained that she and her girlfriend had split up, but that everything was fine and she didn't want to get into it. John showed up late. On paper, he was the assistant director at a factory in town. He'd rented out one of the labs there to Luke so he could use it as a studio. He greeted everyone rather dryly and stiffly and shook Luke's hand for a long while. He slouched even more than he used to, and it seemed as though he'd lost even more weight. A few more people had come along with him. I'd seen one of them at a protest in support of somebody or other, I couldn't remember who. One of Luke's friends, a girl from his past life, buried deep in his memory, came with John. The last one to show up was some really young girl with long, dyed black hair. She was wearing a brightly colored dress and light sandals. She only said hello to Luke, because she didn't appear to know anyone else here. Nobody recognized her, either. At first, they all focused their attention on her, whispering to one another, and exchanging significant glances. Luke noticed, and it made him feel uneasy, so he invited everyone to the picnic table. The girl took a step off to the side and stood alone under the apple branches, and everyone instantly forgot about her. Then she joined them at the table, sitting there and drinking wine, not saying anything.

Everyone started getting rowdy; a heated argument broke out. Bob was especially loud. He sure had some stories to tell his fellow Ukrainians now that he'd had some firsthand experience abroad, felt the otherworldly breath of fire; now he was presenting the incredible details of his recent voyage to the other side of the Atlantic Ocean, to the cold heart of America, interrupting everyone, leaning confidentially toward everyone, and choking on a barrage of words. Eventually all the other side conversations stopped, because everyone realized it'd be best just to hear him out and give him some sense of affirmation instead of interrupting and shouting over him. Luke sat there smiling, his eyes shifting from Bob to the girl who was sitting on the other side of the table.

"Two hot ocean currents sweep against the shores of America," Bob said. "This dictates its climate and the complex character of the locals. This affects its flora, as well as its fauna. In America, animals living in the wild are quite serene, and most of them are tame. Foxes trot briskly into the suburbs and sleep at bus stops, howling at the moon come nightfall, which is quite a nuisance when people are trying to sleep. Birds weave their nests on people's balconies and in children's strollers. Turtles infiltrate the cities' sewer systems, where they live out their famously long lives. Hot ocean currents burst through the soil in the interior of the continent. Take New York for example—it rests on hot water and damp clay. The streets smell of sulfur, and the sun hides away in a warm haze. Twilight is constantly hovering over the city—black seaweed and tall, orange grass grow beneath it. There's only one city that can compete with New York when it comes to twilight—that's San Francisco, obviously, the city founded by none other than Saint Francis himself, who initially came on an official visit but wound up settling on those sandy shores to strengthen the natives' faith and light up the city at night as Russian and Chinese commercial ships sliced through the ocean's blistering heat, heading toward the shore."

"Yeah, yeah, we get that part," his captivated listeners said, "but what about the women? What are the women like in America?"

Bob appeared to have been anticipating this question; he fired off an answer immediately. "The women . . . they're an interesting bunch," Bob said. "Naturally, most of them are Surinamese. Or Ethiopian. As is their custom back home, Surinamese women carry water from the river in large clay jugs. They have big families with no men. They only bring men into their homes to conceive. They mostly work in the service industry, eat fruits and herbs, and age quickly but gracefully. Ethiopians . . . now they're a different matter entirely. They aren't as tight-knit; they only congregate at church—Ethiopian Christians have built more than a hundred churches in New York alone! They don't make love with outlanders," Bob stated in a sad voice. "I tried. They live a long time. It's pretty easy to meet an Ethiopian woman over the age of ninety—really, there's nothing to it. Some attribute their longevity to the water they drink, while others attribute it to all the praying they do—but it's the Japanese women over there that act the strangest," Bob interrupted himself. "There are some who say that they never fall ill, not ever. They just don't have time for that nonsense. It is said that they can treat themselves with their own saliva. They all have marble skin and a barely perceptible glow hovering over them—some of them even have two heads."

Not knowing how to react to what Bob had been pontificating about, they all sat there in silence for a moment. But then Margarita came out of the house, carrying two large plates of fish toward the table, which lightened the mood. Everyone started talking, commenting upon, refuting, or supporting Bob's bombastic story.

Sasha yelled, "That's right, Bob. People are the same everywhere, and it doesn't really matter who you share your hopes and wine with—a Surinamese woman or an Ethiopian one. But an Ethiopian woman would be better." Maria, speaking quietly, argued that family is the most important thing in life, and it's better to leave anything going on outside the family to other people. Pasha Chingachgook agreed with her, while Kira shook her head dissentingly and described the acts of betrayal people are prone to, and the oblivion that enters us and fills us up. Alla ran with the part about oblivion, saying that it doesn't matter how much it fills you up—it's no match for the exhilaration of new love.

"That's right," Luke suddenly added. He'd been sitting there in silence the whole time, listening intently to the others.

Everyone got very quiet all of a sudden, apparently remembering what had brought them together. There was an intimate yet solemn air about the whole gathering. The light coming off the deck was drowning in the leaves and capturing the men's heavy hands and the women's reserved faces. Luke sat at the corner of the table; the falling shadows made his features sharp, his wrinkles deep. Bloody drops of wine faded into his beard. John was on his left and Zurab on his right. They were listening to him but not looking at him. Luke waited for complete silence to set in and then continued,

"What you said is absolutely right. Oblivion doesn't matter. And death doesn't matter either."

"Death doesn't exist!" Sasha Tsoi yelled boldly.

"Death *does* exist. You can't even imagine how close to us it is. But that's not what I'm getting at. Our death, our disappearance, and our passage to the kingdom of the dead don't have any real significance because they're all inevitable. After all, it would be silly to reject the lunar cycle, or the natural course of a river. You have to take it as a given and accept it peacefully, like all inexorable forces. The only thing that actually holds any significance is love, both exhilarating new love and the enduring love we keep inside, the love we carry with us, and the love with which we live. You never know how much is allotted to you, how much you have, or how much is yet to come. Finding it brings great happiness; losing it causes great misery and vexation. We all live in this strange city; we all stuck around, we'll all come back sooner or later. We live, bearing this love like guilt, like our memory that contains all of our experiences and all of our knowledge, and its presence in our breath, on the roofs of our mouths, is what makes life so riveting. Every morning when I wake up, I think of all the women I've been blessed to meet and know—all those cheerful and unsettled, carefree and helpless, virginal and pregnant women. I'd say my exchanges with them have always been the most important thing for me, my ability or inability to share love, whether new or enduring, with them. Everything else was a consequence of falling in love, so it had no meaning, no significance on its own. So there's no sense talking about anything else. That's all I have to say, now it's time to go for a swim!"

That's what everyone did. Our boisterous crew started spilling out into the yard, thanking the host for his words, remarking that they were wise, though perhaps a little overloaded with passion. Somebody grabbed a bottle of wine, some others used their phones as flashlights to guide us down the path toward the riverbank. She got up from the table, too, and started gathering up empty plates.

"Ya coming?"

"You run along with everyone else," she said, gently waving me off. "I'm gonna help clean up. I'll be down soon."

I stood still for a bit, then turned around, set off into the darkness, crossed the street, passed under some trees, and popped out by the river. Clothes and empty bottles were scattered along the bank; from the depths of the evening air, somewhere in that damp black space, I could hear laughing and shrieking, giddy splashing and confident strokes through the current. Women's bodies shone dimly in the silver moonlight and drunken exclamations made everything warm and cheerful. I recognized them, standing there on the riverbank, calling their names right into the blackness. Their answers came back; they approached me or drifted toward the opposite bank. It sounded as though the river had carried all the voices, all the laughter, and all the songs I knew from the city out here, which steadied me and put me at ease. Everything was right here, just a few steps away. None of this could disappear—it wouldn't end as long as I stood there, no matter how much time passed.

But they gradually started getting out of the water—some of them quickly snatched their clothes and pulled them over their wet bodies, while the more foresighted among them dried off with the towels they'd brought, and some other swimmers simply polished off the bottles, grabbed some clothes at random, and plodded toward the yard, back into the light. It was getting late. I heard someone saying goodbye to the host and someone else starting to sing; a certain bitterness tinged the voices of the women and a fire ignited in those of the men. Cars pulled away. The voices went silent. It got very quiet. There was more moon; there was more coolness in the air.

I didn't hear her coming at all. She simply appeared behind me and touched my shoulder gently.

"Well, what are you standing here for?" she asked.

At first, I didn't know what to say. She slipped out of the jacket she'd borrowed from someone or other, shed her sweater, kicked off her sneakers, and struggled with her overalls for a bit, but eventually got out of them, too. She pulled off her T-shirt, hesitated for a split second, tossed her underwear on top of the warm pile of clothes, and stepped into the water, fearfully groping for the bottom of the river with her toes. Then she squealed giddily, dove into the water, and swam out a little bit.

"Hey," she yelled from the darkness, "aren't you comin'?"

"You go ahead and swim," I answered. "I'll watch your things."

"Whatever you say."

I thought, "It's so good to finally find myself here, on this bank, by this water, just standing and watching her undress and step into the river, knowing that you can wade into any river forever. You can hang on to the wet air that enfolds you — you can hold on to it forever; you can wait for everyone you have known and loved to return — you can wait forever. The river will bring you all the different inflections you've heard, the river will conserve all the warmth you've left behind; rivers know how to wait, rivers know how to start anew. Riverbeds abide, currents abide. Nobody can stop this whole mass of damp light, this heap of warmth and cold. All I can do is wait for her, here on the riverbank, and return with her to the city, like the thousands of refugees and migrant workers, sojourners and newcomers, all those crews of manual laborers who roam the earth building towers and prisons, but eventually come here, sooner or later, to these riverbanks, lit by these moon rays."

I thought about how I'd remember the smell of this water, the smell of clay and grass, the smell of smoke and autumn, the smell of life that hadn't ended, and the smell of death that hadn't come yet. "What's she going to remember about all this? Will she remember the silence that hangs over us? Will she remember her breath expanding in the midst of this silence? After all, it's up to us — it depends on our desire to remember something. Or our desire not to remember anything at all."

After she'd come out of the water and I'd grabbed her hand on the bank and helped her find her clothes, and after we'd returned to the house, she said,

"The last train probably left already. Luke has a guestroom, though. Why don't you stay with me?"

"Well obviously I'm gonna stay."

We heard some music playing on our way up to the house. Sharp, triumphant sounds from somewhere behind the apple trees. The yard was empty; everyone had gone home. We headed toward the music but stopped under the trees before we reached it. There were some chairs by the table on the grass. The girl nobody knew was still there, for some reason. There she sat, her hair thrown back and her hands calmly resting in her lap. Luke was dancing cheerfully, yet violently, in front of her. Well, dancing may not be the right word. He looked like somebody bouncing on a pogo stick—happy, despairing bounds into the sky—tearing free of the earth's surface, trying to leap into the darkness. Luke was jumping high, although he was clearly struggling—his shirt was soaked with sweat and the veins in his neck were bulging, yet he continued jumping and throwing his hands into the air, jumping and landing in the wet grass and skipping to the hoarse sounds coming out of his brand-new stereo. It was Patti Smith, his all-time favorite. He'd listen to her whenever he was in a good mood, or whenever he was in a bad mood, for that matter—the one about how Jesus died for somebody's sins but not hers. Luke kept jumping, seemingly enjoying all of this—he probably didn't die for my sins and probably not for yours, girl. What sins could you have committed? What do you have to atone for? We'll pay off all our debts, we'll make arrangements with all the tax collectors of this world, we'll pay for every last word and every last breath.

She sat there, looking at him attentively. She listened to him, nodding, agreeing with everything, not addressing him, not stopping him, not looking away, willing to wait for as long as she had to.

*Part II: Notes and Addenda*

Translated from the Ukrainian by
Virlana Tkacz and
Wanda Phipps

There's nothing there yet. Green night,
each silence has its own measure.
Knowing how many centuries it took
for the first things to appear,
he speaks her name.

Opening a window into the night,
he anxiously listens for any movement,
expecting something—anything,
but the heavy canvas of nothingness
gently falls into his hands.

From now on everything that happens to them—
ocean currents, icebergs in dead seas,
the daily cycles of the atmosphere,
songs of sperm whales, screams of phantoms,
the awakening of scents and colors,

grass roots and tree leaves,
lake ice and bird whistles,
iron ore and coal's tired tremors,
the whispers and roars of obedient animals,
the yearnings of vibrant trading towns,

fires that burn ships,
death on dark silk banners,
dying stars hanging high in the firmament,
the silent dead in the summer ground,
blood, like lava in the fallow ridges of veins:

everything that was meant to come will come,
everything that once was will disappear,
like taxes owed for worlds revealed to them,
for a voice with hints of darkness,
for warmth liberated with each new breath.

Knowing everything that awaits them,
he still speaks her name,
woven out of consonants and bitter vowels,
until love's green current,
a cool shadow of tenderness,
carries him away.

■ ■ ■

Marat died in his sleep
at the beginning of March,
in spring when the snow melts
and rivers run from their banks,
just as children run from their parents' homes
after a hard winter.

Marat trained at the Spartacus Club.
He had technique, tried and tested,
his body was in shape, he looked serious,
he was probably the best fighter
in the welterweight class,
and had a tattoo of Fidel on his left leg.

The imam spoke at the funeral:
"The Prophet was never sad," he said.
"The Prophet knew—evil devours evil.
What shall be, shall be. As far as we know.
Marat will have a different story to tell
about each of his transgressions.
The Prophet invented illnesses like pneumonia
for people like him."

In the corner, Marat's mother was silent.
Marat's brother listened to the harsh words.
Then the imam placed his hand
on his narrow shoulders
and said:
"Everything that disappears, will appear once again."
The brother answered, "Nothing disappears.
I'll take up the mouth guard Marat used when he fought.

"I know why he died.
Every morning he fought against his phantoms.
Every day he beat his fists till they bled.
Every night he felt
the stars burn out overhead.
Only the bravest go beyond this boundary.
Anyone who saw him in the ring knows what I am talking
about.

"How can something that still exists disappear?
He who gives us everything, what will he do with it?

Only fear can disappear.
The rest is on us—younger brothers
who break our hearts,
steadfast to the end."

Then the brother stepped aside.
He was a year younger.
He always considered Marat the leader.
He followed him everywhere.
Now he fell silent and stepped aside,
holding back tears, ashamed in front of us.

When they carried out the body it started to snow.
It fell from the dark sky and landed at our feet.
The imam walked ahead, like an apparition.
Early spring is not the best time to visit a cemetery.
Women started to cry and men could feel
the silent stars above them burn out.

■ ■ ■

Fights without rules—daily wages of the saints,
the referee yells something, the crowd grows silent.
Young apostles fight
against the locals
they consider foreign.

They wrap Jesus's hands into fists,
and shove him into the ring, as into a river.
His opponent, a young dockworker, faces him,
but doesn't offer him his hand.

When Jesus falls on the canvas,
sliding into hell, somewhere near the bottom,
his body becomes brittle, like bread,
and his blood dry as wine.

Then someone shouts, "Come on, get it together!
Remember everything you used to tell us!
Get up or people will hear about this,
everywhere, before you know it.

"Get up and fight, as only you can!
Knock down that scum! Don't let him walk out of here!
Each victory
brings you closer to the goal!

"No forgiveness for those who hide, not in the river or in the
　　　　grass!
No grace from the Lord, no rights!
Come on, you've fallen so many times,
fallen and died!

"They're all traitors and losers!
They don't have a conscience, only gills,
fins, instead of wings on their backs!

Knock them down, Savior,
bloody your fists on them!

"Knock them down for their weakness and tears!
Knock them down for forgetting everything each night!
For watching their own deaths
like spectators!

"Anyway, they don't listen to you or to us,
nothing will save them, they don't give a shit about anything,
destroy them, O Lord, before they
destroy themselves.

"Destroy them for their corruption and laziness,
their treachery in every generation,
their cunning, which they weave
into their prayers!"

. . . and he gets up, spitting black blood,
rises, and falls, then rises again,
and the dockworkers whisper, so again,
by death he's conquered death.

He hits 'em right in the solar plexus
for each sin!
Boxing is really for the stubborn
and the young.

The young dockworker, parting from life,
manages to thank him, happy as a baby,
as if saying, Blessed is he who believes
in salvation and oblivion.

The apostles wipe his face with a towel
and tell him they always believed in him.
And the one who placed his bets on him,
continues to back him,
now
a tested fighter.

■ ■ ■

Uncle Sasha worked in a bar in Frunze[1]
and was wise in the ways of the world, may he rest in peace.
He liked to say, "For a real sailor the honor of the fleet
is more important than the reputation of a ship.

"So no matter what port, or where you drop anchor,
keep your heart open to all winds.
Even if you are throwing up overboard in the morning,
make sure to hold on to what you want.

"Even when you are strung up from the yardarm,
or when you are dragged on the bottom of the ocean,

---

1. A seaside town in Crimea.

always remember that somewhere there's a door,
where someone is waiting for you with wine and hope!"

We are not given that much advice.
And what we do get is not what we need in life.
So I was always ready without a doubt
to see the truth in Uncle Sasha's rants and confessions.

All his wild stories, tales, and drunken yarns,
all his dark curses and pitch-black tirades
had a point: you cannot abandon your friends in a fight,
nor can you forgive anyone who hits you.

I remember everyone who once sat beside us,
who were then led out by surly cops
into the melting snows of March or the freezing air of
      November,
deprived of the joy and sense of justice around every table.

Some of the workers and professors with dark faces
who listened to his stories about the Black Sea Fleet,
now eat from dumpsters;
others have died of hunger or TB;

some left those dissipating places
to defend a lost Jerusalem.
But I don't remember a single one
who was not ready to die with him.

"Hey Uncle Sasha," one of them would shout,
"We dwell in the bounty of the Lord.
This country does not deserve to have its own fleet.
This town, with its rivers and golden sand,
will drink to us with bad brandy when we die.
Our light will be reflected in the distant stars,
black roses will turn to cinders in the hands of girls.
Every heart burns only once.
Death arrives after
life ends."

Then they would step around the corner
and fall into the gutter.
Maybe I alone kept
what they left behind.

Silver sewn into belts.
Animals, children, women.
Trees growing in summer sands.
Springs gushing on the bottom of the river.

■ ■ ■

The team was disbanded before the season started —
the owner cashed in his shares and bought a hotel in Egypt.
Black crows strolled, guarding the lawn.
In the locker room the deflated soccer balls smelled of defeat.

Sania, our right wing, the hope of the team,
cried as he carried his things out of the clubhouse.
He held on to his shoes, as if he had nothing else,
his hands folded like a Sunni saying his prayers.

Well, I didn't believe him, he was doing it on purpose,
behaving like he was the only one who cared.
Sania's brother, a rightist, was sitting in jail, dreaming of
       burning down this town
for electing such an idiot as mayor.

His father also had done time and was right-wing too.
I don't know how he dealt with them.
The only good things in his life were his injuries,
old sports club patches, and his long black hair.

So I say to him, "Enough, Sania, enough whining,
enough lamenting losses.
Why are we standing here like a couple of Sunnis,
come on Sania, let's settle our nerves.

"We'll go to the factory and find some work,
we'll apply to college or sign up to be security guards.
When you have a choice, always choose freedom,
When you're one man down, you've got to lock down the
       defense."

And he answers, "Work, what work?
Guard? What are you talking about?

All my life all I ever saw was the opponent's goalpost.
The only person who ever respected me was their guard.

"All I had was a number on my back,
a place in the lineup, and I gave everything for it.
What can I do now in this country?
How can I tell who's on my team and who's not?

"Why stay, who should I fight?
What the fuck, I'll go to Russia.
I'll play where they assign me, I'll take my chances,
leave this mess, and wait for amnesia."

. . . I knew he would never leave, things would never change.
All our losses are not accidental, they're necessary.
You can't escape from yourself, from your own grief,
from your own hate, from your own love.

You can't change your memories or your dreams,
you can't stop the shadows or the comets.
Things never change, they stay with us,
no matter how long we live or how we die.

Our night skies, our flocks of birds,
our rivers, our towns, our buildings:
no one will ever remember a thing about us,
no one will ever forgive us for anything we've done.

■ ■ ■

So I'm writing about her again,
about the balconies
and our conversations at home.

I remember what she
hid from me,
what she kept in between the pages
of that anthology with all those damned poets
who constantly spoiled
our lives.

"Last summer," she said,
"something happened to my heart.
It started to drift, like a ship,
whose crew had died
of fever.
It moved deep within my breath,
caught by the currents,
attacked by sharks.

"I always said,
Heart, dear heart, no sails or ropes
will help you.
The stars are too far away
to guide us.
Heart, dear heart,
too many men

have signed up for your crews,
too many of them have stayed behind in British ports,
losing their souls
to the tears of the green dragon of alcohol."

So I also
remember her legs, which I was ready
to fight for to the death,
and I repeat after her,
"Heart, dear heart,
sick with fever,
get well soon,
recover quickly,
so much burning love awaits us,
so many beautiful tragedies
hide from us on the open seas.
Heart, dear heart,
I am overjoyed to hear
you beat,
like a fox—
captured
but never tamed."

■ ■ ■

The princess wears
orange clip-on earrings
and carries a dark bag

filled with treasures.
Sometimes she likes to tell us,

"This is makeup my father
bought me. These cigarettes
I took from my older sister.
My mother left me
this silver jewelry she wore
till she died."
"And this," I ask, "who's in this photo?"
"My girlfriends," she answers,
"they really hate me for my
golden hair and black underwear,
which none of them have.
My friends are ready
to tear me to pieces
for all that summer sultriness
that heats up in my
heart."

What is the point of poetry?
To write about what everyone already knows.
To talk about things we are deprived of,
to voice our disappointments.
To speak and provoke
anger and love, envy, hatred,
and sympathy. To talk
under the moon

hanging above us, with all its
yellow reflections looming down.

Every grown woman
has this,
this sweet melody,
which you can only hear
when her heart begins to break,
which can only stop
when you've broken her heart.

■ ■ ■

This fox
howls at the moon all night
and avoids my traps,
acting like nothing happened,
like nothing concerns her.

Once the jewelry she wore
around
her neck
grew in value.
The blanket in which she wrapped herself
was a field of sunflowers
in which birds

found stray seeds
of tenderness.

When she grew angry,
rage rose in her veins,
like sap moving up a rose stem.

When you're in love it is most important
not to believe what's said.
She yelled, "Leave me alone,"
but really meant,
"Tear out my heart."
She refused
to talk to me,
but was actually refusing
to exhale.

As if she were trying to make things worse
for me than they actually were.

As if our biggest problem
was the air
we breathed.


I ask her,
"What are you drawing all the time?"

"These are men," she answers, "and these are women."
"Why are your women always crying?"
"They cry," she replies, "for the wind,
which was hidden in their hair;
they cry for the grapes harvested,
which tasted tart in their mouths.
And no one—neither men in clothes smelling of smoke,
nor children with golden scorpions
of disobedience in matchboxes,
can make them feel better."

The love of men and women
is the tenderness and helplessness we receive,
a long list of gifts and losses,
the wind tossing your hair in May.

Oh, how hard it is to rely on the one
you trust, and how easy it is to be disappointed
in the one who touches your lips at night.

Some things are whimsical and invisible,
no matter how you color them,
they will always stay the same:

a star hangs above you,
the air roils with warmth.
So much light is hidden
in every woman's throat,
so much trouble.

■ ■ ■

The best things this winter
were her footsteps in the first snow.
It's hardest for tightrope walkers:
how can they retain their balance
when their hearts pull to one side?
It would be good to have two hearts.
They could be suspended in the air,
they could hold their breath,
as they closely examine
the green jellyfish in the snow.

The best things this winter
were the trees covered with birds.
The crows looked like telephones
used by
demons of joy.
They sat in the trees, and trees in winter
are like women after breakups—
their warm roots intertwined
with cold roots,
stretching into the dark,
needing light.

It would be good
to teach these crows songs
and prayers, to give them something

to do on damp
March mornings.

The best thing that could have happened,
happened to us.
"This is happening because it's March," she said,
disappointed. "This is all happening
because it's March.
at night you spend a long time searching
your pockets for bits of ads,
in the morning emerald grass
grows under your bed,
bitter and hot,
smelling like golf balls."

■ ■ ■

In the summer
she walks through the rooms,
catching the wind in the windows,
like an amateur sailor,
who can't set
the sails.

She stalks drafts,
setting traps for them.

But the drafts tell her,
"Your movements are too gentle,
but your blood is too hot,
you'll never get
anything in life
with that disposition!

"You lift your palms
too high
to catch the emptiness."
Everything that slips
out of our hands—is only emptiness.
Everything
we have no patience for—
is only the wind blowing
over the city.

The sun in the sky at dawn
is like an orange
in a kid's schoolbag —
the only thing with real weight,
the only thing you think about
when you are
lonely.

■ ■ ■

If I were the postman
on her block,
if I knew where
she gets those certified
letters from,
maybe I'd understand
life better,
how it's set in motion,
who fills it with song,
who fills it with tears.

People who read newspapers,
people with warm
hearts, good souls,
grow old without letting
anyone know.
If I were the postman
on this block,
even after their deaths
I'd water the plants
on their dry balconies,
and feed the feral cats
in their green kitchens.

Then, running down the stairs,
I would hear her say,

"Postman, postman,
all my happiness

fits into your bag,
don't give it away
to the milkman or hardened widows,

"Postman, postman,
there is no death,
and there is nothing after death."

There is hope
that everything will be
just like we want it,
and there is confidence
that everything happened
just like we wanted it.

Oh, her voice is bitter
and imponderable.
Oh, her handwriting is difficult
and indecipherable.
That kind of handwriting
is good for signing death sentences—
sentences no one will ever carry out,
no one will ever figure it all out.


■ ■ ■


She likes to walk barefoot and sleep on her stomach,
so she can feel the oil flowing underground,

the trees being born in the empty darkness
and the water rising to seep directly under her.

She knows where all the courtyards lead in this city,
and the paths that thieves use from cellars to rooftops.
She knows how to catch kites and blimps without anchors
aided by street patrols and air shepherds.

Every teenager would like to catch her by her shoulder,
knowing that she would escape anyway,
leaving behind only her warmth,
and not believing that she was actually just there.

Every killer watches her disappear into the darkness,
hoping that she will come to him in his dreams,
convinced that she will forget his name.
He'll never understand
what I mean
to her.

Because she loves to warm her hands in other people's pockets,
and knows every ticket collector on the night trolley,
she greets them only to interrupt
their loneliness, which lasts till dawn.

Because each of the lost ticket collectors
is chained by their own fear like to a galley,
hopelessly handing out tickets, and looking out the window —
for her, the passenger, who doesn't care

what stop she gets off at to descend into the darkness,
what unhappy love affair she mourns,
what losses she regrets, what losses she doesn't,
and what words she will use to tell me about it all.


■ ■ ■


Her stepfather was odd—
worked as a gardener for a Vietnamese family,
looking after trees, which would have grown without him
in the suburbs, past the factory, in the haze.
He counted off branches, like prisoners count off years,
hunted for foxes,
fed wild dogs straight from his hands.

Everyone thought he was crazy, even she agreed,
but explained,
"I love him, I need him,
so why is he constantly hiding in the trees, in the shadows?
When he steps out into the sun, why does he move so
        strangely,
as if he knew
where trouble was coming from?"

His employers couldn't remember his name,
his friends didn't recognize him, his family rejected him,
and used him to frighten children, who were not scared at all.
They ran after him onto the old railroad tracks,

and when he was sick, they pulled birds' eggs out of nests,
as if they were taking bulbs out of street lamps.

I saw him only once, in the fall,
I noticed him walking, far away, from the back.
He was wandering in the shadows, frightening the stars,
carrying a ladder to cut some branches.
His demeanor was humble—he was simply exhausted.
That's how Jesus carried his cross, I thought.

I also thought—this is easy for him,
knowing what to do, not noticing the emptiness,
remembering everything that was, accepting everything
     that is,
clearly imagining his future,
believing that nothing will change,
guessing that no one will escape,
shifting the ladder from one shoulder to the other.

I said as he passed,
Do what you have to do,
work is only part of our struggle,
faith is the sand that forms the foundation of our years,
and trees can't really grow without gardeners.

■ ■ ■

It's good, he thought, it's good that I'm dead to her,
good that she's forgotten my name,
good that this all happened so quickly,
good that I wasn't there for all of it.

Good that she decided all this for us,
that I didn't have to convince her to stop the nonsense,
didn't have to watch her hesitate,
didn't have to see her dark eyes.

Now it's important to disappear, to choose the right course,
it's important not to return to where I used to live,
it's important not to go to familiar places,
not to frighten friends, or disappoint strangers,

not to wander into their dreams, not to touch their things,
not to look through their books, not to drink their wine,
not to hear their breathing, not to see their eyes,
not to feel what they themselves no longer feel.

It's good that I can fly out of the chimney now,
walk through fire, fall on the grass,
feel the flow of the stuff that fills her dreams,
notice the cables that keep her afloat.

It's a good thing that death is neither an achievement nor a
       loss,
good that our footsteps don't give us away,

that nothing can be turned back,
that nothing can be lost forever.

What was there?
green warmth,
against the orange background
of the evening sky.

Golden moons,
blue fish in the river,
dark shadows
on her face.

■ ■ ■

What to do with the priests?
They graze their churches like cattle,
leading them to emerald-green pastures, watching
how their churches plop down into the river silt
to escape from the June sun.
They follow their churches, chasing them out of the
       neighbor's
wheat fields, turning them toward home, where
evening fires are lit in cottages.
They sleep on bags and books, listening to the breath of
       sleeping animals,
recalling in dreams the faces of women who came and

told them their darkest sins,
asking for advice, awaiting forgiveness.

What kind of advice can he give you?
His entire life is spent herding echoes,
searching for pasturelands, and sleeping under a dark sky.
You can sing with him, you can
sleep next to him, covering yourself with an infantry jacket,
you can dry your wet clothes at the fire,
wash your shirts in the river.
He is ready to hang them in the church like a holy shroud.

What to do with the atheists?
They say, "Truly I believe, I believe in everything said,
but I will never admit it for any reason,
under any circumstances, that's my business,
and only concerns me. Let him take offense
a hundred times and threaten me, get angry, and turn away
        from me on his crucifix,
anyway—What is he without me? What can he do alone?
He must struggle for my attention.
He is destined to fight for my redemption.
He must take into consideration my doubts, my
inconsistencies, my sincerity."

What to do with you? You can sing with us,
stand in a circle with us, place your hands on our shoulders:
we are united in our faith,

united in our love,
in our loneliness,
in our disappointment.

What to do with all of us?
If he had just a little more time,
if he did not have to watch his domesticated church,
if he didn't have to follow it, chase it out of yellow fields,
he would have more time for our
worrisome premonitions.

Love destroys
all our ideas of balance.
We can forget and stand to the side,
we can deny what we once said,
we can kiss the black lips of night—
we are the only ones touched by the flames of night,
we are the only ones who believe,
we are the only ones who will never
admit it.

You can talk about everything that you've dreamt.
You can talk, you don't have to fear the dark:

someone will hear you anyway,
but no one will ever believe you.

■ ■ ■

The city where she hides,
burning with flags, lies under a snow-covered mountain pass.
Hunters chase wild animals out of Protestant churches,
blue stars fall into the lake,
killing slow-moving fish.
Oh, tightrope walkers dangle above the streets.
They balance in school
windows, inspiring awe.
They avoid the gulls on the lake
that grab weightless golden potato chips
out of her hands.

Where we once lived,
we didn't have time for peace or reflection.
We struggled against the sharp reeds of the night,
threw off our clothes like counterweights down dark elevator
        shafts,
so we could be suspended in the air for one more night,
not loving and not forgiving
not accepting and not believing,
angrily experiencing the best days
of our lives.

The city where she finally hides
touches her gently by the hand,
and shows her all its warehouses and storage.
Oh, ports where transported

Senegalese prisoners gather,
dark meat of hearts,
ivory of eyes,
oh, those cellars packed with cheese,
welcoming Protestant towns,
where you can sit out Judgment Day,
where they have such learned lawyers,
such impregnable walls.

Where we once sat with her,
warming ourselves in kitchens
near the blue flames,
not a trace of us remains. Time, that old tightrope walker,
fell a hundred times, then got up a hundred times,
despite broken collarbones and metal teeth,
time doesn't care which way he moves —
he licks his wounds then once again dances with the gulls.

In the city where she managed to hide
there are such bright-colored dresses and blouses.
The Chinese students and pilots have such
velvety skin.
Oh, the fresh mountain air,
the feeling of blood rushing
after exhausting kisses.

She didn't leave anything behind where she came from,
not a single voice or curse.
Life is a joyful tug of rope.

On one side are the angels.
On the other — lawyers.
There are more lawyers.
But their services are more expensive.


■ ■ ■


Saint Francis built this city for surfers and heroes.
He brought ships from royal fleets
to these quiet bays covered with fog.
The Spanish jumped onto the shore,
Russian sailors came by rowboats and Chinese prospectors for
       gold
stitched the night with lanterns, surprised by the shadows in
       the hills.
And each church they established was like a weary voice —
there will be enough freedom for everyone, as long as you
       don't keep it all for yourself,
share the bread and coal during winter,
and look at the sun through the glass bottle of the ocean.
There is enough gold for everyone,
but only the bravest will find love!

It takes a thousand years
to dig out the bounty of the earth.
It takes a thousand nights to learn the ways of the local fish,
a thousand words to commune with eternity.
The plague descends on the holiday port,

young girls and teenagers follow it out of churches,
daring, golden skinned, full of their first secrets
and Catholic hymns—
share your books and bright-colored clothes,
share your coffee and fruit.
This city is protected by moats and fortified walls,
so much joy has been brought here from all over the world,
what shall we do with it,
what shall we do with it?

I know Saint Francis protects her,
when she appears at conferences and in libraries,
protects her every time she walks through the shops,
counting the pennies she has to live on,
protects her from enemies, protects her from friends.
He is annoyed when I advise him,
share your patience with her,
share your weariness, share your joy,
who else can she rely on in this city, if not you,
who else can we talk about in this life, if not her,
who else are we to protect,
who else can we envy,
Francis?


■ ■ ■


What are your sins, woman?
Who will count the stitches on your opaque body

where veins slowly flow into your palm?
Who will think of asking directions from strangers
whose voices possess you in your sleep?
Who will be brave enough to stand at the head of your bed
to watch you choking back the tears,
like snakes coiling around your throat?

What are your troubles and what are your secrets?
Nothing can be hidden
nothing lost will be returned.
Why ask forgiveness from skeletons,
that lie in the garden
under rosebushes?

She answers, "There's always
someone who will remind us about each of our losses.
There's always someone who will not let you be,
who will pull fear out of your body like weeds."

Autumn approaches. Honeyed voices
and songs fill the churches.
All Christians are united by images of saints on icons,
like pictures in a family album—
beloved and familiar since childhood, a light that
        accompanies
us through life; the closest are those saints who
took the splinters from your hands when you were a child.

What are your worries, woman? Where are your men?
Betrayed and contrite, angry and hated,
they pronounce your name like some concoction—
which couldn't alleviate their pain.
Moons waxed and waned in your window—
someone collected and assembled them
like the thick layers of an autumn onion.

She does not agree: "Moons that have waned
cannot teach you anything
and extinguished stars, like the eyes of linguists,
fail to pierce through
the darkness of the world.

"There's no light, no wasteland, no fires on the river,
no name to remember tonight.
Love is the ability to arrange stones in the waters of the
        night.
Love is the ability to see how everything is born,
how everything dies,
how everything is born again."

■ ■ ■

Women who live beyond the river,
where the ground is full of silt
and the streets are paved with red brick,

wake up and go to the river's edge
and wait for what the water will bring them that morning—
laundry that escaped someone's hands,
baskets set adrift with vegetables
or infants.

Water is made up of secrets; you must
be careful or you'll be pulled into deep wells,
where creatures with fish heads
and delicate tails wait—loved and betrayed.

If bridges existed,
if I could cross over to the other side,
I would have done so long ago.
How can I forget about you,
I see the marks your nails made on my arm,
but how can I remember your face,
if you always ask me to turn off the light.

On this shore, past the factories and boilers, the skies burn
and dead girls in bright gypsy skirts
hover in the air above the rooftops, peering into chimneys,
singing into them, like into old vacuum-tube microphones.

No one tells the women, who live on the other shore,
about the young strays,
who hide every night in the spilt
gold of the apples, watching them on the sly,

as they take off their light dresses and take
the pins and poisoned combs out of their hair.

Whoever finds themselves here will fish
every day, throwing their nets into the mist,
and place red hearts at their feet,
plucking them out of the fish
like tulips

If only I could get to the other shore,
walk past the cold shadow of the power plant,
see the birds that steal earrings
and little gold crucifixes set out on windowsills.
Feel the dark rise out of the river at night.
And know it will be gone by morning.

■ ■ ■

Winters are not like winters,
winters live under assumed names,
and unpleasant events are associated with them,
such strange things have been happening to us,

such sorrowful partings, such losses,
such expectations, such returns,
such insults, you want to sort it all out,
but you don't know which came first, or last,

such confidence that everything you are doing is right,
such unwillingness to accept the obvious,
such snow, as cold as the war,
such sieges are planned, such escapes occur,

such blue trees, such green planets,
such bright hills and twilight valleys,
even when you are not with me, I know where you are
and what you are doing right now,

I know what you are afraid of on winter nights,
what you recall with joy, what you recall with sadness,
what you see walking through the yards at night,
what you hear in each voice, each splash and sound,

what you feel approaching this home,
what you find in the dark corridors,
what concerns you, so later, at the front door,
you nervously react to the smallest movement,

you regret that he still waits for you,
you are happy you don't have to say anything to him.
The birds in the sky look like the combs in your hair.
The snow under our feet resembles an engraving.

■ ■ ■

The snows pass, and in the green mist
of every Maytime
women stop time in the kitchen,
cooking moons as if they were cheese.

At night warm smoke rises from the pots
and the yellow moons
endure, and even the heaviest
only leaves ripples in the river.

Every moon has its own space in the kitchen
among the knives, drawers, and scales,
and each name is as long and full as a drink,
drenched with the voices of women.

Their uncertain weights
are lightened with cries and songs,
the women carry them out to the shore
for refugees, runaways, and killers.

The suns of fishermen and the stars of shepherds,
pour light, like song,
on the dark bronze shore birds
and carp heavy with silver.

Because all the women stick to the mist,
forgetting during the day but remembering at night
secrets engravers, weavers, and antiquarians
shared with them,

they stand for a long time by the fire,
taking on thousands of poisons,
as long as the mud lies on the bottom,
and the silence grows cold on the rooftops.

As long as their moons last,
and there is enough light,
grass grows to penetrate the dead,
grass grows to hold on to the living.

■ ■ ■

I say, "So what if nothing is understood?
So what if we have to start everything all over again?
Every soul inhabits a body,
and every door leads to a room.

"Every space is full of its own radio shows.
Every heart grows flowers and algae.
So what if all this could have been predicted?
So what if you have no idea how to talk about this?

"I passed through these twenty-four-hour twilights,
I know how to fight off attacks and trauma.
But I still have so much love left
that it could stop the plague at the gates of the city.

"I know how the fire dies down in a woman's voice.
I carried that poison in my own pockets.
But I still have so much tenderness and anger
that it could raise lepers and hanged men from their graves.

"So they will follow me through the golden nights—
tired clowns, defenseless sleepwalkers.
So what if you have no idea where to begin?
So what if nothing comes of things between us?"

She listens to me, slightly swaying.
She walks out and then returns.
She is silent, agreeing with me about everything.
She smiles, not believing a single word I say.

■ ■ ■

May your delicate throat never get cold
and may your night songs never end.
The devil will stand over you with a bronze military horn,
blocking the fierce tides at your headboard.

Let the smell of wind never disappear from your T-shirts,
let it play in your hair forever.
I will live in the sound of Sirens, like worries,
recognizing your breath in their harmonizing voices.

I will eat bread in detention centers,
sleep with black refugees in gyms,
find your aroma in the dry air and
overripe earth like a testimony at midnight.

I will sing of this ruined country,
disintegrating from the poison in its blood,
I will remind everyone who passes by of their guilt,
I will chew the twilight rich with color.

The sun rises in the east every morning past the market,
there is a different reason for each loss,
there will never be a silence like the one over your building,
there will never be a moon like the one just past your
        shoulders.

May you be warmed by wine someone else opened,
may tenderness fill your careless speech:
children will learn to love when they learn a kind of love
they can understand, untranslated, whether summer or
        winter.


■ ■ ■


What will you remember about these times?
Memory washes out all the voices,
memory doesn't remember any names, any titles,
but you must remember, remember each of us.

Remember how we were in love with your face,
even if you didn't like it, remember it,
even if you didn't believe how serious our diseases were,
even if you didn't doubt the hopelessness of all our attempts,

even if you can't remember our names,
even if the colors of our banners annoyed you,
the language of our declarations of love,
the biographies of our saints,
the weapons, wine, and books in our houses.

Remember everything we wrote to you in our letters,
remember how many of us died in faraway towns,
remember how many of us were broken and sold out,
remember at least one of us,
even in the passing.

Remember how we'd catch your words,
remember our failures and our amazing feats,
our loyalty, our courage, our fears,
and carry our love with you like old sins.

Whether you want it or not, there will be nothing without
        you.
Our hearts rest on river bottoms like naval mines.
Remember each retreat, remember each attack—
if you can, remember everything till death, at least.

■ ■ ■

And then she says,
"I know how this will end:
it will end by everything finally ending.
I will suffer, you will keep catching more and more of the
     dead,
releasing the ones you caught before."

But I tell her,
"No one will suffer.
No one will ever suffer again.
Why does poetry even exist,
why do canals and shafts open up into the air?

"Why do we fill the emptiness
with poetry and holiday carols, why prepare escapes?
Any decent poet can use words to stop
the bleeding."

Then she asks,
"Why do these decent poets behave like children?
Why do they live like aliens and die like criminals?
Why can't they end that
at least?"

So I say, "Because it's hard to live with other bodies,
because the holy men of words have their own
     incomprehensible plans,

because there are no decent poets left,
just thieves and charlatans.

"They chant the pain away in animals and children,
catch feathers entangled in branches,
just live, choosing
between death and unemployment."

That is why everything will end by starting again at the
     beginning,
falling into the throat and lying on the retina,
filling us with love and oblivion,
instantaneously
at conception.


■ ■ ■


It's all up to us.

You touch the atmosphere and disturb the equilibrium.
Everything we've lost, everything we've found,
all the air that passed through our windpipes—
what sense does it all make without our pain and
     disappointments?
What value does it have without our joy?

After all, it's all about your fingers.
You touch her clothes and know nothing

can be taken back, a name spoken once
changes the voice, coils around the roots of words,
so you struggle from now on with dead languages,
as you attempt to use them
to communicate with the living.

You touch her things and understand: behind each word,
behind each deed stands the impossibility of return.
Courage and sorrow push us forward—
love is irreversible, and we can't decipher most
dark prophesies and visions.
What happens to us is only what we wanted,
or only what we feared. The question is
what will win—desire or fear.

The night will ring with music in the web
of our fingers, the room will fill with light
from the dictionaries we've brought.
After all, everything depends on our ability
to speak the dead language of tenderness.

Light is shaped by darkness,
and it's all up to us.


■ ■ ■


Because we have to make this road ourselves
to the very end, because this road is not the last one,

we celebrate work, which has divided us into social strata and
    classes,
we sing of the dead, and the silence they left behind.

We build this road between far-flung cities,
we lay it down in the heat of summer and in winter flurries,
confidently calling out to each other in the fog,
never scrimping on our hate or our cigarettes.

Because every road is our joy and weariness,
because every stop is our silence and solitude,
because we always know who waits for us at home,
we understand dedication and we know there's no going
    back.

Each of us will have lots to tell after death,
although we don't believe it will ever come.
Heaven warms us up in worn-out jackets.
I have a heart, and I understand what it's worth.

I have a voice, and that's why I can communicate,
this road can truly be easy,
because a warm moon hangs overhead
and you can always reach up to touch it.

That's why we build this road from silence and clay,
We stretch it out like a thread behind us,
between sound and silence, between heaven and earth,
between light and darkness, between love and oblivion.

■ ■ ■

Five years standing watch, five years as a worker,
dark sunburnt skin, hot veins.
When I return I will talk till
the last gaping fool walks away.

I will tell him about the cities, countries,
about the seasonal hired hands who
raised walls and towers all these years,
raised them like warriors after convalescence.

I will tell him how sirens called us to work,
how we slept in churches under the trumpets of the
        archangels,
and on the rooftop, crosses were as sensitive as antennas,
so you could listen in on the conversations of the saints.

It made no difference where each of us came from.
The differences were in the heavens above.
In the East we built churches and prisons,
in the West we built hospitals and train stations.

I know the real value of work.
I know hearts have the color and taste of oranges.
As long as there's work, each of us strains,
stretching toward the warm summer air like a blade of
        grass.

I will say that the Lord stood between us,
creating arguments in our guilds and brigades,
dividing us by language, skin color, and names,
forcing us to put up barricades in the streets today.

So now the water in his baptismal fonts is always salty,
and his golden churches are full of Irishmen and Lemkos.[2]
My love, forgotten in the squats of Babylon at night,
weeps for me in all languages and dialects.

But someday, I will say to him, we will work again,
we will drag building stones again,
day workers of the world, mercenaries, rebels.
We are divided by our bosses and our fear.
But we are united by our perseverance and our hate.

■ ■ ■

Always returning here to these hills and rivers,
where guards and tax collectors stand at the gates.
Here the evangelists in churches have such dark faces,
like they've been in the sun all day picking grapes.

Here the men wear so much gold
that it's a strain for death to carry them off.

---

2. People from western Ukraine.

Here the women are touched by such deep fears at night
that they paint their eyes blue.

Here children learn such dangerous trades when they're
       young
that they can't find jobs when they grow up.
So every war for them is like manna from heaven,
since soldiers are laid to rest with flowers.

Trucks from the South bring a plague into the city.
At midnight the beggars count the losses.
As always, it's my fate to remember everyone
and return here.

I tell myself,
Autumn isn't here yet.
But here are its evening trees, like regimental banners.
And here is her dark building, here are her windows.
Maybe she waits here too.
Maybe she even waits for me.

SERHIY ZHADAN was born in the Luhansk Region of Ukraine and educated in Kharkiv. He is the author of twelve books of poetry. His prose works include *Big Mac* (2003), *Depeche Mode* (2004), *Anarchy in the UKR* (2005), *Hymn of the Democratic Youth* (2006), *Voroshilovgrad* (2010), and *Mesopotamia* (2014). Zhadan's books have been translated into English, German, French, Italian, Swedish, Norwegian, Polish, Czech, Hungarian, Belarusian, Lithuanian, Latvian, and Russian. He is the front man for the band Zhadan and the Dogs.

REILLY COSTIGAN-HUMES and ISAAC STACKHOUSE WHEELER are a team of literary translators who work with both Ukrainian and Russian. They studied together at Haverford College. Their debut translation, Serhiy Zhadan's novel *Voroshilovgrad*, was published in May 2016.

VIRLANA TKACZ and WANDA PHIPPS have received the National Theatre Translation Fund Award, the National Endowment for the Arts Poetry Translation Award and twelve translation grants from the New York State Council on the Arts. Their translations have appeared in many literary journals and anthologies, and are integral to the theater pieces created by Yara Arts Group. www.brama.com/yara.

Translations by Virlana Tkacz and Wanda Phipps were supported by public funds from the New York State Council on the Arts with the support of Governor Andrew M. Cuomo and the New York State Legislature.

Special thanks to Svitlana Matviyenko, Sofia Riabchuk, Julian Kytasty, Olena Jennings, and Kateryna Babkina for their assistance with the poetry translations and to Tanya Rodionova and Tania Maiboroda for their assistance with the prose translation.

Printed and bound by CPI Group (UK) Ltd, Croydon, CR0 4YY

06/05/2025

14665531-0001